Hilda Bernstein was born in London and moved to South Africa in 1933. She became very actively involved with radical political organizations campaigning for black people's and women's rights. She also began writing poetry and short stories. In 1964 she and her husband left South Africa illegally, under threat of arrest.

HILDA BERNSTEIN

# Death is Part of the Process

**GRAFTON BOOKS**

A Division of the Collins Publishing Group

LONDON GLASGOW
TORONTO SYDNEY AUCKLAND

Grafton Books
A Division of the Collins Publishing Group
8 Grafton Street, London W1X 3LA

Published by Grafton Books 1986

First published in Great Britain by
Sinclair Browne Ltd 1983

ISBN 0-586-07090-7

Printed and bound in Great Britain by
Collins, Glasgow

Set in Times

*To Toni, Patrick, Frances and Keith*

But man has given a false importance to death
Any animal plant or man who dies
adds to Nature's compost heap
becomes the manure without which
nothing could grow nothing could be created
Death is simply part of the process

*Marat* by Peter Weiss

In memory of Solwandle Ngudle, Suliman Saloojee, Alpheus Malibe, Caleb Mayesiko, Ahmed Timol, Steve Biko, Neil Aggett, and all the others who died as these died.

# Prologue
## *JUNE 1980*

Just for a moment, at the first earth-shaking explosion, Cass put a hand before his eyes as though to shield them from a light too brilliant, a cloud too rounded which billowed upwards into the night sky. Then – no more hesitation – he turned and buried himself in that night. It was done. Years of preparation, years of training. They had succeeded; or partially. To survive, to get away safely, to find the way through the net of security forces – that was part of the total plan.

*THE TIMES, London. 3 June 1980.*
*Simultaneous sabotage attacks on three of South Africa's oil-from-coal plants in the Transvaal last night caused damage estimated at £3.3 million and rudely shook the belief that urban terrorism was likely to be confined to minor bomb attacks by ill-trained insurgents. The attacks, just before midnight, were on some of the nation's most vital fuel installations and in the heart of its richest industrial area – Sasol One, at Sasolburg, south-west of Vereeniging, the neighbouring Natref plant, and Sasol Two at Secunda about sixty miles to the east. The explosions at Sasol One sent up sheets of flame from several huge oil tanks in the biggest fire in South Africa's history . . .*

*Police have started a widespread hunt for the saboteurs who appear to have escaped without trace from all three areas, though at Natref, one of them was stopped by a black security watchman but got away after shooting him.*

*Eye-witnesses said that for three hours after flames from*

*the explosions leapt three hundred yards into the sky, the surrounding urban area was lit as brightly as day. This morning smoke from Sasolburg was drifting over Johannesburg's southern suburbs more than fifty miles away.*

*In London, the outlawed African Nationalist Congress claimed responsibility for the attacks.*

*THE STAR,* Johannesburg. 2 June 1980.
*Last night's Sasol oil refinery attacks are a sobering reminder for South Africa that sabotage and urban terror have entered a new phase . . . A sophisticated operation like this is a far cry from the first fumbling sabotage attempts of the 1960s.*

# 1960

# Indres . . .

When the boy crossed the yard to the toilet, Indres straightened up from his cramped position behind the dustbins and waited for him to come out.

It was early morning, a hot day coming; already it was very warm, with a drone of flies around the rubbish in the corner. Several families with throngs of children, uncles and aunts, shared the toilet. A smell of urine and decay pervaded it. The improvements promised by the Council years ago would now never be made. The homes owned by the Indians were destined for the bulldozer, for the land had become valuable as Johannesburg had expanded and the area had been re-zoned for white occupation only. Soon all the Indian families would be moved far out, to Lenasia. But for Indres what had been a political issue was now reduced to a more simple problem concerning his safety and liberty: too many people lived in those houses, entered that yard.

The boy came out fastening his pants and walked over to the tap. He saw Indres and greeted him without surprise, a familiar visitor. 'They're not up yet,' he said. 'They're still asleep.'

Indres took his arm and drew him close. 'Listen,' he whispered, 'the police are looking for me.'

They went into the toilet together, and the boy closed and latched the door.

'I don't want to go into your house. There are too many people. Can you tell Essop? I want him to help me.'

'My brother's not here,' the boy said. 'He's in the country.'

'When will he be back?'

'Today, I think. This afternoon. You can come into the house,' he added.

'No, it would be foolish. Neighbours come in. I must find somewhere . . .'

The boy said 'There's our servant's room. It's empty. We don't have one now. You could stay there till Essop comes.'

'Don't they use it?'

'Not really. Sometimes my aunt keeps things there, but not much. You see, I could lock you in, there's only one key, and I'll take it to school with me.'

After a pause the boy said 'Well, do you want to? They'll be up soon.'

He was exhausted by the very act of thinking, by the necessity of making a choice. But he could not risk the streets in broad daylight. They would be looking for him.

He nodded.

'Wait here then,' the boy said. 'I'll get the key, it's in the kitchen.' He added comfortingly, 'You'll be all right. It's the best place.'

How old was he? thought Indres. Nine or ten. Small and always serious. He rarely smiled; he seemed to hold a responsibility beyond those few years.

The screen door that protected the kitchen against flies creaked and slammed, creaked and slammed again; Indres opened the latch of the toilet. The boy motioned him back with a gesture of his hand. Peering through a ventilation hole in the door of the dark malodorous cabin, Indres watched him unlock the door of the room across the yard, turning the key carefully to avoid unnecessary noise. The boy pushed the door open, than glanced up at

12

the windows overlooking the yard. Curtains were still drawn. He lifted a hand in a gesture to Indres to come.

The one small window was too high for anyone to see into the room from outside, and covered with a piece of curtain. There was an iron bedstead standing on four bricks, with a striped and soiled mattress; and a wooden packing case next to the bed.

Inside the room it was still cold, the air musty and stale. Later, when the sun beat down on the corrugated iron roof, it would be too hot.

'Can you bring me some water?' he asked the boy. 'Don't bother if they're up.'

In a little while the boy came back with a bottle filled with water and a large pie.

'Hey, that's nice! How did you get this?'

'It's my lunch. Don't worry, I'll buy some chips.'

His serious face relaxed. 'I'm going now,' he said. 'You see, I'll keep the key in my pocket. They can't get in. As soon as my brother comes back, I'll tell him.'

The door closed quietly, the key turned from outside. Indres sat on the edge of the bed. The springs creaked noisily. He lifted the mattress off the bed and on to the floor, and lay on it. He smiled to himself at the unaccustomed luxury of a mattress between his body and the floor.

But he could not purge himself of anxiety. He lay for a while, trying to induce sleep. He had been awake all night. He had learned how to pass days and weeks of doing nothing and now he tried to induce a certain blankness of mind as though he had switched off the mechanism whereby he moved and thought. He knew he could trust the boy, he had more understanding than a lot of adults. Trust the boy. He relaxed and slipped into

13

the state of emptiness, the void in the head. The void became sleep.

Some time during the day he woke with pumping heart. Someone was rattling the handle of the door and shaking it. He heard a woman's shrill voice shouting across the yard, and answering cries from the house. They were debating the absence of the key, which should have been hanging from a nail in the kitchen. He lay rigid in the hot semi-darkness. Sandals slapped across the yard, to the house, back again. She was trying another key. It did not fit. He lay and listened. The screen door creaked and slammed once more, then it was quiet again. He ate the pie. He did not want to drink too much because there was no place to urinate. The water was warm, flat. He took a mouthful, rinsed his mouth, then swallowed it. He went to sleep again.

When he woke, he knew it was late afternoon. He wished he had his watch, the police always took your watch away when you were arrested, it made jail just that much more miserable; you learned to judge the time quite accurately by light and by sounds. He sat up and took another mouthful of water. Water and a mattress. Better than a thin felt mat on a concrete floor, better than their congealed and stinking porridge, but at least they gave you a bucket in your cell, even though it stank and you hated it and tried not to use it.

From the kitchen, through the screen door, came the sounds and smells of cooking, the penetrating spices and garlic, the pounding and slapping of chappaties. The women were frying something, probably samosas. His stomach contracted.

People crossed the yard, the screen door creaked and slammed over and over again. The flush of the toilet. A mingling of voices, music from a gramophone. At some

14

time a note was thrust under the door. In the fading light he read 'My brother is home. He will come later when it is safe.'

From habit, he fumbled for a match to burn it; when he realized he had none, he rolled the note into a tiny tube and thrust it into a crack in the floor, rubbing earth and dust over it.

When he guessed the family were all at supper, he got up and did some exercises. Habit again; when in a confined space try to keep fit. His knees creaked at first as he went up and down; keep the back straight, neck in line with the back, heels together. They must be looking for him. They might come to this house. Whatever happened, he had to find a place that was safe, to hide, to lie low for a while, get some sort of disguise. Most of all, he needed to contact Thabo.

The domestic sounds were his clock. The clatter of plates and the voices at the kitchen sink seemed to go on for hours. The women crossed and recrossed the yard in their flapping thonged sandals. The metal rod of the toilet was pulled again and again. Refuse was emptied into the dustbins. The screen door shrieked and clapped continuously.

After a while the sounds subsided. The women, he knew, would go to bed very early.

In the dark, quiet footsteps. The door was unlocked at last. Essop came into the room, clasped his shoulders and embraced him. 'Cass told me,' he said. 'Come into the house. We'll talk there.'

'Is it safe?'

'It's safe.'

'But won't they hear voices?'

'No, I tell you its safe. I often have friends in. No one

will come, they won't interfere. It will be all right, and you can have some food.'

'The police might come.'

'The boy will watch for us.'

They sat in the living room, on dark-red plush armchairs with heavy curved wooden sides. Essop put a plate of food on the glass-topped table, pushing aside a vase of plastic roses. 'Eat,' he said. 'You look so thin.' And after a pause, 'They let you go, then?'

Indres looked at him for a long moment. 'Why do you think all this caution? I escaped.'

'No. How can such a thing – how is it possible? I thought perhaps they had released you, then you were afraid they would pick you up again. They've done that to others. Cat and mouse game.'

'I escaped,' Indres repeated.

'Are they so careless?'

'Oh, it wasn't too difficult.' He tried to be offhand, to suppress that feeling of triumph. 'You see, they'd finished with me, they'd squeezed me dry, so they pushed me on one side, out of their way; to one of their locals – Booysens. Places like that, it's not like the Fort or Pretoria, they aren't so vigilant. You're under the ordinary police, they're much slacker at the smaller stations. And you have time to look for ways, too much time, nothing else to do. You have to think about ways to get out. There are always chinks. You have to find them and crawl through.'

'But they'll be looking – they will be out in full force.' Essop pushed lank black hair off his forehead, got up, paced around in agitation.

'Yes, they'll be looking. We haven't much time. There wasn't anything in the paper?'

'Nothing about you. Some more raids.' He picked up

16

the Rand Daily Mail and pointed to a small paragraph: *Police raided several places in Johannesburg in the early hours of this morning. They searched homes and carried away cases of documents. It is not known whether any arrests were made. General van der Bergh, head of the Security Branch in the Witwatersrand area, has refused to comment.*

'Sometimes it suits them better to keep quiet,' said Indres. 'When they want to, they blazon things in the press.' He flung down the paper. 'They raid, they arrest, no one knows how many or why. They just take you away. You disappear, that's the end of it. And the press doesn't say a word.'

'How can they?' Essop asked. 'They're not allowed to. Not permitted to give a single name. They must not print a line if anyone has been detained. But you – what are you going to do, man? It's too dangerous for you here. Of course the family can be trusted, but this place is too obvious. It'll be watched, raided even.'

'I must find a safe place to hide for a while.'

'But where? It's all dangerous. This house is dangerous. Do you know any place that's not? They haven't been here since Billy's trial, but that's no guarantee.'

'What about Golub?'

'No, he won't do it. That won't do. He's trying to wangle a permit to stay in his shop. He wants to ingratiate himself. You can't trust him.'

'Just for a few days, some place reasonably safe, until I can . . .' he broke off.

'What?' Essop asked.

'There is someone I must see, it's very important.'

'No, it's more important for you to get out, over the border.'

'All right, get out,' Indres said sharply. 'Let's not

17

discuss it now; in any case I must find a place until it can be arranged.'

'You'll have to stay here tonight.'

'It's too dangerous. I've been out one night already, I've been in your room in the yard, they'll be raiding all around looking for me; places like this.'

'Ja, but I should think it is more dangerous for you to go out tonight; even for me it would be dangerous. It's too late, people are in bed, it would look suspicious. Tomorrow I can see a few people, make some enquiries. Tonight you can sleep with me in my room.'

'I don't need sleep, I've been sleeping all day.'

'All the better. If they come you'll have a chance to get out through the back. I can keep them waiting before I open the door.'

Essop went into the boy's room. Cass was kneeling on his bed, in the dark, peering out into the street from behind the edge of the curtain. 'It's all right,' he told the boy, 'you can go to sleep now. He'll stay in my room tonight.'

'I'll keep watch,' the boy said.

'You can't keep watch all night. You go to sleep. We'll be on the look-out.'

'Your room's at the back. I'll keep watch.'

'Don't be silly, Cass, you must sleep. We'll listen.'

The boy said nothing. He climbed under his blanket.

The two men went into Essop's room. Essop undressed while he talked in whispers.

'How will you get to the border? You'll need a car. Tomorrow I will see Abraham. He takes a lorry up and down that way. You might even get away tomorrow, then we won't have to find a place . . .'

'I can't go tomorrow,' Indres said.

'Can't? What are you talking about?'

18

'I have something to do first.'

Essop sat on the edge of his bed and moved his hands back and forth across his body in nervous agitation.

'Listen, you're mad,' he said. 'You want to be taken again? What did they do to you? Was it nice? Twice you won't get away. Look, man, what's the use of it, it hasn't been worth it. Look what it's all led to. A few bombs, half of them didn't even work properly.'

'They worked very well.'

'Oh yes, and others – and how many people even knew about most of them, anyway? They only let the first few in the papers. And the trials – and punishment! Look at Billy – twelve years!' Involuntarily his eyes filled with tears whenever he thought of his younger brother. 'Twelve years! And he was only nineteen. He'll be more than thirty when he comes out, if they ever let him out, all those years of his youth, how can it be worth it? And it was all for nothing, a trap. Twelve years on Robben Island for walking into a trap.' He shook his head. 'It was wrong to turn to violence. Passive resistance served us well, from Gandhi's time.'

Indres clenched his teeth. 'We can't argue it now . . . anyway, we didn't *turn* to violence. How do you shake off an iron fist with passive resistance?'

'I know, I know,' Essop sighed. 'But it hasn't achieved anything, except to make an outlaw of you. You, who were going to be a lawyer. You were such a good student, gifted.'

'Why do you reduce it all to personal terms?'

'Why did you give it all up? For this? If you were a lawyer, you could also help your people. After all, lawyers are needed more and more. But now – ' he paused, and Indres remained silent. 'Tell me, what are you going to do?'

'First I must find a place.'

'What's the use? You'll have to keep on hiding and it's too dangerous. Why don't you leave?'

'No. there's something I must do first, that's why I had to escape. Later, I may get out, but first there is something I must do, someone I must see.'

Still sitting on the edge of his bed, Essop leant over with hands outspread. 'Indres, listen to me, please, just listen! It will be suicide. They'll simply take you again, and you know you'll end up on Robben Island like Billy – worse, you'll get at least twenty years. They'll torture you. Even . . . you may endanger others. You don't know. There is nothing more you can do. You are dangerous. Not only to yourself, to other people. Think of your family, Indres, please! How can you live like this? We'll find a place for a night or two, maybe a week, then you'll be on the run again. What for? What's the use of it?'

At that moment the door opened and the boy stood there, hitching up his pyjama trousers from which protruded legs like brown sticks.

He spoke directly to Indres.

'Uncle, there's a car parked just along the street with two men in it.'

'How long – ?'

'A few minutes. It's a Volkswagen. I've been watching from behind the curtain.'

Both men rose. Indres thrust his hands into his pockets to conceal their shaking. Essop was also agitated. 'You must go. You can go through the back. What will you do? I'll go and see some people . . . how will you know where to go?'

Indres asked the boy 'Will you keep a look-out?'

'Yes, Uncle.' And he added confidently, 'I can stall

them if they come. They can't get to the back, except through the house.'

The two men went out into the yard. 'If you climb the fence,' Essop whispered, 'you can go out into the next street through the alley at the side of the house, over there. The door in the passage isn't locked, just give it a push.'

'OK.'

'Indres, perhaps it will be better to come back here. If they come once, then they might leave us alone after that. Otherwise how will I know to get in touch with you?'

'I don't know,' Indres answered. 'I'll find some way to contact you.'

He hoisted himself up on to the top of the fence. 'Take care,' Essop whispered urgently, 'look after yourself. Indres, don't do anything, just take care!'

Indres dropped silently down on to the earth of the small yard of the adjacent house. There was no lights on. He pushed against the door at the side, lifting it a little at the same time so that it would not scrape and make a noise. In a moment he was through and into the street.

He thought he heard knocking on a door behind him, but he was not sure.

It was late. People in this district went to bed early. The street was empty.

One way led to the top of the street where, if he turned the corner, he would be back where the car was parked close to Essop's house. The other way led to a dead end. The road petered out. Beyond the road, behind the remaining houses, was open country, a scarred and derelict landscape. He started walking away from the town. Night claimed him as a shadow among the dark shadows.

21

Fear was at his back, fear now undiluted by any sense of noble purpose. He was overwhelmed by a sense of defeat.

From the rutted land criss-crossed with fencing, pitted with ditches and abandoned quarries, reaching the Main Reef Road was like ascending to a mountian top. From there the way became clear, movement easier and swifter, if not so safe. But the road was unlit and at this time of night the traffic was infrequent. Whenever he saw the distant headlights of a car, he left the road and lay in a ditch until the vehicle had passed. First there was a distant glow in the sky, moving up and down with the pitch of the road, then the car's lamps cut like search-lights, emphasizing the blackness of the shadows in the holes behind the humps. Visible from far away before they topped the hills, the vehicles sped by with the purposefulness of those who have a destination.

He felt he had none. This direction, followed continuously could lead nowhere except across the whole country from town to town until the East coast, the last barrier, the sea. And the sea was a dead end.

'A time comes for each of us to leave.' Who had said that? Why should it be so? If he wanted to leave he must go back, and if he wanted to be taken again he must go back and if he wanted to keep his assignment, he must go back.

There was no one left to trust. Even Essop. He was too frightened, for Indres, for himself. But the boy – he acted so simply and naturally and was so totally trust-worthy. *For a day and a night, I replaced Billy, the beloved Billy who had been his idol and hero, who moulded his attitudes without conscious thought, simply by what he was, simply by what he did.*

*As my uncle Aziz moulded mine.*

22

The pungent metallic scent of marigolds was the remembrance in his nostrils, their colour a burning gong of garlands around the necks of brides and bridegrooms. Laced and draped, the brides had sat apart in a packed, hot room, heads bowed above the weight of the flowers, as though stunned by the brash insistence of their smell and colour. The older women surrounded the brides with wailing chants; the children pushed into the room to chatter and stare, then out again into the big marquees in the dusty yard where the dark-suited grooms sat upright on the dais among the honoured guests who had come for the joint wedding of the five men, brothers and cousins, to their five brides

African and white guests sat among the Indian guests and their hosts. Only the women were separate, the brides not even part of the speeches and ceremonies, mothers, sisters and aunts busy in the kitchens. But white and African guests had come from the city. Although the children of the store-owning Indians played with whites, the Indians formed their own community, keeping within the bounds of social and political laws. Their relationship with their customers, all whites and mostly farmers, was friendly; they carried the farmers over hard times of drought and crop failures, with credit extended for months or even years. Friendly, but not extended to any social mixing.

The boys played together on the open veld. Colour consciousness was slow in growing. Even the midwife who had delivered him was white and like an aunt to him. The rules of exclusion seemed to apply only to the girls, whose lives were different. But when he was eight, Indres had to go to school. He could not go to school with his white friends; there was no school for Indian children in Middelburg. He was sent to live with his uncle's family in Johannesburg.

Political awareness, always somewhere close, opened like a red flower, flowed through his veins, pumped by the passionate blood red grief within. *He drowned in his own blood.* Fractured skull and cerebral haemorrhage, multiple injuries to head, and lacerations and bruises all over his body; and the surgeons said 'He drowned in his own blood.'

The leader of the cricket team, white flannels and dazzling white shirts with sleeves rolled up over strong brown arms, those arms swinging back and up through the circle to release the ball . . . he taught Indres to bat, he bowled to him for hours on end. He could hear his voice still, see the smiling, strong-jawed face. Sportsman, Congress leader.

When Constable Visser raided the home of his uncle and assaulted him and two other Congress officials, the three men brought a civil action for assault and were awarded damages of £9,000 against Visser.

*He drowned in his own blood.*

Visser trailed Aziz night and day until one night he found him entirely alone and struck him from behind, beat him unconscious, then kicked him to death.

Visser was arrested and charged with murder, found guilty of culpable homicide, sentenced to ten years and eight lashes, the maximum that the judge could give.

Less than two years later he was walking around, released from jail, a free man, and still in the police force.

This was his initiation. It was also a time of much happiness, a time without doubts and hesitations. There was only one enemy, the apartheid state, its visible embodiment the bulky frames of the Special Branch

24

whom they so delighted in outwitting; with some there was even a cautious familiarity as of enemies who know the ultimate battle must come but who from time to time establish a kind of communication. The SBs, who called the Congress members by their first names, knew everything about them; their dossiers began with births and were never closed, even those who had left the country were watched and checked, thousands of miles away.

He felt all that time of the past seemed beautiful, a time when they all loved and trusted each other, without which they could scarcely have endured the tensions and dangers with which they lived unremittingly. They had a total belief in themselves, in their cause. They were confident, they were united, they were innocent of betrayal.

The road led out towards the townships and somewhere among those never-ending rows of identical little boxes lived Thabo. Indres was not sure of the address, although he had been to Thabo's house once. It would be easier to find Thabo during the day in the bookshop in town where he worked. Cass would take a message. Or Essop. Better Essop, it was more natural for him than for the boy to walk into a bookshop. But the problem remained – what to do now. If he could reach Thabo now it would save precious time, even tomorrow might be too late.

As he walked he went over, one by one, the people to whom he might go, just for a couple of nights, until he had seen Thabo, and maybe someone could get a disguise for him, and then they would decide what he should do. To leave the country as Essop had suggested, on his own intiative, was unthinkable.

Each name, each place, slotted into his mind as though he were calling a register; and each one rejected –

25

family connections, they were bound to go to any house connected with his family; no, not safe, they've already been raided a couple of times; that one or that one . . . too much extended family in a district too crowded. Pila's flat? She should be safe, if only for a night or two, but there was no way of going there that night and the flat itself was a trap. Fifth floor of a large building; once in, no way out except through the front door. And then there would be an extra charge (he even smiled at the thought) under the Immorality Act: a white woman, an Asian man.

Yet Pila and Thabo were linked together, they worked in the same bookshop. Thabo, Thabo. Somewhere in the night, somewhere not too far away, probably hiding out, they could not have him yet, impossible, they would have boasted, gloated. Thabo must be safe still – he was like a rock.

The road turned upwards. Far behind him now were the lights of the city, behind the natural humps of the land and the mine dumps on the Western fringe, a glow in the sky, the richest city in all Africa. Deep dongas pitted the earth, miniature canyons, their sides veined and scored by the rain.

They had had to learn for themselves the knowledge of chemistry already so familiar to guerilla groups around the world. In lunar landscapes such as this they had first tested the weapons, the witches' mixtures of charcoal and saltpetre and sulphur, or aluminium powder and potassium permanganate. It was not far from here, among the ravines on the sides of the sloping hills, that a test charge was packed in a glass bottle. In the impenetrable dark of a clouded night Indres had run down and placed the jar at the bottom of a ravine while his two companions waited at the top of the hill; waited. Suddenly the explosion they had anticipated but not really expected went reverberating through the ravines and beyond; in distant townships dogs began barking.

The explosion of that first test bomb set off both their fears and their confidence. They ran to the protection of their car and sped away along this very road where he walked now with so little idea of where he was going.

His legs carried him relentlessly forward. Each time a glow arose in the sky he stumbled off the road into bushes or a ditch, or simply lay flat on the stony land until the car had passed. Each time he rose again more slowly and with greater reluctance, not physically tired but emotionally so exhausted he could scarcely summon the will to get up and go on walking.

The tests. All resistance became concentrated on those preparations and those tests. Before, he had been simply a student who was involved in politics; one of many. But now he was a volunteer, a member of a new small unit, preparing to work in a different way.

His life became divided. There was the apparent life, the surface. He went to Wits, attended lectures, met with committees formed for protest or for talk. He sat with others on the main flight of steps beneath the massive pseudo-classical pillars, watched the shifting patterns of young women in carefully careless clothes and young men with large thighs, well-fed, suntanned, self-assured. He strove for the appearance of normality while underneath he burned with impatience for the day to end and for the real life to begin. More and more he was pulling himself away from his former associates, feeling their impotence. Students and lecturers, mostly white, were small groups standing against the huge mass of indifference, of enjoyment of white privilege.

A committee calling themselves the Human Rights Council prepared an exhibition of posters and photographs for the main hall of the University buildings, to commemorate Family Day. The exhibition showed black families being destroyed by laws that made a mockery of human rights: the Group Areas Act, the Bantu Laws Amendment Act, the Mixed Marriages Act, the Immorality Act, and all the various pass laws and restrictions on movement which operated in intricate bureaucratic ways to break up normal family life. They had spent some weeks on the preparation of the exhibition, students from many faculties had assisted, young architects, lecturers and ex-students like Pila.

It was all over very quickly.

In the morning students from the Engineering faculty swarmed into the hall where the exhibition was mounted, tore down posters, snatched at photographs, stripping them from their display stands and ripping them to pieces. Scuffles broke out when others tried to defend their exhibition. When some of the senior staff intervened the engineering students went away.

At midday, after they had put up more posters, the police arrived in cars and vans, with huge Alsatian dogs pulling on leashes, and with photographers, some from pro-government newspapers and others from the Special Branch. These took pictures of everyone in the hall, and the Security police pulled out notebooks and asked those holding posters for their names and addresses, and the names of the organizers. The Security men with their own uniform of felt hats and raincoats and their atmosphere of being not the law, but above the law, a law of their own, intimidated the remaining spectators even more than the uniformed men with their guns and dogs. Those who had come to see the exhibition or who had been simply hanging around in the entrance hall drifted tactfully away. Only the militant core remained, aggressively demanding to be told what offence they had committed, knowing they would not get an answer.

In the afternoon Dr Hoogter, the Registrar of the University, ordered the exhibition to be dismantled on the grounds that it was provoking disorders in the main building.

And in the evening the Human Rights Committee met at the home of one of the members and with anger and acrimony discussed the events of the day.

They were meeting for the last time in such a group. Ostensibly they were discussing what to do next. But Indres, for one, and he thought possibly others, had already taken that step forward and away, and regarded the day's disastrous events as confirmation of the correctness of what he was doing. Others hesitated on the brink of conviction, wanting to be pushed forward or to be permitted quietly to withdraw.

Indres knew them all well, they had met together in this and related organizations throughout his student days. Four or five other students, one of them an African, Dhlamini; Pila, who worked in a bookshop, but whom he had met first as a student; two lecturers, Dick Slater and Ralph Stern. The house was spacious, the room where they met book-lined; deep chairs, hi-fi speakers suspended from walls; concealed strip lighting; paintings, batiks. All this light-years away from the shanties of cardboard and corrugated iron, the bull-dozed shacks in the 'removed' townships, the rocky landscapes where shelters were built from twisted metal, beaten out petrol cans, splintered bits of wood – discards from the rich white world.

Beer and soft drink cans, icy to the touch, left moist

rings on a glass-topped table. Somebody put on a record of folk music and turned the sound up in the usual gesture made on the supposition that it helped to confuse listening devices. So everyone spoke loudly, and interrupted each other, their impatience fuelled by the sense of their own impotence.

'. . . need to do something now, immediately, to show we are not intimidated.'

'It might be easier to try from now on to work more individually.'

'We can't just throw in the sponge – bow out . . .'

'Surely there isn't just one way, only one solution. One has to try different things . . .'

'What different things? Arming ourselves with crowbars to protect our exhibitions from the fascists?'

'I wasn't suggesting violence . . .'

'Oh, no! That's an absurd statement, that's meaningless. What happened today? That wasn't violence? What do you want? Turn the other cheek?'

Ralph Stern, who had been sitting back and listening, leaned forward, clearing his throat. He was a good-looking man, popular with his social science students; he had abundant dark hair graying elegantly in wings on either side; the circle of scalp at the back was unnoticable unless seen from above. Even those who shrank from his radicalism gave him their attention.

He always spoke slowly, enunciating his words clearly.

'I would like to make a firm proposal,' he said. 'I propose that we formally dissolve our Human Rights Council.'

They were silenced by something so unexpected. But he did not add an explanation, just let them consider what he had said.

Finally Dick said indignantly, 'That's totally negative!

30

Granted its value has become extremely limited, but it has some use, by its very existence it makes a certain point. Do you just want to leave a vacuum?'

'The Council,' Ralph replied, 'has become an obstacle. Its existence fools people – it fooled us – into thinking there are still avenues of entirely legal action open to us. It fools the world by giving the impression that we're a democratic country. "Look at the lively political life at the universities," they say. We've become a weapon to be used against ourselves.'

With a habitual gesture Dick pushed up the spectacles on his nose with two stiff fingers as he frowned at Ralph. 'You think we're better off with nothing at all?'

'No, of course not.'

'Then – ?'

Ralph was provokingly slow, as though he faced a class of students from whom he was trying to draw their own answers. His glance flickered among the faces, settled on Indres.

'Come on Indres,' he said, 'tell them. Tell them we've picked it clean, the democratic machinery. Tell them it's a dead end, and worse – like people walking unarmed into gunfire, like Sharpeville.'

Indres was not sure what Ralph wanted him to say.

'Tell them,' Ralph repeated, 'what's happening in Middelburg where your uncle lived, the one that policeman kicked to death. What about these chaps in the countryside – Poqo – shooting things up, attacking police stations with a couple of knives?'

'But surely,' Dick intervened, 'that's exactly what we don't want, isolated groups attacking police or whites in small places and getting themselves annihilated . . .'

'Yes, well, there's an answer there, don't you think?'

Indres said suddenly 'I suppose it doesn't really make all that difference in the long run whatever we decide.'

'What do you mean by that?'

'What I mean is, a group like this, we're pretty powerless unless we align ourselves with others, with the real people.'

The voices rose, higher in tone, harder in their uncertainties as though they could only convince themselves of what could be done if they could demolish the ideas of others. Dick clung obstinately to the statement that to dissolve the group was to opt for immobility.

'What's your case, Dick?' Ralph asked him finally. 'What's your answer? Is it simply the problem of keeping your own hands clean in what might be a dirty fight?'

'Come,' Pila said to Indres, 'I'll give you a lift home.'

Her car was parked outside in the street. She held the door open for him, leaning over from the driver's side, and as he slid in, she asked 'Well, what did you make of all that?'

'Of what?'

'Of Ralph and his obscurities. What's he really up to?'

Indres did not reply, and after a pause Pila went on, 'You know, he's been the Marxist guru for more than one generation of students. He had a great influence on me in my student days. That's how I began to learn my politics. My father so loathed that type of person – "an intellectual," he would say – it was a term of abuse, so of course that made me much more interested. I had to find out what it was about.

'They were all mad about him,' she went on. 'That serious, twitching face, and all that sport – he was a sort of hero-figure, all-rounder . . .'

'He was a great cricketer.'

'Yes, and rugby, even swimming. How could someone like that deviate? But mostly, the students who ogled him pretended to be interested in his ideas, but they weren't really.'

'Some of them must have been. You, for instance.'

'Yes. But not at first – I was just intrigued by him. Then he made me begin to think. But tell me, what was he really prodding us to do this evening?'

Indres hesitated. 'One doesn't spell these things out.'

'Not even in this car.'

'Then how . . ?'

'Pila,' he looked at her, 'you'll find a way. I expect you will. If we want to we'll find a way.'

# *Dick . . .*

He returned to his home, a compact, single-storey sub-urban house concealed by bushes and trees in a garden flower-filled at all seasons. His wife Margie warmed up the supper she had put away when he phoned to say he would be home late. He went to wash his hands, thinking of Ralph's scornful remark. They *were* white, unsoiled, long-fingered, clean-nailed hands. 'You would feel different if you were black,' Dhlamini, their only genuine black African member, had remarked. Yes, well, of course, but he was not black. He was a prevaricating white intellectual, not a black victim. He was, in fact, a victim-iser. A white supremacist.

'You look tired,' Margie said.

'They smashed up the exhibition,' Dick replied.

'I know. I saw it in the Star.'

She put a plate of food in front of him. 'I ate without you. I hope you don't mind. I didn't want Elias to wait for us.'

'No, of course not.'

She sat opposite him, elbows on the table, a shake of her head clearing her face of her long, brown hair and revealing the little pearl in her ear, a discreet adornment that tried not to draw too much attention to itself.

'What did the council decide to do?'

'What could we do? That little stooge Hoogter doing the dirty work for the Special Branch. Once he ordered it to close down there was nothing we could do. Ralph wants us to dissolve the council.'

34

'Is that what you've been discussing all evening?'

'Yes. He thinks it doesn't serve any purpose any more. Actually he goes further. He says the existence of such a committee is a hindrance now to more militant action; we deceive people into believing that something can still be achieved through such organizations.'

'What does he want to do, then?'

'That's the thing. He doesn't spell it out in so many words. He obviously thinks the time has come for something more militant and less legal.'

'What does he mean?'

Dick shrugged. 'Some form of underground organization.'

'To do what?'

Dick hesitated to put it into words, even to her. He hedged.

'Somehow I think it must be wrong,' he said 'to accept their morality, to begin to adopt their methods, to take things on their level. There must be other ways. People say "What ways?", and what kind of answer can one give? What ways that have not been tried and blocked and stopped by law, by police interference, intimidation, bannings? Protests, petitions, marches, demonstrations, boycotts, strikes, stay-at-homes, mass gatherings, conferences – you name it – we've done it all, we've watched it all, haven't we, all trodden down, legislated out of existence or gunned to the ground. When Ralph reminds me of this I feel as though his arguments are not just words but what we've all lived, our own hard, painful experience.'

He saw in a vivid remembrance the massing of Saracens down narrow township streets, searchlights sweeping across the rows of matchbox houses, the tension generated when the radio started calling up the military reserves; all the enormously inflated counter-action against any form of protest or dissent; mass arrests; the loss of jobs; families being kicked out of their homes; families split up; banishments, bannings; people thrown away.

'How do you organize for change when organizations are banned and everyone who inspires others is taken and jailed or banned or exiled? When everything you do is either illegal, or is made so by the Special Branch?'

'Is that a rhetorical question?' Margie asked. 'Are you trying to convince me, or yourself?'

'Myself, I suppose. What Ralph has in mind is a different thing, entirely different, from having a group for legal, peaceful activities, even if the police make them seem illegal. Basically, no matter what they maintained, we acted within the law, whatever we thought of the laws. We were always so good, so correct. We obtained permission from the police and the authorities to hold a poster parade, we meekly supplied our names and addresses when the SBs came along to intimidate us. We cancelled a demo if the police banned it, we wouldn't go ahead, it would have been inviting violence. Mostly I think we felt all along we wanted to avoid any violence.'

They went to sit in a room overlooking the garden, and Margie put on a record. On Dick's salary as a lecturer they did not live in luxury by general white standards, particularly since Margie had stopped working and their son was born. They lived in quiet suburban comfort. Not too much to possess, not too greedy in what was grasped; if only it were not for the black servant in the backyard and the far-off townships that rimmed the sprawling city beyond the indutrial areas. Orlando, where the electricity for their house was generated lay in unlit shadows there, beyond a stretch of open veld.

Dick said after a while 'I think our whole way of looking at things has been conditioned by this long association with people steeped in the philosophy of passive resistance. To convert others by the sheer force of example, by the sheer rightness of what you believe. That was Gandhi's idea, wasn't it, fifty years ago when he conceived this gentle, peaceful, determined resistance to unjust laws. And that was the legacy he left us here in this country where the passive resistance thing started. His vision. It's been such a profound influence on generations of political leaders in this country.'

'But Africans are peaceful by nature,' Margie said.

'Are they? What makes you think so? Because they've been quiet or docile so long? Look at their history. What about Shaka, what about Dingiswayo and . . .'

'That's very much in the past. I'm talking about recent history.'

'Margie,' he said earnestly, leaning forward, pushing up the spectacles, brushing back the fringe of fair hair, 'what right have some of us, a kind of self-appointed few, to decide for others? We can start making choices, arbitrary decisions – have we the right?'

'Do we make the choices . . . or are things going to happen in any case whatever we individually decide?'

'Ah yes, I suppose so. That's what Pila said. It's not for us to decide, she said, but we don't have the right to stand on one side.'

Margie thought about Pila. 'She was always definite like that, even at school. She always seemed so sure of her own ideas.'

'And Ralph – he said one can't always be so afraid of taking decisions. Do you know what he said to me? He said your refusal to take part in a decision is also a decision. You influence events by not doing as well as by

37

doing. In the end, refusing to take action, you'll find you haven't kept your own hands clean. No white can.'

Margie looked down at her own hands, resting in her lap.

'I never know what you really think,' Dick said. 'I seem to use you as a sort of sounding board for my ideas but you don't really express your own opinion. You are so quiet. All you do is pose questions.'

'Maybe I have nothing to say.'

Silence. Passivity. The inability to act decisively. She had always admired those like Pila who seemed so direct in what they did. She was overwhelmed by her own crowded and incomplete thoughts.

Last year she and Dick had gone together to Johannesburg's annual jamboree, the Rand Easter Show. What had once been a display of agricultural implements had grown over the years to an outsize exhibition of industrial and national achievement, a commercial showcase and a fun fair.

Easter was the end of summer; cold nights and lack of rain had already turned the veld dry and brown, but it was a shimmering sun-heated day. Margie was pregnant. The heat and pressure of the crowds exhausted her; the inadequate cafés were full. They found a piece of grass shaded by two tall bluegum trees; Margie sat on the ground while Dick went in search of cold drinks.

Next to her on the grass was a woman with a baby on her lap, doll-like in its frilled nylon dress and lace-trimmed bonnet.

Two Indian women in saris approached. One was old, with a wrinkled brown face, and greying hair; a diamond-like jewel gleamed in the side of her nose. The other was young and pregnant, more pregnant than Margie, very large and exhausted, the sweat of fatigue shining on her upper lip. She glanced at Margie and at the other woman with the baby with that habitual sidelong apologetic look, then lowered herself clumsily on to the grass. Margie smiled at her with unspoken reassurance, sharing the fact of their mutual burden. But the woman with the baby turned in fury and cried 'Get up! Get up! How dare you sit here, next to a white woman! Go on, get away! Get up!'

Then she turned to Margie and cried indignantly, 'Did you see that coolie woman? Have you ever seen such cheek, sitting down here right next to me and my baby, right next to a white woman?'

Quite clearly in her mind Margie recalled the heavy turn of the lumbering body clambering up with the help of the older woman. And the two walking away into the crowds, melting into the pattern and the shimmer . . .

And she had said nothing.

She had wanted to speak. But the two women had gone. It was too late.

Not too late to make her feelings known to the woman with the baby; but too late to affect the situation. She should have spoken immediately, taken the Indian woman by her arm, held her down, made her stay.

She had not spoken. She had not acted. Once the two women had gone it did not matter.

But it did matter. What had stopped her speaking? A life of behaviour patterns. One did not 'make scenes'. One waited for someone else to act first. But there was still time to speak her mind, but then Dick was beside her saying, 'Look, there are such queues I couldn't get anything, how about we just go home? Haven't you had enough?'

'Yes, I have had enough.' And those few minutes of silence were an ineradicable stain, and Ralph was right.

'If you remain passive or silent,' she said, 'it's the same as actually doing something, because you connive.'

But to herself she was thinking '. . . and we make excuses. I don't do anything because of the baby, he's too young, I can't leave him, I don't want to put him to any kind of risk.' Only the year before, after the Sharpeville massacre, thousands had been swept into jail for the five-month duration of the State of Emergency. Sometimes both husband and wife had been taken, leaving small children.

Dick, too, did not see her as a participant.

'Any decision I take personally will inevitably affect you,' he remarked.

'Oh yes I know,' she replied, 'but you mustn't be held back by Jonny and by myself.'

And perhaps that's what she preferred – that others took the decision that she did not want to have to face.

Dick felt the burden of these decisions that would weigh on them both and on the child. He felt he did not have the political conviction and determination of Ralph, nor the idealism of Pila, nor the direct personal involvement of those who suffered from discrimination, like Indres.

He was a free man, free to make choices.

# *Thabo . . .*

He made up his mind.

He said casually, just before the lunch hour, 'Miss Pila, will you be going out for lunch today?'

'Yes I will, Thabo. Did you want something?'

'Would it be possible, by any chance, if you went near a chemist's shop . . ?'

'Yes, of course. What do you want?'

'I need some Condy's crystals – potassium permanganate. Would it be too much trouble?'

'No, no trouble at all. How much do you need?'

'I think,' he said, pausing, '. . . perhaps . . . if you could get a pound . . .'

'Whatever you need. Anything else?'

'No . . .' again that hesitation '. . . not at present.'

But she waited for a moment, sensing the silent hesitation with which she had become familiar; a caution, a mental weighing-up. With Thabo it was always like that. As though he was waiting for you to discover some other meaning hidden away inside what he actually said.

Now he felt he had taken a step that might prove dangerous. He could have gone through another channel, or asked someone else to ask her, but where it was possible he preferred not to involve others. The fewer the better, the safer. The day would come when someone, questioned, would reveal her name as a supplier. His request was not abnormal. She had often brought him small items that were difficult for him to buy in the township, or more expensive.

And then, there was still time for withdrawal. But if he could trust her, then he must trust her. And if he could trust her and she did not change her mind, then perhaps he would have established for himself and his friends what they so badly needed, a reasonably safe source of supply. A source that might even expand. She had friends like herself.

Trust? How could he judge their relationship? Despite all the careful cover, the control, the deferential politeness learned over long years, he still shivered inside at any approach to a white person save on the level of work, anticipating the familiar reactions: being ignored, as though you were invisible, or sharpness verging on anger, or else patronizing patience and child language.

Pila was not like that. But she was a white woman, educated, superior to him in her work and her life-style, and he was the black general factotum. However pleasant she had always been to him, however easy, there was still a fear of pushing their relationship just that one degree too far for a white woman to tolerate.

For the moment he would not go any further. He would wait for her to help him take the next step, and that would require her to take a step forward herself.

Two days later he was in the stockroom in the basement of the bookshop when she came to fetch her handbag before going out to lunch. He paused in sorting out books and covertly watched her. She said, 'Is there anything you want while I'm out, Thabo?'

'Well, thank you. I wonder if it's possible to get some more Condy's?

'More Condy's! Whatever do you want so much of that stuff for?'

'It's for my house, Miss Pila. I'm fixing it up. I need it for staining wood.' He paused. 'Not that I wish to trouble you,' he went on diffidently, 'so please not to go out of your way, but if you pass a different chemist, any chemist . . .'

She looked at him in surprise. Staining wood? Cement floors and metal windows in all those township houses. What wood? And Thabo, diligent and consistent as he was in his work in the bookshop, had just never seemed a particularly house-proud person.

But she did not say anything. She picked up her bag and went out.

An hour later she handed him the packet and he paid her. 'I went to a different chemist,' she said.

It was not unusual for her to shop for him in her lunch hour, because she was keenly aware of how a black man had to wait to be served in those city-centre shops, particularly in the rush lunch hour period. If he went himself he would have to stand and wait silently while one white person after another who had come into the shop after him would be served ahead of him. Sometimes she would buy him sandwiches from a shop around the corner. They served the public from separate counters. The whites came up to their counter and were served immediately. The black queue stretched all down the street, even though most of them were buying for white employers who would ask angrily when they returned why they had taken such a bloody long time just to get a miserable packet of sandwiches.

This request, though, was different, and she knew it, although as yet she had not defined clearly the reasons for this knowledge, nor the feeling she had that she was walking along the edge of something unknown, possibly dangerous.

A week later he made the same request but it was she

who had made the opening with an offhand, 'Anything you're wanting while I'm out, Thabo?'

He had replied, 'Do you think you could get me some aluminium powder at the paint shop? I'm painting my window-frames silver.'

'Sure.' Then as she was going out, 'I didn't know you were such a devoted home-lover. I thought you wouldn't have time for all that painting.'

'I like to keep things looking nice, Miss Pila.'

And was not he always the one who kept the stockroom so neat and fresh-looking? Quiet, reliable, self-contained Thabo.

As he hoped, she began to make it easier.

'Some more Condy's?' she asked next time.

'If you don't mind.'

'From a different chemist?'

He smiled politely. 'There are many chemists' shops in this city.'

She was about to say something, but again did not speak.

He knew the question would inevitably come.

# *Pila . . .*

There was the obligation to spend every Sunday with her parents.

One of the reasons she had wanted to leave home to live on her own was to escape the demanding routines of her parents' house. Weekends had their patterns as fixed as those of the week, but when she returned to them for only one day, she could bear them with less misery and irritation. She could relax over the ritual of the large, late Sunday lunch with her mother and father, her sister and brother-in-law; the afternoon visitors, tea on the verandah with gold-rimmed rose-painted china through which your fingers were shadows, and all the cakes that her mother baked and decorated. In the early evening she escaped to the cool privacy of her own flat, leaving behind the tensions that inevitably developed between herself and her parents.

But gradually the Sunday visits became more difficult; living apart accentuated the differences between them. Pila felt as though she were walking a tight-rope; maintaining balance demanded constant vigilance and self-control. The whole family tried to avoid those issues that gave rise to controversy but it was not always possible. The issues remained, part of the Sunday scene itself. They had a way of penetrating into the most seemingly innocent discussions.

This week, she knew, there would be trouble. She had crossed the invisible line that her family had drawn for her; as long as she stayed behind it they would keep silent about the increasing non-conformity of her life. But at the point where her private convictions spilled over into public spectacle, so also would their resentment and anger. Don't involve us – but it was more than that. It meant: stay quiet, keep your views to yourself, don't take part in public demonstrations, don't draw attention to yourself. To argue in private was permissible. To make your views known in public was unforgivable.

Pila drove her car from the garage in the basement of the large apartment block where she lived, reaching for her dark glasses in the glove compartment to subdue the dazzle of light in the summer street. The streets baked in Sunday emptiness. You could park anywhere in town today but no one wished to stay within the confining towers of concrete. She drove past Joubert Park, where black nannies in starched white uniforms sat on the ground watching their small white charges playing on the swings and in the sand-pit.

When the cinemas and theatres had closed on Saturday nights – before midnight, in conformity with the Sunday Observance Law – the city became devoid of human life. The black workers, the messengers, delivery men, sweepers, who swarmed along the pavements all week had gone to ground in municipal compounds or out in the distant townships. The whites were in their gardens, or driving out to country clubs and swimming pools. The streets became sticky with melting tar and swam in the reflection of their own heat.

In the street where Pila's parents lived you would sometimes see a domestic servant, male or female, white-aproned, waiting to talk to a friend, bound to the employer's home by the demanding hours of the job.

Each house in the street stood in its own private park, turning its back to the road or concealed behind flowering bushes. Low, single-storey houses sprawling among carefully placed rockeries, shaded by jacarandas and wattles, gardens filled with indigenous plants.

Her mother greeted her with the lightest brush of her cheek, and her usual flow of talk.

'How are you, darling? That's a pretty frock you're wearing, is it new? No? But I don't remember seeing it before. It is hot, isn't it? The Hedley's are coming this afternoon and maybe Phyllis and Jack. Dad's out in the garden, do you want to get into your swimsuit first?'

'That's a very smart hair-do,' Pila remarked. Her mother's hair, the dark shades of which had long departed, was now a light coppery colour, almost pink, short and curled all over her head, set and sprayed with lacquer until it resembled spun glass. Her mother barely touched the stiff fronds with the palm of her hand. 'Oh, do you like it? It's a new man, in Norwood, he's really so good, everyone's going to him, Mr Pietro, do you know I had to wait an hour and a half on Friday, he kept me waiting an hour and a half . . .'

'Why don't you go somewhere else, then?'

'Oh, he's marvellous, there's no one like him, no one. Everyone goes to him. It really looked fantastic on Friday but I played bowls yesterday and those awful hats! I stuck it right on top of my head, but it was no good.'

'Why wear it, then?'

'Oh, Pila, you know we can't play unless we wear those white dresses and awful panamas. But I've been sleeping on a special pillow, it's a sort of neck thing, it's supposed to be good for your back as well, you sleep straight and it doesn't mess up your hair so much. It is a *little* uncomfortable . . . Go and have a dip before lunch, you're rather late, aren't you, did you sleep late? What did you do last night? What's happened to that nice young man, what was his name, Allan, Evan, something, you know, the one you brought here a couple of weeks ago? Have you seen him again? We went to the Colosseum on Friday night, there's a marvellous picture there, have you seen it? The place was packed, a marvellous film, honestly, it's about this girl who thinks she's just nobody because she doesn't know who her real father is, and she sets out to find him, and then at the end it turns out she's really — no, I mustn't tell you what happens, that will spoil it for you, really you must go and see it . . .'

The voice, the pink curls, the figure shaped like an egg-timer between its firm elastic controls, followed her down the passage to her room, the room that was still her room because her mother wanted her to know that any time — any time — she wanted to come back it was there, it would always be waiting for her just the way it was.

The room was immaculate: pale pink quilted bed-spread, kidney-shaped dressing table with pink frills, silver-backed brush, comb and toilet articles laid out on glass. Pila herself had chosen the furnishings when she was fourteen, but that was ten years ago and her tastes had changed. The room was unchanging, the choice of a romantic teenager, kept fresh for her and ready because that was what she had once wanted and this was what her mother wanted her to want, wanted her to be. Even the same books on the shelf, the ones she no longer cared about.

Pila opened the window wide to the garden. Burglar bars curled in iron leaf and stem prevented her from leaning out, but she could see the rockery pulsating with red and purple mesembryanthemum and portulaca, a wall with trailing bells of golden shower, a blazing bed of zinnias. Beyond the mingling orange, red and yellow gleamed the crystal and turquoise of the swimming pool.

Two little boys, sons of her sister Janet, splashed and squealed in a plastic paddling pool, watched over by their African nanny, in cap and apron, who stood ready with dry towels and clean clothes. It was the same delectable world in which she had grown up, full of visual delights and tangible comforts; it was like living in a great glass ball, polished by others, from which all that was sordid or distasteful had been excluded. She stood in front of the triptych mirror, more aware of herself in this alien setting: hair that was permitted to find its own shape, clothes chosen for ease and comfort first, not fashion . . . but the cultivation of carelessness was itself becoming a fashion, and her cosmetics, although restricted and discreet, were none the less expensive.

How far could a flat in town remove you from this life, allow you to reach out and touch the other world? Perhaps it was a passage leading to an unknown exit.

'How can you bear to be cooped up in a flat?' her mother said, 'I don't know how you can stand it, particularly in summer, I must have space, grass, trees, otherwise I can't breathe. Pila, why don't you come home again, it's not natural for a young girl to live all on her own. What about that young man, Pila, the one who . . . why don't you ask him around again; and do you see that nice boy from . . . oh Pila, what's wrong with you, why are all your friends married and not you, you're as pretty as any of them. Marie's expecting her second baby in March, and Sue's got twins; but you always wanted to be different. They've all settled down so well, nice homes, husbands in good jobs. When I was your age, Pila, all I thought about was tennis and new clothes and planning parties and holidays, but you . . .'

Pila, in her swimsuit, moved out into the shining world

of cool sparkling water, of sun-hot canvas chairs and misted glasses with tinkling ice.

Her sister Janet, wearing a tiny bikini, was stretched out on a garden chair, her body gleaming with oil. Her tan was in the nature of a summer hobby at which she worked as diligently as some pursue embroidery or gardening. Her arms, spread out, were twisted so that the unexposed insides could brown as evenly as the rest. In July she would be taking her mid-winter holiday at the South Coast. The problem was how to retain the tan until then.

Janet's husband Barry was in the pool swimming powerfully up and down. He relaxed with the same purposeful intensity as he worked; into the pool, twenty lengths, out, shake off surplus water, rub-down with a towel, slip on a shirt, tie a silk scarf round the neck, then lie back with a drink and cigarette, hairy body taut and flexed as if preparing for the next plunge.

'Jason! Come here,' Barry called to his elder son. 'Show Pila how well you've got on with your swimming.'

Happy to be noticed, the little boy ran up. 'The deep end,' said Barry. Jason jumped in and with his father pacing along the edge of the pool, he struggled his way down the length, to emerge dripping and smiling.

'You can't start too young,' Barry said. 'He's having lessons with the van der Horst sisters. Janet takes him twice a week.'

Pila had learned swimming with them too, remembering the harshness and anger under the apparent sweetness with which they exhorted their little victims. And the mothers, each watching her own child, tense at failure, beaming with success; as later they would watch their children in competitive school games, seeking through their children's lives something that they had lost; some desire to be noticed, some fulfilment of ambition, some dream of achievement.

Soon the little boys were borne away from the pool to have lunch in the kitchen under the supervision of the servants. Pila went into the kitchen to greet Emily who had worked for her parents since Pila was a child. She was happy to see Pila, assured her 'I am well, I am well. And Miss Pila?' She added shyly, 'I see Miss Pila's picture in the paper this week.'

'You recognized me behind that placard?'

'Oh yes, Miss Pila, we all knew it was you, we say so as soon as we see the papers. We think you do a very good thing.'

'I'm sure my father doesn't think so.'

Lunch was lengthy and formal. Iced soup in glass cups. Phineas in a white jacket and white gloves, handing round the dinner plates ringed with blue and gold. Little pots of flowers arranged down the centre of the table; a brass bell next to her mother's plate to tinkle its summons as each course was completed.

After the soup there was roast stuffed chicken. When all the dishes had been brought in on the dinner trolley with its heated glass top, and when her father had carved and Phineas had withdrawn into the kitchen, Mr Norval cleared his throat several times and Pila knew the row was about to begin. The opening shot: 'So you got your picture in the papers?'

'Not my fault,' said Pila, 'I concealed myself as best I could behind the placard.'

'What do you mean, not your fault? If you hadn't been there, standing there with those protesters, they wouldn't have taken your picture.'

Janet said, 'Really Pila, how could you make such a show of yourself? I can't tell you how embarrassing it's been for me, and for Barry. Judy phoned me: "Isn't that your sister on the front page of the Rand Daily Mail?" I didn't even know about it. Barry takes the paper to work with him in the mornings. I had to send Solomon up to the shops to buy another copy. Really, it was disgusting.'

Mrs Norval said, 'You didn't have to stand there, dear. Why couldn't you just write a letter to the paper?'

'What good would that do?'

'What good does it do to stand on a street corner?' Janet cried. 'We're not objecting to what you think – lots of people don't like these laws – it's the way you choose to register your objections. At best it's pointless and at the very least it's undignified.'

'And what's dignified about forcing young lads out of their homes, taking them out of school, sending them to work as cheap labour on the farms?'

'White boys have a form of compulsory service as well,' said Barry. 'They all do nine months in the army.'

'It's totally different. How would you feel if your sons were taken away from you, sent to work wherever the government chose, locked in compounds at night, dressed in sacks during the day, for a few shillings a week?'

Her father turned his powerful head towards her. 'It's not every boy,' he said. 'Those who are studying get exemptions.'

'Oh, like hell they do! Emily's son – there's an example for you.'

'What about Emily's son?'

'You see, you don't know what's happening under your very nose, in your own home. Emily's boy Willie has been endorsed out, and now he's being sent away to one of the labour camps.'

'She never mentioned it to us,' Mr Norval said.

'Have you ever asked her about Willie?'

52

'I thought he was at school.'

'So he was. He failed his exams, he was ill, and they won't allow him back. In his school if you fail once, that's it.'

'Well, if he failed . . .'

'When Janet failed matric she stayed on and re-wrote the following year.'

'It's different,' Mr Norval said, 'and let's not fool ourselves. The position for us and for the natives *is* entirely different, and you can't change things overnight when it's taken a thousand years for our civilization to evolve. They'll have better opportunities in the future. Bantu education is expanding all the time, there are twice as many at school today as ten years ago. It'll change even more in the future, you'll see. Only there must be patience.'

'Meanwhile Willie will become a labourer instead of a teacher.'

'If your protest did any good, there might be some point to it. But it won't make the slightest scrap of difference and you know it.'

'What I can't understand,' said Mrs Norval, 'is why *you* have to take part, Pila. Let them demonstrate if they want to, but why do *you* have to do it?'

'No, I think the important thing is, it doesn't change anything,' said Barry. 'What's the point of protests if it doesn't make any difference?'

'We feel some people should publicly disassociate themselves from the Act.'

'Well, that's a selfish argument, if I ever heard one,' said Janet. 'Just to ease your own conscience, regardless of what good it does; just to make yourself feel noble.'

'Honestly, Pila,' her mother said, 'if you had your own home and a couple of children to look after, you wouldn't have time to stand around on street corners.'

Mrs Norval rang the bell and Phineas came silently into the room. When he had removed the plates Mrs Norval said brightly, 'Now that's the end of politics for today, I'm sick and tired of politics. Why can't people just enjoy themselves? Politics, that's what's wrong with this country. Promise me you won't start any arguments with the Hedleys this afternoon.'

The visitors arrived. Each couple had a black nanny in tow so that the adults were entirely relieved of the chore of caring for their children.

Pila went to help Emily prepare the tea. Every cup was given a final polish before being placed on the lace-edged traycloth on the loaded trolley. Small triangular sandwiches and orange juice or milk for the children. A large chocolate cake, an apple tart, and a great variety of iced cakes and biscuits for the adults. The kitchen was white-tiled and shining like a laboratory. The pleasure of Emily's warm reception had gone. Easing her conscience? Feeling noble? Just enough truth to make her feel uncomfortable.

Thabo would be waiting there in the basement tomorrow. He would watch her with that narrowed look, and sometimes a half-smile that hovered between obsequiousness and insolence.

Dick Slater walked into the shop on Tuesday afternoon, and browsed among the shelves, asking for new publications. He seemed to be searching for something; he went up to Pila.

'Pila, you had a copy of that UNESCO publication on race. Is it sold out?'

'Yes, we had it, but it isn't sold out. It's been banned.'

'But you had it on the shelves last week. I saw it there. I would have taken it but I was in a hurry and didn't want to wait for a slip to be made out. I mean, it's a scientific publication, it's by world experts.'

'I know. What difference does that make? We had to remove our copies this week. There was a notice in Friday's government gazette. It's objectionable literature.'

'Come on, Pila,' he said, lowering his voice, and with that furtive glance over his shoulder that was becoming habitual in so many discussions, 'you can let me have a copy.'

She also glanced around. Another assistant was talking to a customer. The boss, Mr Swart, was in his office.

'What do you need it for? I'm keeping them for social science people.'

But she bent down and slipped a book from under the counter into a protective envelope.

'You're a dear,' he said.

'No, honestly, we do like to keep things for people who really need them for their work. You're a laboratory and test-tube man, not a sociologist.'

She sealed the envelope and took his money.

'Now I want to ask you something,' she said. She left the counter and strolled to the door with him, far enough away from others browsing among the shelves.

'Tell me, what do you use Condy's crystals for?'

He glanced at her with his rather startled look, as though shying away.

'Well, all sorts of things. A lot of things.'

'Such as?'

'Such as for disinfectant. A mild one. Mouth wash.'

'But you wouldn't need much for that, would you?'

'Only a few crystals.'

'And in larger quantities? Could you use it, for instance, for staining floorboards?'

'Oh yes.'

55

'And what else?'

'Well, if you must know, it can be used for making bombs.'

'Really?'

'Yes. It's not difficult. Mixed with aluminium powder. I'm not giving away any secrets. Anyway, you must have the right quantities, proportions.'

They stood self-consciously at the shop doorway.

'I must get back and do some work,' said Pila. 'Thanks for the information.'

'Oh, any time,' said Dick airily, waving his hand, 'any time you want to make some bombs, just let me know.'

They laughed awkwardly. There was a rumble of distant thunder.

'I must run,' Dick said. 'My car's three blocks away. I'll get soaked.'

The first large, isolated drops of rain began to fall on the city.

Each afternoon the accumulated heat of summer, the tense and burning air, exploded over the city in crashing thunderstorms. Beyond the suburbs the plains of grass paled beneath the mulberry clouds and the brilliant flashes across the sky. Rain poured across the horizon and swept down the canyons of city streets, a wall meeting walls, beating and obliterating. The force of the flood from the sky, the bursts and cracks of the charged atmosphere, the blinding zig-zags of light, were all concentrated into the intense fury of ten or fifteen minutes. Suddenly it all ceased. Thunder became remote, echoing across the distant veld; the pulsating flashes receded. Darkness, clouds, lifted, leaving a dramatic yellow evening light with water muttering in swollen drains, even as the streets steamed and were dry.

# Dick . . .

On Saturday morning he went into town to get a new lamp for the automatic slide projector that his wife's parents had given him.

The baby slept in a pram in the garden under the shade of a tree. The sun shone hotly and the morning vibrated with light.

'I sent Elias to the shops to get some bread about two hours ago,' Margie said when he returned, 'and he hasn't come back.'

'Oh dear! That's not like him, is it?'

'No, he never hangs around gossiping. Either he's had an accident or been arrested or something.'

'Did you phone the hospital?'

'No, I was waiting for you to come back.'

Dick went through the kitchen and out into the back-yard. He knocked on the kitchen door of Elias's room; there was no reply. It was not locked. He went in and glanced around. A jacket hung behind the door. He put his hand in a pocket and found what he guessed would be there – the passbook. He knew what had happened to Elias.

He went back to the house and showed it to Margie. 'He must have been arrested for being out without his pass. There's always a lot of Black Marias hanging around the shops at weekends. They just love to round them all up, handcuff them together. I saw a whole row of them squatting on the ground at the bus terminus last week, each one handcuffed to the next, wearing kitchen suits, overalls, waiting for another van to come along and take them away.'

He did not add that assailed by the sight of these men handcuffed in a chain, with one man at each end handcuffed to the railings, these crouching, sad, anxious, resigned, despondent figures, he had fumbled in his pocket and taken out a packet of cigarettes, and walked down the line giving a cigarette into the iron-bound hand of each man. A cigarette! His own white freedom to dispense so minor a gift, to walk away freely without fear of being stopped and asked for a pass, his superiority of race that protected him permanently from squatting handcuffed in the street, tore at him and so sickened him that he wished they would all disappear from sight, that he could close his eyes, open them again and see nothing, to save himself from such shame and humiliation.

The Saturday afternoon was wasted. He spent nearly two hours on the telephone, trying to get through to various police stations, to find someone who would listen. They arrested hundreds of men, they did not even have a proper record of their names. He spelt the name over and over again, waiting with controlled impatience for some barely literate policeman to write it down; and to keep him waiting; and to come back with the same remark 'There isn't a Bantu with that name here.'

Nor did Elias appear on Sunday. Dick tried the local police station and the central station once again. He phoned the hospital. No Elias Makrake there either.

On Monday Margie phoned him at his office during the morning and said, 'There's someone here who says he's come with a message from Elias. He says he's at the Magistrate's Court, and could you please go there and pay his fine.'

Elias had a black eye, a grossly swollen lip and two

58

front teeth missing. He had been sentenced to a five-pound fine or thirty days for being out without his pass. Dick paid the fine and drove him home.

'Why did they knock you about Elias?'

'No, because I tell them, you must phone my master and tell him where I am, so they tell me shut up, so I say but my master will come with my passbook if you phone . . . so they hit me.'

'I tried to find you,' Dick said. 'They told me you weren't arrested.'

'Oh yes, I am there at Marshall Square. I am there the whole weekend.'

Dick hurried back to the University to give a lecture; later in the afternoon he sought out a friend from the law department.

'Listen, Jimmy,' he said, 'I want to lay a charge of assault against the police. What do I do?'

'Assault? Were you assaulted?'

'Not me; actually it's for the chap who works for us, Elias. He was arrested for being out without his pass – he wasn't more than a few hundred yards from the house, went to buy a loaf of bread. They wouldn't let him get it, of course, and when he insisted that they phone me, they knocked him about.'

'Badly?'

'Well, he lost a couple of teeth and got a black eye.'

'That's not much of an assault, Dick. It's really not worth while laying a charge.'

'What do you need for a charge – that they should half kill him?'

'Well, frankly man, yes. You see, it's really a very minor assault. We could take photographs if you insist on going ahead, but in a couple of days all the marks will be gone.'

'Except his lost teeth.'

'Yes, well, the teeth. But you see it's the cost, Dick, both in time and money. He hasn't been disabled or lost any wages, has he? I tell you, it isn't worth it. It goes on all the time.'

'That's exactly why I want to lay a charge.'

'From our point of view – I mean sympathetic lawyers – it will be a nuisance. We have so many really serious cases to deal with, we haven't time for the little ones, so it would be all out of your pocket. You want my advice and here it is: forget it. Were there any witnesses? The police will say he was drunk and fell against a chair.'

He went home early and opened the door of his house, the house that lay almost concealed among creeping vines, wisteria, bougainvillea, honeysuckle, plumbago. Elias was laying the table for supper. His eye had changed colour and the swelling on his lip had lessened.

He greeted Dick cheerfully. Dick said, 'Don't you go out without that bloody pass, Elias, even as far as the front gate. We can't afford it.'

'Yes, master.'

'Tie the bloody thing around your neck or something, sew it onto your chest.'

'Yes, master.'

He sat with a book after dinner with determined concentration while arguments jumped into his head to exclude the meaning of the printed page. Margie wanted to go to bed early, because Jonny had been giving her disturbed nights. 'Are you coming, Dick?' she asked.

'I'll come later,' he said. 'I'm not sleepy. I want to sort out some of the slides from our summer holiday.'

The new automatic projector took a whole tray of slides and at the press of a switch lifted them one by one.

Another little button focused them without his having to move from his chair.

Photography was his hobby and the new projector a great joy. He closed the gaps in the curtains and put a small table in the centre of the room. The white wall acted as a screen. He fetched the boxes of slides, set up and plugged in the projector; switched on the fan that cooled the box, its low hum like a friendly insect in the quiet room; then the projector light, a strong white beam on the wall. He switched off the room lights.

A tray loaded with slides. He pulled up a comfortable chair and sat back with the switch in his hand. Click, a whirring sound, the slide lifted into place. That's the beach at Plettenberg, God, the surfing was marvellous last year, it was a good idea to go when the schools were not on holiday, the place was empty; shan't be able to do that when the kid is older and at school. Click, whirr . . . Margie coming in so smoothly on a breaker, smiling right up to that swerve on the sands. Memories of learning how to surf, waiting for the right breaker; the unparalleled physical exhilaration when you came in on a big one, all the way from the beginning of the indigo curve to the icy-white churned up dispersal on the beach.

Click, whirr.

That's the sea going through that hole in the rock at Keerbooms – that place is getting spoilt with all the holiday camps. Click – not quite in focus. That's better. Kysna forest. Too dark, take that one out. Click, whirr. The flowering wattles along the road, magnificently crowned with flame and orange flowers. Beautiful.

For the first time since that evening the previous week, the oppression of the groups and the arguments and all the tedious and troublesome discussions were swept from his mind. He felt relaxed and happy. The darkened room, the silent house, the mesmeric light enclosed him. The plastic switch that controlled and focused the Technicolor memories shining on the wall of the room was like a genie, responding instantly to the press of his finger. He was secluded, safe, withdrawn from the world.

Click, whirr.

And suddenly, sharply in focus, in full brilliant colour and larger than life, he saw in place of the slides the face of Elias, top lip huge and distorted on one side, eyes puffed and discoloured. Without thinking, he pressed the switch. The machine made its movements, replaced the old slide with another, but the face of Elias remained as though painted on the wall.

He switched off the projector light; then sat for a long time without moving, staring in the darkness of the room, while the fan cooling the machine whirred quietly on.

'It was foolish of you to phone me,' Ralph said.

'Why ever not?' Dick asked, 'We were on the same committee together.'

'No, but it's not the same thing. You were never in any political party, as I was, nor have you been closely associated with the Congress movement. They must have a file on you, that's true, but you're probably not under regular surveillance. They watch me all the time.'

'Then why did you tell me to come up to your office?'

Ralph glanced at him impatiently. 'Because once you'd phoned me there wasn't any point. Don't you know they tap phones? And bug offices? How would it have sounded if I'd said "Meet me at the café, be sure you're not being followed?" And then of course we couldn't talk in my office, it was just a meeting place. It's better in the open air.'

They were sitting together on a low wall near the main

University block. The sun shone from a cloudless sky and students, singly or in groups, were walking or lying around on open grassy spaces.

'Anyway, from now on,' Ralph continued, 'it would be better if we appeared to be not particularly friendly. But of course, I'm glad you contacted me,' he added to soften his strictures.

'You seemed to be the best person. There were others, but I suppose I trust your experience more.'

Some students came and sat on the wall near them.

'Let's go for a walk,' Ralph said, getting up.

As they walked, he said, 'So you've made up your mind?'

'Always so many choices,' said Dick. 'Which one is better than the other . . . well, I shouldn't complain, it's always easier for us whites.'

'Not always. Our lives are easier, of course. We have money, choice of home, freedom of movement, yes. But as regards moral choices, everything pulls us different ways; we have a vested interest in the maintenance of white supremacy, the way we live proclaims that interest. Materially we risk more if we want to change things. With Africans it's not so complicated. For most of them there's only one way.'

'They have two choices, don't they?' said Dick. 'To accept or to oppose. Maybe a third: actively to collaborate, be a government stooge.'

'Yes, *but* – look at it this way. If you are black and you collaborate with the authorities, you are casting yourself out from your own community. With us whites it's the reverse: we are cast out when we oppose apartheid. Blacks who simply remain passive are not compromising themselves in any way; but we, if we remain passive are actual collaborators, because we derive such huge benefits from white supremacy. Every white draws big dividends on the investment of being white, whether we say we approve of apartheid or not.'

'According to that argument you are still drawing dividends, even if you actively oppose.'

Ralph smiled. 'Up to a point. We are always very much aware of this in the CP, the way we lived, our servants, our holidays, our kids' schools. Sometimes it was painful – to have African friends come to your home, to go to theirs . . . But the position is changing. The risks are much greater now than a few years ago, and prison for whites is still prison even if we get a slightly more varied diet and a thicker mat to sleep on.'

They had arrived at the grounds where a Rugby practice was in progress. The players were all white and hugely muscular. A scattering of spectators on the benches, students with Wits blazers and long scarves. Seating themselves on a bench, distanced from other spectators and from the players, Dick felt the strange contrast between this normal physical display and their own tense and secretive conversation.

'Do you think they're like the Germans and just don't see the transports?' said Dick, gesturing towards the students, 'But how can they *not* see what's going on? I keep asking myself. Well, there are some . . . but so few, such a small minority compared to the whole student body, they should want to be rebellious, not to conform . . .'

'Think of the enormous pressures on the individual today. The Nationalist government *is* South Africa, to oppose them is un-South African. Who advised them, I wonder? In psychological terms it's been masterly, and it doesn't happen by chance. Opposing the government has become synonymous with betraying South Africa, the government is apartheid, apartheid is the South African way of life. To choose to be different is treason; this cuts us off, we are indicted not for opposing apartheid but for betraying us all.'

'Then how do you overcome? If you're correct, the more you proselytize against apartheid the more you drive whites into a defensive response, and their patriotism becomes equated with their ethics. In Germany, only an extreme military defeat . . .'

'But that's just where we're different,' Ralph intervened, 'because here the majority of people, the vast majority, are totally against the state apparatus. Africans don't identify with the government, they loathe apartheid and the Nationalists and everything they represent, loathe them with their hearts and souls. This is where white liberals fall down, they don't think of anything except what whites feel, whites say, white reaction. Whites must come to understand there is no future for them unless they are prepared to defer absolutely to the black majority.'

Dick contemplated the field, the trainer with hand uplifted blowing his whistle, interjections from a group of spectators, and said sadly, 'I don't see them coming to terms with that.'

'Not by logical arguments, maybe, but by the hard logic of events. There is a change coming in the nature of the struggle. It's not simply that things are becoming more difficult, it's a radical change of direction.'

'Change? It's been changing all the time, every time new laws came to suppress what people were doing, they changed their tactics.'

'Yes, but this is radical change, qualitative if you like. A new organization is being formed, an offshoot of the African National Congress, a militant wing, Umkhonto we Sizwe – the spear of the nation.'

65

He said the name slowly and with pride.

'I'm inviting you to join it, Dick, because your expertise is just what is needed. 'We're preparing for a campaign of sabotage. You must know what you are in for.'

Dick gave a little laugh. 'Funny, really,' he said. 'Here I've been hovering on the brink so long and when I finally have to decide – hell, it's not a little step, it's a stride into the unknown. You know, I don't really see myself in this rôle. Can it be done? Where will it take us? What will it lead to?'

'Who can answer such questions? The idea is to attack symbols of apartheid and to do so without killing people.'

'A contradiction, surely.'

'No, not if you go for installations, transformer boxes, or post offices, pass offices, such places, at night when they're empty. The idea is to shock whites into a realization of the despair and impotence of the people, the closing of every single outlet for expression. Whites condone violence, this is a deadly violent society, but violence against blacks is permissible because it's done within the framework of the state and its violent laws; only retaliation must be wrong because it's in opposition . . .'

Dick said impatiently 'I understand that, my doubts are not concerned with that.'

'Then?'

He hesitated. 'I wish I could see where it will lead. I can't persuade myself of its effectiveness.'

'Dick, why did you approach me at this time? I know you were approached once before to join an underground group and you refused. Isn't this the inevitable next step?'

'Yes, I suppose you are right.'

'What did you think? What would you propose?'

'I don't know. I wanted someone else to give me the answers. I just don't know.'

66

'When every single way is blocked? Every effective act illegal? Every organization driven underground? A massive military operation if anyone tried to organize peaceful protest?'

'Yes, of course . . . there's this awful contradiction: fear of doing nothing; fear of involving innocent people.'

Ralph frowned as the players left the ground to shower and change before resuming their studies.

'There are no innocent people,' he said.

# *Indres . . .*

The volunteers were formed into groups of three and began to study how to become saboteurs. Indres was in a group with Kabelo and Sipho, Congress members with whom he had worked in the past. They used pseudonyms, as instructed, although they knew each other well. Sipho was the lieutenant of the group, in touch with the captain, next in the pyramid organization. They knew there were many other groups like theirs, but each group knew only its members. Inevitably this structure designed for security began to break down. Technical information passed from experts at the top through the various levels down to the captain, through to the lieutenant and to the other group members, did not always arrive as accurately propounded or understood as it started, and for such work this was too dangerous. A small error in timing could become a fatal accident. So one of the experts himself would come to give information, and Indres soon had direct contact with Dick Slater. Dick's name was now Harry, but they had known each other in the Human Rights group and using assumed names became a bit of a game.

Dick – Harry – was experimenting with different materials and constructing various timing devices.

The explosive, the detonator, the timing device; three essential components and each had to work reliably. Harry showed how the fuse or primer could also embody the timing device. He took a plastic tube and put filter paper over one end then a layer of Condy's ground to a fine powder, then more filter paper, a layer of sand that had been washed repeatedly, then glycerine poured on top of that; the glycerine dripping slowly through sand and paper would finally reach the Condy's and ignite it. The time taken for the glycerine to seep through the sand, penetrate the paper and react chemically on the finely-ground permanganate of potash was determined by the quantity of sand and the amount of glycerine used. The whole mechanism was therefore a timing device, while the ground permanganate and the glycerine acted as the igniter; the heat and flame generated by these were sufficient to ignite and explode the bomb.

He gave them a simple and spectacular demonstration.

He put some of the powdered crystals in a saucer, then dripped glycerine directly on to them. In just a few seconds they flared and flamed.

'You have five, perhaps six seconds from the time the glycerine touches the powder. So if your detonator fails and you want to set it off yourself, remember – five seconds to get clear, to get away. But you're more likely to blow yourself up this way.'

The group did its own tests, timing the drip through the sand. Too much sand and it absorbed all the glycerine before it reached the powder; too little, and it dripped through too quickly to allow a safe get-away.

One night they made and tested Molotov cocktails. 'Molotov?' Indres had asked their captain, 'What's that?'

'Molotov,' he replied, 'was a Russian general in the last war. The Soviet guerillas used to make these and throw them at the Nazi tanks. They called them Molotov cocktails.'

Old jars, old bottles, any glass container filled with petrol. A little tar or creosote added to make it stick; an airspace at the top, then the neck of the bottle stuffed with cotton waste dipped in motor oil or petrol. They took the cocktails to an abandoned brickfield, ignited the cotton waste, then threw the bottles hard, with all their strength, against the piles of bricks. And exulted. Each imagined himself flinging his cocktail against the Saracens.

Summer ended, the winter passed with trials and tests. The short crisp days, without rain, the early dark and cold nights which kept people at home, exactly suited their needs. They worked feverishly; they had to be ready by the time summer arrived, for the date set in December for the co-ordinated acts of sabotage planned for the main centres throughout the country. They knew that everywhere there were groups like theirs, experimenting and learning, borrowing 'safe' cars and motor-scooters, selecting targets, watching and noting times, traffic, passers-by, other hazards; groups, like theirs, training themselves for that day when it would all begin, the day when they said goodbye to pacifism and opened a new era of resistance.

As the time came nearer, Indres spent more and more of his time on the preparations and less on his studies. Books lay unopened in his room; he skipped lectures, wrote up notes from friends' books. He had not been unaware of the irony of his position, the man studying to become a lawyer, a defender and upholder of the law, preparing at the same time for the most illegal challenge yet to the country's laws. The contradiction amused him for a while, then seemed absurd.

There were painful arguments with his brother Joe who ran the family store and had fastened all his own ambitions on Indres becoming a professional man, the man of education and standing who would break out of the pattern of shop-keeping and trading that had been forced on the Indian community when other avenues were barred, Joe had provided the money for Indres to go to university and study law.

'Get educated first,' Joe told him 'then you can liberate the masses.

'Why can't you wait?' Joe asked him, 'Just wait for these few years while you finish your studies.

'Give me an undertaking,' Joe pleaded, 'that you'll keep out of trouble until you've written your finals. When you are qualified, I promise you, what you do with your life will be your affair. I won't even ask. But until then, don't you think you owe something to your family?'

It was not easy to go to Joe and say, 'I've abandoned my studies, and I'm not going back to them.'

There was the silence of sadness, of disbelief.

Then, 'And how do you expect to earn a living? You never wanted to come into the shop – even if I would have you.'

'I'm becoming a full-time political worker,' Indres said.

'And that's your career!' Joe exclaimed with bitterness.

'Yes, that will be my career. I want you to know how very grateful I am to you for all . . .'

'Grateful? Don't talk like that! Gratitude! It's not what I've done that I care about, Indres. It's what you do with your life. A waste of your gifts, of your life. You, the clever one, such a sharp child. What good will you be without education? How will you ever support a family on what the comrades will pay you? Is this a career? You'll be of more value to the movement, to your comrades, when you are a qualified lawyer. They will need you then. They need lawyers, don't they? And they will need more . . . You, such a brilliant student; you will regret it very soon, it won't be long before you will regret.'

'If I do regret,' Indres said, 'then perhaps I can return

to my studies at a later stage.' He did not really think this, he wanted to comfort Joe.

'And that will be so easy? They won't have you, for sure. You can't come and go as you please. Life's not like that, particularly for you, an Indian in this country.'

In despair he pleaded, 'We were all looking to you, Indres, we were depending on you. How can you do this?'

'How can I not do it?' Indres retorted, misery forcing an angry response. 'Where will I practice law when we all live in separate Group Areas? Stuck out at Lenasia with a dozen other unemployed Indian lawyers, or living five miles outside Middelburg on a spot of bare veld labelled "Indian Group Area"?'

'We'll still need lawyers, wherever we are living,' Joe said obstinately, 'and you and your friends will need them most. Look how much we depended on lawyers in the past.'

'That's how it was; but things have changed, you know it yourself, changed. Every year new laws, there's no real law to practice anymore. It's a joke, Joe, to try and practice law in this country.'

'Go overseas for a while, then. I'll give you the money. Have a look around Europe.'

'Oh, Joe, I don't want to look around Europe, even if they gave me a passport which they wouldn't.'

'Think of yourself and your family for once,' Joe urged.

Teeth clenched, Indres said silently inside himself, 'Get off my back.' Everything reduced to personal terms. Joe couldn't see beyond the family, the individual ambitions. But he, Indres, was pledged to a better, more dedicated life. He was filled with his own moral superiority.

But he remained silent for a while. Then he said, 'How can I ever explain? At what point do I, do each of us, stop thinking about our own safety, our own family, career, jobs, at what point can we stop making excuses?'

'You're young still, you are an idealistic, it's good, I admire your ideals. But men can't live on ideals. Politics is one thing, but there is still the politics of living, of getting up each day and eating and working. I can't see the end. I can't see what will happen to you, except you will end in jail.'

The end was far away, the end would come one day but not for a long time. All that mattered for the present was the pestle and mortar, that prized possession with which they ground the crystals and charcoal and saltpetre. They took turns at the grinding, half an hour at a time. They thought of nothing else except the day when all the alchemy, all the theory and learning and testing, would be made to work in a great circle of acts of sabotage spreading through the land.

## Pila . . .

By the following Sunday the marks of the week's storms had been obliterated from the garden; the massed banks of star-like daisies were reflected in the blue water of the pool.

Janet was once more massaging her legs and Mrs Norval cried, 'What a week! What a week! All that rain – we had some hail one night, I thought everything would be flattened – flattened! but luckily it stopped, just a few large stones; do you remember last year, every flower stripped, bare stalks standing, the whole garden white – but this year it's been just rain, rain, I can't remember so much rain at this time of the year.'

'It always rains like this at this time of the year,' said Janet.

'Oh, no, that's not so. Later on, January, February . . .'

'It rained just as hard and often this time last year.'

'Well, it might have done, it just doesn't seem like it though. Perhaps I've forgotten.' Mrs Norval was conciliatory; past experience had taught her she could not win this kind of argument with Janet.

'You know,' she went on, 'I had to have my hair done twice this week, I went Tuesday, no, Wednesday, oh no, it must have been Tuesday because Phineas was here and he's off on Wednesday . . .'

'I thought Phineas was off on Thursdays.'

'No, it used to be Thursday. It's Wednesday now, he changed with Emily, because her husband gets off

Thursdays, so if she goes off on Thursday they have a chance to see each other every week.'

She continued to talk about the hair appointments, then turned to Pila and said she would make an appointment for her to have her hair done.

'Whatever for?' Pila exclaimed. 'What's wrong with my hair?'

'It's not that anything's wrong with it, but they do such cute things these days, brushing it up on top, so high . . .'

'I hate all that teasing and back-combing,' said Pila, 'and anyway it ruins your hair.'

'Pila's the natural type,' remarked Janet, adjusting a piece of white cardboard, a triangle held in place by her sunglasses to protect her nose from too much sun. 'Barry, tell Nanny to get those kids out of the water, they've been in long enough.'

'She's a new one, isn't she dear? What happened to that nice girl you had?'

'Edith? Vamoosed. Just upped and left, taking all her things of course and one or two of mine.'

'Oh dear, oh dear, I thought she was such a reliable girl, honest and reliable, being older, it's the young ones usually . . . what did she take?'

'She didn't actually steal anything, but I'd given her a very good winter coat I didn't want any more and one or two other things, and I did expect her to pay me something towards them at the end of the month.'

'But she was with you such a long time. What made her do a thing like that?'

'She said her daughter was going to have a baby and she wanted to be with her. I told her she must wait until after the holidays. I can't train a new girl, it would ruin my whole holiday. It's so difficult to get decent, reliable girls these days. Influx control – they stop them coming in to the towns, but we're also affected; it limits our own freedom of choice, doesn't it?'

At lunch time Mr Norval announced that he had bought a farm.

'But you know nothing about farming!' Pila exclaimed, 'Whatever do you intend to do with it? Retire onto it? Mom's hardly the country type!'

'It's a form of investment, my dear,' he replied. 'Many business men are investing in land today. There's a lot of money to spare. Land's always a sound investment, it can only go up in value.'

'Land and diamonds,' remarked Barry, 'the very best investment, they never deteriorate.'

'Where is it? What sort of a farm is it?'

'It's up in the Western Transvaal, Marico district, right on the border of Bechuanaland – in fact, the farm ends at the Groot Marico river which actually marks the border. It's very good land, needs irrigation. The place would be a dustbowl like Bech, if it were not taken care of. That's how the natives ruin the land, crop it into desert with their donkeys and their cattle. We'll mainly grow mealies, I think. Keep a bit of livestock.'

He added, 'I plan to go up there next weekend. Would you like to come?'

'Yes, I think I will if I can manage it,' Pila replied. 'I'd love to see it.'

'Well, it's a bit of a long journey, I must say. They're building a landing-strip close by – security reasons, I think – then it will be a half-hour flight. But it'll take us about four hours by road. We'll have to start early.'

'You'll have trouble getting labour up there, won't you?' Barry asked.

'Oh no, I shouldn't think so. For one thing, they've had this long drought in Bechuanaland; a lot of those boys will be only too anxious to earn some money, they're doing nothing, you know. They can cross the river straight to my farm; it's dry most of the year or almost dry in any case. Then there's the new Act,' he added tactlessly. Realizing a moment later what he had said, he glanced sideways to Pila.

She made a sound of disgust. 'So that's why you objected to me demonstrating against it! You have a vested interest in it now!'

'Oh come, Pila,' her father replied, 'that's hardly fair. I didn't particularly like the Act, but a law is a law. Once it's been passed then you have to accept it; otherwise if everyone decided which laws they would or wouldn't obey it would lead to anarchy. And in many ways it's not so bad to provide work for young natives . . . lots of unemployment . . .'

Barry said, 'Those gangs in the townships, hanging around all day, bone idle, living by their wits – isn't it better that they should be allowed to do a good honest day's work than exist by stealing?'

'We've had this gang down our street,' said Mrs Norval, 'you know, they hang around the golf course, kids, most of them, but they'll steal anything they can lay hands on, food, clothes – you take your coat off for a moment . . .'

'But they wouldn't hang around if they were allowed to work. They won't give them work permits and they endorse them out. There are plenty of jobs in town, they're simply not allowed to take them.'

'Those people with the corner house. The window of their dining room is close to the street, it's burglar-barred at the other end, but one window . . . anyway, she was sitting there listening to her radio and she just went out of the room for two minutes – two minutes! – when she came back, the radio was gone.'

'But if they haven't got permits,' Janet intervened, 'regardless of the pros and cons about not giving them, then isn't it better for them to be in those camps, where they'll be looked after, given food, given work to do instead of smoking dagga?'

'You see, they just stroll down the street pretending to look for work, and if they see a window open and anything they can reach, well, that's that. Or else they go to back doors and beg for a piece of bread. You get it for them, next thing you turn around – the toaster's disappeared.'

'What's more, it's my intention to build proper housing on the farm for my workers, real decent housing. There's a cluster of huts, mud, thatch-roofed, you know; first thing I'll build proper brick houses and use the huts for storerooms.'

'And what about the children? Do you intend to build a school?'

'I'm in favour of it, but I'll have to sound out the local farmers. It has to be done with a group. I'll have to wait until I know some of them; don't want to start by antagonizing the neighbours.'

'You know the Lawsons, just down the road? They went to the Game Reserve for a long weekend, and when they came back their place was stripped. Stripped. Everything – blankets, sheets, clothes, cutlery, even some of the furniture, every single thing they could carry. They must've just driven a lorry up the drive and loaded the stuff on to it, in broad daylight, have you ever heard of such nerve? They lost everything.'

'Surely they were insured?' Barry asked. 'Very foolish if they weren't insured.'

'Well, of course, but you know what happens. You never get back the full value, even if you add a few things. And the nuisance of it all! All those forms, the police, the fuss. Fancy coming back from a holiday and finding . . . And you know those people in Waverley?'

'Anyway, I hope it will become a really pleasant place where we can go and relax, get out of town. I'll build onto the house, it's a bit small, and put in a swimming pool. The pool first, if you like.'

'You know the ones I mean, Marginson the name is – they moved into the house next door to the Hedleys four, no five, no it must have been four months ago because it was just at the same time as the provincial bowls tournament and they had a sister who's married to Gerry Fox, the gynaecologist, and I particularly remember the date because his wife was in the team which came second.'

'Whose wife? The Marginson bloke?'

'No dear, Mrs Fox, that's Gerry Fox's wife, she plays bowls at the Lyndhurst Club, and her sister is Mrs Marginson . . .'

'Never mind whose sister is who. What happened to the Marginsons?'

'I'm trying to tell you, dear, only you keep on interrupting. Lila Marginson, she had her bag snatched in the middle of town, right in the middle of Eloff Street, snatched out of her car. She was sitting at the wheel waiting for her daughter who'd just gone across the road to pick up a dress at the new boutique, you know the one, the place that's all done out in silver and black and they have a counter with cute little stools like a bar; the trouble is, you just can't get parking anywhere near there, so she was double-parked and her bag was lying on the seat next to her. And this native boy came to the window and said, "Excuse me Madam," – very soft-spoken he was, Lila said, very polite – "excuse me, Madam, there's something wrong with your exhaust." So naturally she got out of the car to have a look . . .'

'Oh lord!' Barry exclaimed, 'That's the oldest gag in the book; how on earth could she fall for it?'

'Well, you don't always stop to think,' Mrs Norval cried indignantly. 'Sometimes you don't think, you just react automatically. I mean, if someone told me something was wrong with my exhaust or my back tyre was flat, or something, I wouldn't stop and consider, and say to myself it's all some sort of trick or plot, now, would I? Would you?'

'Yes, I would,' said Janet flatly.

'Well, she didn't, and I don't blame her. She got out of the car and went to the back, and she couldn't see anything wrong, so she turned round to ask what he was talking about, and he'd disappeared, and when she got back in the car, her handbag had gone.'

'She deserves to lose her bag, to fall for a trick like that.'

'Oh, but there's such a lot of crime!' Mrs Norval exclaimed. 'Let's face it, they've become so brazen, they'll steal anything. Look what happened to Jock Weidenfeld's teeth . . .'

'You might end up with Emily's boy working for you.'

'Fine, fine, she could come and visit him, and he'll get good treatment. I've always treated those who work for me fairly. But I'll go into it. Perhaps I can get him a permit to stay here, though I doubt whether they'll take him into the school again.'

'Jock Weidenfeld's teeth! Honestly, Mum, whatever are you talking about?'

'Yes, his teeth. I mean his false teeth, of course. He put them in a glass on the windowsill at night. He put them there one night and when he woke up the next morning they'd gone.'

'They're no use to anyone, it's like pinching someone else's spectacles, you can't wear them, everyone's got different eyes and teeth.'

'You'd be surprised. They flog anything in the townships. They wear glasses when they don't need them, just to make themselves look educated. Next thing, they'll have their teeth out just so they can wear false ones like white people.'

'Fishing it's called. They have this long pole with a hook at one end, and they fish through the open windows, between the burglar bars. He lost his trousers as well, with money in the pockets; and the teeth, they must've just put their hands between the bars and lifted them out of the glass.'

'I think it's hilarious!' Janet cried.

'You wouldn't if it happened to you.'

'My teeth are my own, thank you.'

'Yes, and next thing they'll find a way to steal the teeth from your mouth. As for Jock, it's all very well for you to laugh, Janet, but he had to attend a civic luncheon that day for delegates to the Chamber of Commerce conference and he had a terrible morning trying to get his dentist to fit him a new plate, but of course, it couldn't be done in time. Myra told me, she's Dr Miller's sister, he's the dentist Jock went to. She made me promise not to tell anyone, so don't spread it around.'

'But if he can't get back to school, there isn't much point in him staying, unless you can get him work as well. Dad, it's a terrible law, will you really make use of it to get cheap labour for the farm? Not just cheap labour – it's forced labour.'

'But everyone in town knows about it in any case. He

couldn't eat a thing the whole luncheon, just sat there with his mouth closed and never said a word so no one could see he had no teeth.'

Mr Norval, his heavy face suffused with sun, wine, high blood pressure and anger at Pila, turned his annoyance onto his wife.

'What in God's name are you talking about?' he exploded.

She looked at him in surprise. 'Why, we're talking about the same thing as you are – Jock Weidenfeld's teeth.'

'What on earth have his teeth got to do with anything? We were discussing labour problems on the farm!'

'But it's exactly the same thing, isn't it? You're talking about giving work to the thieves and gangsters, and we were talking about crime. It's all the same thing.'

'What would you do, for instance, if you were in my position?'

'I wouldn't collaborate.'

'You wouldn't collaborate! You do collaborate, we all do, you've been doing it all your life. The way you've lived – this house . . .'

'I don't live here any more.'

'No, you don't live here, and how different is the way you live? So you have a flat without a garden. You still have a flat boy who comes in each day to clean and polish floors, don't you? Who washes and polishes your car for you? A black man! Do you refuse to get on a bus or go to the theatre because the natives are not allowed to? Be logical! You couldn't go and live with them, even if you wanted to, and they wouldn't want you in any case. And let me tell you, my girl, you wouldn't last two days under their conditions, you're not used to it. This is the way we all live. You can't change it, so you want to smash it to bits.'

'Perhaps that's what we should do.'

They were both silent, sitting at the table loaded with the debris of the meal, from which the others had now gone.

'It's OK Phineas, you can clear the things off now,' Mr Norval said, as the man came silently in and paused at the door when he saw them still sitting there.

Mr Norval pushed his chair back. 'Well, then, perhaps it should be smashed and perhaps not. The plain truth is that the native isn't strong enough to do it. Maybe he will be, one day, in fifty, a hundred years. They just haven't got the intellect, it's been proved time and time again. They haven't the know-how, the technical knowledge, the experience.'

# Indres and Sipho . . .

As December drew near, each group selected a target, their 'symbol of apartheid authority, symbol of the state'.

Indres, Kabelo and Sipho chose a municipal office in a small mining town not far from Johannesburg. When they had received the go-ahead from higher-up they examined the place several times. There were municipal police at the main door, and one of them would walk round the building at intervals during the day and at night. But it was intermittent and casual, the sort of inspection that could easily be delayed by some diversion.

In the office were pass records, the files of every single black employee in that area. With their experience still limited, they knew they could not hope to blow up the whole building, but at least some damage could be done, some records destroyed. It was the right kind of symbol to attack.

At a side entrance, along a narrow strip of road, there was a heavy door and a barred window. After watching for some time, they decided that this was the best approach. The blackjacks – the municipal police – strolled round the building in leisurely fashion. Their uniforms had the town's name woven into tabs on their shoulders, and from the wide leather belt that each wore swung his only weapon, a short knobkerrie. Black men were not permitted to carry arms.

There would be enough time to run up to the door and place a bomb against it before the blackjack came round again.

'And supposing it goes off just as he passes?' Kabelo asked.

'Ah, that's a problem,' said Indres. 'We'll have to think of some way of keeping them all round the front for a while, until it goes off.'

'We should put a fairly short time on it,' said Sipho, 'and I'll go round the front and talk to them until it's nearly due to go off.'

'They would remember your face and describe you afterwards.'

'Not necessarily. And another thing, our people have a habit of playing dumb where our own kind are concerned. I doubt if they would give the police a proper description. I could even stay until it goes off, they would never think I had anything to do with it.'

'And when it explodes?' asked Kabelo.

'We'll all dash around in all directions.' Sipho said with relish, 'and I'll dash in all directions too. One of my directions will lead me to the car where you'll be waiting for me.'

Sipho had this way of playing the fool. Indres never knew whether he was serious or not.

'Yes, man, ja, it would work, you'll see . . .'

'No,' Indres was not convinced. 'We must think of something else. Create some sort of disturbance, draw them away from the building.'

The home-made bombs were not very powerful. To make the blast effective at all it was necessary to shore the bomb up with sandbags so that the explosion would not simply discharge itself harmlessly outwards into empty air, but inwards to do the greatest damage to the building.

One night they drove out to a building site and filled four large sacks with sand from a pile. In mid-December they obtained a car, which they drove to the municipal office; then they hauled the bags out and left them next to the door. The building was surrounded with a mass of waste and litter, particularly at the sides and back, a disordered jungle of dried grass, weeds, discoloured newspapers, the bones of old bicycles, rusted cans.

Indres had the responsibility of preparing the bomb. Sipho was to make and set the detonator. Kabelo had the task of arranging safe transport.

The contact who had brought approval of their plan from the Regional Command also gave Indres some Christmas wrapping paper with holly and gold bells. 'Wrap your parcel in this,' he said, 'a Christmas gift for Verwoerd!'

Indres took the train to town, nursing the parcel on his lap. He felt a sense of excitement and triumph. The streets of the city were crowded with Christmas shoppers, the windows decorated with blobs of cotton wool snow, although this was high summer, the hottest time of the year. Even the Africans had extra money to spend – those who were working – and every family stretched its resources to the limits to make a very special dinner and some small treats for the children. Church and charity bodies held parties in the townships, and at these, as at the big stores in town, a white Father Christmas with cotton wool beard and red flannel robe sweated as he dispensed small packets of sweets or promises of toys. In the suburbs trees blinked with coloured lights strung high by the black servants for this ceremony of mid-winter in cold lands, imported to the hot and alien south.

Now it was all beginning, Indres thought, a new era, a new struggle, after all the endless discussions and arguments, the long inactivity, the frustrating delays. How would people respond? Would they be igniting a great veld fire? The spark lay on his lap.

Gazing out of the window as the train came to a station, Indres saw a man he knew walking along the platform; carrying with care a small parcel wrapped in the same gay paper with holly and bells . . . he smiled. On such small things security could break down, for now he knew the identity of someone from another group.

When he arrived at his destination, he crossed over the railway line and saw Sipho walking along ahead of him on the bridge. Outside the station, still walking separately, both turned in the direction of the African location. The passengers thinned out. The two men walked slowly. There were not many people about.

Kabelo arrived in a car, and picked up Indres and then Sipho. They drove to the municipal offices.

Kabelo parked the car some way away, and stayed with it. Together now, Indres and Sipho crossed the road to where they could see the front of the building. They were astonished to see the blackjacks all sitting on the steps of the front entrance, hats off, belts loosened, talking loudly, laughing loudly, arguing loudly, their knees wide apart, the kerries lying on the ground next to them. They were drinking beer from tins, they were all drunk, and would probably be drunk every night now until Christmas. This was so unforeseen but so convenient that Indres and Sipho could barely keep from laughing out loud. They squeezed each other's arms and grinned in the dark.

They were happy. They were nervous.

'Oh boy!' Sipho whispered when they reached the side, 'Oh the stupid bastards, the stupid drunken bastards!'

His own breath smelt strongly of brandy.

'You've had a tot or two yourself, haven't you?' Indres asked.

87

'And you?' came the whispered reply, 'I suppose you never touch the stuff?'

'Not tonight.'

The sandbags were exactly where they had placed them. Sipho squatted down to fix the detonator while Indres kept watch. They heard the bursts of loud laughter, the voices, born on the warm evening wind. They felt confident that they had time, that the men would not get up from their party.

Sipho breathed noisily as he worked. 'It's done,' he said at last, straightening himself up. They gave the sandbags a last pat and went to join Kabelo. It had been too easy. They laughed and sang all the way back to Johannesburg. They felt mad with happiness.

*December 16, 1961*

His small cousin banged on his door next morning. 'Indres, Indres, look at this!'

Huge black headlines: SABOTAGE! The explosions claimed the full front pages of the newspapers. His heart pumped as he read, first skimming the headlines, then studying every word. Bombs had exploded in Durban, Cape Town, Port Elizabeth, as well as many in Johannesburg and one or two smaller centres. But not where they had gone; it was not mentioned. He read the reports over and over again; there was no word of the municipal offices.

They met in bitter disappointment, and discussed what might have happened. They thought it might just have been omitted from the news, but they knew they had to go and find out.

Sipho and Indres drove out one night in a hired car. They saw the whole scene as it had been, totally undisturbed, the weeds, the papers, the rusting spokes, and the sandbags still leaning against the wall. The bomb, untouched and undetonated, still lay behind the sacks. While Indres kept watch, Sipho dismantled it calmly and cautiously. He knew it could still go off at any moment but with steady hands and without haste he detached the detonator; they took the bomb back to the car to examine it. In the light of the torch, they saw it had not been properly set.

Sipho smiled disarmingly. 'I slipped up; don't know how it could have happened.'

He went over everything he had done. 'I just slipped up,' he said.

'You were too drunk,' Indres retorted angrily, 'I told you that night. You drank too much brandy.'

Sipho shrugged. 'It could have happened to anybody.'

After the first fiasco their jobs became more successful. On the opening day of a big political trial they and other groups in their area hit a dozen different places. The disruption caused was not very great and the damage was soon repaired, but they felt they were fulfilling the requirements of the agreed policy – hitting at symbols of apartheid, not risking human life.

They were sure the fear and uncertainty of the whites would grow, and that sabotage would spread across the country. They were becoming more experienced and more daring.

High summer. All over the country fruit ripened on the trees. Oranges rotted where they were dumped in secret piles to keep up prices, while kwashiokor spread throughout the reserves.

Beautiful, bountiful summer, the land lush and prosperous as never before, the little black children with rags and stick-limbs and swollen bellies and hair turning strangely rust-coloured, dying in the remote countryside.

Fires flared on white farms, the dry grass crackled and burned, the ripe crops exploded into flames. Summer heat or sabotage? There were areas of uncertainty. There were many explosions in the towns, each followed by arrests and raids. Sipho and Indres moved around, living in different places, and spent all their time improving techniques.

Gradually they built their store of knowledge, sometimes through information passed on to them, sometimes through their own study and investigations and through experiments. Sipho's unsettled life, the many jobs he had taken, the skills he had acquired and his endless ingenuity and resourcefulness made him invaluable.

They sought the experiences of other people, searching for information on how they had worked; Grivas, the Israelis. A book on guerilla warfare by Ché Guavara became a precious bible, secretly passed from group to group, always kept hidden in safe places.

Others might value furniture, clothes, radios, but their most valued possessions were the pestle and mortar and the pipe bombs they made with 'little three'.

The grinding sessions were social occasions. Sitting on the edge of a bed with a newspaper spread out on the floor they took turns, half an hour at a time, grinding away, while someone sat in the next room watching and listening.

Experience showed the best home-made charge to be potassium chlorate; at first they called it potclor, then later by the nickname 'little three', from the formula, $KCIO_3$.

Getting sufficient quantities of little three was difficult. Chemists required the purchaser to show his licence, and although there were established connections with a few chemists who were prepared to supply them, the quantities were too small.

When they had a problem they could not solve, Sipho would say, 'Let me sleep with it.'

He slept with little three for only one night, then sent an urgent message to Indres the next day: 'Hold everything. In a couple of days we'll be fat.'

When they met, Sipho was almost dancing with joy. Expressive gestures, eyes widening and narrowing, pacing and acting out the episode, he told Indres, 'I was a fool man, just a fool! I knew where there was a ton of the stuff, just waiting for me.'

'Where?'

'They use it in hospitals. Remember I told you I worked once in that hospital near Germiston? They kept it in the storage section where the prescriptions are made up.'

'But how did you get it?'

'Man, it was easy, dead easy. A game. I know that place inside out, every little bit of it. I've done more difficult jobs than that one.'

He stopped abruptly, looking down. Perhaps he had not meant to say that.

'You broke in?'

'Could have done, but it wasn't necessary. My pal still works there. We arranged a burglary.'

And it was Sipho who devised a method for improving the bomb. They had stuffed the formula of little three mixed with sugar and sulphur into fairly large casings, such as empty cans. Sipho packed the charge into ten-inch lengths of narrow metal pipe. Bursting out of such narrow tubes the discharge was far more violent, causing a tremendous explosion. They called Sipho's new bomb 'the terrible one'.

Sipho and Indres became so expert that they were sent

to instruct groups in other areas in their methods. Each time they would contact just one person. They used different names and disguises, an added moustache, a changed hairline, so that the contact would be less likely to recognize them again. But perhaps they were not serious enough about trying to look and talk differently. Absolute trust of everyone they worked with was part of the inspiration that spurred them on.

They went to Durban at a time when the momentum of the sabotage campaign was being met with increased security measures and police vigilance. Every person who had ever taken part in political activity that could be construed as being anti-government, everyone who had been associated with the African and Indian Congresses, trade unions, political parties, fringe movements was under surveillance. Phones were tapped, homes watched, all movements recorded and notes made of all visitors. Each act of sabotage was followed by raids on homes and offices.

Police guards were put on possible targets. At the beginning it had been wide open, simple, now increased police vigilance kept pace with their increased experience.

In Durban Indres found a place to stay with a friend in the suburbs and Sipho went to look up a former woman friend.

'Never stay too long with one,' he would say, 'and never tell them anything, about yourself or anything else.'

They met by arrangement in public places, outside the post office, at busy bus stops, on street corners.

They felt that if they could pull off some acts of sabotage in places well outside the centre of the city, it might force the police to disperse their men to some extent. They had both been chafing at their inactivity, and one night they set out on a venture of their own.

A single-track railway ran down the coast south of Durban for a distance of thirty-five or forty miles. The railway served small holiday towns along the coast. If they could blast the track and derail a goods train it would block all the traffic, both up and down the line.

Indres went by train down to the South Coast to the small resort where he and Sipho had arranged to meet.

In an air-travel bag, he had six sticks of dynamite, a long strip of cordex, a detonator and fuse, and a torch.

He observed Sipho boarding the train at Durban; they travelled in different compartments.

About three quarters of an hour later they reached their destination. Indres walked in front, carrying his bag, Sipho followed.

The small town with its sprinkling of shops lay directly ahead. Indres walked down the single main street to a brightly-lit shop selling fish and chips. It was full of whites from a nearby camping ground: big, red-faced young men in tight and very short shorts, blonde hair close-cropped, children with long brown legs and straight hair bleached almost white.

He put the bag down casually and stood close to the counter protecting it with his feet. He waited unobtrusively until the assistant had finished with all the white customers. He should not have entered the café, but sometimes he was gripped by the urge to be foolhardy; he felt now a sense of superiority at possessing a power of which they were totally unaware, and for once waiting was almost a pleasure.

When he emerged clutching the fish and chips, he saw

Sipho gazing into a shop window a little further down the street.

They turned right on to a road that ran alongside the railway line, away from the town, still walking apart. In a little while the tarred road became a sandy track winding through fields of sugar cane. The tall canes stood on either side. Ahead was a bridge over a river, about half a mile from the sea.

Now the cane fields lay behind them. On one side of the road was the dense South Coast bush, a sub-tropical cave of lush dark leaves, twining vines, bushes and undergrowth so congested that to penetrate it you had to hack a path. Once in that bush, only a few yards off the track, there was complete concealment.

They did not want to start too early. There was plenty of time, there were plenty of trains. They could hear a train passing along the track, invisible below them.

In the thick bush, with the lights of the resort behind them, they ate bread and fish and chips, talking in whispers. They were possessed once again as they had been before by the tension and exhilaration, the adrenalin pumping through them; they were animals, all ears and listening, watchful, cautious, aware.

Unexpectedly, the rain stated.

It was not like the driving downpouring rain of the high veld. It was a fine South Coast drizzle, soft as a mist, but persistent. The moistness enveloped everything for it was this crowded wet air that made the sugar cane and the bush grow so lushly and plentifully. But the rain for them was a nuisance.

They left the bush and entered a small wood from which they could watch the railway line now some distance below them. There was a chemical plant a little further down the line – they could see the lights in the distance just beyond the bend in the track – and guessed there would be a number of trains coming through.

They worked together in the dark and the wet. At least the soft curtain of rain would help conceal them. They went to the track and quickly dug a small hole under the rail where they inserted the six sticks of dynamite. The end of the long piece of cordex that had been wound around the sticks was now trailed along the ground and up into the wood. Indres removed a detonator and a short piece of fuse from his pocket and he inserted the safety fuse into the detonator, using his own private crimping tool to make sure it was well hugged inside – his strong white teeth. He knew a moment of added excitement – if he bit too low the detonator would explode in his mouth.

He attached the detonator to the end of the cordex, binding the two together with insulation tape. The fuse was quick-burning, it needed only about ten seconds to activate the detonator and the shock would be transmitted almost instantaneously along the cordex to the charge under the rails. It would have been so much simpler to have left the detonator under the rails themselves to be set off by the wheels of the train; but if they did that, it meant they could not select their train, and they risked blowing up a train full of passengers instead of just goods. Sipho went a little bit further down the line to where he was visible to Indres, to signal to him when a goods train was approaching.

The fuse needed a sharp flare to ignite it. Indres had found after experimenting that if he reversed the process of match-striking, holding the match steady and striking the box against its head, the flare was more effective. So he stood with the head of the match placed against the exposed part of the fuse and the matchbox ready, waiting for the signal from Sipho, when he would pull the box sharply and run. He crouched over to protect the fuse and the matches from the unremitting rain that fell against him in gentle grey waves. Coat, body, hands, were cupped protectively around the fuse.

In the distance he heard the sound of an approaching train and watched for Sipho's signal. It came – a goods train – he struck the box swiftly against the match head, but it did not ignite. He tried again, trembling with impatience, and the match broke. The train rumbled slowly past as he fumbled ineffectively for more matches. The water dripped off his hands and he tried to dry them. It was too late. The train had gone.

Sipho came pushing through the dark. 'What happened?'

'It's too wet. The match wouldn't strike.'

'Was it the match or the box?' Sipho felt in his pocket. 'I've a dry one,' he said. 'Look, let me dry your hands and then keep them out of the rain.'

'There's a plastic bag there,' Indres told him; Sipho took this from the travel bag and tore it open. He arranged it over Indres' hands to protect them, the box and the matches.

They examined the matchbox carefully to find an area that was completely dry, using the torch and shrouding it with their jackets, even though visibility was so reduced by the veil of rain. Water dripped thickly from the accumulation on the leaves. All around them was the dripping, whispering, sibilant darkness.

'Are you ready?'

'Ready. This time must be it.'

Sipho again went down the line to signal when the next train approached.

At last there came the sound of a train. Indres kept his

eyes on Sipho, but there was no signal. A passenger train came round the bend, passed beneath him and trailed down the coast out of sight.

Indres stayed crouched down, hands stiff and trembling, afraid to change his position in the slightest because of the pervading rain. The air itself breathed moisture into him. Water dripped from his hair, his nose, down his neck.

After a long wait there was another train; again it was a passenger train. As it went past Sipho appeared beside Indres again. 'We should have done it,' he said fiercely, 'we should have blown that one. I nearly signalled to you.'

'But it was a passenger.'

'Yes, and we should have done it. We must do the next one, whatever it is.'

'You're crazy,' Indres told him, 'we can't blow a passenger train. We'd kill a whole lot of people.'

He had never seen Sipho so agitated, so seething with impatience.

'OK,' he whispered angrily, crouched in the dark to be close to Indres, 'what do you think's going to happen, sooner or later? When we're doing things like this? It's dangerous, man, for them and for us. It's not a child's game.'

'Sure, I know that. Accidents can happen. *But we are not murderers, we don't kill people deliberately!* It's against our policy.'

'It's rubbish,' said Sipho between clenched teeth, his lower lip protruding, 'all right, we adopt a policy, we all agree – but can't you see it's nonsense? What did the Israelis do in Palestine? The way I understand it – so I'm not great on theory, but I try to understand – they made it work by that very thing – terrorism. So we blow up a transformer box! Who knows about it except the police and they keep quiet? But we kill a couple of white bastards – the whole country will be on fire! Not so? They won't keep *that* out of the papers! I tell you, it's got to be done.'

'Well, maybe it will come to that at a later date, later on, but – '

'And another thing,' Sipho continued, 'why do we worry so about human life? Look at *them* man, do they care? Sharpeville, man! Langa, man! B-b-b-b-b-bb-'

He swung around as though firing a machine gun.

'Run, you bastards, we prefer shooting you in the back. Easy, isn't it, great sport, standing on top of a Saracen. Like shooting dassies. There – there's a kaffir girl with a baby on her back – look at how she waddles, can't run so fast, watch this, two in one go. *Yirra* man, did you see that? How she leapt in the air before she fell – look, the baby's still alive, we'll – '

'Sipho, stop it, stop it!'

Their hoarse whispers were as violent as if they were shouting. They both stopped and looked at each other, Sipho with anger and contempt, Indres with pain and confusion.

'Get back down the track,' Indres whispered at last. 'The next one's just about due. It's bound to be a goods train. But I trust you, man, you understand? One person can't decide – '

There was still quite a long wait before they heard the sound of another train. He saw Sipho signal and struck the box sharply against the match head. The match flared, the fuse caught and flared up – and died down. Desperately he blew at it to try and ignite the fading spark while the long goods train snaked slowly past beneath him, van after van, in a moment it would be

98

gone. He saw the guard's van in the rear and as he saw it, the explosion took place; he could hear the metal whizzing through the trees and clonking down. But the train continued undisturbed down the track, as though it did not care, and disappeared round the bend.

'It wouldn't catch,' he told Sipho, 'the fucking fuse wouldn't take.'

'Well, it was better than nothing,' said Sipho grudgingly.

'At least we cut the rail.'

'They worked hastily, picking up all the things and putting them into the travel bag. Then they took out plastic bags filled with curry powder and red pepper, slit them open, and scattered the contents over the tracks as they left the bush.

They ran back to the bush once more, then left it again in a different direction that was diagonally opposite to the way they had entered, and they pushed their way through the thick tangle of bush and vines down to the beach. Firm white sands lay between the bush and the sea. They entered the sea and walked some way along the beach in the water. Further on they left it again to walk on dry sand.

When they reached the shore Indres was overcome with a sudden wave of panic. 'Sipho, the torch,' he said, 'have you got the torch?'

'You have it,' said Sipho.

'No, I haven't got it. We've left it. It's there.' He turned but Sipho grabbed his arm. 'You can't go back.'

'I must. I must get that torch. It's got our fingerprints all over it.'

'Don't be a fool, man. You can't go back. They'll probably be on their way there already.'

'I'm going, Sipho.'

'No, no. No!' He held Indres in his powerful grip. He was not very tall, shorter than Indres, but very strong.

There was a distant sound of a dog barking. They both stood and listened. Then Indres turned reluctantly and they went on.

But he could not forget the torch lying in the wood where he had carefully placed it, and with his fingerprints on it. Sipho's too, probably. They had not bothered about wearing gloves because they had intended to leave nothing behind.

The torch lay on his mind with a foreboding of danger.

To avoid roadblocks that might be set up after the blowing of the train – after the big explosion they had planned – they had decided to return by walking all the way back along the seashore. But they had expected to be on their way back a long time before this. Now it was much later than they had planned, and with the passing of time the tide had turned. Along the great stretch of beach the surf was running, and petering, and spreading, each time reaching a little higher on the sand before it drew back again.

They came to one of the many places where a river ran down from the hills and crossed the beach to join the sea. There had been too much rain, the river was wider and deeper that they had thought it would be, fast-flowing with a strong current. Where the river poured into the sea, the sea spread out into a great rough lake across the beach, with clashing small waves meeting, rearing, forming swirling eddies.

They were carrying guns that Sipho had brought, for these days they preferred to be armed; they wrapped the guns in their socks. Guns, socks and shoes were placed in the bag, which they rolled up as tightly as possible. Indres held the bag on top of his head with both hands while

Sipho held on to Indres. In this way they began to wade into the tide-pulling waters of the river.

Air and water alike lay against them, heavy and soft as silk on their skins. Sea and sky and rain and river merged into one, merged into night, became the darkness itself holding the whole world. The darkness was the sea, the darkness was the lagoon, the spreading river that eliminated the land, the darkness was the surf thundering carelessly, proclaiming the power and the indifference of the ocean.

The sea was a bell, sounding along the shore, so insistent, so compelling, so incomprehensible in its spreading force and unknown depths, that consciousness merged with it, dissolved and disappeared in a world undefined by horizons, where their feet lost at last the steadying touch of the eliminated land as they waded step by step into the shift of tide and river and sea.

The sea came rushing in.

The surf rolled towards them. The sand sloped beneath their feet. Water billowed against their bodies. Each knew that alone he would have ceased to resist, for it was as though the river demanded that they relinquish the struggle, join the sea. It was easier to give in and be carried away than to fight against it. It was easier to submit than to resist. It was easier to die. But Sipho's strong hands held and steadied Indres, and the bag on his head to which Indres clung was like a line of life which bound them to their pledges.

Each step was felt first with probing feet. They feared not only the deep centre channel that the river had driven through the sand, but also any holes into which they could disappear. Once their feet were completely off the sand, both felt they would not be able to resist the force of the flowing waters.

Most of all, they feared the unseen presence of the sharks that came up to the swollen river mouths to search for food among the debris brought down by the flooding waters. This was the coast where they attacked swimmers. Dark shapes in dark waters, silent, a mere brush against the legs, – then the thrashing, the blood, the churned up water, a leg or an arm snapped off by a huge triangular-toothed jaw.

*We shall never make it back to the land.*

*You die from shock. That's how they die, on these beaches.*

Indres felt something brushing against his leg – water? – debris? – or – ?

When the water reached up to their chests they felt the sand beneath their feet shelve sharply down, and they knew this was the channel. Indres steadied himself upright while Sipho released him for a moment to test the width of the deep central cut. It was narrow at this point, as they had hoped. Together they managed to step over it and on to the other side.

The river reluctantly gave them back to the land again.

On the far side of the river, thick bush and trees met the banks of sand. The beach curved on, each curve ending in a cluster of rocks. At low tide the rocks were well out of the water so that the long beaches were joined by firm damp sand on which it was easy to walk. Now the sea had reached the rocks, they became jagged barriers, enemies. The sea swirled around them. They had to wait for the receding wave, then wade into the sea to try and skirt the rocks before the next wave engulfed them.

Out of their long silence Sipho voiced suddenly the thought that had never left him: 'We should have blown that train; the first one; the passenger one.'

'And kill all those people, black as well as white?'

'We're saboteurs, aren't we?'

'Yes, not murderers.'

'They murder us – and get away with it,' said Sipho with angry emphasis. 'Haven't they killed people you know? Everyone – '

Immediately a picture of his uncle Aziz came into Indres' mind; lying on a pavement, kicked to death, 'drowned in his own blood'.

Sipho continued, 'We're soft, all of us. You're soft. You carry a gun, but you'd be afraid to use it in case you hurt someone. Listen man, haven't you learned *anything*? Don't you know they are simply ruthless, ready to – anything – no matter what – shoot not one, two – hundreds, thousands if they want to. Sharpeville – it was just a little rehearsal. But wasn't it murder? Wasn't it war on the people?'

'Yes, in a way . . .'

'In a way? In *their* way! Machine guns in the backs of a crowd running away from them? And hundreds of Sharpevilles. June twenty-sixth, all those – riots – they shoot to make us riot to shoot us – '

'But we don't have to have their morals, Sipho; we're better, we're morally different, not just our policy but the way we do things as well, we must not learn to act the way they do . . .'

'That's exactly what we must do!' Sipho cried triumphantly. 'That's it! Until we learn to be like them, as hard as they are, as ruthless, as – as – not thinking of this individual life or that, but thinking of winning a war. OK, so innocent people will get killed, our people through our own action. The time will come, you'll see I'm right. This way is a game. This nonsense – blowing up *symbols*! Playing children's games.'

'But Sipho, we're not at war yet. This isn't war. It can't

103

be, we haven't trained, prepared, equipped. When it comes it will be different . . . I suppose it must come if things don't change. But we are still trying to make them change their minds. We just aren't soldiers, we just aren't fighting in a military sense, our people don't know yet how to start. That's why it has to be simply something symbolic. We limit ourselves, then later on we assess what's happened and discuss the next steps. Together.'

The words pressed against the engulfing night, lonely and absurd.

After a time Sipho spoke again. 'We're wrong,' he said, and paused. Then he repeated: 'We should have blown that train.' They walked on in silence, until Sipho spoke once more. 'Time comes when you got to make your own decisions.'

'I believe in our collective way,' said Indres. 'It can only work if we all agree. We can try and change what's being done, but we must all agree.'

After a while Sipho said, 'In the end, it's you yourself that counts, not the group. What you think is right, that's what *is* right. That's how you survive. In the end you find yourself in spots where there aren't any groups. Like us tonight. You're it, you're number one. Survival.'

Fifteen miles of shore, of rocks and rivers, of night and air like heavy silk pressing against them, still lay ahead . . .

# Dick . . .

A yellow oblong of light shone through the fanlight of Dick's office and onto the wall of the darkened corridor. There was a knock on the door. Inside the office, Dick hurriedly opened a drawer and swept the objects off the top of his desk into it. He wiped off some powdery remains with his handkerchief, glanced around his office. There was another knock, then the handle of the door moved down silently.

'Coming!' he called, and with another hasty glance around the room he walked forward and unlocked the door. 'Oh, hello,' he said to the man outside.

'Hello Dick.' The man wore a checked sports jacket and open-necked shirt. 'Working late?'

'Yes,' Dick replied, 'you know what it's like, exam papers.' He indicated the papers spread out on his desk with a wave of his arm, but still stood in the doorway, not inviting the man by word or gesture to come into his office.

'Man, that's what I've got to tackle,' the man said, 'but I prefer to take them home and work on them there. I just came to fetch some that I'd left behind . . . saw your light on. Thought perhaps it had been left on by mistake. That's why I tried the door when you didn't answer.'

He looked past Dick into the room. 'Mind if I come in?'

'No, of course not.' Dick stood to one side. The broad shoulders swayed sideways as though moving through a crowd.

'Why do you lock your door? Scared of *tsotsis*?'

Dick smiled nervously. 'Habit, more than anything else. When I was a student I always locked the door of my room when I was studying, and now it's a sort of reflex action, I'm not really aware of doing it.'

The man placed one buttock on the desk and sat with one leg tensed against the floor, the other hanging and swinging slightly. He looked around again with his small and thickly-lidded eyes. 'Got a cigarette?'

'I don't smoke,' Dick said, and felt immediately he had made a mistake. Spent matches, barely concealed by papers, lay on the bottom of his waste-paper basket.

'Oh, I thought you did.' The eyes glanced downwards.

'I used to. Gave it up. I do smoke a pipe, though, every now and then.'

'Filthy habit, smoking,' the man commented. He felt around in his jacket pockets and drew out a packet of cigarettes. 'Oh, I have got some after all; thought they were all finished.'

He took out a cigarette. 'Got a match?' Then without waiting for a reply he leaned across the desk to fish a matchbox out from under the papers. Those little puffed-up eyes were extraordinarily sharp. He lit his cigarette and dropped the spent match carefully into the waste-paper basket, leaning forward to see that it did not set the papers on fire. He leaned back again, blew out a long wreath of smoke, and sat silently, but with no apparent intention of leaving.

Dick looked at his watch once or twice, then walked over to the window and peered out. The man unhitched his buttock from the desk and came and stood behind him. 'Not much of a view, is it?' he commented. The office, two floors up, looked out on to an angled brick wall. 'But at least, you're private,' he added.

'It doesn't make any difference as far as I'm concerned,' said Dick. 'Anyway, when you're upgraded you get a better view. The sort of outlook you have is an indication of your status.'

'We're so crowded, we have to share offices.'

'But they are building you a new wing.'

'Yes, it'll be nice when it's finished – *when* it's finished.'

The conversation lagged once more, but still he stayed. Dick went to his desk and began to gather up some papers.

'I think I'll be making tracks,' he said.

'Me too,' said the man. But he did not move.

Dick put a batch of papers in his brief case and fastened it. 'First-years,' he remarked, 'they're really the worst of all.'

'Oh, they're hell, I agree with you. They won't make it, a lot of them, just don't work enough. Too many failures in the first year. Lots of these kids aren't serious, especially the girls. They come to find themselves a nice, educated husband. And some of the students occupy themselves too much with other things – extra-curricular activities – don't you think?'

'Well, I do think they should concern themselves with wider things than just their own particular speciality. It's very confining.'

'Oh, I agree with you, I absolutely agree. As long as it doesn't take them away from their work, become too important.' He paused. 'The Democratic League,' he remarked, 'they've been busy lately, haven't they. I think you are associated with them, not so?'

'I supported their protest against the Bantu Registration Bill.'

'I'm against it myself. Too many laws, anyway. It's just that I don't seem to find time to do anything about it.

Are you planning any more demonstrations? Perhaps I could help . . .'

'I've no idea. I'm not on their committee. It's run entirely by students.'

'Is it? Well, if you hear of anything, let me know. Be glad to do anything to help – as long as you don't want me to stand in a row of students with placards!'

'I'm off now,' said Dick.

At last the man turned his shoulders towards the door. Just before he went out he paused and said, 'Of course, you're quite right to give up smoking. Wish I had the willpower to do it myself. Well, goodnight, then.'

Dick listened to him walking down the corridor. He was wearing rubber-soled shoes that made a loud squeak when they came into contact with the highly polished linoleum. The sound was so pronounced that Dick could not understand why he had not heard it when the man had approached his office.

He looked around once more and was going to the door when he turned back. He opened the drawer and quickly put all its contents in his brief case. Then he locked the drawers and turned off the light.

The corridor was empty and quiet.

His car was parked in a section of an open courtyard marked with white lines and the words: Staff Members Only. The yard was empty now except for his car and another, an old car that had been parked in the same place for more than a week. Someone had said the battery was flat, but no one seemed to have made any effort to move it.

The man who had come to his office was nowhere in sight. Passing behind the parked car, Dick glanced up at the building he had just left and at the row of dark windows, including the edge of his own window, just visible behind the brick wall. He unlocked his car door, looking around once again. He was beset with a feeling of uneasiness, a sense of being watched. But there was no one. The courtyard was quite light, illuminated not only by a tall standard lamp, but also by the flooding white light of the moon. Shadows from the trees, a movement of foliage like curtains parting to the light, closing again. Momentarily – he could not be sure – he had the impression of a faint wavering light on his office window. He looked again, but it was not there. It might have been the movement of the trees, the reflected light from the street lamp, or the moon.

When he started his car he thought he heard another car starting up, like an echo. But when he turned off the parking area to the road he was alone, no car behind him. I'm getting too nervous, he thought, too jumpy. If someone was following me, I would surely see.

But the nervousness persisted. He drove slowly, his brief case on the seat beside him. It had seemed like a light . . .

Thabo stopped in the doorway of a building and took a pouch of tobacco out of his pocket, a pipe and matches from the other. He began to fill the pipe and tamp down the tobacco. His movements were slow and deliberate. He did not particularly enjoy smoking a pipe but he found it a useful excuse for stopping and hanging around when he was waiting for someone. A cigarette was lit in a moment, then you had to move on. But you could stop over the ceremony of filling, tamping and drawing on the pipe for quite a time without attracting the attention of police for hanging around.

Thabo had left his house in the township at six that

morning to catch the 6.30 train to Johannesburg. It was now fifteen hours later; he had worked in the shop until nearly seven, and had already covered one assignment. His strong, bearded face bore lines of fatigue, blue shadows under the skin beneath his eyes. I never see the children, he thought, Rebecca has to bring them up, do everything. He wanted to be home. Rebecca would have some food ready, kept warm a long time, for she never knew when he would come; but the children would be asleep.

As he felt the tobacco in the bowl of the pipe ignite and grow warm he looked carefully up the street. At this time of the evening, not too late, he still had a reasonable excuse for being in town should the pick-up van come past, but the town was closed down, the shops and most of the buildings in darkness. There were few passers-by and only an occasional car further down the street.

Then he saw the car for which he had been waiting, Dick's little grey Austin coming slowly towards him. He spotted it the moment it turned the corner; he was about to step out of the concealing doorway and walk up the street away from the approaching car – their arrangement was that he would be walking along the street and Dick would drive past and pick him up – when instinctive caution made him hold back for a moment. Then he knew why he had waited. Dick was being followed.

A second car had turned a corner far down the street and driven half way up, then pulled into the curb. The lights were switched off, but nobody got out. Whoever had been driving it remained seated inside, in darkness.

Thabo drew back again into the doorway, holding his pipe in his hand, covering the lighted bowl. He saw Dick drive slowly past him, peering anxiously up the street. Dick drew his car into the curb a little further on, waiting with his lights on and his engine running for a few minutes, then drew out slowly and turned the corner beyond.

Now Thabo heard the ignition of the second car, then judged by the sounds that it was backing down the street away from him. He moved to the other side of the doorway from where he could look down the street without stepping out. The car had backed down the street and reversed into a cross street, where it stopped on the opposite side of the road.

He realized why. The street where he was standing was one side of a grid; the road ran up this side, turned ninety degrees at the top, down the other side, parallel to this street. From where the car was parked, whoever was inside could see three streets. They could see if Dick drove down the parallel street without coming past them, and if he did this and drove on, they could again follow him.

Thabo waited in the doorway.

He heard the sound of Dick's car before it turned the corner into the street again. Dick changed gear at the corner, right down to first, he must have come to a standstill. He would be facing the car parked ahead of him on the other side, he could not fail to notice it. Surely he would note that the car had not been there when he first came up the street. Probably not, because he was not looking that way, he was watching the pavement where Thabo was standing, scanning that side of the street for him.

Slowly the little car drove past the doorway again; quite clearly Thabo saw that strained face. Go home, you fool, go home! How many times have we discussed just this sort of situation? For Christ's sake, go home!

Dick turned the corner again at the top of the block.

The other car stayed where it was, in darkness. Of course, all they had to do was wait. He could only pass somewhere in their line of vision.

He heard Dick's car being reversed, then for a third time Dick drove past the doorway, this time in the opposite direction, facing towards the parked car. Again Thabo pleaded silently, Go, go, go, oh you idiot! Go home!

This time Dick drove on slowly towards town. Thabo heard the other car start, watched it move down the street without its lights on. When it was out of sight he waited another two or three minutes, then walked out of the doorway and quickly headed towards his bus stop.

One evening the week before, Dick had excused himself in the middle of an important meeting to go out and phone his wife from a public call-box to tell her that he would be home late.

Apologetically he had said to Thabo, 'You know what it's like? I bet your wife worries if you're late, doesn't she? Might as well set her mind at rest.'

Mind at rest? No telephone in the townships. Home late? For her it could mean anything: delays on the long journey to the townships, breakdowns, accidents on the line; trains so crowded he could not get on; or he might have had to deliver some books after the shop had closed; or been assaulted, by the police or by *tsotsis*; or been arrested and whisked away to jail in the *kwela-kwela*, the pick-up van, for some trivial pass offence or imagined 'cheek' to a policeman; or he might be on one of his assignments.

He felt a surge of angry impatience towards Dick who was so opposed to apartheid yet understood so little of what it really meant. Yet with his life so far removed, how could he? So much unthought-about privilege was invested in just that one thing – the white skin. And they needed him. His expert knowledge was a precious asset that he was sharing with them all. He was, after all, on their side.

Tomorrow morning, first thing, Pila would have to be told to warn Dick that he was being followed. It would be a good idea if he simply stopped seeing anyone for a while. They would also have to decide, in view of this, whether it was safe to go ahead or whether they should delay. Whichever one chose could prove to be wrong

Friday was a busy day in the bookshop. Margie examined shelves, leafed through books, until a moment arrived when she could speak to Pila without anyone over-hearing.

'Dick asked me to come in,' she said. 'He's left a parcel for you. I've got it in the car, I didn't want to bring it in here. Perhaps you could just slip out for a moment and get it. And this note.'

She handed Pila an envelope.

'He's had to go away suddenly. His mother had a heart attack and yesterday afternoon they phoned for him to come, so he left early this morning. It's a long way to go – she's at Nelspruit.'

'Oh, I'm sorry to hear that. I hope it's not too serious.'

'Well, it must be quite bad or else they wouldn't have sent for him; she's very old. I just hope he won't have to stay too long, I hate it when he's away. Especially as it's the weekend.'

On impulse Pila said, 'I tell you what: how about coming away with me this weekend if you're on your own? My father's bought a farm in the eastern Transvaal, we're going down in the morning – I've taken the day off – and we'll come back Sunday evening. There's tons of

113

room in the car – you know the kind of car my Dad runs, and it would be company for me.'

'That sounds like a wonderful idea,' Margie said, 'but there's Jonny, don't forget.'

'Would it be too much for him? It's a long drive.'

'He usually sleeps in cars. He'll probably sleep all the way there and back. I'd like to get out of Joh'burg for the weekend.'

Pila went to the car and fetched the parcel wrapped in brown paper, then opened Dick's letter. There was a second envelope inside addressed to Thabo, and a note to herself: *I was supposed to meet T last night but he did not turn up. I went up to your flat, but you were out. Sorry to have to involve Marge but there was no other way to get this to T as I have to leave early in the morning and it's very urgent.*

When Pila found Thabo alone in the basement, she said, 'There's a parcel and a note for you. Dick's wife brought them. He's been called away to the country, his mother's ill. What happened to you last night, Thabo? Dick said he was supposed to meet you and you didn't show up.'

'I did come,' Thabo replied, 'but I did not show myself because he was being followed.'

'Oh God! Are you sure?'

'Positive. I was there at the place we had arranged, I wait for him. When he come, I see this car following, so I hide myself, I stay out of sight. But I see Dick. He come three times round the block. When he drive off, the car follows him.'

'He came up to my place,' Pila said.

Thabo was upset. 'He should have gone straight home. As soon as he think I am not there, he should go home. How many times we talk about this thing. Now he leads them to you. If they suspect him, now they will suspect you. How long . . ?'

'I was out. I just got this note saying he had called at my place last night. I suppose he was desperate to get the stuff to you because of having to go away so suddenly to his mother. And because of all the close timing on everything for the next few days.'

Thabo was entering books received into a ledger. 'When he come back,' he said after a while, 'will it be possible you warn him? Let him stay away from us; not to contact anyone. You too,' he added, 'better we don't see you too for a while.' His head was down low over the ledger. 'Then tell me,' he murmured, 'is it all arranged with the cars?'

Pila replied, 'Yes. One's borrowed, it's a green Cortina; here's the key and the registration number. The other's hired, it's a black Chev. I've arranged for them both to be at the place we fixed.'

'And who brings them?'

'The owner of the Cortina will leave it there himself. He'll park it and walk away. I will drive the hired car.'

'Is it already collected?'

'Yes, it's parked not far from where I live.'

'Then we must arrange something else. You just let it stay there. Don't go near it. If you can give me the key of that one as well, I make a plan for someone to take it.'

'All right. But don't be too worried about Dick coming to my flat. I'm friendly with his wife, we were at school together, and it could have been purely social, I'm seeing her this weekend. Should I say anything to her, do you think?'

'I think better not. Better not for her. Her husband never tell her anything, I think.'

'Don't you tell your wife anything, Thabo?' she asked teasingly.

He smiled and shook his head.

'And good African wives don't ask questions?'

'Our wives do not have the same lives as whites, Miss Pila. Their lives are like ours. The police come, they pull them from bed just the same way they pull us. What must we tell them?'

She was uncomfortable. 'I know, I know,' she said.

# Indres . . .

Beyond that gentle rise and fall of the land there was the possibility of a refuge. Perhaps he had been aware of this all the time, but not consciously. Some part of his brain had continued to operate on its own while his thoughts were elsewhere, and had directed him along this particular stretch of road.

The cars were infrequent, and he ignored them now; he had become reluctant to leave the road. Once when he had lain down on the ground out of the yellow-white glare of headlights he had found difficulty in rising again and going on; he was not accustomed to being out, to walking along a road, to lying down and getting up at will and not at the dictates of prison routine. But he had to get up. So his legs carried him relentlessly forward and when the next glow rose in the sky, blazed, focused into a pair of headlights, he had kept on without bothering to try and hide. The car sped by without slackening speed.

Beyond the slope was a small isolated store run by an Indian family to whom he was distantly related. They were all related to each other, or so it seemed, here in the Transvaal. They were all descended from those first illiterate indentured labourers who had been brought over from India at the end of the last century to work in the canefields of Natal. Some who stayed on when their contracts had expired filtered into the Transvaal. Indians, Jews, it was a familiar story. Barred from other occupations, they opened their small stores where the whole family worked at all hours.

117

They scarcely knew him, but they would not turn him away. However remotely related, they were cousins. If he could stay there for a few days until the pressure lifted, until he could contact Thabo . . . they would not refuse. The importance of making contact and giving the information he now bore blotted out, from time to time, the desolation, the unhappiness.

And the fatigue. He had not known how much all those weeks had drained him physically as well as mentally, that now he was not capable of sustained physical effort. What impelled him forward was this necessity, the thought of Thabo and Sipho, and at this he laughed aloud, a harsh angry laugh, for after all it was from Sipho himself that so often he had drawn his own courage.

If it were not for the time when he had watched Sipho dismantling the timing device, calmly and with such steady hands, perhaps he would never have dared to go back to the transformer himself that other night, to walk as it were into a cage with a savage and unpredictable beast that might attack at any moment, and whose attack would certainly mean death.

*I thought of Sipho. My hands were as steady as his.*

There had been three of them in the group that recced the transformer. It stood on the railway line in the heart of Vrededorp, a transformer to boost the power for the electric trains. Heavy power cables ran from the box that looked like a steel radiator, enclosed by a fence of strong diamond mesh, eight feet high.

They used a charge of dynamite, eight sticks tied together, and for the timing device one of the small meter timers, with numbers running from one to sixty, that motorists carried around to warn them when their parking time was up. The timer could be set to ring at any time up to one hour. It had been wired to two batteries, the connection soldered to thirty minutes at the base of the dial. Half an hour to get completely away, to establish their alibis, before the whole thing blew up. After thirty minutes the current would ignite the fuse and set off the detonator.

There was one thing that raised this particular act of sabotage above the others. There was a forty-four-gallon drum of oil standing close to the transformer.

The materials were in a plastic bag, which he set down carefully on the ground at the base of the fence. The other two members of the group were on guard. The job itself – that was all his own affair.

The first thing was to cut through the steel mesh of the fence. Someone, somewhere, had bought these steel cutters that now clicked their way so purposefully through the mesh, someone had passed them on to another person, another link, and eventually they had been left in a certain place, and he had received a message, and from that place he had collected them.

A whole chain of events led away from one pair of wirecutters.

He cut through the mesh just sufficiently to raise a triangular piece, and he tested the ease with which he could get through.

Distantly yet distinctly came the mingled sounds of the city, trains shunting in the yards at Braamfontein, cars hooting somewhere down under the dip beneath the bridge at Vrededorp, dogs barking, a voice that separated itself from the muted clamour and cried out and died away.

In the dark filled with these muted noises, he rolled the oil drum against the transformer box; on it he placed the charges, packing clay around the dynamite to drive the force of the explosion down into the drum. He worked quickly, but without any feeling of undue haste. They could not afford to waste time, for their alibis would fall to pieces if they were away too long; but by now he had also learned that each step must be done deliberately and with consideration, for one small omission or slip would bring complete failure.

He set the dial on the timing device for the half-hour, and wound the key, waiting to hear the tick-tick-tick like a tiny voice speaking to him, and to see that the hand had actually begun to move. He took the bag with the wirecutters, looked around for the last time to see that nothing had been left, and then (having practised this and reminded himself so many times) he slipped the piece of insulation tape off the wire prong on the dial, the tape that prevented any chance contact completing the circuit. And crawled out again through the hole he had made in the fence.

The instructions were that as soon as he was clear, all three were to disperse. He signalled to his companions, Ntite and James, and he saw them go. Then he walked to a place he had prepared at a safe distance from the transformer and placed his bag with the wirecutters in a small cache under a rock. He sat down and waited.

Now that the barrier of his intense concentration on fixing the charge had been eliminated, the city sounds swelled out, and he heard the hooting of the trains, the voices, a call, a laugh, like music charging the night air. He glanced at the dial of his watch and let the minutes slip past him, and waited.

Then the half-hour had all but gone. His body tensed. He crouched on one knee, he became aware of his own heart beating as the seconds passed, a metronome inside his body softly marking the fleeting time. The drum, the box, were clearly definable by eyes long accustomed to the dark. They were etched on the zinc of the night sky.

Those steady heart-beats, that steady watch, the seconds doubly measured. Five minutes after the half-hour; quiet; and stillness; and the inexorable transformer with its black entrails, still, quiet.

He acted now with deliberation and with a sense of the enormous reality of what he was doing. Anything could have happened. The timing devices were not instruments of good quality, the mechanism could fail – or be out by several minutes; or it could have stopped, and as inconsequentially have restarted to set the whole thing off at any second, any split second.

But all that was pushed to the background, only making him acutely sensitive and aware of each action and of the ticking seconds warning of imminent destruction.

First, the wirecutters. He clipped a few more strands and pushed the mesh outwards so that he could move out easily from the inside of the fence without restraint. He ran away from the fence again and flung the bag with the cutters into a bush.

Then back to the transformer. Is this how a lion would stalk his prey, treading so softly, not to frighten or disturb it in any way? He was at the drum, and taking the timer in his hands he pulled out the wires that had been twisted together at the back, wrapped in adhesive tape. Having disconnected it, he turned the tiny mechanism on the dial back to nought.

He breathed again. The explosive was momentarily disarmed.

There was a piece of ordinary commercial fuse, not longer than three inches. He reckoned it would give him at least three, perhaps five seconds to get clear.

He lit a cigarette, took two or three deep draws, then

touched the lighted end to the fuse, flinging the cigarette away as in one movement he dived beneath the wire; he had run perhaps thirty paces when a violent force seized him and flung him to the ground.

Stunned by the blast, he was dimly aware of things falling from the sky and plunging into the ground. And behind him a great light, a great heat, a volcanic eruption, the flames consuming the oil in a huge conflagration, as tremendous and as terribly beautiful as if the whole city were on fire.

He had to get away. He had to get right out of the whole area as quickly as possible. He stumbled, stopped, told himself not to panic, think carefully. Take the wire-cutters . . . then you will run slap into the police with them in your hands. Leave them . . . they may be found, it may be possible to trace them back to the shop where they were bought, perhaps even a description of the purchaser . . .

He compromised, seized the bag, ran some distance, then hurled it into a dump of old and rusting cars, not far from the main road. It would be possible for someone to retrieve it in a day or two.

He reached the road, brushing down his clothes as best he could, steadying himself – to be picked up now for being drunk – that would be ironic. And he laughed. Great black clouds proliferated, swarmed up and out to fill the sky. Beneath these swelling clouds of smoke, the fire leapt, glowing at its heart with the white intensity of the heat.

He thought yes, he was like a man who was drunk, drunk on his own pride, his own harsh courage, and the power that he had in his two hands. He felt like a giant striding down the street while behind him oppression crumbled and was cremated in the flames of that beautiful fire.

It seemed only yesterday they had been on a rising curve of success. But already it had flattened out, and now there was a sense of slipping as though a deep descent had begun.

First it was the silence. Sabotage, like justice, must not only be done, it must be seen to be done.

The first acts had been greeted with a blaze of publicity, of outrage, speculation, discussion. At some unidentified time, the newspapers shut down on all reports of acts of sabotage, or even of accidents that sounded as though they might have been sabotage. They had enough security laws to make sure the press obeyed; the editors needed only one visit from the Special Branch. In the face of silence the deed was not simply diminished, it was virtually wiped out.

All the anguish and tension now became augmented by uncertainty as to whether the deed had gone as planned and was simply unreported, or whether it had totally failed.

Dangers multiplied as the saboteurs were drawn back to try and check, knowing they might walk into a trap.

There were many incidents now known only to the police and a handful of officials concerned with investigations and repairs. From the point of view of the public, sabotage had ceased. If there was a delay on the suburban train line, after all, that was not unusual; the railways were notoriously inefficient and prone to accidents. That sub-station, local post office, transformer, damaged and put out of action for a day or two, affected only a handful of people.

Now they did not even know themselves how good or

how wide-spread were their activities. Each knew only of his or her *own* particular operation. Even the most dramatic events were muffled by doubts. An explosion at a dynamite factory? Was it, as they claimed, just an accident? A wave of fires on Transvaal farms. Were they no more than the results of careless cigarettes in the dry grass?

With silence the doubts multiplied, first about the efficiency of the operations, then about their validity. Indres was a victim of such doubts. In spite of all that had happened, the deep-rooted antagonism to violent political action was hard to overcome. The joyous moments of triumph did not entirely still the long nights of doubts.

Many times he had defended what they were doing against the attacks of his family. A purely social visit would end, inevitably, in fierce political controversy.

Sometimes Indres attacked. 'You think it's wrong,' he told Joe, 'because you have such an exaggerated respect for property. You can't bear an attack on property.'

And Joe was equally angry. 'And you, you like to see things destroyed? Blown up?'

'Yes! We have to destroy apartheid otherwise we can never build anything else.'

'On ruins?'

Even then, Joe did not suspect that his own brother was deeply involved in acts of sabotage. He thought Indres was simply defending in principle what others were doing.

Essop was there one evening, and among others an old man, Sironivar, who had been an associate of Gandhi in the very first passive resistance campaign in South Africa, and who had continued to wear the little white cap all his life.

'What is wrong,' the old man said, 'is that such weapons harm not only the enemy; they harm also logic, reason, truth. You argue with explosions? You convince with bombs?'

Sironivar had an air of wonder about him; he shook his head. He still believed in the ultimate good of all men. He believed in those words he used, logic, reason, truth; their ability to overcome; the only reasonable weapons for reasonable people.

'Even the whites, the Nationalists,' he would say, 'yes, all people are subject, in the end, to reason. You will see.'

And the following week he and his whole family had been served with an order compelling them to move from the home in which they had lived for fifty-seven years, because the Group Areas Board had re-zoned their street for white occupation only. They were all under notice to move, Sironivar, Essop, all of them; running to lawyers; preparing briefs, appeals. Trying to employ the machinery of the courts to delay execution of the orders. Another three months, six months, a year's grace, and they would feel their time and money had not been wasted, they had achieved something. In the end, it was nothing. Better if they had joined the liberation movement, or at least given them the cash.

It was a measure of success, all the same, that these fierce arguments and divisions shook people all over the land. In spite of the silence.

He had not seen Joe since before he went to Natal. There were many arrests in Durban and Sipho and Indres had to separate. They left the languid town with its heat and humidity, its towering hotels and apartments on the sea-front, its segregated bathing beaches; and went back to

125

their own high, dry, glittering city where the sun burned through the thin mountain air and the nights were cool and sharp, Sipho to disappear into the townships and Indres to establish for himself a respectable front, some sort of legitimate day-time activity to conceal his real work.

Inevitably, in spite of all intentions, the shop where he began work as a counter assistant became a depot. It was too convenient; not far from the centre of town, with Indian owners known to have given donations to Congress, knowing when to ignore the customers who did not buy anything, and passing messages on when requested.

One morning when he opened the shop, Essop was waiting for him, so pale that his face seemed almost green; and obviously very upset.

'It's Billy,' he said.

He came into the shop with Indres and stood with clenched fists, speaking in a rapid, low voice. 'Billy, Solly and Ismail. They've taken them. They beat them up, assaulted them . . .'

He had to struggle to go on. Billy had been only a baby when their parents died, and Essop had cared for him and brought him up and loved him not simply as a brother, but with the deep love of the parents he had replaced.

'They brought him in this morning,' he said, his voice thickened with tears. 'He had blood all over his face; his arm in a sort of make-shift sling. They broke his arm. He was all dirty, bruised, torn . . . They turned everything upside down. They searched from top to bottom, tore up floorboards, ripped open mattresses. I've never seen anything like it.

'We couldn't talk to them,' he went on. 'One of the bastards stood next to Billy the whole time. We were

126

frightened. They shouted when we tried to ask them what it was all about. Only as they left, Billy managed to whisper to me: "It was a trap."'

He could not go on. He was crying.

'What are we going to do?' he whispered after a while. 'I've been to Suliman already, he says it's this new law, ninety days detention without trial. He says he can't do anything, the law excludes everyone, no contact with the arrested person, no family, not even a lawyer . . . court applications a waste of time and money, he says, they can hold Billy and the others. You are not even supposed to talk about them! We're not even supposed to tell anyone he's been arrested! Ninety days! Indres, what am I going to do?'

Indres said stupidly, 'I don't know.'

'But what were they doing?' Essop asked. 'What were they up to?'

'I don't know, Essop.'

'What do you mean, you don't know? If you don't know, who would know? They went out on some – some enterprise, the three of them. You must know, it's your outfit, isn't it? You can't just stand there and tell me you don't know, you're right in the thick of it.'

'Essop,' Indres said earnestly, 'please listen to me. I don't know what Billy was doing. I've never had any contact with him, in a political sense, I mean. I didn't even know he was . . . If it was something planned together with others, I can't tell you, I don't know anything about it. Maybe it was something the three lads decided to do themselves, I simply don't know.'

Essop calmed down. 'I'm sorry, it's just that I'm so upset, I don't know what to do next. I thought you might . . . or one of your friends, perhaps; you could ask? You mustn't think I am blaming you. Not blaming.'

127

He paused and thought for a moment. Then he burst out again. 'But it's what you wanted, isn't it? You didn't know what Billy was doing, but that's what you wanted, that others would follow your example and go out and do the same sort of thing . . . They admired you so much, they wanted to be like you . . .'

Silence now lay over those who had been arrested, and there was danger for everyone. When the arrests had been observed by wives or husbands or other relatives, and they passed on the word, that was bad; but the wound could be cauterized – the meeting places known to the one who had been arrested could be abandoned. But sometimes people simply vanished. Had they been arrested? Had they simply gone away for a little while, hiding out somewhere? Silence obscured the fate of those held. Stories began to circulate about beatings and torture. Ex-prisoners sometimes came out of jail and passed on a message tapped on a wall, or a story of groans heard in adjacent cells.

Steeped in the legends of Fucik and Alleg, they believed that their comrades would not talk. Each said, *Well, you can't tell until it happens to you*, but each secretly thought *They will kill me before I'll say a word*.

And out of the widespread net of silence and uncertainty, suspicions began to grow. There were informers, of course, there had always been informers, but they were outside the magic circle of the alliance; many were known by name, their activities simply aroused contempt. Action had to be founded on mutual trust, on belief, on love. But now it was different; suspicions of informers penetrated right through their ranks, and this cut the ability to plan easily and act.

The worms had begun to crawl in.

# The Unit . . .

'At this stage,' said Thabo slowly, 'it seems to me, it is as difficult to delay it as it is to go ahead. In some ways, more difficult. So we have to talk this over very carefully.'

'I don't see that it alters things,' Kabelo said, 'I don't really understand. They arrest three boys who went off and acted on their own, they were not part of our organization, there's nothing those boys can tell them about us or our plans.'

Ralph paced up and down as he habitually did during such discussions. Tall and active, he liked to think on his feet. When he stopped pacing and stood motionless, or sat down abruptly, it usually indicated that he had arrived at a decision. Now he was still pacing.

'Listen, Kab,' he said, 'there's even added danger in the fact they acted on their own. The SBs are going to be on the alert for a while: mass raids, swoops, haphazard arrests – you'll see, they'll want to try and find out or uncover any more independent groups, whether they know they acted on their own or not. Think what they want to know; where for instance, did they get their explosives?'

'Made it themselves, I expect,' said Kabelo.

'Maybe . . . But how did they find out? Who taught them? Perhaps it isn't as simple as we think. I'll tell you something I've never mentioned before. I went to the public library to read everything I could in the Encyclopaedia Brittanica about explosives. Under that heading, twenty pages had been cut out, sliced out with a blade, I guess. That was the first time I realized there were other organizations than our own making such preparations. Then, all the stuff we've got stored; if they have very widespread searches, they're going to uncover some of it. It's all terribly dangerous.'

'And if we call it off, what are we going to do with all our lovely things, the stuff we've made ready, that each group's got?'

'We'd have to jettison it. Dump it somewhere.'

Kabelo looked at Ralph as though he thought he were mad.

'Dump it?' he exclaimed, 'Throw it away? Do you know what risks those chaps on the mines take to get it to us? It would be . . .' he searched for the right word, but could not find it, 'an insult,' he said.

Ralph said, 'We are responsible for a lot of people. We can't play with their lives. I keep putting everything I can in one balance and then another. Not only the difficulties and dangers in having to contact so many people in such a short time, but the void with which we will be left. I keep thinking of the effect at a time like this, with Ninety Days and all the new Security laws, their tremendous demonstration of power; then if we pull it off, if we literally cut the power all over the city . . . but then what are we asking people to risk?'

'We know the risks,' Thabo said.

'Of course. But to send people into possible traps? The miners will get us more stuff. Indres, what is your view?'

'It's not easy to take a detached view,' Indres said. 'I desperately want it to go on, we've been preparing for this for such a long time, and as Ralph said, it would be exactly right at this time. Everything's ready, we've been over it and over it, we've even dress-rehearsed, if you can call it that. I almost can't face calling it off. Yet I know it does seem terribly risky at the moment. I try to take a long cool look, but really I can't. Perhaps the truth is that there isn't one absolutely right decision.'

'Thabo,' Ralph said, 'it's up to you. We all think you're the most balanced among us. Let's bring it down to practicalities since there's so much doubt. You're the one who will have to contact the groups, arrange for disposal and so on. If we decide to call it off now, how difficult will it be?'

Thabo said, 'In my opinion as difficult as if we go ahead.'

'Kab?'

'I agree,' said Kabelo.

'Yes,' said Indres, 'I agree too.'

Ralph sat down. 'Then it's decided. Now we must just go over one or two things before we break up . . .'

He did not say what he himself had decided, but had he been strongly opposed he would have spoken more forcibly against the project. He was always aware of the handicap of being white, highly-educated, articulate and competent. He knew he had to control his own forceful personality so that he did not dominate their discussions.

The last decision, to be passed on to as many people as possible, was to take all steps to avoid being arrested.

'Don't sleep at home for at least a week,' Ralph warned. 'If we get an arrest warning, then go underground completely, break all contacts, remove yourself. If they're looking for you and you can't stay underground, it might be necessary to leave the country.'

And Thabo emphasized solemnly: 'If you are free, you can always come back. Or do something useful outside. But if you are in jail for years and years . . . we've lost enough people. Do not take unnecessary chances.'

\* \* \*

131

*That is what keeps me going now, Thabo, in the face of
my own confusion, my own sense of disillusion, because I
must find you, the steadiest, the truest and best and I must
tell you what I know, my brother, it is you I must think
about. They can take me again then, I will hear the gates
clang once again and be glad if I have succeeded in this
one thing. Then they can come for me.*

He was close to the place where he hoped to find at
least one night's refuge. The shop with the house attached
had that look of neglect that settles so swiftly on a
building when the occupants have gone. The windows of
the shop were boarded up. The house wore a silence, not
of sleep, but of life departed.

For a moment, to dispel his own disbelief and despair,
Indres ran to the house and began banging on the barred
door. All around was the menacing night, the road
narrowing away into the distance, the fear that soon they
must come, their cars fanning out along every road out of
the city, and so much time already tossed away! He
banged on the door calling hopelessly, 'Asvat! Let me in!
Open – it's me, Indres. Please!'

And a man stood watching him, a dark figure that had
barely emerged from the darkness, naked to the waist
and barefoot.

'What you want?' he asked. 'No good knocking.
Nobody here.'

'Where are they, then?'

'Gone, these past four, five months.'

'Where have they gone?'

The man shook his head. 'Don't know. Somewhere.
This is white area now. They build factories here. All
Indians gone from here.'

He took a couple of steps towards Indres. 'You did not
know? They don't tell you?'

And Indres was afraid of him. It was not what he said, he spoke easily enough. But there was no friendship in his looks, only suspicion and hostility. He did not want Indres there. It would be a lot easier, Indres thought, if you could trust all black men and know only whites as the enemy.

He stood silent and undecided. Again the man looked him over, then said, 'I look after this place. No one come here.'

Indres raised his hand in salutation and turned back to the road, walking towards it as though he was going back in the direction of the city. He felt the man standing and watching him even though he did not turn round to look. He wondered how long it would take him to report the encounter to someone in authority.

He reached the road, crossed to the other side, walking some way into the veld before changing direction once again, away from the city. There was nothing left for him but to go straight on until he reached the townships. Just to keep walking and find Thabo's home, as though he were a free man and could go wherever he chose. To walk fast, to walk steadily, to forget about looking for a place to hide. At least when they searched for him they would calculate that he would be heading towards the border, not into a black township.

Giant ghosts, a row of pylons, rose from the landscape to march away across the distant curves of the land. The pylons, their triumph and their downfall.

There were two main power plants, one close to the city and one some miles outside. The plants operated on a grid system of alternatives, so if something went wrong with one, then the other would take over. What they had to do was to work out the grid system so that they could cut the circuit between the two plants.

Over this land where he now walked he had once ridden out like a man on an adventure trail, starting from the power station and following one of the lines of pylons until he came to a branch, and then each night following a different line of pylons; eventually he came to a point ten miles away or more where many other branches took off for distant places.

He and Sipho were partners, sharing a borrowed scooter, discussing their routes, their maps, with distances marked and all the features of the countryside, both natural and man-made. They worked weekends, late nights, early mornings, for many weeks until they both bore in their heads a picture of the pylons and where they stood and how they could be reached.

They became close, the tall, athletic Indian youth and the older, energetic African man. Sipho never revealed his age; in fact, he spoke very little about himself, except in bursts over glasses of beer, providing brief glimpses of a life that embraced widely diverse experiences and ranged over many parts of the country. He astonished Indres with the extent of his unexpected skills, annoyed him with his sometimes erratic behaviour, his excessive drinking, and his tendency to take his own decisions. He was scornful of the bureaucracy of organization. He was in the organization as deeply as anyone, yet always one part of him stood aside and made critical or cynical remarks, mocking the sacred committees that Indres so respected.

The circuit had to be cut in three different places to be effective. In the end, after the mapping had been completed four striking points were selected after eliminating those too close to populated areas, or too exposed to roads. Four groups were detailed, two to travel further out, two who would tackle the pylons closer to town.

The chemical unit had estimated the amount of dynamite needed for each strut, and the detonators required. Work was distributed throughout the organization, from the stealing of dynamite and detonators from the mines to the purchase of electrical tape and putty; from details of prime importance, such as the nature and accuracy of the timing devices, to smaller matters such as obtaining the bags in which the charges would be carried. There was a technical unit, a transport unit, a unit concerned with supplies. The network of people involved spread out, from the women who carried the stolen dynamite into town on their heads in bundles of washing to the youngsters who dug holes in the dark beyond Soweto to hide the stuff until it was to be used. While the Security police enormously increased both their vigilance and the number of their informers in the townships, the activity increased under their noses; notes slipped from hand to hand as people passed in the street, a message left in a street waste-paper basket, three people standing in one of the interminable bus queues, holding a meeting, a young woman chatting up the uniformed guard at the gates of the mine compound while a passing miner placed a plastic carrier-bag bearing the letters 'O.K. Bazaars' next to the one she had put down nearby.

James Magofe was driving the car, Indres, Ntite and Sipho were to attach the charges. The car had been hired by Pila who had passed it on to Thabo, who had given Indres the instructions as to where the car should be fetched and to where it was to be delivered later on. Their pylon was one of the distant ones, not far from where a railway line crossed a road. A small dirt road ran from a cluster of houses a little distance away, and passed

135

close to the pylon. There were bushes nearby, and that was all.

Summer was almost over, the leaves drying and crumpled on the trees. Although the days were still warm, night came swiftly and early, and when it came the earth delivered up its warmth into the high, thin air. If there was an autumn in the Transvaal then this was it.

Indres emerged from the suburban station and began walking along the main road. In a few minutes he heard a car. It was James; Ntite and Sipho were already in the car, collected at different points. All four wore dark clothes. Indres was nervous and on edge, but Sipho was completely relaxed, sitting back and relating some never-ending anecdote about a woman.

They left the main road and hit the dirt track, James switched off the headlights of the car, and drove carefully with only starlight to see by. He stopped the car near some bushes. The three men pulled on balaclavas and thin cotton gloves as James drove the car away.

From the dirt road the huge pylons had seemed so near, only a matter of yards. Now they found the distance had increased, and they had not realized how rough the ground would be, broken and hard with the sharp dried grass and each sound – breathing, stumbling, even just walking – enlarged in the quiet dark.

But suddenly they had reached it, a colossal metal structure, rising above them; and they could feel the hum, the power flowing through it. The great wires pulled from one pylon to another, shining in the starlight like polished silver. It was almost as though there was communication between the vibrant pylon and the sky, as if it drew its power from the immensity above.

*It is this we are going to bring down.*

The angled steel was cold and sharp. Indres touched

136

the great bolts at the base of the legs. Big, beautiful bolts.

They took four prepared charges from the bag and working very quickly they placed each charge on a leg of the pylon, fixing them in place with insulation tape. Then each charge was linked with cordex which was wrapped around the first, the second, the third, and then linked to the fourth. They used putty to contain the explosive force. Sweating inside his balaclava, Indres could hear Sipho whistling very softly between his teeth, and Ntite's breathing; it felt like some sort of game, playing with the putty, slapping it with his hands.

Now he inserted a detonator with a short length of safety fuse carefully into one of the charges, the initiating one.

All was ready, except for the last vital element, the time-delaying device.

He took from his pocket a condom, which already contained a small amount of potassium chlorate and sugar, finely ground and mixed together.

*Sipho had roared with laughter when I first produced one to test it out. 'What's that, man? What's that you got? What on earth you propose? What's this thing?'*

*'Don't tell me you don't know what this is.'*

*'Me? Not me, man, I never use them, never. It spoils their happiness.'*

*'What are you trying to do then – scatter the whole world with little Siphos?'*

*'Let me tell you, my women are proud to carry the results, they can boast they've lain with Sipho. No, it's not irresponsible,' he had insisted. And laughed again. 'So you've found a good use for a really useless object!'*

They had worked so quickly and well that there was

time to spare. Indres had checked his watch with Thabo's earlier in the day. All the pylons would go together.

He looked at his watch once more. Sipho was holding a small capsule, the kind used to house tiny multiple coloured pills. The capsule was now to be filled with sulphuric acid and placed inside the condom. In exactly half an hour it would eat through the capsule, flow through onto the potchlor and sugar, which would ignite.

Sipho had been selected to fill the capsule with the acid in a test they had carried out a few days previously to see who had the steadiest hands. Sipho's hands were as steady as rocks.

With an eye dropper, Sipho carefully put the acid into the capsule, then closed it. Indres stripped off a glove and Sipho placed the capsule on to his outstretched palm. 'It's OK,' Indres said. If there had been any acid on the outside, he would have felt a burning on his skin.

Indres then held the condom while Sipho dropped the capsule into it, whispering as he did so, 'Fully charged! Home, baby, home!'

The fuse rose like a stem, upwards then curving round and down slightly. Indres sheathed the safety fuse, drawing the rubber on so that the fuse was fully inserted, binding it tightly with string.

They had to march once more round the pylon, to see that it was all linked up, that the cordex was flowing freely, that the charges were taped at different heights to make certain the pylon would actually topple, not simply be sheared and come to rest again on its splayed legs.

The night throbbed. Above the humming of the pylon they heard the car coming back to fetch them, and ran to get in, tearing off their balaclavas as they ran.

They were gripped by a wild happiness.

138

They began to sing:

> Sizakubadubula ngembayimbayi
> Bazakubaleka,
> Dubula ngembayimbayi!!
> Izakunyathel 'iAfrika
> Vorster shu!!
> Uzakwenzakala!

And finally:

> Nants 'indod' emnyama Vorster
> Basoba nants 'indod' emnyama Vorster*

Happiness, a release from the build-up and the temsion, and a sense of power, of changing history. '*Pas op! Pas op!*' were the last words of James as he dropped Indres near the station further down the line, 'Basopa! Mind out, take care, beware!'

The others were to go straight to whatever place was now home for them, and stay there. When James had driven on, Indres left the station and walked back along the road in the direction of the pylon. It was getting close to the time. He found a clump of thick bushes and crept inside them, and waited.

This was his secret addiction, the need to see it take place, the only way he did not follow out instructions to the letter.

The explosion came out of the innocent night with ferocious suddenness. The size and the violence of it

---

* We shall shoot the oppressors with cannon, they are going to flee before us, shoot, shoot, with cannon!

Africa will trample you underfoot, Vorster, beware, you shall die!

Behold the advancing Blacks, Vorster, beware the advancing Blacks, Vorster.

stunned him. He saw the flames and the distant smoke. And then, as the noise died away, he was aware once again of the incandescent sky, the emptiness, the quiet; the stillness of the void, the barely audible clickings of tiny insects, a slight abrupt wind, grasses rustling just a little beneath his feet.

All those weeks, all that work, all the network ranging over the city and out over the townships and even embracing the distant white suburbs; Dick and Ralph and Pila and others; Salim and Farid and Rahima and Farima; Thabo and James and Kabelo and Ntite . . . and Sipho. What had it all come down to? A couple of big bangs, and their whole countrywide organization in disarray.

Laws now held them in a vice, the Terrorism Act, the Sabotage Act, Ninety Days. The State seemed stronger than ever before, while they had lost what they had. Not only were their groups broken and so many arrested and so many forced to flee; not only were they unsure whether the small fires they had lit, their explosions, had spread all over the land; but also they had lost more than that, their faith in their own comrades. That that should have been destroyed as well . . .

Sipho. The man who loved women and boasted about them; who stole little three and invented better ways of making stronger bombs; who had walked with him along the seashore that night in the misting rain, who had supported him when the sea wished to take them both, who slept with him in a hole they had dug with their hands in the sand; Sipho, the man with the strongest nerves and the steadiest hands, who had a story about everything, a joke about everything; who was afraid of nothing, whom he trusted with his life, whom he loved . . .

# Pila . . .

Quite fortuitously in the middle of the week Mrs Norval phoned Pila to ask if she would accompany her to a charity performance of a new play. 'I've two tickets, your father was supposed to be coming, but he has to work late.'

It could not have been more convenient. 'I'll come,' she said promptly.

Outside the theatre little black boys who looked about eight or nine years old, stood begging with one eye on the gold-braided commissionaire. Beneath their ragged jackets their skinny black legs ended in bare and cracked feet. They held cupped hands under the pancake faces of the women, they crouched and darted and chanted over and over again their monotonous demand for bread. The first-nighters held their fur stoles more tightly, their diamond rings glittering in the light from the foyer. They kept their thickly-mascaraed eyes averted from the children.

'Bread!' snorted a large man whose neck and head were held to attention by his stiff shirt, '*Hamba, hamba, hamba! Dagga* more likely – go on, *voetsak*, scram!'

The little boys scattered behind the black trousers and satin dresses, to reappear a little way away, holding their birds' claws together and reiterating their chant.

'They work in gangs,' Mrs Norval murmured apologetically, with some memories of recent discussions. 'They don't actually use the money for bread, Pila, they give it all to a gang leader and he takes it . . . drink . . . drugs . . .'

'Kids of that age?'

'They're probably older than they look. It's the clothes they wear. And they don't show their age like . . . Do you remember John, the one who worked in the garden when you were still at school? He looked about sixteen, and then it turned out he already had two wives in the country!'

Pila's hands tightened in the pockets of her jacket. The cars had both gone when she drove past earlier this evening. Something must be on, it must be all right. Is this how they feel, muscles aching with tension? And it had not rained! Thabo had said, "Pray it doesn't rain tonight", a momentary relaxation of his usual tight sense of security. She looked upwards. Above the theatre lights the stars were shining. It was not going to rain.

At twenty-past nine there was a ten minute interval. 'Let's go outside and get some air,' Pila said.

The foyer was congested; the women tottered past on their high heels, exuding their sharp expensive perfumes, calling greetings to their friends.

'I'm so glad you came with me, Pila, but I do wish your father wouldn't work so hard. He can't neglect the factory, you know, it's the busy season, he comes home late night after night. I get worried about him, there've been so many heart . . . they seem to be on the increase, Margery Foster's brother-in-law died,' she clicked her fingers, 'just like that! Such a young man, they say it's worse when you're young, I don't understand that, I would have thought – they'd only just moved into a new house, her boy's at an expensive school, she'll have to . . .'

The voice trailed happily on. She did not require any

real replies. She simply said her thoughts aloud, scarcely aware of speaking at all.

The theatre-goers bunched on the pavement outside, breathing the cooler air. The skeletal boys were still there with their sing-song pleading that persisted beneath the loud white voices around them.

It was half-past nine. The bell rang for them to go inside.

They turned from the brilliantly-lit street to the semi-darkness of the theatre.

At that moment, silently, the lights went out.

The darkness was intense. Voices were raised, people jostled against each other. Pila turned and pushed her way back to the street. Except for car headlights there was complete and utter blackness, not a single light to be seen. It was as though some hand had lifted a giant switch to plunge shops, flats, hotels, streets, into darkness.

She heard her mother call, 'Pila, Pila, where are you?' Cigarette lighters were held up in the foyer. 'Pila – oh, there you are, good heavens, what a fright it gave me! It's a power failure, I expect, it'll be all right in a minute. Stay near me, dear, or I'll lose you.

A fountain of joy spurted up within her. This was what it had been about then. She could have run down the street shouting out 'It's not a power failure – it's sabotage – they did it, and I helped them!'

They would be out there in the night, with the cars, rushing back to pre-planned places. It was the most spectacular of all their operations; and she had had a part in it, not knowing exactly what, yet still an essential part.

Mrs Norval said, 'It's terribly hot in there, I suppose the air-conditioning's failed as well.'

'I'll take you home,' Pila said, smiling at her mother

with gentle toleration, 'it wasn't a very good play, was it?'

The noises of the confused and dislocated city, cars hooting at intersections where they were snarled up without traffic lights, voices shouting, rose around them as they walked along the blacked-out streets.

'Do you realize I'll have to walk up all those stairs to my flat? The lifts won't be working,' Pila said.

At midnight it rained, an earth-pounding storm that would help to obliterate any traces left by the saboteurs. In the morning the city was gleaming once more, the air polished. Buildings shone like crystal in the sunlight, the sky was a pulsating arc above the plain.

Security police, operating with the precision of an army, fanned out into the townships, plucked people out of their beds, teachers from schools, students from their classes, arrived in force at the University, searched offices, detained a number of students and two of the staff members, raided a few houses in the white suburbs taking quantities of books and papers. And an unknown number of people.

The shop was not busy in the mornings. At lunch time she would fetch the hired car and return it. She sat behind the counter on the ground floor, copying book titles into an order book. Someone walked up to the counter. She raised her head. There were two of them. One of them took a card from his pocket and held it in front of her. Det-Sgt. J. J du Plessis.

She said quietly, 'What can I do for you?'

'Miss Norval?'

'Yes, I am Pila Norval.'

'We would like to ask you one or two questions. Will you please come to headquarters with us.'

'Then I must tell the manager.' She turned quickly towards the steps leading to the basement, but for all their size they could move swiftly; one of them barred her way.

'I will inform him. You stay here.'

All she wanted was that Thabo should know, should be warned.

In the car she tried to compose her thoughts. *What I must work out now is, why me? How did they get on to me? Was it the hired car? I might have been seen, or traced.*

She began to answer, in her head, the questions she thought they would ask. She tested each answer against the next probable question. She was pleased with the simple and logical explanation she had prepared.

She had never been raided before. They took her to her flat and were quite polite, extremely formal and cold. They asked her to be seated while they searched the front room. They opened cupboards, cabinets, looked into the back of the radio, lifted chairs, ran their hands beneath them. They examined books, took a few at random from the bookcase and riffled through the pages. They spent time at her small desk, searching through papers and reading letters from friends.

'They're purely personal,' she protested.

One of them ignored her and continued with his reading. The other looked up at her. 'That's for us to decide,' he said. She felt that the very privacy of her thoughts was subject to that slow, hard, probing gaze.

They moved to the bedroom, asked her to come with them. They lifted the mattress, examined the edges; went to the wardrobe; put their hands in the pockets of the clothes, looked inside shoes. Their eyes shifted continuously about the room. They held up the book that had

145

been next to her bed and shook it; they began opening drawers, lifting underwear, feeling with large fingers among flimsy garments, even opened a packet of tampons and examined the contents. At other things they simply glanced, looked at the curtains, looked at the floor, turned a slow gaze on everything within sight.

The search in the kitchen and bathroom was also slow and painstaking. One sifted some talcum powder onto the palm of his hand, sniffed it, dipped a finger in and tasted it. In the kitchen they emptied packets of flour and sugar onto sheets of paper, sniffed and tasted, put them back again. Finally they told her to pack a bag.

'What for?' she asked. 'Are you arresting me?'

'We just want you to come along to headquarters to answer a few questions,' one of them said.

'It may be necessary to keep you for a few days,' said the other.

'I want to know if I am being arrested. I want to know what you are charging me with, and I want to see your warrant.'

The expressions on their immobile faces did not change.

'You will be detained for a few days,' one of them said, 'and you should know we don't need a warrant. We are holding you for questioning under ninety days.'

# Dick . . .

The night before he returned Dick phoned Margie to say he was coming back the following day, and to ask if everything was all right. He felt she would have enough understanding to warn him if the police had come for him.

Margie sounded cheerful and said everything was fine. Jonny was missing him, and so was she. At his request she met him at the station the next day and he drove her home, then went on to the University. There was a message in his office that the head of his department wished to see him as soon as possible.

The professor was lighting his pipe, the flame shooting up from his lighter at each release of his breath. He stood up when Dick came in and asked politely about Dick's mother's health.

'Please sit down,' he said.

He went to the door and made sure it was closed, walked around the office and adjusted the angle of the venetian blinds. He was ill at ease.

'We had a bit of trouble here while you were away,' he said at last. 'I suppose you heard about it?'

'I saw in the papers that there had been raids, here as well, and some of the students were detained.'

'Yes, and two staff members.'

'Oh. Who were they?'

The professor said nervously, 'They told us we are not to disclose any names to anyone.'

There was a pause while he put the lighter to his pipe again, puffing clouds of smoke into the office.

'I thought I had better let you know, Dick, that two of them were asking for you.'

'Oh. Did they say what they wanted?'

'One hardly asks in such a situation, does one? But they did say they just wanted to ask you a few questions. I'm afraid they had a thorough search of your office. Took some papers and things away. Did the same to some of the others, you know.'

He went on, not looking directly at Dick, 'I said you'd be back some time this week, but I wasn't sure exactly which day.'

'Well, thanks,' said Dick.

The other man looked down at his desk. 'I just thought you had better know.' He cleared his throat. 'I trust you will respect my confidence. That is, if you should see them again, it would be better not to mention . . . I . . . ah . . .'

'Of course,' Dick said. 'I quite understand.'

He had no lectures to give until the following day. He looked around his office, but could not actually make up his mind what they had taken. He took his car and went to town.

He spent some time looking in the window of the bookshop. The interior was visible above the display of books in the window, and while he pretended to look at the book titles, he searched for Pila. He should not go in and ask for her, but he could not desist. He tried to walk in casually, wandered over to the shelves, looked at some books, chose one, then finally went over to a corner of the shop where the owner, Mr Swart, was sitting.

'Is Pila Norval around?' Dick asked.

Mr Swart looked at him. 'I'm afraid she's not here.'

'Will she be back soon?'

'She's gone away for a short while,' Mr Swart said.

'Oh? Is she on holiday?'

'I'm afraid I do not know,' said Mr Swart coldly and turned his head away.

Dick stood resolutely for a moment or two. 'Umm, she promised to get me some books,' he said at last, 'perhaps Thabo would know if they've come . . .'

'What books were they?' Mr Swart asked.

Dick named two books he had seen reviewed recently.

'They're not in yet,' Mr Swart said. 'Perhaps they'll be here next week. Shall I notify you?'

He drove home in the late afternoon trying to work out what to do. He bought the evening Star on his way home. Parking his car by the side of the road, he ran quickly through it to see if there was any news of those arrested, or of more arrests. Nothing that had not appeared in the morning paper.

He started the car and drove slowly along his street, looking for any cars that were not actually parked there; wondering if he would be able to see if they were waiting for him.

The street was quiet in the afternoon sun. There was no one about.

Margie greeted him and said, 'Someone phoned for you only half an hour ago. He said his name was Robert.'

Robert was Ralph's pseudonym.

'Did he leave a message?'

'He said I must tell you that he has to leave town for a while, urgently. Then he said something peculiar. He said, tell Dick he should join me. I said, join you where? And he just repeated, please tell your husband it would be a good idea to join me, as there is no time left. And then he hung up.'

'Did you recognize the voice?'

'No. It was muffled. And he was speaking from a call-box. Who was it, Dick? What is it about?'

He shook his head. 'I don't really know.'

'But who's Robert? Do you know anyone called Robert?'

'Well, I used to know a chap . . .'

'Why should he want you to join him somewhere?'

'It must have been some sort of joke.'

'It didn't sound like it,' she said in an uncertain voice.

She was troubled all evening. She had never intruded on that territory which he had kept entirely for himself, she knew that he wanted to protect her; but now she felt impelled to voice her unease.

After supper they sat in the room overlooking the garden.

Because it was colder now at night, the doors were closed and the curtains drawn across the large glass windows. Dick put on a record and Margie brought in her sewing box and picked up some work. A typical domestic scene, she thought. But after a while she put it down on her lap and holding her hands tightly together, looking directly at her husband, she said, 'Dick, I've never asked you to say anything about what you've been doing.'

'No,' he acknowledged.

'I'm not asking you to tell me anything now, I don't want to know . . . it's not that I want you to tell me anything. But if there's trouble, Dick, wouldn't it be better to go away?'

He said, 'Where should I go?'

'How should I know? It depends on you, on what's happening. I just want you to know that if it's necessary, then I won't mind if we have to leave, even if we have to go overseas.'

He did not answer. She said finally, 'I'm so worried, Dick,' and she lowered her head.

He came up to her then, and sat on a stool close to her chair.

'I'm worried too,' he told her.

'Are you in danger? Do you think you might . . ?'

'Yes,' he said.

'Then wouldn't it be better to go? Even if you just go and stay somewhere else, for a while, until things have sorted themselves out here? There've been a lot of arrests. Nobody knows just how many people have been taken. Whites and blacks. They could take you for ninety days even if you haven't done a thing.'

'Where could I possibly go?' he asked again.

'Take a room in a hotel, under a different name. Just stay for a week. We can make some sort of arrangement to keep in touch. I could let you know if they come for you. If they don't come, you could come home again.'

'How could I do that?' Dick replied. 'It's the beginning of the term. There's a huge pile of work on my desk. I can't just walk out on everything.'

'We could make some excuse, illness or something.'

'And what about you and Jonny?'

'Oh, I'll be all right. I'll ask Esther to come and stay.'

'It's not so easy to go,' he said.

'Dick, please,' she urged, 'your work won't get done in any case if they arrest you. Is it worth it, taking such a chance? Just stay away for a few days to see what's going to happen. Everything might blow over.'

'It won't blow over,' he said. 'Nothing will blow over. It will get worse.'

She did not speak. She was very close to tears.

Eventually she burst out, 'Are you afraid? Afraid of running away, I mean? Is that it?'

'No, it's not just that. Perhaps in a day or two. There are some things I must do first.'

'It will be too late,' she said urgently, insistently, and added, 'other people go.'

Her brown hair fell forward to cover her face, and he leant forward to smooth it back gently, so he could look at her. She was trembling.

'If this man, this Robert, has gone, and he's warned you – that's what it was, wasn't it? A warning? Then why not you? He's given you a warning, he's told you . . .'

*Then why not me?* Inertia seemed to settle on him. His limbs felt heavy, his throat constricted. He wanted to sleep, just to go to bed and sleep. He could not possibly summon the energy to pack a case and find a place to stay. *Why not me?*

His hand held hers, and now he lowered his forehead until it touched the back of his hand. He wanted to think, but his mind had stopped functioning. It was a blank. 'Margie, my dear,' he said at last, 'let's sleep on it for a night. It's a big decision. Perhaps tomorrow we'll have a better idea . . .'

She did not move, nor answer him. He got up. 'I'm going to bed. Will you come?'

'In a moment.' She picked up her sewing, as though there was something she had to get finished, and did not look at him as he walked out of the room.

He came back and stood in the doorway.

'Margie?'

'Yes?'

'Don't worry dear, everything will be all right.'

When she went into the bedroom he was already deeply asleep, breathing like a drugged man. She thought that if he went to sleep so quickly and easily, then perhaps she was making too much fuss. He should know. Perhaps tomorrow . . .

She lay awake for an hour, two hours. Then she left her bed quietly and went into the kitchen. She made herself a hot drink and took it into the lounge without turning on the light. She drew back the curtains and sat looking out into the silent garden. The suburb was very still at night.

She went back to bed and eventually she slept. At two o'clock there was a hammering on the front door, and the bell was ringing. She sat upright. Dick was also awake. He switched on the bedside light. 'It's all right, Margie,' he said, 'I'll go, you stay here.'

'Dick,' she whispered, 'perhaps you could get out . . . the back garden . . .'

He was putting on his dressing gown, carefully tying the cord, moving with deliberation.

'I wouldn't be able to get away,' he told her. They were banging on the door again.

'It's just too late,' he said, and walked along the corridor to let them in.

# Indres and April . . .

From far off he heard the chugging of an ancient lorry, slowing painfully on the hills, the pause, the grinding gears and grating start. It took so long to reach him that he thought he must be walking faster than it was being driven, but eventually it was rattling and chugging just behind him, and then a face as yellow and wrinkled as an old apple appeared above an elbow resting on the door next to the driver's cab, and a voice called cheerfully, 'Hey, mister, you going somewhere or just taking a little stroll?'

Indres hesitated. The man went on, 'Awful dangerous to walk alone round these parts at night, mister. If you're going my way, why don't you hop up?

'Late to be out,' he commented as they proceeded along the road.

'Well, you see, I went to see some friends of mine back along the road there to get a place for the night, and when I got there I found they'd moved.'

'So where you heading now? Looking for a place to shack down for the night?'

'Yes.'

'Care to come to my place? It's not far from here, mister, you welcome to come. Though it's not exactly the Grand Hotel.'

'Where do you live?' Indres asked him, 'In Noordegesicht?'

'Noordegesicht?' The man laughed. 'I don't stay in any of them municipal townships. They don't want me, I

154

don't want them. All their rules and orders and the rest. No, I got my own place, whole township of my own.'

Further on the lorry turned off the road onto a dirt track, turned once more, and bumped across the veld along the faint grass-covered remains of what was once a dirt road. The lorry swayed and heaved, leaping in the air and rattling down again as though each part had independent life, but the man drove with the confidence of long familiarity, undeterred by darkness and the roughness of the track.

He changed down to second gear and drove down an incline leading to a quarry. They entered an arena where once fleets of lorries had driven to cart away the red sand. They stopped and the driver hopped down. 'Here we are, mister.' He opened the door for Indres.

Indres jumped down from the lorry and looked around. There was nothing to be seen except deeply eroded cliff-sides. The driver grinned, seeing the puzzlement on Indres' face, and said 'This is just my drive-in, mister. Drive right up to me front door.'

He walked directly into a gully in the cliff-side, motioning Indres to follow, and held aside a curtain of sacking. They entered a cave dug out of the side of the quarry.

His host hopped along ahead using a torch to guide the way. He showed Indres to a chair, and lit a paraffin lamp. When the white glass chimney was in place, Indres saw the room, the roof and sides shored up with pit-props and with corrugated iron. It was densely furnished, the floor covered with layers of hessian and pieces of carpet. There was an iron bedstead, chairs, a table and rows of old packing cases converted into storage cupboards. The room was warm and in spite of the assortment of disparate items, remarkably tidy.

Indres helped his host unload some paraffin tins from

the lorry and bring them into the room. 'My water supply,' he explained. He lit a primus stove and put a kettle on.

'Everything in this place I made myself,' he said proudly. 'That chair you're sitting in, look at that wood,' he stroked it fondly, 'railway sleepers, old ones, thrown away. I had a job to bring them here, they weigh a ton. Lovely hard wood, hard to work, but look at it. That table, too.

'Picked up that bed on a rubbish dump. Those chairs there, they was all broken and thrown away. But as long as there's a bit of wood, I can do something with it.'

'You're a carpenter, then?'

'I was a carpenter, once. Not here. They don't need good carpenters here. Where I come from, in the Cape, I used to be a carpenter. Here, I'm an independent operator, self-employed.'

'You live here alone?'

'All by my self, mate, just me. Funny, when you come to think of it, I came from such big family. My mother had thirteen children. I was number four, so she called me April, that's my name, April Petersen. Number five was called May, that was all right because she was a girl, but number six turned out to be a boy and me Ma insisted on calling him June. He hated that name. Soon as he was old enough he changed it to Jules. Do you blame him?'

'Where are your family now?'

He waved his arms. 'Scattered around the four corners of this country. I got a wife and kids, too. Never see them.

'I'm a Capey,' he said again, 'born a Capey, lived a Capey, I'll die one too. Even if my bones rot in this miserable dry Transvaal, my soul will go flying back in the teeth of a Southeaster. They're all there, my wife and

156

kids. We was all right there too, until they started that new Population Registration Law. She had a good job as a typist, my wife, she was real white, a real whitey. We had two kids working, two at school. The two younger ones favoured her. They was going to a white school. So then they started this classification business and I knew what was going to happen. There was a kid down our street, his Ma and Pa took him out of school and hid him in the house because he was dark and the others was white. He hanged himself.

'So one day I decided to leave. I just up and left. She would have lost her job, the kids chucked out of school. What for should I ruin their lives? They've got most years to live; me, I've had my life. I had plenty good times. So I left.'

'Don't you ever hear from them?'

'They don't know where I am. You see I reckoned my wife, she was sort of loyal, she'd want . . . I never told them anything. Missing, presumed dead. I want her to think I'm dead. Maybe she'll still find someone, she was a good-looking woman . . . good luck to her. We was married twenty years. I never liked living alone, I've often wished . . . but you know how it is; twenty years. I couldn't think of being married to anyone except her. Well, that's life for you. You got to live. You married?'

'No.'

'You looking for a place to stay, mate? You could stay here a while if you liked, you're real welcome to stay. I'd get you a proper bed, like mine. I know where there's one . . . It's cosy here, mister, even in winter. And cheap. No rent, no rates, no taxes. Isn't any flush toilet, I just dig a little pit, only problem is water, have to cart that here in tins, but I manage.'

157

'It's kind of you, very kind, but you see . . . well, I just came out of jail. I've got a few things to do . . .'

'Oh, I understand!' April exclaimed. 'Oh yes, I suppose you got to see your folks again. Takes a little while to settle down. You always feel strange at first, hey? You got to adjust, like. I never been in one of those Transvaal jails. I suppose they'll catch up with me one of these days: "Where's your registration card? Where'd you live? Who employs you? Who's your boss? Where you work?" What'll I tell them, man, hey? You got to be registered, you got to be entered up in their books. You got to be official.'

Later in the night, when they both went outside before going to bed, April said, 'Look how nice it is here, beautiful, quiet. What would I want in them townships? I just wish they leave me alone. You got to live.'

And just before they went to sleep, Indres felt impelled to ask something that had been bothering him all evening.

'April,' he said, 'tell me, what did your mother call number thirteen?'

He heard April chuckle in the darkness. 'Well, that was a problem. I remember the arguments. I was quite a big boy myself then. Lucky the baby died when it was only two weeks old.' He laughed again.

Indres felt himself smiling. He could not remember when he had felt so completely relaxed.

# Indres . . .

There was a pause in living, a hiatus, a time of inactivity.
The newspapers, self-censoring for fear of reprisals, kept
to the safe news. Angrily Indres crumpled the pages of
the Star and flung it on the floor. He had gone through it
column by column, swiftly at first, then with endless care,
and – not a word. Yet he knew for sure that certain
arrests had been made only last night, and someone had
reported them to the Star. They knew. Were they afraid
to publish? Had they had orders from the Special Branch?

He had been waiting for four days, keeping out of sight
during the day, filling the ashtrays with stale stubs and
the room with stale air. At night he walked down to the
Greek shop, the café on the corner, and bought more
cigarettes. And woke the next day with that dark brown
taste in his mouth and swore to give up smoking . . .
tomorrow. Next week. When this particular crisis was
over.

He knew the police were looking for him. They had
been to his flat more than once. The news was passed on
by a neighbour and eventually reached him. 'She says
there's a chap been hanging around the building all the
time. She thinks he's waiting to see if you come back.'

*All these years you kept talking about wanting a time to
read, a time when there would be nothing else to do. Well,
read then. What's stopping you? Farid will get all the
books you want. And for once in your life you've got the
time . . .*

He found difficulty in concentrating. He read for short

159

periods during the day; listened to voices through the thin partition that divided his small room from the doctor's surgery. Then tried not to listen; after all, it was entirely intimate and private, what went on between doctor and patient. When the surgery finished, always at least an hour after the stated time, the doctor would bring him some food and stay for a short while to talk.

On Saturday he went out to make a phone call.

The phone box on the corner two streets away was out of order. The instrument was there, even the coin box seemed to be intact, but there was no dialling tone. Indres pressed the receiver up and down and waited, and tried again. Silence. Most of the phone boxes seemed to be permanently out of order.

He walked back to the corner café. He bought his usual packet of cigarettes, then asked the proprietor if he could use the phone. 'I'm terribly sorry to worry you,' Indres said, 'but the phone box on the corner is out of order.'

The man asked abruptly, 'Local call?'

'Yes.'

'Well, all right then,' he muttered.

Indres dialled his number, and waited a long time, listening to the burr-burr of the phone ringing somewhere in the Blue Moon. Surely they could hear. Surely someone would answer.

At last there was a woman's voice, 'Hullo?'

'I want to speak to Sipho,' Indres said, holding the receiver close to his mouth and speaking softly.

'What?'

'Is Sipho there?'

He could hear the sound of music in the background, and the hum of voices. The hubbub of that distant

160

shebeen came clearly through the earpiece, distinctly into the quiet café.

'I can't hear you,' the voice said. 'Can't you speak louder? Who do you want?'

He said, enunciating the name as clearly as he could, 'Sipho, Si-pho! I want to speak to Sipho. He said he would be there tonight.'

He saw the café proprietor watching him from a corner where he was wiping glasses with a cloth that hung from his waist. Straight hair plastered down across a dead white forehead. Dark suspicious eyes. A kind of resentment seemed to emanate from him.

There was a burst of laughter through the phone, then the music rose louder again. 'No!' the woman's voice shouted. 'No! He's not here.'

'Has he been there this evening?'

'What did you say?'

'Has he been in?'

'No, haven't seen him. Didn't see him all week.'

'If he comes, will you tell him Jerry phoned?'

'OK' and the receiver slammed down.

He realized he was perspiring. He put some money on the counter. 'Here's the money for the phone,' he said. The man moved his head, watching Indres with his dark, unfriendly eyes, but said nothing.

He decided he would not go to the café again.

In the middle of the week, Farid came to the surgery, slipping through the back room.

'Well, it's all set up,' he said. 'We've moved the hand duplicator over to the room behind Mohamed's shop. It's all ready.'

'And the stencils?' Indres asked. 'Who is typing the stencils?'

'Rahima. She says she can get them done at work, when her boss is out.'

'God, that's a joke!' Indres exclaimed. 'And he's such a big supporter of the government!'

'Yes, that makes it better. It isn't likely they'll ever trace the typewriter.'

'And the leaflet? Is it OK? Have the others agreed?'

'It's fine, it's all agreed. One or two small alterations, nothing much; more or less as you drafted it. And we've got three groups ready to handle the distribution. Now, the running off: we can only use the machine during the day. It's too quiet around there at night, and it makes too much noise. Someone might hear it. We tried it out today while Mohamed was in the shop. He says you can barely hear it. So tomorrow morning Meshack will come here with a van, and he'll take you over to Mohamed's. You'd better bring a blanket with you, you'll have to stay there one or two nights. It'll take a couple of days to run off all we'll need.'

In the evening, when the doctor came, Indres said 'I'll be leaving you tomorrow.'

'So you've found another place? Is it better than this, then?'

'No, not better,' Indres replied. 'But I'll be able to do some work that I can't do here. Anyway, it's not a good idea for me to stay in one place too long.'

'And may I ask what are your intentions? You can't go hiding for the rest of your life.'

'Well, no, obviously one can't go on living like this forever. In a couple of weeks we should have a clearer picture, we should know more about who has been arrested, and try and work out how much they know.'

'You know they look for you, Indres. Whatever you work out, they still look for you.'

162

Indres laughed. 'They've been after me most of my life,' he said.

'This is different,' the doctor replied. 'You know it is different. It's one thing they're after you because they think you went into the townships without a permit, or they're chasing you about a meeting, or if you were talking to people you've been banned from talking to . . . All of us do that sort of thing. We've all been going to meetings we are not allowed to have, and meeting people we are prohibited from seeing. They know it, too, but they have to catch us at it. But this is different. Breaking a ban is one thing, a year or two at the most. Sabotage can mean . . . death.'

'What makes you think . . .'

'Oh, please, Indres, I'm not such a fool.'

'They'd have to catch one at that, too.'

'No, you're wrong, Indres. They've arrested one helluva lot of people. They only have to break one or two . . . Once it starts . . . I'm sorry to be a prophet of doom. You'll see.'

'They won't break our chaps,' Indres said.

'No? You're so sure?'

'As sure as I am of myself.'

'I hate to say it, but if I were you, I would not be sure of anyone, even myself . . .'

After the doctor had gone, Indres read for a while, then he realized he had smoked his last cigarette.

It was only a little after eight, and he would not be able to sleep until twelve or later. The thought of so many hours ahead without cigarettes was intolerable.

He walked round the room restlessly. He could go out and buy some. But the thought of returning to the café on the corner filled him with disquiet. Tonight he should not take a chance, when everything was ready for him to do the leaflets tomorrow.

He reconstructed the locality in his mind. The nearest alternative shop that would be open at this hour was some distance away, and on a busy and well-lighted street. That would be foolhardy.

*Do without, then*. But it was impossible. If he only had one, or two. If he had one, he would break it into two. It was knowing that there was not one left . . .

He put the door on the latch, and slipped quietly out into the yard. He waited in the darkness alongside the house for a while, watching the street. It seemed empty. He stepped out and began to walk quickly towards the café. Not too fast. To try and hide in the shadows would look suspicious if anyone happened to look out of a window. To run would attract attention.

He turned the corner. The shop was just a couple of hundred yards up the street. Its lights shone brightly, a patch in the darkness. There was a van parked further up the street. Nothing odd about that. The Greek shop. All the cafés that stayed open so late at night were Greek shops. They worked hard, those Greeks, but they kept to themselves. They liked to keep in with the government, otherwise they might lose their trading licences. There was something hostile about that chap. Perhaps it was his manner. Perhaps he was just tired.

There was someone else in the shop, a youth wearing jeans and a T-shirt. He stood with his back to the door playing at a pin-table that stood near the furthest window. He did not turn round when Indres entered, only paused to insert another coin, then began to push and pull the handles vigorously so that the whole machine shook. The lights flashed on and off, the balls bounced around noisily.

The Greek stood behind the counter, unsmiling.

'Tweny Rothmans, please,' Indres said.

'Cork?'

'Filter,' Indres replied. The activities at the machine seemed to be reaching a climax, with lights and bells and twangs. The balls fell back into the base of the machine, the lights went out. The youth remained with his back to the door, fumbling in the pocket of his jeans for another coin, then turned quickly and placed a note on the counter. Indres caught a glimpse of heavy brows meeting above the eyes, a scarred and pitted skin. The proprietor took the note and pressed the buttons of his cash register. A bell rang, a drawer sprang open. He counted out the change slowly, placed it on the counter. The eyes of the man and the youth met and held for a moment in a look of mutual understanding.

The packet of cigarettes was slapped down on the counter, and again the cash register gave a ping. The pin-table also sprang to life once more. A zig-zag of coloured lights flashed first on one side, then on the other. In the black mirror of the window, Indres saw the frowning face as the youth shook the handles and slapped at the side of the machine, trying to manoeuvre the balls into the right holes. Indres stripped the cellophane off his packet and took out a cigarette. He felt his hand was a little uncertain of itself. *Whatever you do, behave in a normal way*. He picked up his change and said goodnight. The man behind the counter did not reply, standing with his arms folded, looking at him.

Indres reached the door and paused for a moment to light the cigarette. Suddenly the shop was completely quiet. The machine had stopped. The lights had gone. The youth stood, unmoving, looking at the window, looking at the reflections of the shop interior in the window.

He hurried out. He saw a car approaching, turned to go the other way, swinging round so abruptly that he almost bumped into a man who stood in his way.

The man wore a raincoat and a felt hat. Indres looked up, and knew who he was. At the same moment, a pair of hands came down from behind and seized both his arms.

The man smiled.

'Well, well, well,' said Sergeant Wessels of the Security Branch, 'this is a surprise. Fancy meeting you here!'

# Pila . . .

Pila had examined her cell and all it contained, taken a measure of everything, and worked out a routine for the day.

They had taken her to the prison at Pretoria, the massive complex of red brick that fronted the main road from Johannesburg to the north; they had entered the iron gates between fortress-like towers. They passed through corridors lined with cell doors, each with its judas-hole. Doors were ceremoniously unlocked and locked, until finally the wardress left, locking the door behind her. Pila was in her cell. She was in jail.

All fears and uncertainty had subsided. Her suitcase and its contents had been inspected; after some items had been removed she was allowed to have it with her. A change of underclothes, toothbrush, toothpaste, face cloth, soap, comb. No lipstick, no cosmetics, no mirror. The mirror would have been useful. No pen, no pencil, no paper except a roll of toilet paper. You could still write on that, if you had anything to write with, if there was anything you wanted to write. Keep a diary? Remember everything, keep it in your mind.

There was an iron bedstead with dark and very heavy blankets that seemed to have been pressed out of some coarse fibre. There was a bucket with a lid. A tin mug with water. A stool. She climbed on the bed and precariously on to a small ledge in the wall to try and see through the high, dusty and barred window. It seemed there was nothing outside except another wall.

Life took on a pattern dictated by the prison procedure, and security rested in the repetitiveness of this routine, which also provided a measure of time since her watch had been removed. She was taken out of her cell twice a day; in the mornings to empty the bucket, to shower and use the toilets, and to exercise; and then in the afternoons again for exercise. All cell doors were shut when they took her out, all signs of other prisoners eliminated. She could have been the only one in the whole block, except that while she was in her cell she heard the rattling, the grinding, the opening and slamming, the *Kom!* and the shouts of orders; and at night she heard voices calling through the walls, sometimes singing. African voices. Words that could not be deciphered. Other women prisoners.

But the corridors would be empty when she was escorted by two wardresses to the yard. They did not leave her, stood next to the shower, beside the swinging half-door of the water closet, watching every movement as she walked around the small yard. Through a gate into another yard she could glimpse black women prisoners, hanging up washing or scrubbing the cement. Sometimes she heard a baby crying. Always, whatever the time of day, there were the crashing reverberations of great iron doors and gates, the exaggerated jangling of enormous rings of keys and the harsh voices of the wardresses shouting with venom and angry hate. It was like an incomprehensible opera with an alien but repetitive chorus, an opera built on discords and dissonance.

The metal dixie with food was placed outside her door by an African woman prisoner. The prisoner was dismissed, then the wardress opened the door, and Pila had to lift the dixie off the floor and take it into her cell. Supper, which was always a cold congealed mess of fat and gristle with pumpkin or cabbage, came early in the afternoon. She would spend the next few hours listening to the pattern of sounds and trying to construct the events that caused them. Later it would become very quiet, and when the judas-hole had been lifted and flapped shut again, and after the departure of the wardress the voices would begin. At eight the cell lights went out, although a light burned all night long just outside her cell.

One day, presumably, they would come and take her away for questioning. They did not seem to be in any hurry. She knew that sometimes people who had been detained for questioning were kept for weeks and weeks. She was prepared to go on like this for a long time and she thought with quite pleasurable anticipation of what she might start to do in a little while: try and make some sort of contact with the African prisoners; see if she could breach the wall of silence of the least unfriendly-looking wardress; attempt in some way to make a slow and cautious contact. One of these days. Plenty of time. No point in trying to rush things.

Had they taken Thabo? He was out of the shop when she was arrested. And who else, and what did they know? Her thoughts about this were also remote and in a low key. Whatever had happened, nothing would make any difference now. It was all out of her hands.

She slept well each night on the sagging bed. She welcomed the physical discomforts. She had a bed while Africans, she knew, slept on a thin mat on the floor. She had different food, and she had the privilege of not being sworn at by those hoarse angry voices. But she was a prisoner, as they were, and like them deprived of freedom. She had earned the badge of honour of Africa – jail for political reasons. Whatever came in the future, this was enough. She slept, and cleaned the cell, and exercised, and listened to the voices, and she was strangely unapprehensive – even content.

The sounds that denoted each day's activities were so regular that she was able to programme her life by them.

But after some days, there came a disturbing event, the sound of footsteps at the wrong time. Keys, the door swinging open. A small tremor of fearful expectation that the time for questioning had arrived. Two wardresses came into the cell.

'Take your things,' one of them ordered.

'My things?'

'Yes, everything.'

'Am I being moved?'

There was no reply. They never answered questions.

In the matron's office she had to sign a receipt for the return of her watch, ring, and money which they had taken when she was booked in; when this was done the matron said, 'Your father is waiting for you.'

He was pacing up and down in the waiting room. He greeted her briefly and took her case; a wardress unlocked the front door. 'Where are we going?' she asked.

Her father replied, 'I am taking you home.'

'Home?'

'Yes. Didn't they tell you? You're being released.'

Outside, in the full glaring sunshine of a Pretoria noon, stood the big black Cadillac which her father had bought only recently. They were on the road to Johannesburg before either of them spoke. She had glanced at the set lines of her father's face, and hoped that he would give some sort of explanation.

Eventually she said, 'I'm afraid I'm in a bit of a daze. I didn't know they were letting me out. They never tell you anything. I thought perhaps I was being moved somewhere

170

else. You're the last person I expected to see. What happened? How was it you knew to come and fetch me?'

'What do you mean, what happened?' he said angrily. 'What do you think I've been doing ever since you were arrested? Why do you think you've been released?'

She said, with a growing feeling of something disastrous exploding around her, 'I've no idea. I don't know why I was arrested and I don't know why I was let out.'

'You should know why you were arrested, but you were released because of me. And damn difficult it's been, too. I had to go to the Minister personally. I've had to plead, to make promises on your behalf. What a ghastly business. But I had to get the Minister's intervention, otherwise they would never have let you out.'

She was stunned. 'I don't understand,' she said. 'Are you telling me that you went to the Minister of Justice to beg for my release? Is that it?'

'That's it. If I hadn't had that kind of influence, known the right person to go to . . .'

'Oh God!' she cried. 'What did you do it for?'

'What do you mean, what did I do it for? You're my daughter, whatever I think about what you've been doing, whatever it's done to my position, to our family, you're still my daughter. I couldn't leave you there, rotting in jail. But I made promises, and now I'm going to see they are kept.'

'What did you do it for?' she repeated. 'What did you want to do to my life? What right had you to do it?'

As though he could not comprehend what she said, he did not answer her. The car sped smoothly along the tree-lined road.

Further on, his hands relaxed a little on the wheel. After all, she had been in jail for more than a week. She was

171

shocked, she would need to rest and recuperate. He felt there was nothing to do but to ignore what she had said.

When they reached Johannesburg and were approaching the suburb where her parents lived, her father said, 'I suppose you can respect a confidence even if we don't see eye to eye? Do you know how you were released? It was through Vorster. He, personally, ordered your release.'

'It doesn't make sense to me. Why? What for? What sort of relationship do you have with him?'

'Matthias arranged it. He got the Minister's ear, they were at law school together, and Vorster's got a soft spot for all his old legal colleagues. He's always ready to listen to them. People say some pretty harsh things about Vorster, but I'll say this for him, he's a reasonable man. He's not ruthless, and he was very decent about this whole affair. How many Ministers can you name who would bother themselves about some idiot daughter who got herself mixed up in very shady politics?'

'I don't even want to discuss it with you,' she cried. 'I can't even begin to say . . . He's responsible for putting thousands of innocent people in jail. Why should I be favoured? Who else has he released? Just because my father's got pull, got an ear to the Minister . . .'

'We'll discuss it later,' he said as they reached the house. 'You'll have a chance to rest, a chance to get over this, and then we'll discuss it.'

'I don't need a rest. We'll talk about it immediately, right away.'

'If that's what you want.'

'Yes, immediately. So that I can go straight back to my flat.'

He said, 'Pila, you're not going back to your flat. You're staying here for the time being. That's one of the conditions.'

\* \* \*

172

She was in the room with the kidney-shaped dressing table. The room was a cell, the house a prison. That other cell with its high barred window and massive door with the peering eye was less of a prison to her than this one with its frilled valances and draped curtains and curling iron bars.

In spite of the storm that had blown up in the house a few hours previously, a great disturbance starting with her mother's tears and her father's barely-controlled anger, and ending with her own great screech of misery, the house was quiet now, locked in its inevitable domestic routine from which no personal disaster could shake it.

Sounds of the servants, sounds of the kitchen and the kitchen yard, the late afternoon sounds that began when the sun had moved downwards towards the hills. Johannes sweeping the back yard. Emily sitting on the kitchen step, preparing the vegetables for the evening meal. Pila in prison.

'I won't stay here!' she had cried.

'You'll stay, my girl, because I've given my word that you will be under my constant supervision until you leave the country.

'I have no intention of leaving. I'm not leaving South Africa! What makes you think I'll leave?'

'I'm thinking of you and your future. They've given you an exit permit. But later they'll probably let you have a passport. In a few years, when all this trouble has blown over, you can come back. We hope you will. We don't want to send you away for all time.'

*They cannot make me go. They cannot keep me here in this house. I will do as I wish. I have not given any undertakings, there is nothing legally binding as far as I am concerned. I'll return to my flat, my job . . . perhaps a different job. Where is Thabo? How can I find out if he has been detained? How can I make contact again? Ralph? Perhaps Indres?*

'They won't arrest you again,' her father said. 'Not immediately, anyway. Vorster says he doesn't wish to create martyrs.'

No, they would not arrest her. She would be trailed everywhere she went, every encounter would be noted, every conversation monitored. She realized that whatever evidence they had of her activities must be very slight, otherwise she would not have been released, no matter who had the ear of the Minister. He did not act without consulting his Security chief. It probably suited them better this way, to have her under supervision.

Bit by bit the full implication of her position came to her as she tried to think of what she could do. Not only would it be far too dangerous to try and contact any of her former associates, but more than that, they would not, ever again, have anything to do with her, because they would believe that she had in some way bought her release.

She remembered how others, who had been detained for short periods and then released, had been isolated. He might be innocent, Thabo would say, but how can you take a chance?

She might be innocent, Thabo would say when they learned that she was out, but on the other hand, she might not. Wherever she went, she would be marked. White and a woman. No way of sinking unidentified, back into a dark pool of humanity. A woman, and white. Odd, conspicuous, branded.

*Believe me, it's true, I didn't even know where I was going until my father took me outside to his car. I had nothing at all to do with it . . .*

'Even if we believe you,' Thabo would reply, 'it's better for us all if you keep away.'

She saw his strong and unrevealing face. He would look at her without hate or contempt, without compassion or sorrow. She would not exist any more. They would simply wipe her completely out.

Bitterness and hopelessness pushed knives through her heart. Her father had said at last, still unable to comprehend, 'But how could I leave you there? Your mother was ill with worry, Janet's taken the children and gone to hide herself somewhere down the coast, she couldn't bear to face her friends. If I had the means to get you out, how could I leave you in jail?'

And it was then that she had screamed at him in a voice hoarse with pain, 'Oh, why didn't you leave me alone? Why couldn't you have left me alone? I was happy there – do you hear me, do you understand that? I was happy, I was happy, I wanted to be there!'

Just for once, for a few short days, she had been at one with them, sharing their hardship and their punishment and bearing, she had believed, for ever afterwards the proud stigmata of political prison.

'Thabo,' she whispered, 'I didn't betray you, I didn't talk. I never had the chance. Thabo, you must believe me. How can I make you believe me? I did not even want to get out. I wanted to be like you. I wanted to share everything.'

Even if they believed that, the rest would be as incomprehensible to them as it had been to her father. They, too, would never understand it if she said to them, 'I was happy there. In jail, I was happy.'

# *Dick . . .*

At certain times a kind of blankness would take possession of his mind.

This had begun not long after his arrest. At first there had been fear, and this surprised him since his arrest was so expected that he had simply been waiting for them to come. All the earlier calmness had disappeared; he became jittery, small things upset him. The handle of the old green suitcase into which he had packed socks, underwear and shaving kit, broke as he lifted it. He had to carry the case under his arm. The search had upset him. They were very thorough, and after they had searched the house, they searched the garden; they woke Elias and made him stand outside while they searched his room.

It was dawn when they finished and drove into the city. Clouds streaked with pale golden light lay across the sky. Lights were glowing in the servants' rooms in the suburbs.

He was taken to police headquarters at Marshall Square and locked in a large cell with black walls.

There was a lot of activity, keys rattling and doors constantly being locked and unlocked, footsteps and voices in the passages. Someone began whistling 'We shall overcome' and others joined in before angry shouts silenced them. So there were others. It had been a busy night for the police.

Later in the day his cell was unlocked, he was handed his suitcase and taken down to a van. In the van were four other white men, detainees like himself, warders attached to each.

He recognized two of them, and ventured a nervous 'Good morning,' thinking how ridiculous it sounded; a warder yelled 'No talking!'

They were driven to Pretoria; here he was put in a cell with walls painted in two shades of brown, and innumerable things scratched into the paint, words, names, symbols, dates. He looked around and thought there would be plenty of time to read those walls. There was a small pool of sunlight in the middle of the floor. As soon as the door was closed and locked, he took the felt mat that was rolled up in a corner and lay in the sun; it was then that his mind became suspended. He lay and thought of nothing at all, not of his arrest, nor of any of the others, nor of Margie nor of the baby. He just lay in the sun awake, and aware, but empty.

They left him alone for a long time. He was terrified that they would come to take him for questioning. What did they know? What would he say? He would say nothing, but he was frightened at the thought that today might be the day, this particular morning or afternoon or evening. Gradually the prison routine settled down around him; there were those certain times for sounds, for comings and goings, and he knew that he need only fear if they came at unusual times.

He would get up early, put on his shoes and walk fifty times around his cell. The shoes were rubber-soled veldskoens, and grit and dirt became embedded in the cracks of the rubber so that the morning walk was a method of helping to clean his cell. Every morning as he was completing his routine pacing he would hear the head warder beginning his rounds; first the rattle of keys, then cell doors opening, the sounds approaching nearer; then the head warder at his cell. His blankets and sleeping mat were rolled in the manner prescribed, he stood at attention as he had been ordered. He knew now that it was against the rules to unroll the mat or to lie down during the day. He obeyed the rules.

When the inspection was over, his breakfast was put down on the floor outside his door. He was kept from all contact with others, and was permitted to go outside the door and pick up the dixie only after the African prisoner who had brought it had gone. Then the door was locked again.

Coffee and mealiepap. He was satisfied. When it was finished he picked up the Bible. All books for detainees were prohibited, except the Bible. As it was the only book permitted, he rationed his reading, allowing himself only a certain number of pages each day. He read twice a day, conserving the book for all the days to come.

The Bible had been sent in by Margie; it was a new one, in a smart blue paper jacket with white lettering. With his thumb-nail he cut out the letters to make a word game. He devised a number of word-games, and particularly delighted in making anagrams. The tiny paper letters were precious. He was afraid that one of the warders, peering through the judas-hole, would see and take them away. He was afraid that they might in some way be an infringement of the rules. He kept them hidden in a folded handkerchief and only took them out when he thought it was safe.

His only point of contact with others was at exercise time. The prison routine, so strict at other times, was flexible as far as exercise was concerned. He knew he was supposed to get two half-hour periods every day. Some days he was taken out only in the mornings, and usually it was for less than half an hour.

Emptying the sanitary bucket, using the toilets, showering, shaving, and smoking the one permitted cigarette –

all these had to be done in less than half an hour. It did not leave much time for walking round the yard.

Four detainees were taken down at a time, kept apart by warders. Talking was strictly forbidden. Even winking or smiling or the slightest gesture was forbidden. With sanitary bucket, dixie, shaving and showering kit, he would walk silently down the stairs to the yard. In the centre of the yard was a brick square which housed the urinals, one shower and one lavatory. A warder climbed to a position from which he could look down into the square and see and hear everything. One man would be showering, another on the lavatory, and a third washing his bucket and dixie at the urinals. In the yard they paced around in single file with warders watching them from both sides. They walked quickly as though all of them had pent-up energy. Dick thought of a silver fox that he had once watched in a cage, padding back and forth, back and forth, very quickly without a pause at the turn, in a continuous controlled movement.

He observed the other three white detainess, but with a certain detached interest. He knew them all by sight. One was a surprise, a university colleague whom he had never suspected of having any interest in political affairs; one was a newspaper reporter who had written sympathetic reports on political trials; and the third was an older man who had long been associated with left-wing political activities and who had been in prison before. But there was no Ralph. There were signs that others had been in the yard immediately before Dick's group, and he had seen other white detainees in the van. Perhaps Ralph was amongst those. Or he could be held in a different prison. Or he might have got away.

Dick had now entered into a routine; anything that did not fall within this known pattern was disturbing. He had been taken and shut away from the outside world; he in turn had shut the world away from him. He found he lacked curiosity, he did not seek information. He had his own ways of passing the hours, and this internalized life became so important that he began to resent intrusions of any kind.

The exercise inside his own cell; pacing the cell in the mornings with his rubber-soled shoes; other exercises, simple remembered ones from school days, touching toes with rigid legs, gradually extending flexibility to touch the floor with palms flat down; arms outstretched on either side, turning from the hips, arms on hips and bending knees, back held straight; push-ups, two or three to begin with, then more and more, until he could do twenty without a pause; all these he performed at a certain period each afternoon before eating his supper, which was brought to his cell at half-past four. They had, of course, taken his watch, but he judged the time from the reflection of light across his cell, spreading over the floor and then to the other side. He could see himself doing his exercises, he was like a spectator watching his own figure, reduced as through an inverted telescope, stretched on the floor, up-down, up-down, up-down, the tiny figure flickering through its exercises as though on an unreeling film.

He worked a little time each day at an extended mental game of chess. But apart from the two sessions of Bible-reading that were like a special treat for himself, he liked best of all a game he had devised in which each day he invited a different person into his cell for conversation. The art was to keep the conversation on the level of what would be normal for the chosen person, and on subjects which would be the ones they would like to discuss. He had to be sure not to project his own views on to the guest. He chose personal friends, relatives, colleagues,

180

people with whom he had held discussions on many topics in the past. He decided that when these more intimate friends had each paid him a visit, he would move on to people not personally known to him, but whom he knew through their public work or writings – scientists, writers, sympathetic politicans. The thought of having these people, many of them world-renowned, to visit him person-ally and spend the day in his cell, quite excited him. The imaginary conversations, the simulated arguments, stretched out for weeks, months in the future. He saw no end to the stream of visitors, nor to the pleasure he would derive from them. There was a moment of pure delight each day when he selected his guest. Now today, who will come, who will it be? Names, faces floated through his head. For some reason one would persist above the others. He did not consciously decide, he did not even know how the choice was made.

Because this world of his own making had become so complete, he sought no means of establishing contact with the others. On the contrary, after the morning exercise period in the yard, he was impatient to be safely locked in by himself once more, away from the pacing prisoners, knowing that a new visitor awaited him. Some-times his conversations with the visitors would be very amicable, sometimes acrimonious, but they were always interesting. Often it would be time for the afternoon push-ups before the conversation had been satisfactorily rounded off, and he had to propel his visitor out of his cell as politely as he could, with the promise that they would meet another day.

The prison was unbearably noisy and very quiet by turns. The noise started early in the mornings when African prisoners were being herded out of their cells and put in gangs for a day's work outside the prison walls. For extended periods the noise would be continuous. When the warders went off for their own meals, and at those times when the locking and shouting and unlocking and shouting had ceased, silence came like a mist and lay over the walls and barred windows of the prison. Silence after the noonday meal. Silence after the early night-time lock-up. Yet it was a silence outside of himself. Inside his head there was no silence; voices and whispers came and went like the rustle of bird wings.

When the tapping began on the walls of his cell, he was annoyed. He did not wish to be disturbed, he did not want to reply. He knew the taps were some sort of code and he listened with growing irritation, wishing they would stop. Then he felt stupid because he did not have any idea what sort of code was being used, and he searched his memory for boy-scout formulae, morse or something else. It did not occur to him that the code could be as childishly simple as a straightforward counting of taps, and he only realized it when Peter, the reporter in the cell next to his stood boldly at his door and began to sing, to the tune of *Where have all the flowers gone*: 'A is one and B is two; C is three-ee-ee; D is four and so it goes, long time away; A is one and B is two, Z is twenty-six.. . .'

Fortunately for his peace of mind, tapping could only be undertaken at a time when the prisoners were reasonably sure that the corridors outside their cells were deserted. They had no way of knowing, except by the pattern of sounds and the obvious round of duties of the warders. There was a period when the warders all went away to get their own meals. On weekends, there were fewer warders on duty, and on Saturday afternoons when there were rugby matches, even those on duty would sneak away to listen to the reports of the match on the radio.

Dick felt impelled to communicate because he did not wish to offend the others. By this slow and cumbersome method, Peter passed on small snippets of information; there appeared to be as many as eight or nine whites detained in this jail, a sign of how extensive the detentions must have been among other sections of the population; that none of them had yet been questioned; and so on. And Dick replied as briefly as he could, having no information that he could pass on, as he had not established any kind of contact with anyone else. Then someone shortened the code: the alphabet was divided into five groups with five letters each. Four taps followed by three taps, for example, would be R – the third letter in the fourth group.

But one day, standing by the wall with a comb in his hand, listening to the taps and waiting to begin his reply, the cell door was unlocked and swung open.

A particularly unpleasant warder, van Wyk, who never lost an opportunity of yelling and screaming at the detainees, shouted at him, 'What are you doing?'

'Nothing,' Dick replied, 'I was reading the Bible.' And he put his hand on the book which lay open on his small table.

'No you wasn't, you blerry liar, do you think I'm a fool? Do you think I don't know what you was up to? I been listening, this is what you was doing.' And the warder seized the comb from Dick's hand and began banging it on the wall.

'If ever I catch you at it again,' he shouted, 'you'll be up before the Colonel, I promise you!'

The incident upset Dick a great deal. Twice a day van Wyk came into his cell and walked along the wall, examining the paint and plaster for any new marks. But Dick refrained from tapping again. He wanted to placate

183

van Wyk. He felt no defiance, only the need for his own kind of survival.

When the conversations started again, he generally ignored them, hearing the taps somewhere in the background; not his life, not his friends. The tapping violated his solitude, dragged him back into the realities of jail life, of being a prisoner, of all the uncertain and fearful future.

He was never bored. He had thought about solitary confinement in the past, thought of the empty hours without end, but if he had wondered then how he would be able to endure such a condition, he did not think about it now. He had, in fact, so many different things to do each day that the time was finished before he had completed them all. He had the word game tied up in his handkerchief. He had problems of other kinds to solve. And sometimes it was music. Very softly, under his breath, he half-whistled a concert for himself, a concert of carefully selected items, chosen for their familiarity. Orchestral music was, on the whole, better than vocal because he would become troubled by an inability to remember words, whereas with the orchestra he could visualize the different instruments, each one coming in, the movement of the bows, the raised horns . . . music was a deliverance, a solace. After lights out he would always listen to at least one piece of music before he went to sleep.

Food also became important to him. The first few days, he barely ate at all, finding the appearance and smell of the food so appalling that he could not get it down. Then as the days went by, he became accustomed to it, and he even began to look forward to the mid-day mess of vegetables, gristly meat and mealie-rice. In addition he was permitted to receive a food parcel once a week with a limited number of items, and these included such luxuries as chocolate. He knew that Margie prepared the parcel and brought it to the jail, because the choice of food was very much hers; and once a warder had relaxed the rule about not talking to political prisoners sufficiently to say, 'Your wife was here. She said she and the baby are very well.'

For about a week after his arrest he had carefully excluded Margie and the boy from his mind; he deliberately refrained from thinking about them and if they came into his thoughts without his volition, he would consciously switch his mind over to something else. Then, one day, he found they had become so removed from him that he could think about them entirely without any disturbing emotion and without a hint of pain, as of acquaintances he had known in the past. It did not occur to him to try and find a way of communicating with his wife.

He knew that everything was opened and carefully inspected before being brought in to him: the bars of chocolate were broken into small pieces, sausages were slit across. There was no point in looking for any concealed message after they had gone over the stuff. He was glad that Margie remembered him, pleased she always knew the foods he liked best, but that was all he wanted of her. Nothing more.

For some weeks he lived sunk in this internal existence; he had forgotten his fears of being called for questioning, when one day the thin membrane that held his life together was violently torn apart.

Except at weekends, when it could be as early as three o'clock in the afternoon, supper would be at half-past four. That day he had taken into his cell his dixie of soup, but had not eaten it because he had received a food

185

parcel and was not hungry. He undressed and unrolled his mat. It was cold now, and although he did not wish to sleep yet, it was much pleasanter to lie under the blanket than to sit upright on the stool.

He had a beautiful sensation of relaxing as he stretched out on the floor and pulled the blankets right up and over his head. He was going to continue an important conversation begun the previous day with Buckminster Fuller who had once visited the University and delivered a series of lectures. But he was immediately disturbed by the sound of gates being opened, the great keys rattling. Were they coming to him? Must he get up, fold up his mat? There was not sufficient time – what would his excuse be for lying down before supper time?

So he was already upset when they unlocked his door, and a warder and a man in plain clothes entered the cell. The man said, 'Dress,' and the two of them stood silently while he hastily pulled on his clothes. Then the man said, 'Kom.'

*This is it; they are taking me away to be tortured.*

The car went through Pretoria. He was sitting in the back with a man on either side. Although preoccupied with fear of what was going to happen, he was astonished to see the streets packed with people and traffic in the brilliant afternoon sunshine; so absorbed had he become in his own life that he had forgotten that at half-past four, when prison supper was served, people outside were only thinking of their afternoon tea. But he could not take in anything. The sights were too bright, everything too animated and crowded. He turned his eyes away from the windows of the car and looked at the back of the man in front of him.

They took him to an old building and conducted him through a maze of winding passages. He thought the maze would never end, but eventually, at the end of a corridor, they entered a large room and sitting behind a long table were a number of men – nine or ten of them – each with a file open in front of him.

'Stand there,' said his escort.

The man in the centre of the table was leafing through his dossier. At last he looked up and said, 'Yes, Slater.'

Dick said quickly, 'I want to know why I'm here. If I've done something wrong, why haven't I been charged? I want to know the charges against me.' Then he lapsed abruptly into silence.

They did not reply. They watched him.

'Are you friendly with Pila Norval?' It was the man in the middle who spoke first.

'I know her, yes. She isn't a close friend of mine.'

'No? What is the nature of your relationship, then?'

'I knew her when she was at University, and I was on the same committee for a time . . . I see her sometimes when I go to buy books at the shop where she works.'

'And that's all?'

'That's all.'

'Why do you visit her flat, then?'

'I don't.'

'No? Yet you went to see her on the third of June.'

'I don't remember.'

'We'll refresh your memory, then. It was about eight o'clock in the evening, you left your car at the corner of West and Beit Streets and walked to the end of the block . . .'

The speaker began to fire a number of questions at him, fast, scarcely waiting for any coherent reply. Then, abruptly, he stopped, and another of the men began, standing up to question Dick, and speaking more slowly.

*When they ask me about any activity or any relationship*

187

*that is perfectly legal, such as the University protests and Human Rights Day, I'll tell them. I'll be frank and open. But when it comes to anything else, I'll not answer a thing . . .*

The questioning was taken over by number three. He started by coming round the table to Dick and hitting him sharply on the back of the neck with a newspaper rolled up to make it into a weapon. Then he unrolled it on the table in front of Dick, so that the black headlines flared up – POLICE SWOOP IN MASS RAIDS.

The paper was three weeks old. He managed to read a few phrases: sabotage suspects held . . . many taken in early morning raids . . . this action will bring all sabotage to an end, says police chief.

'Look! You think you're so clever, you lot. We've got you all, every stinking little cowardly saboteur. What made you think you could get away with it?'

'I don't know what you are talking about,' Dick said, trying to sound dignified.

'Oh yes you do, Harry.'

At this name, his group pseudonym, known to only three or four other people, he felt a pang of fear. But he tried to look puzzled and did not reply.

'Did you hear me, Harry?'

'My name's not Harry,' Dick said.

'You idiot!' The man took up the newspaper and folding it, he struck him again. 'Do you think we don't know what you've been up to? We know everything about you, everything.'

Then he walked back to his place behind the table, and the next man began, throwing at Dick a number of questions that seemed irrational. They did not fit into anything he had been doing.

After that came number five. His technique was entirely

188

different. He began by reminding Dick of his wife and family, and delivered a little homily on the morality of one's actions, and then he appealed to reason. The whole strange performance, so completely unexpected, so unlike anything he had anticipated, seemed to be comprehensible in only one way. It was a sort of trial performance, a test-run. They were trying out their different techniques and all watching him the whole time to see how he reacted and which method disturbed him the most. There seemed to be no other reason for such a large display, such a splendid array of important Special Branch men altogether at one time.

The questioning continued until each man had had his turn. Then they gathered up their papers and all except two left the room.

These two began firing questions at Dick, repeating them over and over again, – Why did you go to the shop where Indres Ramjee works on the third of June? What is the name of your contact?

*It is clear now they know something, but not all. If I say anything at all, I will be reinforcing what they know, or giving them new knowledge. Therefore there is only one thing to do, to keep quiet. If I admit I was at a meeting at Indres', then they will want to know who was present and what we discussed. I cannot divulge any names. Therefore I cannot possibly say anything. Under no circumstances will I make a statement.*

And then, without volition, came the thought but what if he did. Even the consideration of such a thing was in itself like a betrayal. He would not talk. He had the responsibility of keeping quiet. There was always the possibility that once he said anything at all, he would let something slip. They would trap him if he spoke. He would not talk.

Lights had been switched on as early winter dark arrived. A tray was brought in with two cups of tea. Both men smoked a lot, the ashtrays were overflowing with stale ash and cigarette stubs. The air was old, stuffy. One man walked to the window and raised the venetian blind. He opened the window and a blast of sharp, fresh air entered the room.

'Close the window, Hennie,' said the older man.

For some time now there had been sounds of people leaving the building, office doors closing and being locked, voices and footsteps in the corridor outside. It began to get quiet.

The younger man walked out of the office. The one remaining, older, plumper, sat down behind the table and picked up a dossier. Then he put it down and leaning forward he looked straight at Dick and began to speak to him in a quiet, pleading tone of voice.

'Now, Dick,' he said. 'I am going to tell you something, and I want you to listen very carefully to what I have to say. I want to tell you that they'll get from you everything that they want in the end, this I know from years of experience, and I assure you it is true. Everything they want. Be sensible. You're only harming yourself by being obstinate. If you sit down here and begin writing, all this will be over. The longer you stay standing there, the harder it will be for you in the long run.'

Dick said, 'I have nothing to say.'

*Have I anything to say? What do I feel? Nothing. I am not going to say anything. I am just going to go on standing here. I have nothing to say.*

The man shook his head and sighed. He rubbed his hand over his thinning hair. 'I want to help you,' he said, 'I really want to help you.'

The second man, van Zyl, returned, his breath smelling

190

of liquor; the man sitting behind the table rose and left the office.

*This one is going to bash me about. He is fiercer, he shouts, gesticulates, comes up close, shakes his fist. Scared, but keep quiet. The silence seems to infuriate him.*

'I'm sorry, but I have nothing to say.'

*That was a silly thing to say. I should have said I am not prepared to talk about what I don't know.*

At about nine o'clock, the shift changed. Two went, two more came. For periods of time they ignored him entirely and talked among themselves. Was he tired? Not really. He could go on like this indefinitely. He stood with his hands clasped behind his back and his mind went blank.

The new interrogator paced up and down. He took a dossier and began reading bits of it aloud. A sentence or two here and there. It sounded like a statement made by someone, Dick could not guess who. The man was selecting pieces that might have had some relevance for Dick.

Then he dropped it, and picked up another file, and from this he began to read to Dick a full and detailed account of his political activities, from the time that he was a student.

He paused in his reading and glanced up. 'Your eyes lit up,' he said, 'you admit all this, then?'

'It was all perfectly legal, and there is nothing there to hide.'

The man gave a smile, and resumed his reading. *He knows I am interested; he knows I am even enjoying this recital.* Dick tried to move back a little, so that he could lean against the wall. The interrogator went on reading, then suddenly he stopped and shouted, 'Stand up! Get away from that wall! What were you doing when you went to visit Indres Ramjee on the third? What's the name of your contact?'

What made time move? He strained for the sound of clock-chimes. Sometimes there were prolonged periods of silence lasting for what seemed like an hour, and then, faintly, he would hear a quarter-hour strike.

They changed shift every four hours. This would help him to guess the time. It must be about one in the morning. The newcomers came in freshly washed, tidy, full of energy. They had been eating and drinking. They were renewed, and he was more tired.

'Still here?' the new one asked jovially. 'Are you trying to earn the Springbok colours for standing? We thought you'd be gone long ago.'

'I'd like to know what you have against me. I want to go back to my cell.'

'Ah, your cell! That's the Savoy Hotel to you now, isn't it? It's comfort you want, isn't it, Dick?'

The sameness of it. Sometimes long periods of quiet. One man would walk out, one man would remain leafing through papers, asking inept and irrelevant questions. Just killing time.

*Don't think of anyone or anything.*

'What about your mother, Slater, she's ill, isn't she? You wouldn't want us to detain her.'

'If you want to detain her, you will.'

'Aren't you being very callous? Why should you let her suffer for you? And your wife – Margery, isn't it? It would be awkward if we pulled her in, wouldn't it, with that young child? I suppose someone you know would take the child for you?'

They were just playing with him. Marge knew nothing, they could not hold her for long. But nevertheless he was afraid.

192

'You'd like to see your wife, wouldn't you? I tell you what, I'll arrange it for you. You know, we can arrange anything if we want to.'

He concentrated on blankness, on excluding everything, not even trying to think up stories to explain going to see Indres. Because once he started telling stories, they would catch him out, and that would be the end. They could disprove things. They had information he didn't know about.

It would be better during the day. The nights would always be harder because of the quiet in the building and the dark, because of the quiet outside, the knowledge that everyone was sleeping, indifferent and unknowing, and he alone was standing there beneath the harsh office light.

It was a long time since he had heard the chimes of the clock. Four notes for the first quarter of the hour, eight for the half, twelve for when it was three-quarters past the hour, then the full sixteen-note chime, followed by the slow, gong-like notes that would tell him the hour. If it would get light . . . Sometimes the chimes had come through clearly, but if they were talking and laughing and making a lot of noise he would miss them. If it would get light . . .

He asked to go to the lavatory. They escorted him down the corridor and he was surprised at the difficulty he had in moving his legs. Just to walk – incredible that it should require such an act of will. His ankles were swollen, and his feet painful.

The few minutes of change were over. It had become very quiet again. A long time ago he had reckoned that it was past three in the morning. Two new men came into the office. One was short, with red hair; the other tall and dark, was called van Rensburg. He wore a dark brown suit, a beige shirt, a brown tie. From his crisp shirt-sleeves his wrists protruded, very thin with a prominent bone, and long-fingered hands. He was sallow, lanky and unsmiling. Nothing he did was casual, he was conscious of each of his actions however slight and it seemed as though no movement he made was without intention.

The two men talked briefly, then the short man went out. Van Rensburg sat at the desk and taking a pencil up he began to tap it against the edge of the desk, at first lightly, then with some force. He watched Dick. Stopped tapping; sat for a while allowing the quiet to pervade the office again. The two of them formed a tableau, Dick standing and van Rensburg sitting like a statue without moving, with the pencil poised in his hand.

He rose from the chair with a movement so swift that Dick felt menaced. He walked around the office, then he came to a halt behind Dick and stayed there absolutely still for a couple of minutes. Dick could hear his breathing.

The expected blow did not come. He came round again, he sat down and taking a piece of paper, he began to write. Every movement of that long body, of the thin wrists, somehow suggested controlled violence.

The short man came back, 'Is he talking?'

Van Rensburg snorted. 'Talking? No man. I'm just making notes for my sermon on Sunday.'

'Your sermon? You preach?'

'Ja, that's it. I'm a lay preacher. And what's more, I'll tell you, I not only write my own sermons, I often write the sermons for our predikant as well.'

He picked up the paper and walked around to address Dick. 'Would you like to hear my sermon?'

'I'm not interested,' Dick said.

'Oh, ja, of course, you're not interested, you commies are all the same, you're hot on politics but you can't be bothered with morals. All the same. I suppose you never told your wife how you used to visit the Norval girl in her flat? She'll probably find out, just the same. She's been here, your wife, you know, she says she wants to see you. I daresay she'll pick up some information about you she never knew before.'

The short man said, 'I'm going to get some coffee,' and he walked out.

'Entirely without morals,' van Rensburg repeated. 'Now me, I'm just the opposite. I keep quiet on political questions, I leave those things to the politicians. They're not my field at all; I just do my job. But I'll talk about any other subject under the sun, anything. That's why the predikant comes to me, he knows I can put things properly. It's because I've read a lot, I read anything. He knows I believe in morals, in moral principles.'

Suddenly he slapped the table three times with his open hand, a startling noise in the silence around them.

'It's torture, isn't it, Slater?' he said, and for the first time he smiled. 'Just standing there, that's the thing, just standing becomes torture. Not doing a thing to you, are we? You won't have a mark on you. We won't touch you. We don't have to, you fix yourself for us, just standing there, we won't have to fix you. We know. We've studied the methods, we've tested them, and they work, too.'

He smiled again.

He picked up his pen and began to write. He wrote a few lines, talking at short intervals. 'Not a mark, not a scratch, not a bruise, not even a hair out of place.'

He wrote a few more lines.

195

'Works on everyone, every single one. You too, you'll see.'

He put down his pen and picked up a rubber band. He began to stretch the band and release it, watching Dick all the time. Then he began to fling questions at him one after the other, fast, not waiting for answers. The questioning had a surreal feeling; a particularly astute question would be followed by one that was really stupid, something way out, not connected with anything Dick had done. Then there would come another question, sharp as a whip, dangerous. All the time he kept his unwavering eyes on Dick, who had to exert a physical effort not to show any reaction.

The other man returned and handing van Rensburg a thermos flask, he went out again. Van Rensburg carefully unscrewed the cup and placed it on the desk, then poured out a stream of hot, strong-smelling coffee. He put the flask on the desk next to the cup, and abruptly walked out of the office.

The stream from the coffee rose in the room. Dick took a cautious step backwards and leaned on the wall behind him.

Van Rensburg must have been watching at the door. He stepped into the office. 'Stand up, Slater!' he said sharply, 'Stand up! If you want to make a statement you can sit right here at this table, and there's coffee for you. Otherwise, stand up!'

He took a piece of chalk out of a drawer and bent down to draw a circle on the floor close to Dick's feet. 'Stand in there,' he ordered. 'Don't know what they've been thinking about, letting you loll around just anywhere. That's right, in the circle. Now, there you are. And that's where you will stand until you are prepared to make a statement.'

He took a book and he sat at the desk facing Dick, pretending to read. Dick watched him; his eyes were not moving. He was not reading, simply waiting. How long could this go on for? If he could think up some sort of explanation about going to see Indres . . . But not with this man, not with this man.

Four o'clock. He asked to go to the lavatory again. Twelve hours since they had taken him from his cell. In twelve hours they had reduced his physical activity to that of a very old, very arthritic man, bent over and unable to straighten out properly, shuffling along putting one cautious foot after another a few inches at a time, and suffering fierce cramps and pains with every step.

Back in the interrogation room again, van Rensburg took off his jacket, placing it precisely over the back of a chair. He unstrapped the holster he wore under his jacket and putting it on the table, he removed the revolver and pointed it toward Dick, a half-smile on his face, watching for some reaction.

*He will shoot me 'accidentally'. There are no witnesses. He can concoct any story he likes, he can say I made a lunge at him, he can get his mates to bear him out.*

But there was a kind of remote coldness in the thought that was less than fear. Almost a longing, for this would remove the unendurable responsibility of decision.

The revolver was moved from right hand to left, from left to right. The gestures were loving, deliberate. The eyes in the dark, narrow face watched continuously.

A flood of brilliant morning light. The strong arms supporting him were a humiliation. This was what they wanted, to humiliate him, an old man fumbling with the zip on his trousers, staggering and swaying in front of the urinal.

*Afterwards there will come a time when I will want to remember what happened, people will ask me, I will try to relate it. But what is there to relate? How can you relate nothing, how can you describe nothing? If there were physical assaults, ah, now, that would be the thing. Something dramatic, something to explain . . . If van Rensburg had let his finger slip, if there had been a shot, even if they had slung me up and beaten me . . .*

*Listen for the chimes of the clock. Impossible to concentrate. Try to remember the names of these men, which one did what. But they came in droves, hard, healthy, red-faced, having slept and showered and fed . . . the smell of stale sweat. Even their best friends wouldn't – how could they have any friends, how does it feel to be so hated? They are impervious to emotion.*

When they moved away the smell remained. A stubble of beard on his face, a pair of grossly swollen feet and the stale smell of his own sweat.

The Major came. Red eyes, head wedged down on bull neck, hair cut like a Nazi. The Major stood before him and read sentences from a dossier. 'You drove round the block three times, Slater,' he said, thrusting his face forward. 'Who were you waiting for? Was it your contact? Why didn't he turn up? Then you drove your car up Twist Street and at the corner of . . .'

Such a lot of details. They knew so much. But there was a lot they did not know, that was why he was standing there. The careless and stupid things he did; how hopeless it all seemed.

'You put yourself there, you put yourself in that circle, and you can get yourself out of it just as simply. You can walk out any time you like because we're not keeping you there, you're keeping yourself there.'

And yet the day was not so bad. Things happened

during the day; the procession of people, the noise and the light were all reassuring. What he could not bear was the thought that it would get dark again.

During the day he had been permitted to sit down for a short while, given some food and some tea. Now it was late afternoon, and once more the activity was diminishing.

Each one who came made a remark about him, poked fun, a coarse threat, a coarse joke that made the others laugh. They examined their faces in a small mirror that hung on the wall, smoothed back cropped hair, straightened a tie, turned their heads this way and that.

In the evening he collapsed three times, and three times they flung water on him and hauled him up again. In the night van Rensburg came again and walked up and down the office with his sudden shouts and sudden silences, turning with those calculated and menacing movements, watching him like an animal waiting to pounce.

On the morning of the second day two new men came. One swore at him with words that stuck and smeared, and then began to hit him, slapping him across the face, the side of his head, stinging blows, shouting, 'I'll wake you up, you communist swine, I'll wake you up!'

The first man, who had walked out of the office when the assault started, now came back, and taking the other man by the arm he said, 'It's enough, Willy, enough. Leave him.'

'God!' Willy cried, 'You got to do something! The stupid bastard's been standing there for more than forty hours now. Look at him, what a sight he is! And he just stands there. Someone's got to wake him up, someone's got to knock some sense into him!'

And he stormed out of the office, as though in a fury.

The second man looked at Dick, then went to the desk. He took a chair and placed it on the other side of the desk.

'Slater,' he said, 'come along. Sit down for a while.'

It could not be a trick, because his voice was genuinely kind. Through swollen lids and the unendurable burden of sleeplessness and pain, Dick saw his face, not young and thick and hard, but older, lined; greying hair; deep-set eyes. Then he went into the next office and came back with a cup of tea, which he put in front of Dick. 'Here,' he said, 'drink this.'

He did not speak while Dick held the cup with two hands, trying to steady their excessive shaking. After a minute or two he took a packet of cigarettes out of his pocket and offered them to Dick. 'Smoke?' He lit the cigarette for him.

The first pull on the cigarette made his head spin. There was a singing sound in his ears and he felt he was suffocating. Through the smoke haze he saw again those tired and friendly eyes looking at him with what seemed extraordinary kindness, understanding and sympathy.

A wave passed over him, and when he emerged from it, he heard his own voice saying, 'It was Thabo. That's the name they want, he collected the parcels I left . . . Thabo.'

And he joined his hands together on his forehead to hide his face, and began to weep.

# Thabo . . .

As Pila emerged from the shop with a man on either side of her, Thabo was turning the corner at the top of the street and saw the three of them get into a waiting car.

That moment was like the closing of a book; he knew that his life as Thabo, the man with a house and family in Orlando, who worked every day at the bookshop, had ended. These years, the years of precarious legality, were gone; the passbook always signed, stamped, in order; the taxes always paid in time and duly receipted; the house rent delivered promptly to the municipal offices. The fabric of rectitude in which he had clothed all his activities had now finally to be discarded. The balance, maintained with such difficulty all these recent months, between the legitimate days and the clandestine nights, had finally broken down. He would not now return to the shop. He would not again return to his home.

He boarded a bus to Alexandra; alighted in the heart of a respectable white suburb. There, in a servant's room in a back yard, he was transformed from Thabo Motjuwadi into the Reverend Thomas Khumalo. His thick black beard was trimmed down to side whiskers, ending in a few tastefully-grouped hairs on his chin. His moustache disappeared. His workclothes were discarded for a black suit and a preacher's white collar. When he emerged he had in his pocket a new passbook, essential for establishing his new identity, and in his hand a crumpled notebook stamped 'Orlando Mission for Christ the King' which he would use to beg small sums of money from white householders.

Thabo plunged into the mud-brown obscurity of the townships: anonymous doors of identical boxes opened to let him in, closed to conceal him. Friends, and friends of friends; relatives, and friends of relatives; working men and women, old women, children; into the confusion of the enlarged multiple families who addressed him only as Brother, who knew no other name, and who worried for nights after he had gone, satisfied only that they had been able to help him for one more night, the man who could not go back to his own home.

Among all these brothers there were also informers. He kept on the move.

Messages were taken by the women and children criss-crossing the township. Bit by bit, after the shock wave of arrests and raids had subsided, the remnants of the groups began to come together.

'You haven't been able to make contact yet with Sipho?'

'Either he's been arrested, or else he's in hiding. Me, I think he's been picked up, but with Sipho you never know. Could be he's simply lying low with one of his women somewhere.'

'He would have got a message through to us by now.'

'You would think so.'

'Who do we know definitely?'

A catalogue of names, the ones known for sure to be in jail, the ones suspected of having been taken. Most of the older ones, known to the police for activities in the past, had been detained, but many of the younger ones were still free.

He read the papers. 'You see this? That woman, they've released her. It's rather strange.'

'Who?'

'A white woman, Pila Norval, she worked in the bookshop with me.'

'Then she told them something they wanted to know?'

'Perhaps. But why would they release her so soon?'

'If she talked . . .'

'Yes, but so quickly? Why should she talk so quickly?'

'Why should anyone? Perhaps she was an informer.'

'Then they wouldn't have arrested her in the first place . . .'

Paper was spread out on the table in the candle light and names scribbled in pencil, grouped together, ticked, crossed out. Two from this group, one from this, and this, and this.

'Our trouble is not the ones we know about, it's the ones we haven't yet heard about. There are some houses where we dare not go. Try to work out some pattern in the arrests.'

The days passed. After two weeks a message came that Sipho was back.

'He was not arrested, then?'

'No, he says he has been lying low. He says he thought it better to stay in hiding for a while.'

'How did he contact you?'

'He came to the house where I am staying. He knew that I used to go there sometimes when I wanted a place for the night.'

'We must meet him.'

'Yes, he wants to see you, but I would not bring him here without asking you first.'

Thabo thought for a moment. 'Can you contact him tomorrow?'

'Yes.'

'Then bring him here to this house. I will not stay here another night, but we can meet here once.'

When Sipho and Thabo met, they embraced. 'How are you, comrade?' Thabo asked; and Sipho replied with a laugh, 'Like you, I'm fine, we were sharper than they were!'

'This time.'

'Yes, this time. How did you manage it? Who warned you?'

'I saw them when they came to the shop to pick up Pila Norval. I decided it was time for me to go.'

'Why did they arrest her? Was it because of you – did she have some contact with you?'

'She – well she bought some things for me, once or twice.'

'Then it was you they wanted?'

'I don't know – it might have been, or she may have been active with white comrades. But she has been released.'

'Can it be true?'

'It is true,' said Thabo.

'A white woman,' said Sipho contemptuously, 'to talk so quickly!'

'But even so, they would hold her as a witness. There's something strange there.'

'Strange? What do you think with the whites? They have influence, they pull strings. Her father's a wealthy man. We make a mistake to trust such people in the first place.'

Sipho brought a bottle out of his pocket, and went into the kitchen to fetch cups. 'Have a drink,' he said to Thabo and Kabelo, pouring out a generous amount of brandy for each of them. The raw spirit burned their throats and brought tears to Thabo's eyes. 'Man, this is strong stuff!' he exclaimed. 'Where did you get it?'

'Oh, I have my suppliers,' said Sipho. He drank his liquor in one sharp fling of the cup to his mouth, head back, a continuous strong gulp, then reached for the bottle to pour more.

'Not for me,' Thabo said, covering his cup with his hand. He looked at Sipho. 'And you had better lay off it too. We have to keep our heads clear these days.'

'My head is clearer when I've had a few tots,' Sipho replied.

'Come, let's get down to business, it is not good to waste time. We must not meet for longer than half an hour.'

'Right!' Sipho banged the bottle on the table. 'And I have a suggestion to make that I think we should discuss first. I think we should make a gesture, a really big gesture, to prove that they have not smashed our organization. To show the people. I think we should plant some bombs at some place, some place important, really big – Marshall Square, perhaps, or the Greys.'

'That's wild talk, Sipho,' Thabo said. 'First, we must wait a bit, they have not yet finished with the arrests. Then we must re-group. They are too active at the moment. Every place is being watched. It is more sensible to lie quiet for a while. We must also re-establish contact with other areas.'

'More sensible!' Sipho's eyes were bloodshot. He was still wearing the large black overcoat with collar turned up to protect him from the cold outside. His shadow was thrown, huge and distorted and wavering in the candle-light, onto the wall. 'Sensible! What we want now is not timidity but real boldness. To strike now! And we must be armed.'

'You are talking wild, man,' Kabelo said.

'I know what I am saying. I know what I mean. Armed. And we've got the arms, too. Yes. Thabo will tell you. Listen!' He spoke across the table to Thabo, 'You're the one. We're just a region, one region. What we do must be co-ordinated. How soon will the Supreme Command meet? How soon can we get a decision? You're the one.

What's the use of beating about the bush, man, you're the only one who can tell us, because we only operate on the regional level, we do not know how to make contact. Listen! What will happen if they pick you up? We will be lost. We have to make arrangements now, now. I'm sorry, man, you are not being honest with us.'

He reached his hand for the bottle again, and Thabo also grabbed it, so that their hands met on the bottle and they both sat for a few moments holding it tightly.

'If you drink too much at a time like this,' Thabo said, 'then it is better if you do not come to me. As for what will happen if I am detained, that you should know by now. You will wait until someone approaches you in the correct way.'

Anger flared in Sipho, but he suppressed it as best he could and tried to appear calm, as Thabo was calm.

'I know how much I can drink, brother, I know what I can hold. You don't have to lecture to me like a Jesus-lover.'

'Come,' Thabo said evenly, 'we are wasting precious time. Let us not make any big decisions tonight, we will sleep on it, and meet again in a few days. Meanwhile, the most important thing is to keep contact with all the units and collect all the information we can.'

He indicated the paper. 'These you will try and see, and you, Kab, must take these under your wing. I will try to deal with the rest.'

There was a soft knocking on the front door of the house. The three men froze, hearing a whispered conversation, the door closing again.

Marie came into the room.

'My neighbour sent his son,' she said, 'there are vans out tonight, road-blocks on the main roads.'

They prepared to go. 'Kab, you go first,' said Thabo, 'I

will leave a message with Marie within the next two days. She will let you know where to contact me. Be careful.'

When Kabelo had left, Thabo said 'Sipho, how will I know where to find you?'

'It would be easier if I could find you. I do not know where I am making my bed each night. Shall I come to you here?'

'No, then let us make an assignment. I will meet you on Friday morning at the north entrance to the station, next to the sign that says "Left Luggage". At half-past ten. Read a newspaper and wait for me. If I do not come, then someone else will bring a message.'

When Sipho had gone, Marie brought in a mug of strong tea, and sat down at the table watching Thabo as he sipped.

'He is drinking too much,' she said.

'Perhaps he needs it tonight. It is cold.'

'No. He needs to keep his head clear. Where has he been hiding this whole time?'

'Oh, lying low with one or other of his women.'

She made a contemptuous noise, a small explosion of air. 'Huh!'

Thabo smiled. 'What is it, Marie? You are angry with him.'

She said in her firm, low voice, 'He drinks too much and he boasts too much about his women.'

'But he is a good comrade, he did very brave things. And he always has so many plans, new ideas. We need people like him who are not always waiting for others to tell them what to do. Maybe he's a bit reckless sometimes, but he's daring – he dares to do things.'

'That may be so,' she replied, 'and we need, also, people who have discipline, who work with others and do not set themselves up above the group. What he has done, he has done. I am concerned with what he is now.'

Thabo shrugged. He finished his tea, put down the mug, and rose to go. 'We will not come again,' he told her. 'But you must know where I am. Tonight with Ramotse, but tomorrow I make some other arrangement. I meet Sipho in town on Friday. Will you come? Then I tell you where to make contact with me again.'

'I will come,' she said. He took her hand and pressed it softly. 'Go well,' she said. 'Stay well,' he replied, '*amandla!*'

As soon as the door had closed behind him she ran to the window, and in the darkness of the room she watched him walking down the street. His footsteps crunched on the hard winter earth.

She let the curtain drop. She stood for a while, thinking, then she went to fetch a coat and tied a scarf round her neck. She let herself silently out of the house. With hands thrust deep into coat pockets to keep them warm, she walked swiftly away, her anxious breath rising in small white clouds as she hurried along.

# Indres . . .

The big man took off his hat and put it on the desk. He opened a drawer in the desk and took out a piece of white chalk. Bending down so that his huge haunches strained his trousers almost to bursting point, he drew a small square on the floor.

'You stand there,' he told Indres, indicating the square.

Indres stood in the square.

'Now you can talk.'

'Talk?'

'Yes, talk!'

'What must I talk about?'

The big one, Nel, walked over and struck him a sharp blow across his mouth.

'Talk, coolie!' he said. 'You know what to talk about. We want to know everything. Start with your own group. When you meet, where, and all the names. Talk!'

'I don't know what you mean.'

'Don't come that stuff. You know. You know exactly what I mean.'

'It's all right,' Nel said. 'We want some lunch, anyway. We've got lots of time. Just you stand there and think about your statement. The sooner you talk, the sooner we'll let you go.'

Nel walked out of the office. Two other Security men stayed in the room.

Just stand there. And what would happen if he sat down? He thought about it, he wanted to do it, but he realized that in spite of everything, in spite of anticipating the time when he would be in their hands, in spite of his hatred for them and his contempt of them, he was afraid. He was afraid of being assaulted. His lip was swelling and his mouth still stung from the single sharp blow of Nel's huge hand. They wanted him to stand. All right, he would stand.

He stood, shifting his weight from time to time. The two men ignored him, yet he knew they were aware of his slightest movement. One sat at the desk looking through a file of papers. The other swung on a chair, picking his teeth and pushing himself backwards and forwards.

In less than an hour, Nel came back to the office. He took off his jacket; Indres saw the revolver in a special pocket of his shirt. His face was red and his breath smelt of beer. He stood in front of Indres, close to him, hands on hips.

'Look, Ramjee,' he said, 'we know a great deal about you. But we're not so much concerned with you. You were one of the pawns, and we want to get our hands on those at the top. We want to know exactly who you worked with, and who were your contacts. You make a statement now, and things won't go too badly for you.'

Indres said, 'I want to speak to a lawyer.'

Nel looked at him with contempt. 'I've been in the police force for twenty-five years,' he said, 'and I expect to stay another twenty-five before I retire. I don't care if you're still standing here the day I retire, but you're not moving from there until you talk. Talk!'

Then they ignored him. Men came and went the whole afternoon but there were never less than two in the office with him. They talked to each other, but scarcely looked at him. He remained standing in the square.

In the late afternoon the building began to empty. Security men walked past, glancing into the office, passing a remark to the men sitting there, cracking a joke. 'Have a good time!' they told Nel, laughing as they said it. Innumerable doors slammed shut, voices and footsteps receded.

Traffic sounds outside the building seemed to thicken and invade the office. He heard the home-going cars revving and hooting. When the full force of the traffic began to subside and the sounds became intermittent, he began to register clearly the chimes of the town-hall clock.

Night came. It was dark outside, but lights burned in the office. A new man came in, Erasmus, tall, handsome, with icy-blue eyes. Suddenly, without planning his action, Indres felt he could stand no longer and he sat down on the floor. Erasmus went to him, caught both his arms behind him in an iron grip, and yanked him to his feet again. He gave the arms a painful twist, then using the side of his hand, struck Indres several blows across the head and neck.

'Don't make things difficult for yourself,' he said.

A third man came in, bringing a tray with tea and sandwiches. Two of them sat on chairs, rocking backwards. Erasmus sat on the edge of the desk. As he bit into a sandwich he spoke to Indres once more.

'You're going to be a mess unless you do what we say. I'll tell you something. We break people like you, we know how to do it, and we do it properly. I could do it now if I wanted, but we're in no hurry. We prefer to let you do it to yourself. See what the courts will say when you start whining to them "They made me stand during interrogation".'

The other two men laughed, but Erasmus did not smile. He stared at Indres with his cold, light eyes with their blond lashes and white brows.

The men drank their tea. 'I long for the earth,' Erasmus said. 'I bought some plants on Friday. Winter stocks,

Iceland poppies, sweet peas. They're just sprouting. Planted the lot over the weekend. Beautiful. Pressing the earth down, the way it feels under your hands, it's beautiful.'

'My wife does the gardening,' said Nel. 'I like the things that smell, carnations, tobacco plants.'

'They're too messy. They sprawl too much. I like my borders to run straight, to look tidy. You can't have a good show with tobacco plants, they look dead all day.'

'Yes, but at night . . .'

'I have a pretty good winter garden, but you should see my border in summer. Colour – you've never seen anything like it. And not a dead petal or leaf. The boy does the digging, but I keep the border the way it should be. I just love the earth.'

Nel had taken a pair of binoculars from a drawer and was standing at the window looking out through them. He let out a guffaw and handed them to the other man, Muller, who stood staring, then cried 'God, man, that's good, that's good!'

'We'll raid that place one of these days,' said Erasmus.

'What for?' asked Nel. 'You want to spoil our fun? What's there to look at night after night if we raid? Look at that, man, there's that fat one, just look at that! Striptease in front of the window with her boyfriend lending a hand.'

'You'd think they'd have the decency to draw the curtains,' said Erasmus.

'Why should they? No one overlooking them. So they think, anyway.'

Erasmus said 'My kids want a dog. They keep nagging me. But if we get a dog he'll ruin the garden. Do you think it's right to stop them having a dog? But he'll just dig everything up. You can't keep a garden tidy with a dog. I just love that garden.'

Nel put the binoculars away. 'I was going to meet my girlfriend tonight but I had to call it off. She's good and ready, but her parents are so strict I can't get her up to my place.'

'I want to go to the lavatory,' said Indres.

They walked him down the corridor and stood on either side of him. His legs were very stiff, he could hardly walk. When they went back to the office his feet were shot through with agonizing pains. 'Stand there,' Nel said.

'Do you think this bastard will still be alive at the end of the week?' said Muller. 'I've got a big match on Saturday.'

Nel said, 'My girl always rubs me down after a good match.'

'A proper massage?' Muller asked.

'A good rub-down, anyway.' They both laughed.

The office was stuffy, but all the lower windows were closed. Indres felt he needed air. Outside, the traffic had ceased and only an occasional car passed. He waited for the clock chimes. Sometimes the periods between the quarter hours were so long, he thought he had missed them. Then they would come, four descending notes . . . The shifts changed. There were never less than two of them in the office. They smoked a great deal and his eyes smarted. He felt himself swaying. Outside, the night flowed on.

Another man came into the office, a short, thickset man, very soft-spoken. He handed Indres a mug. 'Have some tea,' he said.

Indres wanted to refuse it; he felt it was a trick to keep him awake. But he could not resist it, and gulped it down.

The other two men wandered into an adjoining office.

The new man leaned against the desk and rubbed his chin with his hand.

'You're being very obstinate.' He paused. 'Even stupid, you know. You should stop being so hostile. You should try and understand that we want to help you.'

'Help me?'

'Yes,' said the man, 'whatever it may seem like to you, it's the truth. Shall I tell you something? I phoned your brother Joe this evening, to tell him you'd been arrested. He wanted to come straight to Johannesburg, he wanted to be allowed to see you. Don't you want to see him? I told him we would arrange it just as soon as you were prepared to co-operate. I told him not to worry about you – you don't want to worry him, do you? You think about that statement, Indres. Your brother Joe wants you back.'

Indres did not reply. He heard the clock chime the three-quarter hour. A wave of disappointment swept over him when it did not complete the hour. He wanted to know the time.

The building had fallen silent. All the objects that came to life during the day, the lifts, the stairs, the moving doors, canteen trolleys, filing cabinets, telephone bells, had now reverted to the soundless substance from which they were constructed. At long intervals, rubber-soled shoes squeaked on the polished floors, a tap ran, a cistern was flushed.

'Make up your mind,' the man said after a long while, speaking in his soft, almost kind way. 'You know, it's awfully silly, the whole thing. You were involved in a toy organization, now the toy's smashed, the game's up. Why do you want to try and protect others who are criminals? I tell you, they're not worth it. They don't protect *you*, you know, they're only too ready to talk. We already know your rôle. You weren't one of the top ones, you

214

were one of the ones they sent out to do their work while they stayed safe in hiding. They planned blasting the pylons, and you were just one of those in the groups who carried it out.'

'If you know anything about me,' Indres said, 'then why don't you charge me?'

'Do you want to go to jail, then? I wouldn't have thought so, It's one thing being kept for a month or two, or even serving a year, two years . . . when it's years and years . . . growing old . . . there are more things to do outside. You only live once.'

He went to the desk and started writing on a piece of paper.

'Why should you throw your life away?' he went on, without looking up. 'You can't do anything while you're in jail. What happens to all your ideals then? You know, we're here to do a job, we're not really concerned with politics at all. We're not concerned with who's in the government. If another government came in, we'd still do our job. We're just here to implement the law. To see others do the same. I've never cared a damn for politics. Most of us here are the same, we're only interested in seeing the law is observed.'

Quiet.

The clock struck the full hour at last. The suspense of waiting for the number was almost agonizing. Two strikes. Two o'clock. Quiet.

'They let you down badly, your friends,' the policeman said. 'Do you know who it was who gave you away? I'd better not tell you – not yet. They don't care what happens to you. Your brother Joe cares, but not your political friends. The leaders, the real culprits, they run away across the border and live it up in other countries, leaving you people holding the baby. Do you know who gave you away?'

Quiet.

The others returned. Their conversations went on, voices around him, words that he could listen to no longer. The sound of the voices was there, the meaning had gone. The meaning had shifted from mind to muscle. The meaning had become the intolerable pain in his back. The meaning was in swollen feet, puffed and tightened so that the flesh swelled out over his shoes. The meaning was to remain standing.

The shifts change. The new shift lets the venetian blinds spring upwards, a man opens a window and breathes the outside air. It is beginning to get light. They ignore him, but if his eyes drop, or he sways, then a hand is slammed sharp on the desk or slaps his face.

The telephone bells begin to ring. There is a period of complete blankness. Suddenly two men are holding him, one on either side, ordering him '*Kom!*' He cannot walk. Supporting him, they drag him to the lift, take him to a car outside, and drive him back to jail.

In the reception office he holds on to a chair. *Kom*. The warder is young, brown-haired, dark-eyed, soft-featured. Beneath the shadow of his peaked cap his face is faintly troubled, questioning. Indres shuffles along the corridor, inch by inch, supported by the wall. The warder waits, watches him. At last, the cell, and now no wall, only the floor rushing up to meet him.

The young warder stands at the door. After a while he calls an African warder. 'Take this man and help him have a shower,' he says.

Balancing like a doll on enlarged and wooden ankles, cold water stabs reviving needles into his painful skin. The black warder helps dry him with a small cotton cloth – the prison towel; holds him upright; takes him back to his cell. Indres unfolds his mat and lies down.

'I'll send you in some food,' the warder says.

216

He shakes his head.

'Yes, you'll feel better if you eat something.' Then he adds 'You should do what they want. You shouldn't make them angry.'

One moment, it seemed, the brown-eyed warder was standing there; there was a moment of blankness, and suddenly he woke again to see that two Security men had entered the cell and were looking down at him.

'*Kom.*'

They drew the little square again. Three of them approached him belligerently.

'You'd better start talking this time – now!'

'Who is it brought the parcels to you?'

'I don't know.'

Immediately Erasmus hit him hard on the jaw.

'Who collected the parcels?'

'I don't know.' Another, harder blow.

Muller, sitting at the desk, said, 'Now listen, Ramjee, I'm going to read something to you: "The timing devices and other materials were delivered in parcels to Indres Ramjee at the Naicker's shop in Vrededorp. He kept them in the shop until they were collected by his contact." You know who told me that? You know his name? What's his name?'

'I don't know.'

This time the blow sent him staggering back against the wall. Erasmus seized him angrily and pushed him forward 'Stand there!' he shouted. 'He's your friend, isn't he, your nice white friend? You know who it is. Dick Slater. A nice friend of yours. What have you got to say?'

'He's framing me.'

'But he's your friend, why should he do a thing like that?'

'It's a lie.'

'Oh, that's fine! So he's been lying to us! Listen to this,

217

Koos, that white commie bastard has been lying. You know what we'll have to do, we'll go and beat him up some more and see if he'll tell the truth this time.'

Indres felt angry. *Well, fuck this guy Dick, if he's going to talk, let him. If he's made a statement, they can do what they like to him, he's not my concern any more.*

Erasmus went on, 'And what's more, we're going to deal with you, too. You're not going to play games with us, we're not here to play games.'

As he spoke, he punched Indres in the back; Muller stood in front of him so that as he jerked forward, Muller punched him in the chest, on the arms, in the stomach.

Between the blows, he said, 'I'll lay a charge of assault.'

They laughed.

Suddenly Indres sat down on the floor, putting his arms up over his head to protect himself. They pulled him up and hit him harder. He sat down again. They pulled him up and beat at him, swearing at the same time.

He was half-conscious when they stopped; one opened a book of photographs. 'You know these people? They're all your friends, aren't they? This one came to the shop regularly. Here's another friend . . .'

Erasmus was smoking a cigarette. 'Like a smoke, Indres?' he asked, and thrust the lighted end of the cigarette between Indres' lips. He spat it out. Erasmus picked it up and forced it back, burning and scorching the thin skin of his lips – he spat it out again.

After a while they tired of playing around with him. He was standing in the square again. They left him standing. Men walked in and out of the office; he was never left alone; the pain was intense.

They ignored him for some hours. Two men would stay in the office, talking or writing. Then they would go and others would come. Once he was given some sandwiches, but his swollen lips, aching jaws and sore mouth made it impossible for him to eat. He had to stand again, and it was even harder than before. It was better not to sit at all, just to forget you were a human being and go on standing like a tree. A tree with nerves that ran from the top down to the very roots. The nerves ended in the floor; from the floor grew the pain, the agony of standing.

In the afternoon, when it was once more beginning to get dark, a man came in whom he had not seen before. He was tall, an older man with a shining bald head. He started to discuss Indres' case with the others as though Indres was not present, reviewing the evidence they had against him. He read aloud bits of statements made by others – informers? prisoners? One, Indres knew, must be Dick, but then there was information about some things that were completely unknown to Dick. It was so hard to concentrate on what they were saying, but either they were reading little scraps deliberately, or else they only had odd bits of information.

The older man came over and stood in front of him with a file of papers in his hand. 'Ramjee,' he said, 'you have a chance to get out of some of this mess you're in, because you're in one helluva mess, and it will be years and years before you see the sun again. But we're still prepared to give you a chance. Now, are you going to make a statement?'

He did not reply.

Erasmus, who had come back a little while before, exclaimed, 'God, this coolie is just making me mad!'

He pushed Indres forward towards the desk. 'Put your hands on the desk,' he ordered, 'flat, palms down. Hold him there.'

The fingers of his hands were splayed out. Erasmus took a pair of tweezers and started pinching the flesh between the fingers. At first it was not too bad, but each time he pinched a bit of flesh, he bruised it slightly so that it became tender, then more tender; every time he tried to withdraw them, two men held his hands down with all their considerable weight.

The older man sat and watched.

When they were tired of this, they made him stand in the square again.

In the night the long empty periods alternate with times of great activity. There are men, sometimes writing, sometimes leafing through papers, sitting for hours on end. At times they seem to remember why they are there, and read over and over again passages from statements made by different people, repeating bits of information that are damaging to him. He is afraid now not of their acts of violence, but of his own thoughts over which he no longer has control, the names and deeds floating through his head. He feels that if they only stand close enough to him, and keep quiet, then they will hear. He shuts his mouth and holds his teeth together in case words spill out. He sleeps sometimes, or so it seems, standing in the square, periods of blankness, waking to his own swaying. It could have been only half a second. It could have been an hour.

*In the kitchen the women are preparing the chickens. They have cleaned them, discarding the long grey intestines, laying aside the gizzard and liver and the fat, and now they are holding them over the earth of the yard, with burning paper to singe the last of the feathers and hairs – the smell of burning feathers, the sting in his nose, clogging his brain . . .*

He is lying on the floor, a piece of burning cloth is held beneath his nose. He is awake. He is standing in the square.

But he can no longer keep awake. They devise new ways to prevent him from swaying and falling. A bag

220

burst next to his ear; the clang of a bell, a school bell ringing. He is late, he begins to run, stumbles, he has to get there. The bell rings and rings. From somewhere he hears raucous laughter. He falls against the desk. 'Where do you think you're going?' they say. 'I'm late,' he mumbles, 'let me go now. I'll be late.'

Roars of laughter. 'Go back. There is still time. Go back for the torch. It has our fingerprints. Sipho, Sipho!' he cried, choking, drowning, 'Hold me, I'm going under!' Water pours over his head. Gasping and choking, trying to breathe with the water flooding his mouth and nose, Sipho flashes the torchlight straight into his eyes.

He is awake again. A bucket of water, the water dispersing itself on the floor, the light swinging above his head. He is standing once more, wet clothes clinging to his body. He is in the square.

Thick, red-faced, tight-skinned men press round him; faces are thrust forward, withdrawn. They come, rested and showered and fed, determined to finish the whole thing off. Someone seizes his shoulders and shakes him, he is made of rags and collapses; then he hears running footsteps and the crunch of the boot against his head and cries out, or tries to cry out.

*He drowned in his own blood.*

The blows land on his head and face. Blood spurts between his teeth.

He is standing. He is in the square.

He begins to breathe heavily. He feels his painful heart labouring inside him. 'Leave him,' a voice says, 'it's enough.'

He lives again the terrible intensity of de-fusing a failed bomb. Sipho has not set the fuse correctly. 'You were drunk!' he cried accusingly, 'You mucked it up because you were drunk.'

221

Suddenly there was silence. Far away a voice said, 'I was not.'

'Yes,' he mumbled, 'yes; that's why it didn't go off . . .'

His voice trailed off. The other voice prompted him softly, carefully, 'Why didn't it go off? What was wrong?'

He tries to think.

'What happened?' the voice said. 'Who mucked it up?'

But he cannot think. Someone else has been talking from his mouth. He does not remember. Words, disconnected, incoherent, stumble out.

He is sitting at the desk. The interrogator says 'When did you join the Regional Command?'

'When I came back from Natal.'

'Who were the other members?'

His head falls forward.

Someone seizes him and jerks his head up again.

'Who were the others?'

He stares at them, not knowing where he is or who they are. He cannot remember. He knows there are names, names he will not repeat. His mouth closes. His head drops.

The light blazes in his eyes. 'Who were the others? What are their names?'

Who were they? What are their names? 'The names, Ramjee, the names.' A blow again, arms like iron that prevent him from falling, that force him to stand beneath the blows. The words repeat and echo and boom and recede, the words themselves are iron blows striking against his head. The names, the names! His head swings helplessly against the knuckles of a giant fist.

'That was a bloody stupid thing to do,' the older man says. 'What use is he to us like that?'

* * *

The young warder says reproachfully, 'You should eat your lunch, it will help you.'

'I can't eat.' His mouth is swollen; two teeth are missing; the skin of his lips is burnt and raw.

Sometimes the warder stands at the cell door, and looks at Indres with brown, puzzled eyes, a young man with faint dark hairs on his upper lip. He asks questions: 'Why don't you tell them what they want? What's the point of it? Go on, tell them, they'll only come back again and again, until you tell them.'

He would go away, then come back again as though he had been thinking it over. 'What difference does it make?' he asks. 'Tell them what they want to know. Tell them anything.'

And again, 'You won't beat them, they know too much. You coolies are clever, you're *slim*, then why don't you tell them what they want to know, and they'll leave you alone?'

'I'm one of the dumb coolies, not the clever ones,' Indres says.

# Indres . . .

Something has broken the time sequence; his mind, disorientated, confuses past and present. Another man, very thin, very pale, with that same white-blond hair and light eyes; 'The coolies and the Jews think they can tell the kaffirs what to do. They think they can get the kaffirs to run the country, then they'll be able to make as much money as they like. Own all the shops. Coolies and Jews. Jews and coolies.'

Joe said, 'If the rains don't come soon, the whole crop will be ruined. The farmers owe us so much money already, I don't know how we'll be able to carry on for another year.'

The tender mealie plants were already drooping under the blazing sun. The sun seared the top of his head, blinded his eyes. Farmers crowded into the shop, all huge men, all fair, red-faced. Thick arms, thighs bulging in khaki trousers. Joe was a small dark figure, lost among them. The farmers pressed around him. They made Joe stand in the square. Joe did not do anything, he did not know anything. They would keep him in the square forever. He begins to tremble. 'Let Joe go,' he says, 'he doesn't know anything.'

'Joe who? Is he in your group?'

Joe? Joe? What did they mean? He shakes his head. 'Joe wasn't in my group.'

'Then who was? Who collected the parcels from your shop? Where did you meet?'

'What are we wasting time for?' a voice says. 'Hang him.'

Another voice says, 'Listen, coolie, when you're ready to talk, just raise your hand. Don't leave it too long, though, or you won't ever be able to raise it again.'

Laughter.

Something is placed over his head, it becomes dark, he can scarcely breathe. Something is tied round his neck, pulled tighter, tighter, he is being lifted in the air, choking, struggling – and the sound of their laughter, fainter, but still there behind the roaring in his head. The horror of dying to the sound of their laughter. If only he could relinquish the thought of living, if he could succumb . . . but he cannot; once again they pull him up and hold him there as his struggles weaken. Twice he feels himself dying to the sound of their laughter, to the awful sound of their laughter. They lower him again and he recovers his breath in agonizing gasps. The third time, without conscious decision, he raises his hand.

The bag is removed.

'No fooling, coolie,' the voice above him yells. 'Are you going to make a statement? We're not playing games.'

He is unable to talk. But lying on the floor, he nods his head.


They wanted every detail. His name, date of birth, where he was born – it was nonsense, they knew all this. But meticulously, for the record, it all went down on paper.

'What organizations did you join?'

'I joined the Youth League of the Transvaal Indian Congress.'

'What date was that?'

This was all harmless, this was public knowledge. But eventually the questions changed.

'When did you first hear there was going to be sabotage?'

'Some time in the middle of 1961.'

'When precisely?'

'I can't say precisely. Everyone had been talking about it for a long time.'

'Who talked about it?'

'All of us.'

'Who did you discuss it with?'

'With Jassat, Solly, Yusuf – all the Congress people.'

'And who told you it had been decided?'

'Yusuf Naidu. He came to a meeting in my flat . . .'

They were driving him back to prison again. 'They're born liars, coolies. They'll do anything to make money or save their own skins. Known for their lies. Jews and coolies. Coolies and Jews.'

Sleep was destroyed by nightmares. He longed so much for sleep, all he wanted was oblivion, but as soon as he went to sleep he heard terrible gasps and screams and sat up bolt upright, drenched in sweat, listening, trembling. Silence. He was alone in a cell. His throat was dry and sore. He was afraid to lie down again.

He walked around the cell in the night. He forgot where he was, what he was doing. He forgot why he was there. He sat down and tried to calm himself, to arrange his thoughts in order, to be logical, but he was overtaken by a strange obsession – *Who am I? Who am I and where do I fit in to the whole sequence of life? Where do I connect? Nowhere, nowhere.* He felt himself crying.

*Kom.*

'You obstinate bloody coolie you!' yelled the man with light eyes. 'Everything you said here is useless. We want the truth! It was Thabo who collected the parcels, wasn't it? He's the contact. Where is he? Where did you last see him? Where were you going to meet? How did you get in touch with him? The truth, this time you'll tell us the truth.'

'You'll get a minimum of twelve years, the rate you're going. And still you are lying. You say Peter was in your group, but we know he worked with a different lot, we have their names. You can't get away with these names you've given us – that's an old trick, to use the names of people who've left the country. They all try it.'

'Do you know what the charges will be? You'll not see the world again until you're an old man. We have the evidence we need, we've got your fingerprints. Sit down there, you're going to write it out yourself, and you're going to write the truth.'

This was the third statement. He still tried to write only the things they obviously knew. There was a blank in their questioning covering the whole period in Natal, but they knew something. He wrote, 'When I came back from Natal, I worked with Dick Slater. He was the technical man. He did not take part in sabotage, he helped us prepare the materials.'

Physical weakness clouded his ability to write, to put his thoughts down on paper. After some time they said, 'You go back and think about it. Tomorrow you'll come back here and tell us the truth about everything, about everybody.'

In the night he thought about it very carefully. For a while his mind seemed to be working with tremendous clarity, the vagueness and lack of control that had plagued him seemed to have disappeared. He felt he was being logical. If he did not now give them a statement that would satisfy them, they would reduce him once more, and very quickly now, to a condition where he would again have no control over what he said. There were a lot of things about which they knew nothing at all. Christ, they knew a lot! A whole lot of people must have talked, not only Dick Slater. Sipho? Kabelo? The names had come up, but from the urgency of their questioning, the man they wanted was Thabo, and they had not yet found him. *If they once more get you into that semi-conscious condition when you cannot control your thoughts or even your speech, you are likely to give them some real clues as to how to find Thabo. But if you can say enough to satisfy them, tell them some things they do not know but not the most important things, then it will still be possible to protect him, and some others.*

In the morning, when they came, he would sit down and write out a proper statement.

# *Thabo . . .*

A car drew into the kerb, and the driver switched off the ignition. He and the man sitting next to him lit cigarettes and sat idly watching the crowds pouring out of the station.

Marie might not have noticed them, but at this hour of the morning parking was not permitted along that street; as she waited, a traffic warden came along, put his head in the window of the car, and said something to the driver. The driver put his hand in his pocket and pulled out something – a card or a piece of paper that he held up to the warden. The traffic warden smiled, nodded, and walked on. The car, with the two men, stayed parked by the kerb.

Marie moved back into the doorway of a corner building and looked anxiously up the street. There was Sipho. He was wearing a woollen hat, strolling slowly along, walking against the main rush of people who streamed out of the station and headed towards town. The crowds jostled and dodged around him.

Not far behind him were two more men, Africans. One wore overalls and a cap with the name of some firm on it. The other wore the usual drab clothes of a working man. There was nothing about either of them to attract a second glance except that they, too, were walking against the flow of the crowd; neither of them appeared to be in a hurry. This was not a time of day when working people strolled down the street to take the air. When Sipho paused and bent down to tie a shoe-lace, the two men also stopped. One leant on the wall, the other turned his back on the street and stood talking to him.

Frowning with anxiety, Marie rushed back towards the station, turning her head this way and that, in an attempt to locate Thabo. Most people arriving by train from the South-West townships converged along this passage before streaming out into the streets and dispersing into the city beyond.

At all costs, she had to intercept Thabo before he reached the street.

She peered and peered, straining to find him.

She went to the corner again. Sipho was still there. He had opened a newspaper, and was standing against a wall, as far out of the way of the passers-by as he could get; he held the paper up before his face. And the men were still there. One leant against the building; the other, cap pushed to the back of his head, looked indifferently at the passing crowd.

And the car was still there. Its two occupants had not moved.

Once again she turned back to the passage to look for Thabo, and ran straight into someone. Muttering an apology, she was about to turn away, when his hand gripped her arm. The deep voice said, 'Where are you going in such a hurry?'

'Thabo! I am looking for you – quickly, follow me.'

Responding to the urgency in her voice he hurried beside her. 'What's the trouble?'

'They're watching Sipho.'

'Watching?'

'He's being followed.'

'You are sure?'

'Yes, and there are two white men sitting in a car there, I'm sure they are SBs. He should have seen he was followed.'

They circled the station completely, walking a considerable distance around the complex of buildings.

'Then we have missed our rendezvous,' Thabo said eventually.

'Do you want me to go back? Do you want me to speak to him?'

'No of course not, that would be stupid. If you are sure . . .'

'There was no doubt,' she said flatly. 'I know what I saw. I saw – there were two *mafokis* and the car. I could see you walking into a trap.'

'Then they will take Sipho.'

'Perhaps. Maybe not. Perhaps they are using him as a decoy. Then they would want him free.'

'If he's under surveillance, we must get a message through to him, to keep away from everybody for a while; or perhaps he should go into hiding. He was too careless if he did not suspect he was being followed.'

'*If* he did not suspect,' she said, then lapsed into silence.

They were walking away from the station, towards the northern suburbs. 'I have a suggestion to make to you,' Marie said. 'I think you should not go back to the townships. They keep raiding, night after night. It is not only the homes of all the people who ever had anything to do with Congress. They are becoming haphazard, they take first this area, then that; a few houses in this street, a few in that. You are not safe there.'

'Where am I safe? One must just hope to be lucky.'

'No, we do not rely on good luck. I have a place where you can go in Alexandra.'

'My dear sister, they are raiding there as well. Maybe not the political squads, the ordinary police, but if they pick me up there with no resident's permit, they simply find out who I am and hand me over.'

'No, it's not so bad there. And this house, the woman there has a permit. They leave her alone. She is by herself in a house, and she is to be moved in a few months, but meanwhile she stays legally.'

She gave him the address.

'Give me time to speak to Florence,' she told him. 'I can go to the place where she works.'

'I have in any case something to arrange,' Thabo said. 'I will go there later this afternoon.'


He was a preacher again, collecting for his obscure church in the white suburb of Parkwood. He went to the back doors of two houses, waiting patiently while the black servant went and spoke to the white madam, cupping two hands gratefully and bending in obeisance as he received a few coins from one, smiling politely and retreating in the face of cold refusal from another.

He arrived at the street where Dick Slater lived.

He walked slowly, alert to everything around him. At this time of day the street was empty and quiet, the men in their offices in town, children in school, babies asleep in prams in the sunny gardens. Each house had its own screen of bushes and trees, its lawn, its gate, its path to the front door with a branch to the kitchen at the back. He passed a house where a servant in his uniform of white jacket and shorts was skimming leaves and debris from a kidney-shaped swimming pool.

Everything he did now meant taking risks. He had to calculate the severity of the risk and weigh it against the pressure of their needs. This one was going to be tricky, because he was walking into the unknown. All he knew for sure was that Dick Slater had been detained, and that Pila had mentioned her friendship with Dick's wife. He had given careful thought to his approach.

All his life had been a battle for survival, and caution

and restraint were essential in that battle. Thus his polite, almost deferential way with white people had never quite reached the point of caricature, never really slipped into obsequiousness. He knew that whites liked blacks to speak to them in a way that acknowledged that blacks were inferior beings addressing their masters. Somehow, Thabo had managed to fulfil such requirements, at least in form; the forms of his address had been correct. Some whites had felt uneasy with him, almost as though they knew he was saying to them, this is what you require of me but both you and I know it is a lot of nonsense. Yet if a white became hostile, alerted by some flatness or slight emphasis in speech, then Thabo would display a face and manner so apparently deferential that it could not be faulted. In speech and in deed, he had surrounded himself with caution.

He stood at the gate of the house, hesitating, and looking. He walked up the path, took the turn to the back and knocked on the slightly open kitchen door. Elias appeared; they greeted each other formally in the vernacular and Thabo asked, 'Is the master in?' Elias shook his head.

Margie came into the kitchen. 'What is it, Elias?' she asked.

'He ask for the master.'

She said to Thabo, 'You want my husband for something?'

'I wish to see Mr Slater. But your servant tell me he is not here.'

'He's never here at this time of the day,' Margie said. 'What do you want to see him about?'

Thabo took out the little collection book; Margie, somewhat irritated, took a coin from her purse lying on the table and was about to give it to him when a thought struck her.

233

'Why did you ask for my husband by name?'

'Mr Slater used to give me help sometimes,' he replied. 'He said he would have something for me today.'

The baby, Jonny, was lying in his pram outside the kitchen; he started to cry and Margie went to pick him up. Holding him to her shoulder, and patting him gently on the back while he grizzled sleepily, she turned back to Thabo and said, 'What is your name?'

Thabo walked towards her, but kept the correct deferential difference between white woman and black man.

'Khumalo, Madam. Thomas Khumalo,' he said.

Her face was puzzled. 'I didn't know my husband supported your church. What society do you represent?'

Thabo said, 'Your husband supported our activities among my people. We do more than just preach.'

'You said he had something for you. What was it?' she asked.

'Money, Madam,' Thabo replied.

'How much money?'

'A lot.'

'A lot,' she repeated, 'but how much?'

A pause, then looking down, Thabo took the plunge. 'A thousand pounds,' he said.

She was totally taken aback. She had thought that he was leading up to a request for a fiver. Now her thoughts became disorganized. Perhaps this was some sort of trap, designed not to catch her, but Dick.

'You see,' Thabo went on after some moments silence, 'he was just keeping it for me. Because such money is not safe in my house. Now my organization needs that money, urgently.'

'I don't know anything about it!' she exclaimed. 'Did he give you a receipt?'

They had walked a little way down the back garden.

234

Margie sat on a bench, and motioned Thabo to sit. But he remained standing, not too close, not too far.

'You know why he is not available?' she asked eventually.

'Perhaps I can guess, Madam.'

'Well then, you can understand I can't help you. But I'm hoping to be allowed to see him in a few day's time. I could ask him . . .'

Thabo was shaking his head.

'I might find a way to ask . . . Why don't you come back next week? Say Tuesday or Wednesday. I'll have a good look . . . although you know they searched the house, and they didn't find any money.'

'They do not always find everything.'

They had begun to move closer to an understanding.

'This organization of yours – is it really a church?' she now asked him.

'Not a church, Madam,' he replied.

She waited as though she expected him to add something. 'You don't tell me very much, do you?'

'What is there to say?' He looked as though he was about to leave. 'I am sorry they have taken your husband. This is a heavy time, for all of us. But if you could look . . . only I don't like to come here again too much – for both of us.'

She rose from the bench, the child's arms firmly round her neck. She said, 'You understand, I don't have that kind of money, personally, I mean, even if I knew what it was for. I'll look. I'll see if I can find out anything.'

The white family for whom Florence worked lived in the northern suburbs where each house was surrounded by extensive gardens. The front of her employers' house was a wall of glass opening onto carefully designed lawns and rockeries. Inside was space and elegance: polished wood floors with small Persian rugs and a *khelim*; rooms lined with books, images in wood and stone by acclaimed African sculptors.

Florence was the cook, and a general assistant. There was a male servant as well, who did the heavier work, such as polishing the floors and the large areas of glass windows, and working in the garden in the afternoons.

Her employers were generous enough to Florence, 'liberal' in the local interpretation of that label. They saw her as a human being with feelings like their own, and were uncomfortably aware of the contrasts between the way they lived and her home in Alexandra. When she found out that Florence liked to read, her employer encouraged her to borrow any books she wanted from their library.

Florence's own house in Alexandra had two small rooms and a tiny entrance that was also the kitchen. The water tap and the closet were in a yard that had been shared by a group of houses, now all empty as their occupants had been sent to the reserves, or, the lucky ones, given a house in Soweto. In a few months all the homes in Alexandra were to be bull-dozed and replaced by blocks of multi-storey single-room hostels, some for 'single' men, some for 'single' women, which did not denote their marital status but the fact that they would no longer be permitted to live with their families.

She came home from her work early in the evening. She handed Thabo the evening paper and some books she had borrowed. She took off her winter coat, unwound her *doek*, and went into the kitchen, where she lit a small paraffin stove, unwrapped some meat, and began to prepare a meal.

The living room was lit with two candles, an extravagance for the sake of her guest. Once the house had been wired for electricity, but then came the plans for eliminating the township and all improvements were stopped.

She placed in front of Thabo a plate piled with mealie-meal, with meat and gravy over it. 'Eat,' she commanded him.

'And you? You do not eat?'

She sat down at the table with him. 'I eat a big meal at the place where I work, two, three in the afternoon. They give me plenty of food. Then, before I leave, bread and tea. It is enough for me.'

She made tea for them both, and sipped it while they were talking.

'I knew your husband Obed well,' Thabo said, 'and his brother, Jeremiah. It is a tragedy both should die so young.'

'Yes.'

'What happened to your family? They have all gone?'

'My daughter is married; she lives in Soweto. My sons . . .' She broke off.

'Your sons?'

'One went away, I think to the Cape. The other is in jail. When he comes out, they will endorse him out, off to the reserves, to starve or work on a farm.'

'What happened to him?'

'What happened? What happened to all the children of Alexandra. Ask all the mothers who are left. We saw them grow up here. At least we had a house. A few years of schooling for the lucky ones. Then, nothing. No permits to work. I saw them walking the road to the city, they waited all day in the queues at the pass office, they came back at night hungry and empty-handed. Then they had to learn to eat without money, to dodge the pick-ups. To live without a pass. Nothing.

'You remember what it was like here?' she went on after a pause. 'You never lived here, but you used to come here for Congress meetings. Remember, we could never meet at night, only in the daytime, all the meetings had to be on Sunday mornings because it was too dangerous for anyone to go out at night.'

'I remember,' he replied.

The gangs ruled the streets, armed with the knife and the *tsumantsu*, a bicycle wheel spoke ground to the fineness of a polished needle, to plunge into the back of the victim and sever the nerves of the spine leaving a lifelong paralysis. Thabo had once read in the newspaper that there were more men sitting in wheelchairs at the big hospital in Baragwanath than in any other hospital anywhere in the world.

Florence said, 'They did it for a few pence, for the coat off your back, for nothing, sometimes for nothing at all, just to practise maybe. They should have stabbed the men in the pass office, the policemen in the pick-up; no, they took revenge on their own people. Whatever we did, we had to do during the day. We could never leave the house at night. To visit someone who was sick, to go to church, to go to a meeting, it all had to be done when it was still light.'

'I remember those meetings on Sunday mornings,' Thabo said. 'Number One Square, Number Two; a wooden box for a platform, or we had a lorry. The women brought chairs for the speakers and umbrellas to keep off the sun. The children, and the penny-whistles. Were you here that day when Chief Lutuli spoke, the last time they let him speak? Thousands and thousands. That was a great gathering.'

But Florence said angrily, 'Why did we never do anything? We just let them take power away. Why could we not act together? We could not act together to stop the police, to stop them taking Chief from us, to stop them breaking down our homes. We could not even act

238

together to protect ourselves against our own robbers, the gangs.'

'The people did try to form a citizen group,' Thabo reminded her, 'but they made it illegal.'

'Do you know what they used to do?' Florence went on, absorbed in her bitter memories, 'Later on, when there were more and more of them? They would break into our houses at night, when we were home; they would break in with weapons, beat up everybody, rob us all, leave.

'I'll tell you what it was like. One night there was a gang down this street, nearly twenty of them; they came choosing this house or that, no reason; battering down the door. It was early evening, dark inside the houses, but still a little light on the streets. There were still people coming home from work. The *tsotsis* had guns, they were always armed by that time. They stole the guns from the men in the white suburbs. And knives, and axes. Makadine, just down the road, he enters the yard of his house when they jump on him, they chop off all the fingers of his right hand, they gash his head open. They see someone watching them, a man just stops at the top of the street, not saying anything, not moving, so they go to him, and he struggles, and they split his head open down to the shoulders and leave him dead in the gutter.

'Then to the next house. They burst in, they flash torches, they order everyone to stand still, big torches like weapons, torches to blind you like the car lights on the Pretoria road. Then they demand money, one of them collects it all. If they think you hide something and not give it to them, you can be stabbed or have your hand chopped. Before they leave they hit everyone, old women, children. One with an axe would smash the table – that is to warn you not to go to the police. Anyway, we know, the police will not do anything. The police need the gangs, the gangs help them to keep the people down, they spread terror. Each house they went to, they had one man with a flick-knife or a gun standing guard at the door.

'Violence!' she cried, 'It makes me sick when I hear people talk about violence, the priest in the church, be gentle, be meek, submit – what do white people know about our lives? We were squeezed to death between the gangs and the police, next Friday the same gang in another street, the third Friday the very same gang. Some people never got their pay back to their homes on Fridays, it was taken off them on the buses. You could hide it in your shoe, anywhere, they knew where to look – even here – ' she thrust her hand down the front of her dress. 'Some of us went to the police, even though we were afraid. But the police? They came in their Black Marias and arrested our husbands and sons for not having passes. They never acted against the gangs, they only took our own men away. This way they controlled the whole township.'

'People could have stopped them,' Thabo said, 'if . . .'

But she interrupted him. 'We held meetings, we decided to organize a civil guard, we even started to patrol the streets at night, and the gangs left them alone, they did not attack them. No, the police came, the police attacked the patrols. The police broke them up, they jailed the organizers. The gangs they left alone.

'If you saw the gangs coming, you melted away. The ones who fought back, they are the ones sitting in those chairs at Baragwanath. Or lying under the ground. Those of us who wanted to go on living, we hid in silence when we heard someone else being attacked. We were just glad it was not our house.'

She stopped speaking abruptly. A terrible memory assailed her, the memory of an incident that was so painful to recollect that it was like a flaw in her life. And nobody knew about it. The only other one who knew had died in prison. The whole thing did not exist at all, except in the depth of her faltering heart.

It had been late at night, past midnight. There had been a shout and sounds of a scuffle outside the door of her house. She woke at the noise, and flinging back the blankets she seized a dress and began pulling it over her head. Obed also woke, and sat up, saying in a whisper, 'What is it?'

'Someone in trouble, right outside,' she replied as she began to unlock the door.

He sprang from the bed and grabbed her. 'Where are you going?' he demanded. 'Are you mad You will be killed.'

'Obed,' she said, struggling to be free of him, 'someone is in trouble. Don't leave him. Let me go.'

'No!'

'You go, then.'

'No!'

She tried to reach the door, but he held her with both arms. He was a big man, very strong, and she could not get away. She did not want to make too much noise and frighten the children. Held against his body, the sweat of her body mingling with his, she whispered passionately, 'Let me go, Obed, let me go!' But he remained silent, concentrating all his attention on holding her, and listening. The grunts and scuffles outside the house stopped. There was a sound like bubbling water; she ceased struggling, and also listened. Not only the two of them were standing in the dark, but in rooms in all the houses down that street people were holding their breath, not making a sound, listening.

There was the tattoo of rapid retreating footsteps. In the distance the dogs were barking, angry township dogs.

241

The barking went on for a long time, trailed off to a single bark, stopped at last. He released her. 'It's too late now,' he said.

She felt the people in the houses around her lying awake as she lay, filled with the poison of their cowardice and their shame.

In the morning an ambulance took away the body of John, eldest son of a family down the street, the only one in his family with a job – shift work. Obed never mentioned the incident but she could not forgive herself, and because of that she could not forgive him.

Out of the long silence Thabo asked, 'You are tired, sister?'

'No,' she replied, 'only thinking of things in the past. We were cowards, not so? Obed used to say, "Be cowards sometimes so later on we can be brave."'

'Surely he was right.'

'How can it be right? You act when you must act, you help people when they need help or else you stand on one side and let their lives run past you.'

'But to me it is not so simple,' he commented. 'People don't always know, they have to learn . . . they only need to be shown, the right leadership. We are too many. They can't lock the whole country up.'

'At what stage have we ever been able to stop them? Look at this place – dead now. We never stopped anything.'

'Oh yes, and there was success too. Remember the squatters' camps, and the bus boycotts? How the people overflowed from the houses and made their own homes out of tin and cardboard?'

She smiled. 'Those women, walking nearly twenty miles every single day, nine miles to town, nine miles back, to stop them adding one single penny to the bus fares. All the old washer-women with their great big bundles. We all wore through our shoes, we walked on holes stuffed with card.'

'Such unity,' he said, 'such strength.'

'And in spite of it all, they proved stronger. Too strong for us.'

'No, not so. Each time we learned a little more. We have to fight many battles, isn't it? We shall win. When people understand how strong they are, we shall win.'

'And will we be alive to see it? We used to shout: "Freedom – in our lifetime!" Our lives are not long enough; theirs too long.'

For the first time his face changed. It had been stern, now it softened, became sombre. 'It's a long road,' he said, 'we always knew it. But at the beginning you do not decide, I will leave my family, my job, hide away . . . you just start going in one direction and the further you go, the less you know any way back; it seems to happen quite naturally. We always knew it would be hard, but not how hard, how far each one of us – listen, it is not easy for anyone. For me, also. If you have a job, a permit . . . wife, children . . . you can make a life, perhaps, Then I know, what kind of life? Listen, I also had many times . . . but for our people it is not really a choice. To be black gives you no choice.'

Her elbow rested on the table, her head on her hands. The candles flickered down silently, their shadows swayed on the wall. Soon he said gently, 'This is not a time for weeping sister, but for working. We had many hard times, defeats. Now we have work to do.'

She raised her head, her face controlled, unsmiling. 'My tears are finished long since,' she told him. 'No, you will never see me weep now.'

'Then I need your help. Will you work with me?'

'I will do whatever I can.'

'Even if it ends with defeat?'

'Even so. I, like you, don't start out to be a hero. But to fight is the only way. If you stop fighting, you die.'

'Good,' he said. 'Then I am going to show you something, no one here knows about it, and if I am taken, then you will know, and you will understand what you must do.'

# *Margie . . .*

At first she had sat with her hands clasped tightly together, but now she was more relaxed, and the small familiar gestures that Dick knew so well began to appear.

They were separated not only by the strong wire mesh screen, but also by a counter on either side of the mesh, holding them four or five feet apart. He moved his head from side to side to try to see her more clearly. 'You've done your hair differently,' he said.

'No, it's the same, only it's longer, that's what makes the difference.' She smiled at him, and he was overwhelmed with longing to touch her hair.

Now they had overcome the worst part, the first impact of seeing each other, the exchange of trivialities; his questions about her domestic life and her slow, gentle replies, trying to put unspoken loving into the words.

Would she be able to ask him about the thousand pounds? All time this was at the back of her mind; she told herself to wait, be patient, an opportunity would come.

They wanted to find things to say that would be significant, that each would remember. Yet they could only say the most ordinary things.

'I tried to get to see you before, many times. Rosa and I have been plaguing the Special Branch.' She paused. 'Rosa Miller, that's Jack Miller's wife; he was detained . . .'

The watching, listening warder stepped forward and waved his hand from side to side.

'I mean, I met her at the SB headquarters when we

were both trying to get visits. She's very nice. We became friends.'

She was trying to say it in a way that would not cause the warder to intervene. Domestic and family matters only, the Colonel had said with great emphasis, or the visit would be terminated immediately.

'She's very brave. She helped me a lot. I couldn't have done it by myself, I didn't know how to – she gave me courage.'

'That's nice', Dick said, trying to focus on to this wife who had developed new relationships and new ways of acting while he had been sitting in a cell.

The warder stood half-turned away from them, seemingly indifferent. He had been standing with his head lowered, cleaning his nails with a pen-knife. Now he leant back to talk to a mate through the open door at the back of the visiting room. He was not paying much attention. Now, she thought, ask him now, but because of her care for him she found herself asking softly, 'Was it very bad, Dick?'

'Not so bad.'

'All that standing, I mean, keeping you awake and standing. It sounded terrible.'

He was startled. 'How did you know?'

'I, oh, I forgot they don't let you read the papers. There was a court application.' She spoke hurriedly, the warder could turn back to them any minute. 'Jack Miller smuggled a note out to Rosa and she brought an application to court to try and get an order to restrain the police from continuing to question him in that way. There was a lot of publicity. They did it to you, too, didn't they?'

He was astonished. 'He did that? Got a note out?'

'Yes. It opened the whole thing up. There hadn't been

a word in the papers until then. It really was a marvellous thing, because it opened up the whole ninety-day thing.'

He thought how terrified he had been, how anxious not to infringe any of the rules or incur any unnecessary wrath. He marvelled at a fellow-prisoner who had the courage to rebel.

'So we knew a bit of what was going on. She wasn't allowed visits, she hasn't had one yet. We thought we wouldn't be allowed to see any of you. Until you were charged.'

Now she would ask him about the money. But before she could speak again he said, 'They may not charge me.'

The warder came back into the room and was watching them again. Domestic and family matters.

'I'm going to start work again,' she said. 'Only in the mornings.'

He saw her life slipping into a new mould; things were changing, she would change.

'Why not wait a bit to see what happens?'

'We need the money, Dick. We didn't have much saved. Apart fron that it's really better for me to work, really it is, I need to get out, to be in touch with people.'

Now was the time to ask him – speak, she told herself. But as she opened her mouth to frame the words he said, 'Tell me, how have people reacted?'

'Oh, they haven't been bad at all, not bad really. Some of the most unexpected people – very kind. Really, the ones you would least expect.'

'I was afraid, I thought they might ostracize . . .'

'Some yes, they try to avoid me, I don't really blame them, they're scared, you know. But others, honestly, I've been taken out, entertained . . .'

The warder said, 'Time's up.'

'So soon?' she exclaimed, 'Oh, please, just one more

minute.' Then to Dick urgently, 'Dick, that thousand pounds we had put away, I need it, please tell me . . .'

He looked at her blankly, in genuine bewilderment. 'What thousand pounds?'

'You were keeping it,' she said, 'for an emergency. I have to know . . .'

Realization dawned. She saw he understood; then his features contracted. 'Margie,' he said, 'whatever you do, think first of yourself and Jonny. I just couldn't bear it if – you mustn't think of me, my friends . . .'

The warder said, '*Kom.*'

'Please Dick, you must tell me – just this, nothing else, I must know.'

The warder was jostling him out of the visiting room. For one second he turned his head and mumbled, 'Bio-Chemistry two.' She was not even sure if that was what he said, it just sounded like it. They had gone, the visit was over.

All the way back to Johannesburg she was blaming herself. It had all gone wrong. She should have asked him at the start of the interview, but they had had to establish a new sort of communication first, and then all those messages, his parents, chat about Jonny . . . She drove the car scarcely knowing how far she had gone, trying to think what she could do. Who were his political associates, who could she ask? It was too dangerous, anyway.

She searched the house and all the outbuildings. She even walked around the garden, looking for places where he might have concealed a packet or a box; perhaps an envelope, wrapped in cellophane. Every drawer and every cupboard was turned out. She found old letters, papers, the manuscript of the technical book Dick had begun to write but abandoned. She turned all the pages, and thought and thought.

She had arranged to meet the preacher at the end of the week, Saturday morning, at the municipal market at Newtown. He had not wanted to come to the house again. On Friday night there was a concert at the University. She decided she would go to the concert and take the opportunity of going up to Dick's office some time during the evening.

She dressed herself as one did when going out at night in Johannesburg: a pretty dress, smart patent shoes, a ribbon to hold back her long hair; and she pinned to her shoulder a tiny bouquet of real flowers from the garden.

Many people she knew greeted her in the entrance, where the boards proclaimed: TONIGHT IN THE GREAT HALL, at 8 P.M. The Cape Symphony Orchestra, conducted by Marius de Leeuw.

Bright lights, smart clothes, mingled voices – how normal it all was! Nothing had changed the surface of this rich and pleasant life. The arrests, the detentions, the man who had just died under interrogation – the police said he had leapt through a window, but that window was barred – the bombs, all that was like an underground stream flowing beneath this smooth surface. It must all break down one day, she thought, it will collapse.

She waited till the interval. People strolled in the foyer and walked along the corridors to the toilets. She walked further, turned the corner, and climbed the flights of stairs to his office. The corridors were dimly lit and deserted.

She unlocked the door of his office and went inside, locking the door after her. A faint light seeped through the slats of the venetian blinds. She turned the blinds to blank out the windows, put the desk-lamp on the floor, and turned the light on. She began a systematic and thorough search for the money. She started with the obvious, the desk drawers. They were locked, but she had the keys. Time went by as she found the right key for each drawer. Faintly she heard the sound of the orchestra beginning the second half of the concert.

After the drawers, she looked quickly through the two baskets on his desk. The SBs, of course, would have looked there also. They would have searched every drawer, looked at every bit of paper. The filing cabinet. This took some time, she knew she must be out of the office before the concert came to an end. There was a cupboard that yielded nothing. She even took some books from the shelves and looked behind them to see if there was any sort of hiding place. But why would they have not found it, if it were a place obvious to her?

Below, the concerto was faintly but definitely in the last movement. Reluctantly she decided she had to leave. At the door she paused and went back again and sat behind the desk in Dick's swivel chair and thought. Her eyes moved round the office. She swung backwards, and from side to side. Her eyes scanned the bookshelves, mostly technical; suddenly one title seemed to spring out at her: Bio-Chemistry II.

She got up slowly and took the book from the shelf, placing it on the desk, and opened it, turned the title page – and there was the money. The book had been hollowed out completely to hold the carefully wrapped wads of notes.

She hastily turned off the desk light and locked the door. She walked along the corridor with the book in her hands as the sound of applause rose up the stairs.

The market was in two sections. One was for the retail stalls, selling every variety of vegetables and fruit, together with meat, poultry and eggs. The other was the wholesale section where boxes of fruit and vegetables and sacks of citrus fruit were piled high beneath the arched iron and glass building that looked like a Victorian railway station.

The traders were whites, Indians and Africans, but there were more whites than others. Housewives and traders mingled here; individuals could bid against the traders, provided they bought by the box or sack. The white housewives were trailed by small black boys who haunted the market at the weekends to earn pennies carrying heavy loads of fresh fruit and vegetables out to the car park, and then packing them away in the boots of the American cars. The housewives bought oranges by the sack, and pineapples, avocado pears, mangoes, nectarines, lichees and apples by the box.

The Newtown market was one of the very few places in Johannesburg where blacks and whites met on the same level. It was an ideal place for Margie and Thabo to meet.

Margie walked through the retail section first, glancing at the piled up displays; carrying her shopping basket and shaking her head at the small black boys who followed her chanting 'Carry, Madam, carry, Madam.'

In the wholesale section, where boxes of fruit were piled six feet high, she stopped by a black man who was lifting boxes from one pile to another. An Indian standing there greeted her with the barest nod of his head, and gestured to one side. And there was the preacher, without his dog collar. They stood behind the boxes, concealed inside a cave of fruit, while the Indian posted himself with his back to them.

The sounds of the auctioneers, the shouts, the trolleys being wheeled back and forth, seemed to recede. She said suddenly, 'I recognize you now. You work at the bookshop, with Pila Norval, don't you?'

'I did work there.'

She put her hand in her basket and took out the book. She handed it to him, and he looked at her. 'It's all there,' she said. 'Take it, it's all there.'

He did not know what to say. He stumbled over his thanks.

'Perhaps you had better give me back the book,' she said. He appreciated her understanding of the need for security. He pocketed the money, and handed back the book. They looked at each other.

'Tell me,' Margie began, 'no, never mind.'

He understood the unasked question. He trusted her now. It was as he had said to Florence, you start walking along a certain road . . .

'Mr Slater was going to buy a van for us. I don't know who can do it now.' He paused.

At last Margie said, 'Are you asking me to do that? Why don't you do it yourself?'

'I am just saying,' Thabo replied. 'It is more difficult for us. Black people do not have this kind of money. They should not have it.'

'Car dealers will take cash from anyone,' she replied.

'They want names, licences, records.'

'They would want the same from me.'

'I know a man,' he replied, 'who will accept cash like this from a white without asking questions. He will not keep a record. It just needs someone to take the money to him and drive the van away.'

'If Dick knew all this,' she replied, 'then the police may know it now. He's been in detention for a long time.'

'It is a chance. But no one tells everything. Even under torture no one tells everything. Always they hold onto something; something the SBs don't know. It proves to them that they are not completely destroyed.'

'But still, this they might know.'

'Then they would have collected the money.'

'Or they might have left it,' she told him, 'to trap whoever came to get it.'

'Then they would have arrested you.'

'And if they had, and I had told them about you?'

'And what would you say? That a preacher called Khumalo came to see you? They would not have kept you long. They would soon know there is no such preacher.'

'I could have led them to you.'

'But you did not.'

A look of deep understanding passed between them. She took the book from her basket again and handed it to him. Without a word, he replaced the notes between the hollowed out covers.


She had another visit to Dick in the following week; and then when she was going to see him for a third time, she met, by arrangement, Rosa Miller.

They always met in public places, in cafés or department stores; Rosa was afraid of closed rooms and homes that might be bugged. Rosa had tried very hard to get a visit to her husband, Jack, but she had been refused. 'You'll see him when he's been charged,' she was told.

She said, when they were seated at the restaurant table, 'Margie, I have something to say to you. I've been thinking about it for a couple of weeks. It's rather difficult . . .'

She had a long, intelligent face; she used no special shampoos or tints to hide her greying hair. An efficient woman, wearing efficient clothes, well-dressed, self-assured.

But at this moment, not so self-assured; she fingered her handbag. 'You know, Margie,' she said, 'there's a battle going on for your husband's soul, and I think you should help him.'

She looked at Margie with deeply-troubled brown eyes, enlarged by the thick lenses of her spectacles.

Margie remained quiet, but felt a tremor of fear.

'You know what they say he is going to do, don't you? You know why you've been permitted visits, why they've relaxed things for him. You even told me, they let him have a book to read. You must know. Gifts don't come free from the Special Branch. There's a payment to be made. There's a price for your visits – Dick will be a state witness. That is what I hear. Is it true?'

Margie said, 'Rosa, I haven't discussed it with him.'

'But surely! You've seen him twice in two weeks. How can you *not* discuss it? You must have known?' She paused. 'How do you feel about it yourself?' she asked abruptly.

Margie felt like a snail trying to curl back into its shell.

'I don't know. I try not to think about it.'

'You must speak to him, Margie. It would be a terrible thing. Listen, it will be more terrible for him than for others. As far as I'm concerned personally, it doesn't matter a damn to me, I know that Jack never worked with Dick, he never had anything to do with him. So it's not that I have any personal axe to grind. But for him – do you realize what this can do to him? It's something that destroys you, absolutely; everything you believed in – it becomes a sham. He would never recover. You must speak to him.'

Tears filled Margie's eyes. 'I can't speak to him,' she said urgently, 'how can I? How can I tell him, don't come out, keep yourself in jail for however long, ten years, fifteen, twenty. I can't tell him that. He must decide for himself.'

'And you? You'll have him back on any terms?'

254

'On his terms, whatever they are,' she replied, trying to stop the flow of tears down her cheeks.

Of course she had realized that Dick had given them information. The Colonel had said, 'Your husband is a sensible man. Since he's reasonable, I'll be reasonable too. When would you like to go and see him?'

She felt confused. 'What makes you think he's going to be a state witness?' she said at last. 'Maybe he's made a statement, but that doesn't mean . . .'

'It's what we hear,' Rosa answered flatly.

Under the layer of trivial things which she spread between them on her next visit, lay the tension of this confusion and uncertainty. She waited until the warder became bored with their conversation and relaxed his attention.

'Dick,' she asked him, 'are you going to be charged?'

He simply looked at her, his face pulled by lines of strain. The small silence became a wall that had to be breached.

He moved his head finally and said, 'I don't know what the outcome of all this will be.'

'You have thought about it?'

'How could I not? One thinks of everything, of every possibility.' And with a dour laugh, 'There's enough time to think.'

'And – ?'

'There are no absolute answers.'

She said, 'There's something I want to ask you, I've thought about it so much, I wanted to know the reason, why did you stay that night? Why didn't you . . ?'

He felt that even if the warder did not intervene, he would never be able to describe the heavy lethargy that had descended on him that night, the fatalism, the feeling of inevitability; the reluctance to face up to the necessity of leaving; the fact that it was easier to do nothing than to decide, easier to let things happen than to act.

He said, 'I don't know. Sometimes one can't bring oneself to . . . we've always had so many privileges, so much advantage . . . so easy for us to turn our backs and run away . . .'

She was carried away by the intensity of her own feelings. 'You know how it seemed to me, afterwards, when I thought about it?' she asked him. 'It seemed as though you almost wanted it. You know, as though you almost . . . welcomed it. Is that unfair?'

'No, I don't think so.'

She started talking about other things, the new jersey she was leaving for him because it had become very cold; there was even frost on the garden at night . . .

But when it was time for her to go, she said hurriedly, 'Dick, I want you to know that whatever you decide, we'll manage. I mean, not to think too much about Jonny and me, not to make us your reason for doing anything. It must be for yourself, for your own good reasons. You do understand?'

After she had gone, Dick sat in his cell and tried to put together all the things they had talked about. He thought first about their home. The job she now had, the mornings out, the afternoons with the child in the garden. She had said, 'It's such a nice job, really, and the Head said he'd put me on the temporary staff, that way he didn't have to fill in forms and answer too many questions.'

She had said, 'I like going out in the mornings. Jonny goes to sleep at about eleven anyway, and doesn't wake up until I'm back. I meet people and talk to them. It's good for me, quite apart from the money.'

She had said, 'I thought I'd paint the spare room myself, and I didn't make a bad job of it, but I haven't tackled the ceiling.'

She had said, 'I wanted to know the reason, I've wanted to ask you all along, what made you stay that night? It was almost as though you wanted to . . .'

And finally 'It must be for yourself, for your own good reasons.'

Sometimes there are questions for which no answers can be given.

There had been only one short period when he had been free from doubt, and that had been at the beginning, when he had taken the decision and they first started doing things. They had seemed to be so successful; before the clamp-down, before all the arrests and the ninety-day law. Did the doubts only arise because they had failed? If that was so, was the morality of the decision determined by success or failure?

Ralph had said people would come to terms with what was happening only through the hard logic of events.

If the events had been more effective . . . the amateurishness and even childishness of everything they had done! All the time the SBs had been on to them. Most of the time they had followed people, taped their conversations. They had unlimited means at their disposal, such highly-developed electronic instruments. What was the use of covering the telephone and putting on records, when they had powerful devices for picking up conversations across streets, through walls? To blow up white supremacy with those few feeble explosions? It was really laughable.

Therefore, why now make oneself into a martyr? If it would influence anything . . . but it made not the slightest scrap of difference. His evidence would be mere corroboration, simply a small added weight to the mass of things they already knew. They knew it all. Now he had the choice of sending himself to prison for years and years, – and if he could further the struggle for human rights one iota by that act, it would be worth doing – or of stating in public, in a witness box, what he had already told them fully in private.

He felt nothing but deep disgust, a disgust which spread to all those he had worked with, and everything they had done.

# Indres . . .

When he was moved from Pretoria Central Prison to the small police station on the outskirts of Johannesburg, Indres knew they had finished the interrogation; and probably not only his, but that of a whole group of people. The papers would be in the offices of the Attorney-General where the charges would be finally drawn up.

To be moved to a police station from the central Prison was in itself a kind of verdict. It meant you had talked. As long as the Security Police needed you available at any time of day or night to be brought out for interrogation, as long as they wished to confront and confound you with new information extracted from someone else, as long as there were incidents not fully explained, your home was Pretoria jail. When they had finished with you they sent you to some small station where political prisoners could be effectively isolated from each other and looked after by the local police.

There was a high brick wall with an entanglement of barbed wire laid along the top, and within the wall a small two-storey building. On three sides, between building and wall, was the passage where Indres was taken for exercise.

Into this quieter and more remote environment, he came with an obsession that amounted to an illness. His preoccupation with this brought him back from the abyss of break-down. He had to find a way of reaching Thabo, and reaching him quickly.

Many things were scribbled on the walls of this cell, and among the ordinary prison graffiti were the marks left by political prisoners: Philomen Matalong, arrested on 4 March, 90 days + 90 days. Beneath that, Mary Macleod, 26 June, and next to that in very tiny letters that must have been scratched with a pin: *Freedom Day*.

He found a small pin in the lapel of his jacket, and this pin he would keep, so that when he had decided what he wanted to scratch on the wall, he would add his name and his mark. Each day he thought of something new, a slogan, perhaps a declaration, an assertion. Even simply the name of the organization so that others who came to the cell afterwards would feel a sense of comradeship.

Nothing quite satisfied him. He kept the pin. He used it to clean his nails, to pick threads out of a handkerchief, to clean his comb, to clean his teeth. But the statement of faith was not written. There was always tomorrow.

He guessed that now they were piecing together all the statements they had obtained, looking for where they did not tally, or for any noticeable gaps. When they had everything they wanted, they would charge him, and then he would be moved to one of the central prisons.

All over the Transvaal, he thought, there must be others like himself in solitary confinement in small police stations waiting, hoping to be charged. Looking forward to the day they would be charged, and brought to court.


Light filtered from the barred fanlight over the cell door. In a recess at the opposite end was his own flush toilet, with an old chain hanging from the cistern. It was a luxury that immeasurably raised his standard of living. Even the sounds it made were a source of pleasure, the companionable slow trickle as the cistern filled and the glop-glop as the valve finally closed.

Behind the lavatory bowl and cistern was a wire mesh from floor to ceiling, and behind the mesh a high, recessed window.

Time moved in and out, was handed to him on a tin dish, crept under the door in the form of footsteps, shouted orders and jangling of keys, less strident and persistent in this small station. The measure of time was the cell door opening to let him out each day to shower and to exercise, the precious half-hour when he could smell the sharp air, the morning frost on the strip of earth next to the wall and even the dry grass beyond the jail. It was winter now, the winter of early dark and late dawn, crisp days and freezing nights.

The Sergeant in charge of the station, a man neither hostile nor friendly, gave him extra blankets when he complained of the cold, and brought him a stool to sit on so that he did not have to squat on the naked cement floor. There was, of course, the lavatory, a place to sit at all times. With stool and lavatory he reached the top of the cistern, from where he could see out of the dirt-grimed window to the landscape of small figures walking across derelict land in the world beyond the prison. Between the white suburb onto which the jail faced, and the black township two miles further away lay a waste-land. This separated the homes of black and white, and the blacks crossed it twice a day to go and work in the homes and factories of the whites; figures, miniature in the distance, larger but still remote nearer the prison wall, sometimes detached themselves, walked right up to the wall where they passed out of Indres' line of vision, then strolled away, doing up their flies. If he could reach one of them . . . he had to find a way.

No other prisoners stayed more than a night or two. Sometimes a drunk sang or vomited his way through the night in another cell. Pass offenders were taken in batches from the prison vans, but after being booked in were usually transported to larger jails. The local Sergeant had to keep up his tally of arrests.

He noted the periods during the day and night when he was likely to be left entirely alone. One night he examined the mesh above the cistern, and found that the top section, independent of the lower part, could quite easily be removed; wedging himself between sill and cistern he slowly loosened the frame holding the glass, using a link prised from the lavatory chain as a tool.

Outside the window the corrugated iron roof sloped sharply downwards, ending in a gutter. Below, at ground level, was the passage, only a few yards wide, in which he exercised. Beyond that was the wall with its rolls of barbed wire.

One day, after the police had brought his evening tin of food, Indres unrolled his mat and blankets; putting the felt mat to one side, he made up his bed without it. Using the carrier bag in which he kept a change of clothing, he arranged the blankets as best as he could to simulate a sleeping form. Only really bad luck would bring anyone in now before morning, and even if the Sergeant did happen to come up to the first floor that night and look through the judas-hole, he would possibly be satisfied with the dark shape lying in the corner.

Taking the matting and a rope made of strips of towelling and his spare shirt, he used the stool to climb onto the cistern, removed the mesh, and eased the glass out of the frame. Head first he worked himself slowly through the narrow aperture. The fabric rope was tied beneath his arms, the other end fastened securely to the cistern.

Once outside, he used the rope to lower himself carefully down the steep slope of the roof to the gutter, making as little noise as possible. He dragged the felt mat behind him. He untied the rope, stood upright in the gutter; and measured the exact distance of the next move.

He was clearly visible now to anyone outside the jail,

but the veld was empty. He paused on the threshold of this landscape of snares and traps, fearful of a return to the world of self-reliance after so many weeks of the protection of prison.

He flung the folded mat onto the barbed wire on top of the wall, looked once more over the gap that had to be bridged, made sure of his balance, then, drawing a deep breath, made a single leap across the space; he landed on the mat-protected wall and with one movement, without any pause, sprang on and over the wall into the blackness beyond, letting his body relax as he fell, rolling over immediately on impact with the ground.

It had all been soundless, except for the single hard thud when he landed. Heart thumping, he walked quickly away from the jail across the veld. He was out, he was free. Now he had to find Thabo.

# Thabo . . .

The code they used for communicating with the other regions was easy to master, but slow to use. Words were transposed into numbers. For this purpose they used a paper-backed novel.

Florence had become a reliable contact passing messages back and forth on her way to and from work.

One night she handed Thabo an envelope. 'Marie brought me this,' she told him, 'and said I should give it to you.'

He opened it and took out two identical keys with a piece of card tied to them. On one side of the card was written: P.O. Box 52170. On the reverse: These are the keys to the box taken in the name of Sterling Enterprises.

He was excited. 'Where did Marie get these?'

Florence said, 'She said to tell you a woman came seeking your wife this week. Rebecca was at the clinic. She went to the clinic and she told Rebecca that she, Emily, works for the parents of the girl Pila Norval, and that Pila asked her to get them to you. Is it important?'

He was animated. 'Ah, this is . . .' he held the two keys out in the palm of his hand, 'with these keys we can establish our contacts again. We were looking for other ways. You see, they are for a box at the central post office.'

'The main post office in Jeppe Street?'

'Yes. She used to do this, Pila Norval, who worked at the bookshop; the one who was detained, but then released again.'

'Then give them to me,' Florence told him. 'I will go there for you tomorrow.'

'Well, there is some risk. Suppose it is a trap. Then they will be waiting to see who opens the box.'

'That is why I will take the keys. Give them to me.'

'Wait, wait. You are my protector. If you do not return? I would rather you do not go, Florence.'

She thought for a moment. 'Give me the keys,' she repeated. 'I will arrange to collect the letters with no risk to myself. I assure you. I will take no risks.'

The next evening she brought him a batch of letters.

He was overjoyed. 'How did you do it?'

'You see, I took Ma-Meni with me, from down the road. She's old now, her hands are all twisted with rheumatism. She went up to one of the messengers at the post office, just someone who was collecting letters for his firm, and she said to him, "My son, my hands are feeble and the key is too stiff. Can you open the box for me?" Then we both waited, we were ready to go away if anything happened. But he just unlocked the box, put his hand inside, took out these letters and gave them to Ma-Meni. That was all.'

'Nobody seemed to be watching?'

'Nobody. But they could be waiting their time. Have you thought they could have opened the letters and read them, then put them back in the box?'

He smiled. 'These letters they cannot read. They are in code.'

'Perhaps they can find the code?'

'No, it is not possible to solve it without the right book. Look, this is what I am going to show you.'

He fetched the book published by Penguin in its familiar orange cover. It was *The Ministry of Fear* by Graham Greene. He opened the first envelope and spread out the thin piece of paper on the table.

'Look, the first number, the one that stands there, that's the number of the page in the book; in this case twenty-six. The second number, that's the line on the page, counting down from the top; line five, one, two, three, four, five. Now the third set of numbers, after the semi-colon, those are the letters in that line, counting from the beginning of the line, and each number after that is a letter in the same line, until you have a new line-number, like this.'

They began to count and to translate each number into letters of the alphabet. Slowly the messages took shape.

'It takes a lot of time,' she said.

'Yes, it takes time, it is not easy to write, but it is very safe. They can never read these messages, never, until they have the right book, and they will not find that book unless someone tells them. If anyone is arrested who knows the book, then we simply change the book. You understand how it works?'

'I understand; but if they raid your house and there are few books, it would not be too difficult for them . . .'

'Well, we are aware of that. If it is in homes with not many books, then the code-book must be hidden in some way. One of us has got a small library near him that he can use. He never even has to buy the book. When he needs it, he goes and looks it up in the library. Then we have made use of white friends who have hundreds of books in their homes. When I worked in the bookshop, I used a copy of the book in the shop.'

'And the white woman, Norval, she kept the key?'

'She used to fetch the letters. She hired the box, but she knows nothing at all about the code. So even if she tells them about the box, she cannot say to them how to read the letters.'

He was enveloped in a calm happiness. Everything was coming together as it should, and it would all be over in the next few days. All he needed was to keep out of their clutches during this coming period. The young men were due to arrive soon, from Natal, from the Western Cape and from Port Elizabeth district. They would be the first volunteers. Now he could get the van and could receive the men without further dangerous delays . . . It had to work. He clasped his hands and bowed his head, as if in prayer. But he did not pray to any god. Only to fate, to let this new way, the beginning of this new era, proceed successfully in the next few precious days.

# *Indres . . .*

He cried out, and woke trembling.

He was drenched in sweat. Someone stood over him with a torch. He was seized again by the same terrible confusion, the mingling of past and future so that the present was devoid of stability.

Thabo was fleeing, running into a trap. Thabo was surrounded by a posse of the Security police . . . He had failed to reach him in time.

He flung back the blankets and began to rise. There was a restraining hand on his arm and a voice saying, 'You had bad dreams, huh? You lie down again and go to sleep.'

He saw April's small, deeply-lined face. He said, without thinking, 'He was the one closest to me, my real buddy, the best I knew . . . and now I'm sure he is betraying us.'

April rubbed the back of his head. 'I'll tell you what,' he said, 'let's you and I have something nice to drink and then we has a little talk, and maybe you'll be able to sleep better.'

From the depth of one of his cupboards he produced a bottle of wine and poured a generous cupful for each of them.

'Got to have something to keep out the cold. Now, you was saying about your friend?'

'It's just so hard to believe, when you've known someone for a long time, been close to them, shared all sorts of things . . . What makes him . . . how could it happen?'

April shook his head, drank, wiped his mouth. 'I know

what you mean,' he said. 'It's hard to believe, but it happens just the same. I'll tell you something. When they started with all this race classification business there was lots of them would go in and denounce their own friends, just so's to protect themselves. This man was my neighbour and my friend, he and his wife were in and out of our house, chatting about this, borrowing that. But it was his kids who started on our kids at school – your Pa's Coloured, our Pa says you shouldn't be at this school . . . They grew up together. He wasn't no better than me, but he got his white card. He was the same as me. I got no proof, but I just know for certain he reported me.'

'What did you do, then?'

'I didn't do nothing. I was so mad at first, I was going to donder him up. I was raving mad. I could've killed him. Then I just didn't do nothing.'

'Why not?'

'Look, man, it wasn't his fault, was it?' April said, leaning forward. 'Suppose I went to him and asked him "What makes you act like that, what you doing it for?" he couldn't tell me, could he? I knew better than he did; at least I knew what he couldn't say to me. He was just plain terrified, he was shit-scared. He was scared because they was stronger than us. He joined the stronger side. But it wasn't him made the laws, was it? It was the laws that were wrong. We were all right until they started with those new laws. So you're mad about it, but you can't beat up the government, you go and beat up your neighbour instead. That's not the answer. One day I'm going to get my own back, but not against him. I'm going to smack those punks that made the laws – pow, boom, one-two, one-two! I'll find a way. Me, I'm waiting for a chance to get my own back. But not against that poor, scarified, trembling, arse-licking half of a man.'

'But this man I was talking about,' Indres said, 'My

friend, he wasn't like that. He was the bravest of all of us. Really brave, a lion. He'd do things I was terrified to do.'

'So?' April was not impressed. 'Maybe he was trying to prove something. Maybe he was always trying to show everyone else, just because all the time he was really so scared. Some people can play hero when there's a crowd to cheer them on. Maybe you thought you was the only one who was frightened. If he's betrayed you, mate, you got to face it, he's changed sides. That's what you got to face up to. He's on the other side now.

'He the one who got you in jail?' he added abruptly.

'Yes.'

'And now you been thinking you want to get your own back?'

'No, it's not that. There are others. I have to get to them and warn them. They don't know what I know about him. And I've wasted too much time already. It might be too late.'

'And that was why you was walking along the road by yourself so late at night? Trying to get to your friends?'

'Yes, that's why.'

April thought for a minute. Then he said, 'You can't go strolling along to Soweto, you're the wrong race. They'll just pick you up and take you back to Number Four. Now, I go in and out with my lorry. Tomorrow I've got a whole load of stuff to take down to White City. Why don't you let me take a message for you to your pals? Would that help?'

'Do you know where the Orlando clinic is?'

'Yep, I know it. I know my way round the whole blooming Soweto. Day or night. Anywhere.'

Indecision gnawed at him. April was right, he could not go into the townships. But tomorrow he must get a message to Thabo. Even now, at this house, the skeletons

of his nightmare might be armed and riding out . . .
Words flickered around his head, jostled each other for
possession of him. Trust this man. Who is he? A stranger,
a light-skinned, grinning, talkative eccentric clown, living
in a cave in the side of a disused quarry. Trust this man.
After a few hours? Hand over to a stranger the thread
that held the organization together? Trust this man, he
will help you. Or else bring the police to his hessian
door. No, not that, what would he stand to gain by that?
You can trust him. Twenty-four hours ago he had felt he
would never trust anyone again. And now he was preparing to trust the first stranger encountered on the road.

Time had already run out. There was no longer a group
with its discussion and joint decision. Once you were
arrested you were on your own. You had to decide by
yourself. At all costs, he had to reach Thabo.

# Thabo . . .

A small gas lamp hisses quietly on the table which has been pushed into a corner of the room. There are two chairs at the table, and Thabo and Ntite sit there. The rest, men and women, sit on the floor. The room is small and the place seems crowded.

The last to come in is Sipho. He is led into the room blindfolded; only when he is inside does the woman who holds his arm take the bandage from his eyes. He blinks in the light and looks round the room, nodding in greeting to those he knows.

Two women sit uncomfortably, trying to lean against the wall. One man has lowered his forehead onto arms that rest horizontally across bent knees. Sipho sits a little apart, watching the faces of the others.

'This is the last time we come together like this,' Thabo says, 'before you disperse to your own places. From now on, everything we do has new significance. That is not to say we now abandon all we have been doing, but bit by bit we must concentrate everything, all our forces, on the new necessities.'

They talk. Many times Sipho shifts impatiently, examines his watch, holds it to his ear, winds it, sits back again.

Finally Thabo says, 'You will understand now what is to be done? First, in each area you will establish arms depots that will be known only to one or two people. The person in charge will leave information with someone else in such a way that if he is arrested, or put out of

272

action for some reason, then immediate steps can be taken to move and safeguard the depot.'

One of the women says, 'We have not discussed properly the question of how we obtain the arms.'

Thabo smiles. 'You will each have to find your own ways. Remember what I told you about the Vietnamese? How they armed themselves from the French?'

One of the men comments, 'You will find many with experience who will be willing to help. It's not only *dagga* one gets from the *tsotsis*.'

There is a murmur of laughter.

'Secondly,' Thabo continues, 'you will begin now to select young men for the second batch of volunteers. We want particularly those who are without any family responsibilities; these are not only a burden for us, but will also in time to come be a burden for the men themselves. Each one must understand completely what sacrifices will be imposed on him. We will not do anything until the first lot have arrived safely. When we have word, then we will let you know and you will proceed.'

'And the first lot, they have gone?'

'They will be gone soon. Everything is ready now. If we are successful with them, then the programme we have all agreed on can go ahead. If we fail with this first batch, we shall have to reconsider it all. Failure now will mean more delay.'

After the meeting is over, Thabo approaches Sipho. 'We have something to discuss with you.'

'Sit here.' Ntite offers him his chair, and leans against the table. 'You were late.'

Sipho explodes angrily. 'I? Late? I was on time, exactly on time. It was your messengers! I was driven around – I don't know for how long. Blindfolded like a prisoner. I lost all sense of what was happening, where I was going . . .'

273

'But that was the idea, of course.'

'You have to take such precautions with me? Has the time come when you no longer trust me? Why bring me here at all, then?'

'Why are you so angry these days?' Thabo asks. 'If we didn't trust you, we would have no more to do with you, you know that. But there is no doubt that you were followed, that day at the station. Now we have to be absolutely sure, one hundred per cent certain. Can we afford to leave a trail that will take the police to all of us?'

'We have a special task for you,' Ntite says, 'and we want to know one or two things first. Where do you sleep these nights, brother?'

'I stay at different places. To tell you where is as dangerous as if you tell me where you stay. You Comrade Thabo, where are you staying these nights?'

Thabo shakes his head. 'One night stops, here and there.'

'And I too,' Sipho says. 'Thabo, you know. Whenever there have been dangerous times, I have many rooms to which I can go. So why do you ask me now?'

'Look, brother, be calm. We don't want addresses. We just want to be sure that for the next week at least you will be absolutely safe, in no danger of being picked up. No backyards where there are likely to be raids. We also want to be able to reach you quickly if necessary. You can drive a car, I know, but have you ever driven a truck?'

'Everything, trucks, lorries, big or small. I can drive them.'

'We want you to drive the van with the volunteers. Can you do it?'

Sipho sits up straight. It is the old Sipho, ready for anything. 'To the border?'

'Yes.'

'And then?'

'Arrangements are being made now. Our people will meet you at the border, the men will be taken across, and you will come back with the van. Now, are you prepared for such a task?'

'Of course. When must we leave?'

'So far we cannot give the exact date, because we have to get the OK from the other side. It will be about a week, maybe a little more. What we want from you during this time is that you stay absolutely quiet . . .'

'And keep off the hard stuff.'

Sipho turns as if to speak, but changes his mind.

'Whatever happens, comrade,' Thabo says, 'from now on we depend on you. The whole organization and our work for weeks, maybe for months to come, depends on you, that you can deliver these young men safely.'

They shake hands. Is it true he looks changed, Thabo thinks, or am I imagining it? The drinking is dangerous. He has promised us he will not drink during this time. Perhaps he is losing his nerve. He never lacked for courage, he had more than that of three others put together. Can one's nerve just go?


Marie said 'I beg of you, isolate him for a while.'

'We need him,' Thabo replied. 'What makes you dislike this man so much? I have worked with him for a long time now. He has had information for years that could have put us away for life. What is different now?'

'I tell you, there is a period during which he disappeared, and it is from this time only that I became worried about him.'

'How do you know he disappeared? He has his own hideouts.'

'I went to try and find out,' Marie said. 'I know most

of his women. I know the ones he usually goes to. I went to each of them and asked for him. They all gave me the same answer, that they hadn't seen him for a couple of weeks or longer.'

'So? Is it not possible he found new companions?'

'I did not tell you everything. One night I followed him, from my own house. You had been there, and left. Did you know he has a car? He walked several streets, as far as the main road, just before you get to the petrol station. A car was parked there by the side of the road, and he got in and drove off. After that he was sleeping around his old places. Where had he been for that week or two?'

'He did not tell me he had a car,' said Thabo thoughtfully. 'I should think he just borrowed it for one night.'

'I'll tell you what I think, Thabo. I think he was arrested, and then they let him out so that he could lead them to others.'

'If that is so, then you must answer two questions. First, why should he make such a bargain with the police, a man like Sipho who has fought them all his life, and why should he make such an agreement in a matter of days? And secondly, then why has he not led them to others?'

'Only because of our vigilance. He was definitely being followed that time at the station. Since then, we have all been too careful not to arrange anything with him, only to bring him, as we did tonight, after we have taken all kinds of precautions.'

'And my first question?'

She was deep in thought. 'I find it hard to answer. I do not know why. He is a man with many weaknesses.'

'Women and drink? Many people drink a bit too much. We cannot all be perfect people. We all have our faults.'

She shook her head impatiently.

'You women in the Women's League!' Thabo said smiling. 'You don't like him because of the way he behaves with women.'

'Where would you be without the women from the Women's League? Look at us!'

'Yes, OK, you may be right. But listen, Marie, I will not see him again until next Sunday. It is arranged now. He will come to church and I will give him final instructions.'

He came at night to the home of Florence, walking entirely alone along the empty streets, his footsteps muffled by the dry dust.

She was disturbed. 'Is it right that you come by yourself? Is there not one who could come with you?'

'Why should there be?' Thabo asked. 'Can one man give me my safety?'

'It is possible. Alone you have no chance, whatever happens.'

'But alone I am safer, because nobody knows where I am tonight.'

She clicked her tongue and shook her head.

He sat down and removed his shoes while she went out to make up his bed. He was exhausted tonight in a way he had not been before. The exhaustion came from all the tensions of the past days, in which there had been so many meetings, so many things done.

She made him a cup of strong, sweet tea.

'But if anything goes wrong, Florence, you will know what to do, you will know how to contact the National committee, and all the regions.'

'I know,' she replied, 'because I have written it all in numbers, but it is better if nothing goes wrong.'

She had written everything in rows of numbers: instructions to each region; on what date the volunteers would arrive; to what places they would disperse. At night she had pored over the book that she had read in strange disconnected snatches. She flicked the pages over with her thumb to find the lines with the letters she needed, and read a few lines here, a paragraph there, first on one page, then on another. It was as though the whole book had been made up of these lines and sentences, written haphazardly, beginning in the middle of one event and finishing in the middle of another. It had become a book she could never really read, its significance resting not on the author's intentions but in the chance placing of the right variety of letters on one page.

'Florence,' he said, 'what I will never understand is what can make a man betray his own people.'

'Then you are as innocent as a child. I can think of many reasons.'

'Give me some.'

'For his own survival, first. We all fight for our own survival. Sometimes we fight together, sometimes we survive at the expense of others. Money, that's another reason. Or perhaps it is the same one. But there is greed as well, over and above the money one needs to survive. And fear. Or a wish to seek revenge. Or ignorance and stupidity. Is that enough? People do all sorts of strange things to others. I have seen them sometimes like a man who is drowning, who clutches at the hair of his best friend and pushes him under so that he can climb out and save himself.'

He shook his head.

'Who is it you are worrying about?' she asked.

'Marie has spoken to me more than once about Sipho. She does not trust him any more. I see no reason to suspect him, but still, she has passed on to me at least a few seeds of doubt. And it is our intention to place everything in his hands.'

'If she does not trust him, she must have reasons?'

'There was a week or ten days when he disappeared. It was the time of all the arrests. He said he had been lying low, with one or other of his women. Marie does not like the way he plays around with women, goes from one to another. What do you think?'

'I don't know him. What can I say? But if there is even the smallest doubt about him, any doubt at all, it would be better to find someone else to take his place.'

'He knows too much already.'

'Perhaps some things could be changed.'

'But I couldn't believe . . . we have worked together for years. I would not be able to understand . . . yet there is no doubt he has become very touchy and surly. His anger is always close to the top. Perhaps he is tired. After this, we will give him a long rest. That is the best thing. We are only human. Why should Sipho be any different? He, too, must sometimes long for another kind of life.'

Rebecca's smiling and familiar face at that moment came into his mind's eye, the thought of the night-long warmth and softness of her became a momentary reality, then disappeared. At what stage had the life so carefully constructed within this race-dominated society become less important than his inner convictions?

*I am a stranger, standing outside the home that once was mine, remembering my relinquished past. I am an alien, walking in fear and danger in the land where I was born.*

# Indres . . .

April came back at midday and said that Rebecca was not on duty at the clinic, and would not be there until the following day. Indres knew that he had to go out into the world again. He could not stay any longer in the protection of the cave, too far from town to be able to make contact with anyone else. To remain safe for the sake of remaining safe . . . no, there was no point.

April agreed to drive him into town. They had some bread and coffee, then set out in the lorry.

The day which had started deceptively mild and still, as though winter had already wholly departed, changed and dimmed; a sharp wind came in erratic gusts, stripping layers of dust off the mine dumps and dispersing them over the whole of the Rand. The sun became a lurid red eye behind a dusty halo.

They drove away from the quarry, taking a winding route towards the main road. Some distance from the road April stopped the lorry, and pointed ahead; beyond a cluster of trees there seemed to be a number of cars and men at the side of the road.

'What do you think's going on there?' he asked. 'Could be an accident. Or it might be a road-block.'

He looked at Indres. 'We don't want to be bothered with that kind of thing, do we? Well, it's all right, because I know another way.'

He turned the lorry round and drove across the veld. They skirted some mine buildings, then reached a dirt road leading away from the mine. Soon the road petered out, and once more they were bumping across the grass until, driving round the side of a mine dump, they emerged on to Commissioner Street which bore a mass of city traffic.

He drove through the city and across the complex of railway lines towards a suburb just to the north of the city itself.

'This where you want to go?'

'Yes. You can drop me over there, on the corner.'

'Sure you don't want me to wait?'

'Sure, thanks. I'll be OK.'

'Well,' April said, 'I'll go out again tomorrow to the clinic, like I promised you, and then tomorrow evening I'll wait for you down the bottom of Jeppe Street, after six.'

Indres watched him as he drove away. *He did not even ask my name. He called me mate, or pal. Whatever he guessed about me he did not probe or question or try to find out.*

When she arrived at her office in the morning, Elaine Stern found a note on her desk addressed to her and marked: By Hand. It read: *Can you come to my office as soon as you receive this. Urgent, Sydney.*

Sydney. Her husband's respectable brother, the one who kept his distance from Ralph and his radical associates, so that he could preserve the purity and moral standing of his flourishing criminal law practice. What on earth would Sydney want?

She told her secretary she would be out for an hour, then took the lift from the glossy corridor to the cement vault beneath the office building where her car was parked.

She drove up the steep ramp and into the city's morning congestion. She could easily have walked over to Sydney's office, but she always felt it was safer to take the car.

Portly and unsmiling, Sydney rose from behind his desk and said, 'I think we'll go to another office to talk.'

He knew enough about police methods to mistrust the privacy of his office – after all, he was Ralph Stern's brother, however detached he might be from Ralph's political views.

Sydney unlocked a room further down the corridor, and they settled themselves in the large leather armchairs.

'I asked you to come,' Sydney said, 'because a man came to my home last night, late. An Indian. He wants to get hold of Ralph. He keep saying it's very urgent, a matter of life or death.' Sydney said the words in a tone that conveyed disbelief.

'Who is he? What's it all about?'

'I had hoped that you would know. He says his name is Indres Ramjee. Do you know him?'

'Not really. I know who he is, I've probably met him, but I don't really recall . . . I thought I heard that he had been detained about the time that Ralph disappeared?'

'He was. He says he escaped from jail. He's on the run. I want you to take him off my hands.'

'Where is he now?'

'I let him stay overnight in our servants' quarters. It isn't safe for him and in any case, I am not prepared to risk harbouring an escaped prisoner.'

Elaine thought for a while. 'Look,' she said eventually, 'I will fix something up, but I need a few hours. In any case, it wouldn't be safe to move him during the day. I tell you what, we'll meet this evening. What time does it get dark? You bring him from your place, I'll have a car to pick him up.'

They completed details of where they would meet, then Elaine rushed back to her office, and in turn wrote a note marked *Urgent, By Hand*.

* * *

Outwardly they were two ordinary middle-aged women meeting for an early lunch. The restaurant was almost empty. They had a table under a window; there was nobody within earshot. Their eyes were always watchful.

'Sorry to bring you out like this,' Elaine told Rosa, 'but it is really very urgent.' She told her about her conversation with Sydney.

An Indian waiter in a white suit and cap with a scarlet sash draped across one shoulder took their order.

'How on earth did he get out?' Rosa wanted to know.

'He was in one of those suburban jails and he says he managed to get out of his cell onto the roof of the building, and then he jumped over the outside wall. It sounds hair-raising. But the thing is, I must pick him up later on today, Sydney won't let him stay, it isn't safe, and I don't trust Sydney in any case. Have you any suggestions?'

'Surely he would be safer among Indians? He must know someone who'd take him in for a short while?'

'He told Sydney the Indian homes are being raided too often.'

'This is difficult,' Rosa said. The waiter brought them bowls of salad and starch-reduced rolls.

'They taste like cardboard,' Elaine commented.

'Not if you put enough butter on them,' Rosa replied, and they both laughed.

When the waiter had gone, Rosa said, 'The problem is that he's an Indian. An African can be tucked away in someone's yard pretending to be a servant. Not an Indian.'

She looked at her watch. 'I haven't a great deal of time. I'm meeting Dick Slater's wife and driving out to Pretoria with her.'

'You've become quite friendly with her?'

'Yes, I like her. She's been pretty good – after all, she wasn't involved.'

'Can she be trusted?'

'Trusted? In what way?'

'Well, is it just loyalty to Dick?'

'She's certainly no friend of *theirs* . . .'

'Then what about asking her if she knows anyone . . . one of her "clean" friends?'

Margie had been waiting for more than ten minutes and was beginning to think she had made a mistake about the time or place, when she saw Rosa's car draw up.

'Sorry I'm late,' Rosa said, opening the door for her, 'but something cropped up at the last minute.'

They drew out onto the Pretoria road.

'It's such a boring trip on one's own,' Margie remarked. 'Forty miles each way just to pick up some dirty washing and drop clean clothes. It's good of you to come with me.'

'Oh well, I like to take an afternoon off sometimes; an excuse to get out of town, for a run in the country; to breathe some clean air. Anyway, I rather like this road, up and down and changing all the way; all these rows of wattle trees with their bark peeling off, and views of the veld beyond. Pity it's such a dreary day.'

'Last winds of winter.'

'Summer's coming.'

'Yes, it's nearly here. All the willows are out at the Zoo Lake. Swimming baths open next week. And it's the end of ninety-days.'

'Yes. Three months.'

As though preparing herself, Margie said 'Of course, they could do what they've done to some of the others – that dummy release, then re-arrest, slap them back into jail for another ninety days. But I don't think so. I think they're all going to be charged by next week. The Colonel as good as told me.'

'When did you last see Dick?'

'A couple of weeks ago.'

'I suppose he wasn't able to tell you what's happening?'

'Only what I've already told you.'

They had reached a place where the road curved down towards the Jukskei river, and then rose steeply again on the other side. For a while Rosa concentrated on her driving. Then she said, 'Listen Margie, you know why I was late? Elaine – that's Ralph Stern's wife – wanted to see me. She told me something . . . look, I want to ask you something, but please understand, if your answer is no, just forget about it, eh? Just forget I spoke.'

Margie felt herself tighten, on guard. 'About Dick?'

'No, not about Dick. Something else. We've got to find a place to put someone for a few days – someone who's on the run, hiding from the police. Do you know anyone, one of your friends, who might be prepared to take him just for two or three days?'

'Yes,' Margie replied without hesitation. 'I will.'

'Wait, wait. I didn't mean you. It must be somewhere safe.'

'I think my place would be safe.'

Rosa considered for a while. Then she asked, 'Have the police been there – since Dick's arrest, I mean?'

'No.'

'Not at all?'

'Never. Not once. They've got him. They probably know there's nothing on earth they can get from me. If they had thought so, surely they would have tried by now.'

'And you don't think your place is watched?'

'No. It's a very quiet street; you'd notice any cars going up and down, or parked nearby.'

'They mightn't be in cars.'

'You can't see into our house from the street. Anyway, the police have been quite decent to me.' As she spoke, she felt herself blush. The remark seemed to imply something of which she should be ashamed. She amended it by saying, 'Well, what I mean is, that they wouldn't be so polite if they thought I was mixed up in anything. I think your friend would be as safe in my house as anywhere.'

'Let's think about this first.'

'I have thought about it.' She looked at Rosa's anxious face. 'I've thought a lot about some such situation, doing something to help someone, I mean. I've never approached you because of Dick's position . . . I didn't think you actually trusted me. But I've hated not doing anything.'

'You surprise me,' Rosa said. 'I always thought you didn't want to be dragged into anything. You kept right out of things when Dick was becoming involved. At least, that's what I've been led to believe.'

'Yes, I did.'

'So you see, one would naturally assume . . .'

She said with some fire, 'You assumed, and Dick assumed, and all my life people have been assuming things about me.'

'Then why didn't you . . .'

'It was never expected of me. And I was never asked.'

Rosa considered this. Then she said, 'Of course, if you really want to do something you don't wait for others to ask you, you reach out to them.'

'That was all right when things were still operating on some sort of legal basis. It isn't easy when it's all secret. Then there's the business of being protected. I've always been protected by someone – my parents, boyfriends, husband. Perhaps I've always been standing on the edge, waiting for someone to come along and push me in.'

'Can you swim?'

'Oh, a little!' she answered smiling. 'I can keep my head above water, splashing around somehow.'

'It might be deeper than you think, Margie.'

She was going to add 'This man's not white,' but for some reason the words would not come. Instead she said, 'He's a friend of Dick's – Dick knew him quite well. What about your servant?'

'Elias? He's been with us ever since we were married. I would have to speak to him, of course, but I really feel I could trust him.'

'Any visitors?'

'I have so few. But in any case, it shouldn't be too difficult. There are places where he could go if someone came. Dick's dark room, for instance; I could lock him in.'

'There could be consequences for you. You must also think about your child,' Rosa said. The car crested the hill near Voortrekkerhoogte, and the angular arms of the Air Force monument high up on their right cut into the sky. 'Serious, perhaps. This man has escaped from jail.'

'What will happen to him, then?'

'I think he'll have to leave the country. He says no. But whatever it is, it would only be necessary for you to have him for a few days.'

'You see,' Margie said after they had been travelling in silence for a while, 'I do think about Jonny. There are too many reasons for not doing anything, aren't there? At what stage do you stop saying, my child, my job, my home, my possessions? How do you decide what is the most important thing, your personal safety and that of the ones you love, or the need to be human, to have integrity, courage, in the face of so much evil? Who can help you weigh it up? I don't know. I only know, I want to act in a certain way, now.'

Rosa said, 'How you've changed in these last three months! Could you have made such decisions before Dick was arrested?'

'It's been forced on me,' she replied quietly. 'Before, there was always someone to consult, someone to advise. I leant on others and respected their opinions. Now I have to form them for myself, I've had to make my own decisions. I used to rely on Dick for everything. Well, that's what's happened. I've had my own kind of ninety-days.'

She was surprised, sometimes, to see her own face in the mirror and notice the sameness about it, the unrevealing surface calm, the reflection asserting that she was the quiet and compliant wife who had never been suspected of thinking very deeply about anything, who had allowed life simply to take hold of her and flow all around her, almost as though she had been a spectator all the time, even in the one area of her life that was specifically hers, her marriage.

'Her house?' Elaine said in surprise. 'Isn't that taking a helluva chance?'

'I think not. In many ways it's a lot safer than you would think. Just consider it for a minute. They won't raid – they have no reason to raid. They know she wasn't mixed up in anything, ever. They've got Dick where they want him, and they've got him co-operating, that immediately takes them off guard as far as she is concerned. And it's such an unlikely place to put a non-white. Almost like putting him under their very noses, but where they wouldn't think of looking.'

'But in a very white suburb! Servants? Neighbours?'

'No, no. The house is really secluded. She doesn't have neighbours coming in. If her parents call, she says, she'll lock him in Dick's darkroom, where they wouldn't go in any case. He need never be seen at all by anyone who comes to the house.'

Elaine considered this for a while.

'Well, what do you say?' Rosa asked.

'I suppose it will do, as a stop-gap. There really must be a better place, among the Indian community. But it will take a little while to make contact, and find an alternative . . . Did you tell her who he was?'

'No, I just said it was a friend of Dick's, on the run.'

'But you told her he's a non-white?'

Rosa hesitated. 'I will tell her. I thought the less she knew about him, until you'd agreed, the better,'

'But she must be told that! It could make all the difference, she might refuse . . .'

'What difference can it make? I'll tell her. The big step for her is taking in a fugitive, becoming involved herself.'

'No, you're wrong there. The big step is having a non-white in the house in any capacity other than as a servant. That's the thing. Just because you yourself have black friends, you've forgotten what it's like for all the other whites. She may be starting to think differently, but she's never had any contact . . . it's a very big step, I tell you.'

He had arrived under cover of darkness, concealed in a car that drove right up to the house. Rosa had made the arrangements, and when it had been settled she said, trying to make it casual, 'Oh, his name, by the way – it's Indres Ramjee.'

Margie was startled. 'An Indian?'

'Yes. I hope you . . .'

'Oh, of course not.'

'I mean, once you had decided, I thought . . .'

'Doesn't make any difference at all.'

They were both speaking together. They stopped, and laughed in embarrassment.

No difference at all.

Except that she had never taken the hand of a brown-skinned man in her white one. Never consciously touched a dark-skinned person, except the black maids who cared for her when she was small. No difference at all, just a question of pigmentation. How could mere pigmentation make such a difference? But during her whole life she had been conditioned to react in a certain way to that difference.

They spoke to each other shyly, nervously, formally. He called her Mrs Slater, and she avoided using a name, the saying of his name aloud would establish some sort of relationship. She showed him to his room and asked him if he needed anything. Then went to her own room and waited.

She heard him go to the bathroom and listened, waiting for everything to be finished. When he returned quietly to his room and closed the door, she ventured out in her dressing gown. The house was still, as always at night. She knew she wanted to avoid casual contact and thought, it's shyness, we're both shy and awkward.

She always slept with her door open so that she would be sure to hear Jonny if he cried in the night. Now she returned to her room and drew the door until it was almost closed. Then pushed it slightly more open. How foolish! Would she feel like this if he were white? She climbed into bed and reached for her book. He spoke beautifully, and he was very good-looking. She focused her eyes on the printed page and read determinedly.

In the morning no one came to the house. Elias was there, polishing the floors, wiping away invisible dust, and talking to the little boy until he lay down on his cot and slept for the rest of the morning. Elias was an ally who watched the front of the house while he worked. The house opened onto a lawn at the back, facing north towards the sun. The garden was screened by trees and bushes, but Indres did not go outside; he could sit in the sun in his room.

'What will you do all day?' Margie had asked him.

'Read, sleep, wait until you come with news for me.'

'Just like being in jail, except for the books?'

'Ah no! You don't know what it's like – you can't imagine, unless you've been in jail. It's all luxury, everything. Beautiful clean sheets, the blankets, the pillow – all soft to the touch, so soft and clean. The smell of them – I can't tell you.'

She watched his face, and nodded.

'Everything. Knives and forks. The china; plates, cups. Then the garden, grass, flowers, bushes, trees, the spray of the hose in the sunlight. I could watch it for the rest of my life!' He laughed. 'Sun, air. Doors standing open. No slamming, no keys jangling. The choice of things. I can just sit here. I can look at the sun outside. I can take a book from a shelf, open a drawer, make some coffee, have a bath. Just waking in that bed in the morning – it's like being reborn. I wouldn't want anything else for the rest of my life . . . if it wasn't for the others.'

Jonny suddenly grasped Indres around his legs and looking up into his face, the little boy laughed and said 'Da-da-da-da.'

'He thinks you're his father,' Margie said, then blushed with furious embarrassment.

Indres took the child on his lap. There was an immediate rapport between them. All at once she felt relaxed, at ease, even light-hearted, as though some burden had been lifted from her. She wanted to say 'I'm glad you're here'. She wanted to touch the brown hand lying on the table.

'Be patient,' Elaine had said, 'we are doing what we can. It is not so easy, you know, to make contact these days.'

In the afternoon she had sent a messenger down to meet April who said that he had found Rebecca in the clinic and passed the message on to her.

April had written a note to Indres: 'I come by this street almost every day about this time. If you want me for anything, you will find me here.' April might have seen the story of the detainee who had escaped, for by now his picture had appeared in all the newspapers.

He tried to read, listening all the time for the sounds of Margie's car and her key in the front door. For two days she brought no news, other than the report from April. But this was not enough. Rebecca would probably not know where Thabo was staying, and she in turn would have to reach someone else to pass the information on to him.

On Monday Margie brought him a note: 'We will meet tonight and hope to see T there. M will bring you.'

He was pleased. 'You will be taking me, then?'

'Yes. I met Elaine today at a shop in town. You will come in my car, and then we will transfer to another one. And this afternoon someone is coming here to help disguise you.'

'Who is it?'

'A friend who is in the theatre. You can trust him.'

'You are worried about it?' she asked him.

'Only because there has been the publicity.'

'That's why the disguise is so important now. Without it, you must be more afraid of being seen by chance than anything else.'

Adam came in the later afternoon and looked him up and down.

'Yes,' he remarked, 'Margie is right. You will make a good Portuguese.'

He walked round Indres, who stood awkwardly.

'The hair,' he said. 'We will cut it differently, dye it brown. It must be thinned out a lot. That will make a great deal of difference. You will need a different kind of moustache, a long drooping one.'

'It would take too long,' Indres said anxiously.

'Oh no, don't worry about that. We won't wait for nature. We'll make it grow for you. Your skin is quite light actually. I've seen lots of whites on Durban beach with skins a darker shade than yours. You'll be surprised what a difference it makes when the hair is a different colour and the line is changed.

'And your clothes, of course; something cut differently, change the shape, that's important. And you must practice changing your walk, even the way you stand. I'll show you.'

'There's little time.'

'It's up to you. It would be better to have more time, but if you apply your mind to it you can make yourself into someone else. After all, actors do it every night of their lives. You must enter into the part.'

Jonny tottered over to clutch Indres' leg. He smiled and bent down to pick the little boy up.

'The teeth, too,' Adam remarked, 'they're too white. That's not difficult. And what about gestures and habits? Do you smoke at all? Pipe or cigarette? A pipe's a useful thing, we'll make you into a pipe-smoker.'

He arranged to come the following day to dye the hair, and said he would bring clothes with him.

'I promise you,' he told Indres, 'that you'll be able to walk down Eloff Street in broad daylight, and those Security boys will walk right past you without recognizing you.'

# *Thabo . . .*

Throughout the night there was the sound of drums and singing of hymns. In the morning the congregation of the Church of the Gospel of Zion gathered for a service in one of the rooms of the small primary school facing Number Two Square, just on the edge of Alexandra.

Dressed in their gleaming white and deep blue robes, carrying wooden crosses, the women filed slowly across the winter-scorched grass singing all the time; over and again a single voice rose high above the rhythmic chanting of the full chorus. There were a few men dressed in dark Sunday suits and at the head of the procession, bearing the largest wooden cross, the tall minister in a flowing white robe with bands of dark blue and gold, and a hat like a high priest of the Greek Orthodox Church.

The procession started in the street in the heart of the township, the women parading before the gates of the houses, pausing and prancing slowly, and singing as they drew their followers out of their homes. There was no given time for starting nor for finishing. Some had been singing and praying the whole night long, and some would continue the whole day and into the evening. The congregation shifted and changed, some left, others joined; from time to time during the day they would all leave the church to parade round the streets. It was this coming and going, this free and easy movement in and out of the service of the Church of the Gospel of Zion that made it possible for people to meet and pass on messages between the singing and the prayers.

Thabo marched in the procession and sat with the

singers on one of the low wooden benches in the school room. This morning the Church had gathered many followers; the room was packed.

A girl stood in the corner behind the preacher, striking a large drum from time to time. The drumbeats marked the rhythm of the singing. Then a long roll would bring an end to the repetitive chorus; and there was a second, longer roll like a warning before the minister began to speak. Single strokes on the drum punctuated his rambling sermon that seemed scarcely to have a beginning or an end; his stream of words drew murmured responses from the hearts of the congregation. In the confusion of mingled voices and soft repetitious drumbeats the preacher's voice maintained the tone and shape of a prayer.

Sometimes the congreagation sat on the benches, heads lowered, while the priest's voice rose loud and clear. Sometimes they slipped forard onto their knees and with heads in hands, voices filled with the poverty and grinding hardship of their lives, they wove into a tapestry of words their cries and petitions to God to help them and save them. Oh lord, find my children who have run wild and will not listen to their parents' pleas, and bring them home again. Oh lord, help my husband who lives only in the shebeen and has drunk away what small savings I had scraped together all these years. Oh lord, I pray that my son should be admitted to school for he will study hard, if only he can get a place, two years we have waited, next year he will be too old. Oh lord take this burden from me that is too heavy for me to bear, too heavy for me to bear. The prayers became louder and louder, the women rose and prayed and chanted, eyes closed, some standing by themselves, others moving in a kind of dance and calling out all the time. Sometimes they were just inarticulate cries, the sounds of their sufferings, longings, hopes, faith. Where would they be without this Sunday of singing and crying? What would they do if they could not believe in some higher and better and more benevolent life? How could they go on without this small crumb of hope? Without the chance to unburden themselves of the intolerable weight of their lives, their grief at families scattered and broken, their helplessness in the face of work unrewarded and children destroyed, their misery at being unable, by any means at all, to influence their own destiny and the fate of all those they loved?

Once a week they purged themselves, then took up their burdens again and endured.

There was a sound of singing from afar, increasing in volume as a new group approached the little school. Soon the chorus from outside joined with those inside, and for some minutes Thabo too was carried away on the wings of this soaring sound. Then a small shock of recognition: Rebecca was kneeling beside him.

He knew without looking at her the familiar shape of her face, the full lips flaring outwards, delicately delineated at the edge, her smooth skin, her dark eyes. 'Something is wrong?' he asked urgently. 'The children?'

'No, no,' she whispered between clasped hands, 'the children are fine. *U-khalipha ukungcatshile* – it is the bold one, he has betrayed you.'

The voices rose like a release:

> Lizalis' indinga lako
> Tixo Nkosi yenyanise
> Zide zithi zonk' ilwimi
> Ziluxelu' udumo lwako . . .

'I tried to reach you last night, but no one could find you.'

'Didn't Marie . . ?'

296

'Marie has been arrested.'

She saw the clasped hands form into fists; his head remained down as if in prayer.

'My husband, I am very much afraid for you. I am afraid.'

'I must leave then,' he said, rising to his feet. 'Sipho was here already. You stay until other women leave. Don't go alone.'

At that moment they both heard, clearly above the singing, the barking of a dog and a sharp order that silenced it. Through the window they saw the shapes of the men outside.

> Bona izwe lako wetu
> Uxolel' Izono zalo
> Unga tob' ingqumbo yako
> Luze luf'u sapho lwako . . .

'Find someone,' he said desperately in the few moments left, 'Peter or Ramishayo or Maponye, you must tell them first of all, above all, to take care of the volunteers. Listen, he does not know where they are staying, nor the day and the places where he is supposed to pick them up. *He does not know this.* Before all else, see they are kept out of his hands. They must get them away.'

The whole congregation rose to their feet; the chorus was punctuated by the sharp grind of boots. The minister turned towards the door, then back towards his congregation as though making up his mind about each one in turn until his gaze focused on Thabo and for a moment or two they stared at each other and understood. The priest shifted his eyes to the window and made a small gesture with his hand, then faced the door again as his congregation began to gather behind him.

'Care for the children and yourself,' he said. 'Stay safe. Go now, Rebecca. *Hamba kahle.*'

297

He plunged towards the open window and leapt out onto the hard ground.

Sunlight on metal reflected in blinding flashes. The procession of women moved slowly out of the door as the men came in, weaving a pattern of bright robes and dark suits, of warm dark faces and the grey and pink skins and close-cropped, capped heads of the men.

He ran across the square. He heard the choir of voices rising into the thin air:

> Yala Nkosi ingadeli
> Imfundiso zezwi lako;
> Luze luf' usapho lwako . . .

The singing and the noise faded into the wind, the wind pressed against his face. He was driven forward by all those years of secret struggle, impelled by the strength of resistance. Desperate chance . . . if he could reach the houses at the bottom across the gully . . . if they did not shoot, if they did not shoot . . .

A great weight struck him to the ground and as he tried to turn on his back a massive Alsatian stood over him with teeth bared. There were more dogs. Running down after the dogs, the men, with guns held ready. Behind the men, the minister with moving lips and hands, like the conductor of an orchestra.

> 'Zonk' intlanga zonki zizwe
> Mazizuze usindiso . . .

They came forward with handcuffs ready. The flood of sunlight dazzled his eyes and the sound of singing was like fire leaping in his heart.

# Pila . . .

There was a black man on the plane. He looked in his fifties, a well-built man with a broad face and a very black skin. He wore a felt hat and carried a bulging brief case. He was allowed on the plane after everyone else, and as they packed coats onto the rack above their heads and hand-luggage under their seats, the white passengers watched him coming aboard. To ensure segregation a row of three seats had been kept for him at the very back of the plane.

'I wonder where he's going?' Mrs Norval remarked.

'To London, like everyone else,' Pila replied sharply. 'Where else could he be going, on this plane?'

'Oh, that's not exactly what I meant. Of course I know where the plane's going, but I wonder what he's doing on it . . . I mean, what would a native be going overseas for?'

*You are my mother, and we are together for a while, therefore I must not make it worse for both of us . . .*

'He's a professor from Fort Hare,' she said evenly. 'He's probably going to a UNESCO conference in New York that I read about.'

'A professor! Fancy that . . . a native. And you actually know him, Pila?'

'No, I recognize him from his photo. I knew his son, though. He was at Wits the same time I was, but he left the country. He wanted to study nuclear physics and they wouldn't let him.'

'A professor. Well, it bears out what you've always

299

said, doesn't it dear? Although of course, it's different when they're educated.'

'What's different?'

'I mean, an educated man, even if he is black, is more like . . . Bit by bit, I expect, they'll begin to get more . . . I do agree with your father, it's education that will make all the difference, given time, of course, and it does take time. Even then, we can't all be professors, can we?'

The words flashed on in both official languages: Fasten your seat belts. No smoking.

Members of the crew walked along the aisle looking downwards at the peoples' laps, and occasionally leaning over to show a passenger how one end of the seat-belt clipped in to the other. Hostesses with enamelled faces and little caps perched on lacquered hair offered trays of sweets. The plane moved slowly onto the runway.

The airport buildings came momentarily into view, with a fringe of tiny figures on the viewing platform.

'Of course you couldn't see him from here, even if he had waited,' Mrs Norval said. 'And if I know your father, he's half-way back to his office by now. It would have been nice if he could have come with us. Still, next year, he promised, we'll both come over together to visit you.'

'I should think he's more likely to stay with those Special Branch friends of his, to see I really do get off.'

'Oh now, dear, they're not exactly his friends.'

'You both behaved as though they were.'

'And you were very rude, running off like that to the Ladies and not coming out until the last moment. After all, they're only doing their job, aren't they? And they kept all those nosy reporters away, you wouldn't have wanted to be pestered by them, I saw one of them confiscate a camera. Why should you have anything against them personally? I thought they were very polite, very polite indeed. They asked all about our trip, where

300

we were going, and where we thought we'd be staying. The older one said he knew London, but he didn't like it. Couldn't stand the climate, and dirty! People never bath, nothing to do, tennis only for two or three months in the year, soft courts – grass – the ball doesn't bounce the same, and you swim indoors! He thinks there's more to do in Joh'burg than in London. But I must say, I'm looking forward to seeing the West End shops.'

Now the engines were reaching a pitch of frenzy, before the race that would lift the plane with its load into the air. It was a long stretch, the dry grass and distant small buildings rushing madly away. Pila sat with her face turned towards the window, watching the ground, watching the red earth where the cement ended. Suddenly, they were looking down on tilted corrugated iron roofs. *At this moment I leave my country, my people, everything I care about; but that's just sentimental, the moment of departure is not now; it was when they released me, without any interrogation; it was when my father went to the Minister; it was when they put me in a cell with a bed, and sheets. It was when I was born with a white skin.*

'Perhaps you'll change your mind and come to Paris with me.'

'Please, Mum, you know I do want to find a place to live first.'

'Yes, well, and I want to see you settled before I return, but it would be nice to forget everything and just be like tourists, carefree, seeing all the sights. We could find a good hotel. No worries.'

Ochre earth and tawny grass – the true colours of the high veld. And there below, there in the featureless, empty, open land, was a black man dressed in a respectable dark suit, white shirt, tie, sitting upright on a bicycle in the middle of the open veld, pedalling silently from nowhere to nowhere – oh, Africa! Features merged,

301

tracks disappeared, single clouds appeared below them, casting motionless shadows of blue ink on the dry red-grey earth.

'Miriam told me about some fascinating little boutiques in Paris, but you know, I do think it takes a lot to beat the shops we have in Joh'burg these days, but of course it is nice to see the clothes at the actual season, the time they first come out, instead of always being six months behind because of the different seasons. You know? Winter in Europe when it's summer at home. They can't be so bad, Pila, can they, if they actually let him travel overseas?'

'Who?'

'The . . . native, the professor, there at the back. You said they won't let them have passports.'

'Oh, he's never opposed the government. He's one of their good boys.'

'Well, and what's wrong with that, I'd like to know? Do we all have to be rebels? Why do you always have to be opposing something? There's good and bad in all of us, that's what I've always said. Oh, we did agree not to talk politics, didn't we? We're putting it all behind us, all the unpleasant things.'

*Emily had come one morning and said, 'It's all right, Miss Pila, I hear they get your message all right.'*

*So perhaps later on it will be possible to make contact again with Thabo, or Indres, and do something from London. There are others there, voluntary and involuntary exiles . . .*

> I am that exile
> from a future time,
> from shores of freedom
> I may never know . . .

302

*'If you keep away from those anti-apartheid groups,'* her father had said, *'just keep your nose clean and you'll see, in two or three years I will be able to fix it so that you can come back.'*

*Back to what?*

*Perhaps there will be things to do. Perhaps it will all happen sooner than anyone thinks.*

# Indres . . .

'There,' Margie said, 'there it is.'

She slowed down and parked behind the stationary car; turned to smile at him. 'Good luck, and take care!' And she drove away.

Indres put his hand on the door of the other car. A woman's voice said, 'In the back.'

She waited for him to open the back door and climb in. 'Nice to see you again,' said Elaine Stern as she drove off. 'How are you, OK?'

'Oh yes, well looked after. But I'll only feel really OK after tonight, when I've seen him.'

'Yes, I can understand that,'

'It's been so difficult to get him.'

'That's the way it should be.'

The journey was a short one. They arrived at a part of the city towards the east where commercial and industrial buildings mingled with small garment gactories, sweatshops, a few general stores run by Indians, cafés with disordered windows obscured by steam and dirt. The council would probably clear the area of its Asian shopkeepers, it had to be re-zoned, to be made over into the kind of conformity that separated races and purposes. Not far away was the Albert Street Pass Office where ragged crowds of blacks spent weeks of their lives trying to obtain the right jobs, the right permits, the correct stamp on their passbooks that would enable them to survive legally. But at this hour it was locked up, dark, quiet.

Elaine stopped the car close to a corner where three

streets came together. 'There, you just walk along there, the first door on your right, it's marked Kat Klub. It's a night club, but they're always closed on Mondays. Go straight up the stairs, someone will be waiting for you. I'll be back in exactly one hour. Check your watch. I make it eight o'clock. I'll meet you here at nine. Be on time, I can't hang around here.'

And like Margie she added, 'Good luck!'

He turned the door handle and pushed; it was not locked. He mounted carpeted stairs, heart beginning to pound. On the landing were a number of doors, but a man emerged from the shadow, nodded in greeting and said, 'This way'.

Indres followed him into the clubroom. There was a stage at one end strung with coloured lights, and littered with a jumble of drums and amplifying equipment. Partitions sprouted from the sides, forming cubicles which each contained a table and wooden benches and lampshades swathed in pink tulle. The windows were blacked out with boards and draped with pink, mauve and blue netting. Faded coloured streamers, remnants of some wedding or special occasion, trailed from the ceiling.

They crossed the floor in near-darkness. A man sat at one of the tables, face in shadows, coat collar turned up. As Indres slid into the seat opposite him, he half-rose to greet him.

'Welcome, brother,' said Kabelo, putting his arms round Indres' shoulders and hugging him.

They both spoke together. 'It's good to see you,' Kabelo began, and 'I thought that – ' said Indres, and stopped.

'Is he coming?'

'Sit, sit. You've had some adventures, isn't it? Man, we were proud you go away.'

'We haven't much time,' Indres said, 'Will Thabo be coming, Kab?'

Kabelo shook his head. 'He is not coming, comrade. Yesterday he was picked up.'

'Yesterday! Oh God, and I got out Thursday.' He drew his breath. 'I wasted time, I could have warned him.'

'It was not so easy to reach him.' Kabelo stretched his arm across the table. 'Rebecca got the message you sent through the other man. But even Rebecca did not know where to find Thabo.'

'Where did they get him?'

'At the church of the King of Zion in Orlando.'

'Then someone must have told the police he would be there. Someone who knew.'

'It must have been.'

'But who knew? Did Sipho know?'

'Sipho knew. He was to have . . .'

Indres interrupted passionately 'It was Sipho who betrayed him. Do you realize that?'

'It could have been. But what makes you so sure?'

'Is there any doubt?'

'Sipho was not the only one who knew he would be there. They surrounded the church. Rebecca went to warn him. They let everyone through, they only wanted him. Tell me what you know, tell me what happened to you.'

'About Sipho?'

'About the whole thing. We must know how much they know.'

'They know a lot,' Indres said, 'but there's also a lot they don't know.' And he related to Kabelo the days of questioning, the torture, the decision to make a statement.

And finally he said, 'And now I will tell you about Sipho. When Sipho and I were in Durban together we

306

went out one night on a job we had arranged ourselves. Just the two of us. No one else knew about it. We went down the South Coast and tried to set a train on fire. It rained, and it didn't go too well. We had a torch with us and we left it behind, in the bush. I wanted to go back for it, because we hadn't been wearing gloves, but Sipho wouldn't let me go. But I worried about it afterwards, I couldn't stop thinking of that torch lying there with my fingerprints on it. To be so careless! The next afternoon I took a train down the coast and decided to recce. I thought the police might be tramping around, but there was nobody. I found the torch exactly where I'd left it, put it in my pocket and took it away. Now, Sipho didn't know I'd gone back for the torch. I never told him.'

'Why not?'

'I think we were both ashamed of the amateurishness of the whole thing. And we had quarrelled that night. We just did not speak about it again. Now, all the time they were trying to get me to talk, they kept on letting out little bits of information they had about me, just to show how much they knew. And one of them kept on saying, "You'll be up for sabotage. We got your fingerprints." Then this chap started saying, "That was stupid, wasn't it, leaving that torch with your prints lying around in the bushes. We matched your prints." When they let me go back to my cell I would try and work out what they'd been saying. But the torch – what torch? I'd taken the torch. But I could not believe that Sipho . . . then you gradually put different things together. They frighten you with what they seem to know, but they're playing a game, they want you to fill in the gaps. Then you begin to see who else they've got, who they could have got information from. They taunt you, this one's talked, he's spilled the beans, that one's going to testify against you. But they never talked about Sipho. But how could I believe Sipho had talked? Why would he tell them about that night? Not unless he was really talking.'

'Wait,' Kabelo interrupted, 'could it not have been possible Sipho told someone else in Durban about it? And that person talked?'

'Kab, you know what happens? You have all the time in the world to work it out. First, you know Sipho, how he hated failures, he never even wanted to discuss our mistakes, he would rather hide mistakes. And we were pretty good on security by that time. We never told anyone anything they didn't need to know. Why should he speak about this? But then, if he had, then that person had been picked up and forced to make a statement and to have described this incident, and not first-hand. And that just isn't on.'

'Why not?'

'Because it doesn't work that way. They force something out of you. You give. You decide just to confirm things they already know. Maybe just give them a little bit more information that doesn't involve someone else. But you don't talk about jobs they have never mentioned. You don't volunteer new information. Mostly what you are doing is putting your own head more tightly in the noose.'

Kab nodded his head. 'I'm going to tell you now what's been happening. Listen. We have this first group of volunteers – they're going outside for training. If they get out, others will follow. These are the first. Sipho was to have driven them out. Thabo arranged transport; he and Sipho were to meet at the church where Sipho would get his final instructions, where to pick up the van, where to pick up the men. But at the last minute Thabo didn't tell him. We know that. We don't know why, something must have alerted him; when Rebecca came to warn him Sipho had already left; Thabo said "Sipho doesn't know

308

the day and the places." He told her "Above all else they must get away".'

'Will it still be possible?'

'It's not finally decided, it looks too difficult. We have to find other transport for a start – only Thabo knew about the van. Then there will be road-blocks out . . .'

'They won't stop the van,' Indres said. 'They'll be waiting at the border. If they stop the van, what can they charge them with? Sipho's evidence in a court would not be enough. There must be independent corroboration. They'll try to get them in the act of crossing.'

'There are many things to consider,' said Kabelo. 'We had everything arranged on the other side. It isn't easy, it's a long way to go, all that way through Africa. You know? Some of them don't want us coming through. We had it arranged the whole way.'

'But if they don't know the day . . .'

'And supposing . . . I think Thabo'd never talk, but supposing they break him?'

'It takes time,' Indres said. 'Even if they really torture you, you're strong at first. Even if Thabo should crack, it would take four or five days – more, with Thabo. It's not the violence, that's bad enough. It's being without sleep. Your mind gets confused, you lose control of your own thoughts, even your words. I spoke in my sleep. I woke and found myself standing there, speaking. I had been dreaming, in my dream someone spoke to me and I answered . . . but that takes a few days.'

'So there's still the possibility,' said Kabelo, 'if we can move them soon – but the problem is how to get transport.'

He was transferred from one car to another in a suburban street, and lay on the floor covered with a rug while Margie drove him back to the house.

Inside she put her hand on his arm and exclaimed, 'I was so worried! I felt you were safe as long as I knew where you were, but once you were out of sight . . .'

Her face was eager, fresh, young. He felt attracted to her physically and began to forget his misery over Thabo. He followed her into the room, seating himself away from her in the semi-darkness.

The rain clouds had rolled up that evening, indigo clouds that promised the rains of summer, but as night came the sky cleared, the clouds massed and disappeared beyond the horizon. Lightning flicked along the rim of the veld.

'You look tired,' she said.

'Not tired, depressed. It was bad news. The man I spoke about – they've picked him up.'

'Oh, how awful! When did it happen?'

'Only yesterday. I should have reached him. I wasted time.'

'But you tried. Maybe you couldn't have prevented it; you can't blame yourself.'

'Oh yes, we are all to blame. Cowardice, carelessness, whatever it was, we are to blame. Sipho and myself and Dick.'

He looked at her. 'I'm sorry. I didn't mean . . .'

'No, it's all right, Indres, I know about Dick. The Special Branch think he will be a state witness.'

'He still has a chance to change his mind. There is time. Sometimes, at the moment they are in the witness box and stand up in court, before all those people, then they refuse to testify. It will be terrible if he doesn't. Worse for him than the ones he testifies against. He has to live with himself.'

'Do you think he might refuse?'

'I don't know. You are married to him. You must know him better than I.'

'But you worked with him.'

'Yes, off and on. Ever since I started going to Wits I had something to do with him. He had a lot of doubts all the time. He seemed more sure of himself in the past few months.'

'I think he was happier.'

'Yes, maybe. We are all happy when we are active, when there is work to be done. It's doing nothing that kills you. We were very happy for a while.'

'I keep worrying, wondering what will happen to him.'

'He will be released if he does what they want. Not at first. They'll take their pound of flesh. They'll make him pay not just once, but over and over again. But perhaps he will refuse.'

'You say that to comfort me.'

'Or to comfort myself. It's so hard to believe. Nothing hurts so much . . . you just get to love someone, so you can't believe that person . . . you keep saying, it's not true, I don't believe it. Then they show you statements . . . They set out to destroy you, to break you completely. To humiliate you so you can no longer live with yourself. They must prove they are stronger, more powerful, and for that they have to annihilate each one of us. It's not only that they make you feel so utterly powerless. I began to feel everything we had done was worthless. They break your life into small fragments. Then you are completely without hope. Maybe that's how Dick feels. Perhaps he'll find a way of recovery later on.'

'And the other one?'

'Sipho? It was different. I don't think they held him long enough to break him. They let him out to act as their stooge. He changed sides. As though it were a game.'

'Perhaps he was playing for time, trying to outsmart them.'

'That sounds more like Sipho. He might have thought that, but then it goes wrong. They set traps, you walk into them. Sipho was always a very fearless man, but you have no idea of what fear is until you are truly in their hands.'

'I think Dick was pretty frightened, but I didn't really know how involved he was.'

'Didn't he tell you? Sometimes husbands and wives . . .'

'Partly his own discipline, I expect, but mostly he wanted to protect me and Jonny.'

'You never asked anything?'

'No.'

'What did you think then, about yourself?'

She turned away, rose and walked across the room, picked up a newspaper, folded it carefully, put it down again.

'It's something to do with the way we whites live,' she said in a low voice. 'We live double lives, on different levels.'

'When I was young,' Indres said, 'I played with white boys, I went into their homes, we were friends, real friends. It is that way in country areas. My family were traders and the adults didn't mix socially, not at all, but we children started without any kind of colour-consciousness. Until we were old enough to go to school, then suddenly we were separated, I didn't really understand that, and one day I saw my best friend, a white boy, I hadn't seen him for some time. He was with two other boys. I ran across the road calling his name – Piet, Piet. He turned and looked at me – the expression on his face! "Coolie," he spat at me in disgust, "what do you want, Coolie?"

312

'But really,' he continued, 'I wanted you to know that I didn't have strong feelings about colour at first. And even now. I have very good friends who happen to have white skins.'

'Oh no!' she said. 'Those who are your friends – they're not the ones I'm talking about. How many whites in this country have Indian friends? I mean the rest, all the others, not your exceptions. All of us, the whole nation of whites who know, and conceal what we know. It's so perfectly simple. We live by a lie, we cushion ourselves from the truth. From the moment we start to walk and talk.'

She lay in bed, unable to sleep.

She was a small child with fair straight hair, plaited and tied with bright ribbons. She climbed onto the wooden base of the gate and swung back and forth.

An old African came down the street. His clothes were a series of rags, each held by some connecting link to another, but giving the impression that if you pulled lightly at one the whole would disintegrate and fall to the ground. A face like a dried prune, intensely black, was crowned by crinkly hair that was almost white. She had never before seen a black person with white hair. She could not even believe that the black hair of a black person could turn white. She stopped swinging and stared, fascinated.

He stopped at due distance from her, deferential in posture, and put one hand to the strange white hair in greeting.

'*Nkosasaan*. Is the big missus home, little missus?'

She stared without answering.

He genuflected slightly and said again, 'Could the little missus call the big missus?'

She aroused herself, remembering her rôle. 'What do

313

you want?' she asked in the autocratic tone used by white people when talking to blacks.

'Work, little missus,' he replied.

She ran into the house calling, 'Mom! Mom! There's a boy at the gate. He wants to know if we have any work.'

'Tell him no,' a voice replied from somewhere in the house.

She ran outside again, feeling important. The old man was sitting on the kerb, his back towards her. 'Jim!' she called, 'The missus says there's no work.'

He rose stiffly from the kerb, he saluted her humbly, he walked away slowly with bent legs, down the street. *There's a boy at the gate* . . . There were many boys and girls in her life.

She was on a bus with her mother.

'Why are there so many nannies standing around there?'

'It's their day off. They're waiting for a bus to go and visit their friends.'

'They can't get on this bus, can they?'

'No, of course not. They have their own buses.'

'But Sophie comes on the bus with me when she takes me to school and fetches me.'

'That's different. When she has a white child with her she can go on a white bus and sit with you upstairs, at the back. But when you're not with her, she has to walk to the school.'

Her parents went out a lot. The maid, Sophie, stayed in the house to look after her. She was afraid of the dark, and used many ploys to delay the moment when Sophie would turn the light off and leave her alone in her room. She called her back many times. 'I'm thirsty, Sophie, please bring me a glass of water. Sophie, I'm too hot, I can't sleep. I want to make a wee, Sophie.'

Sometimes she would get up very quietly and creep

along the passage into the kitchen, where Sophie would be sitting on a chair doing some crochet or knitting; or perhaps just sitting, upright and silent, her hands on her lap, her dark face plunged deep in some unknown reverie.

One night she opened the kitchen door and without premeditation, moved by that shrouded face, those burdened eyes, and by her own inexpressible fears and loneliness, she climbed into the lap of the African woman and put her arms round her neck. Then she saw with amazement that tears came to Sophie's eyes. All her young life black servants, boys and girls, moved around the perimeter, cleaned, gardened, dressed her and made her bed, cooker, laundered, sold ice creams or delivered the bread, the gorceries and the milk. Some were silent by nature and some were cheerful, but it was not like whites, it was on a different level. Africans were like children, her father often said, that was why they remained boys and girls all their lives. They liked to talk in loud voices, and at Christmas they all had noisy parties in their backyard rooms and drank too much, and at midnight when the New Year came, they banged with sticks on the metal telegraph poles, making the white suburbs resound.

But that their hair could grow white, that they were capable of feeling happiness in the same way as whites, or sorrow like whites, this had never occurred to her.

'Why are you so sad, Sophie? Don't be sad!'

The woman held her close. 'When you came in the door like that,' she said, 'you reminded me for a moment of another little girl.'

'Who is she? Was she a little girl you used to look after, before you came to look after me?'

'Yes, I used to look after her.'

'Where is she now?'

'She is far, far. She lived in the country, far from here.'

'Is she as big as me?'

'As big as you. Just the same.'

'Who looks after her, now that you are here?'

She felt the warm protecting arms around her, the heaving of those large and comforting breasts. 'Her Ouma cares for her, but she is very old.'

'I wouldn't like my Ouma to look after me.' The young voice was very firm. 'She's too old and too fussy. I like you best, Sophie, better than my Ouma.' She thought for a moment, then said defiantly, 'I like you better than Mom and Dad! You won't leave me, will you? You'll stay here with me?'

She was enfolded by dark flesh whose warmth and smell had become so familiar to her, she was rocked gently to sounds that hummed into her head, she drifted into sleep, aware of being carried and placed carefully in her own bed, aware of being covered; too far gone to move or utter a sound other than a sigh, but aware, too, beyond the border of her own comprehension, of the tears of some unbearable sorrow of which she was an indissoluble part.

She was a feminine child who never tried to be a tomboy. Her mother said she was a good little girl. She enjoyed the rôle of being a good little girl. Her school reports were predictable, she joined in all the sports, she was pretty without being beautiful, nobody was ever made to feel inferior by her looks or her achievements and for this, as much as anything else, she was well liked by both sexes. She fulfilled all expectations of her. Her mother said 'She'll make someone a good little wife.' The piano she bought after she was married was a reminder, perhaps, that she had wanted to study music but had been discouraged by her parents. 'Unless you're a genius,' her father told her, 'you can never reach the top; and then what do you become? A music teacher . . .' It was obviously more sensible to take a course that would be of some use after she married.

She studied domestic science when she first left school, and excelled at cooking and baking. She could produce exquisite flaky pastry, she loved kneading and baking bread, she created in her own kitchen delectable little ravioli filled with spinach and brains, she could decorate cakes with whirls of chocolate or sugared violets or even real flowers. She designed and made her own clothes. She was so capable, so clever with her hands. Then she did a teachers' training course.

The years were punctuated with few sorrows – an aunt who died of cancer, a dog run over by a car – and with the spectacular pleasures provided by climate and land, mountains and sea, prolonged summers, routines smoothed by the removal of all unpleasant chores. The years unreeled with lenitive ease; what they said she would be, she became, and she herself reflected her own life, gentle, subdued, tranquil, seemingly content. The wounds of all the incidents remained, scarcely observed and yet absorbed: the incomprehensible loss of that other child; the dark eyes of the Indian girl who walked away; servants who came and went trailing their portions of trouble, police raids in the backyard rooms, husbands sleeping illegally with wives, dragged forth and put in the pick-up vans; imprisonments; lost passes; homelessness; the scent of poverty.

His words echoed in her ears: 'You never asked anything?'

There had been no reason to ask.

*I knew always, but I concealed the truth.*

She switched on the light. She heard a door open softly and the sound of someone moving around. She put on a dressing gown and opened the door of her bedroom.

Indres came from the direction of the kitchen, wearing

only the shorts of his cotton pyjamas, and carrying a glass of water.

'Oh, I'm so sorry,' he exclaimed, 'did I disturb you?'

'No, it was not you. I couldn't sleep.'

Becoming aware of himself, he muttered 'excuse me,' and went to his room to put on a shirt.

'It's impossible for me to stay inactive like this,' he said, as he came back to her.

They went to sit in the lounge in the dark, not wanting to switch on lights so late at night. The curtains were drawn back a little on the glass doors that framed a garden immobile in the moonlight. A single cricket chirruped irregularly, a small sound that seemed to emphasize the silence.

He said suddenly, 'They want me to go.'

She did not understand. He saw the questioning turn of her head.

'To leave the country, they think I must leave.'

'And you don't agree? How can you stay?'

'I thought if I could get disguised, find some sort of cover job . . . maybe move, go to Natal or down to the Cape . . . I think enough people have left the country already.'

'But you would always be living in fear and danger.'

He shrugged. 'The real thing is, it's easier for Africans, they are surrounded, covered, concealed by their own people, wherever they are. For us Asians it's much more difficult, we're a small group and there isn't unanimity . . .' He broke off, then added 'For whites, of course, I would think it's virtually impossible.'

'So what will you do?'

'I think I will have to leave. As soon as something can be arranged.'

She said suddenly, 'You knew Pila Norval, didn't you? The girl who left on an exit permit?'

'Yes, I knew her.'

'Well, her father has a farm right on the border. I went there once; it was the end of summer, just before the arrests. All those business men are buying great big farms, it's one way to avoid super-tax; huge tracts of land. It would be dead simple to cross the border from that farm.'

'Where is it?'

'I'll show you.' She jumped up and went to the bookshelf, then squatted on the floor to withdraw large art books that were piled on the bottom shelf. Her loose gown fell away revealing rounded thighs.

She stood up holding an old school atlas. 'Here it is, I knew it was somewhere there.'

She put it on a small table, and they drew up chairs side by side as she flicked through the atlas until she came to a full-page map of the Transvaal.

'It's at a place called Derdepoort in the Marico district. The Groot Marico river marks the border between the farmlands and Bechuanaland. Here it is' – she pointed at the map – 'just around here. The river would be bone dry at this time of the year – most of the year, for that matter, they hardly get any rain. You simply walk across the dry river bed. It's a simple as that.'

'Who lives on the farm?'

'Well, there's this house, the farm manager lives there with his family.'

'A white?'

'Yes, a white. Then the farm labourers live in huts some distance from the house.'

'Any dogs?'

'Yes, two or three big dogs. They all keep dogs on those farms. The road runs like this – ' she drew an imaginary map on the floor with her hand – 'there's a gate here, the farm buildings are not visible from the road. There's a barbed wire fence all along this side. The house is here, the African huts just over here. We walked down to the river, along here, and because of the slope of the land it's completely hidden from the farm buildings. If you go, Indres, this might be the way to cross over. If they have patrols along the border, the only places they won't be patrolling will be the white-owned farmlands.'

'How do you reach the farm?'

'You go through Rustenberg, then turn off the main road. Then it's dirt roads all the way, mostly through reserve country.'

'It would be difficult to find. If one landed up on the wrong farm . . .'

'Not too difficult.' She bent forward and her hair swept softly over his arm. 'The scale of this map's too small, but we could get a map of the area and make straight for Derdepoort. You don't pass a town the whole way. There's a concession store at the crossroads a few miles from the farm. You can recognize the farm by the row of trees planted on either side of the gate. It wouldn't be difficult to leave a car and approach the farm on foot. I would know the way to the farm, after you leave the crossroads . . . I would take you, if you wanted me to.'

Their arms lay side by side on the table, on the atlas. She looked down, suddenly aware of that smooth, almost hairless, brown arm now touching her own, seeing the tendons that moved beneath his skin and radiated out to his long fingers. She took his hand and pressed it gently into the cleft between her breasts.

She had always held back something of herself, even with Dick. Now it seemed as though the reserve had melted away.

He was deeply moved by her words and her gesture. He heard himself say, as though from a distance, 'You are prepared to do that?'

She rose and walked to the window. 'I don't want you to go, only I know you can't stay.'

He went and stood behind her. She remained without moving, her face averted.

'Margie,' he said softly, 'what is it?'

He began to touch her, to stroke her hair, to let his hands wander over cheek, neck, shoulder. He said, 'You are so beautiful.'

'It's not true,' she whispered. 'It's an illusion.'

'I think you're beautiful.'

He held his face against her hair. 'You don't know what it's like,' he murmured, 'you don't know what it's like.'

'What don't I know?'

'Not to be able to touch someone. I never knew how marvellous it was just to touch someone's hand, someone's hair . . . your skin is so soft. The worst thing is this killing of human contact. When you're in jail you forget what it means. You know something is lost, you ache with it, you don't know what it is. What incredible cruelty, to put people into little cells, to shut them away from each other! To separate men and women . . . I wish I could stand here, just touching you, for the rest of my life.'

Her tears spilled over.

'Oh please, please, Margie, don't be sad, don't cry! Is it because of Dick? It's hard for you, it's always hard for one who is left.'

She shook her head, clinging to him. 'No, it's not Dick. I'm not sad. It's happiness, really. I never felt alive. I feel as though my life has only just started. I so much wanted you to touch me, I wanted . . .'

She felt that in this house, and because she was white and married, she had to take the initiative. Her hands moved over his bare body beneath the open shirt. She

321

felt her love go out to him as though it were to all those from whom once she had stood aside.

He said, 'Margie, Margie, you've brought me back to life.'

'No,' she said. 'It's you – you've made me feel alive. I couldn't live like that any more. I was so isolated. I need you, Indres, I need you.'

She was surprised at her own passion.


Lying in bed beside Margie, he remembered how he and Pila had trembled on the verge of an affair, both afraid to make a decisive gesture. Pila always seemed so sure of herself, but he suspected it was protection against deep uncertainties. Sipho once teased him about her. 'Do you sleep with that girl?' he asked. 'No'. 'Why not? Is she not to your liking?' That was the one thing about Sipho, more than his drinking, that had annoyed him, the way he talked about all his women. 'If I go to one of those mixed parties,' he would say, 'you know, the *liberals*,' – and the voice was scornful, 'I can lay any woman in the place if I choose.'

He had replied, 'Why do you talk like that, Sipho? Why should you want to, in any case?'

'To show how easily those high-class white dames lie on their backs and open their legs waiting to be fucked by a black man . . . Yes, man, some of them can hardly wait, they want it so bad. They think this thing has something different. So I give it to them.'

He was laughing. He went on, 'And then there are others, they haven't found a way of rejecting a black man in the same way that they would refuse a white. They think to themselves "If I refuse, he'll think I'm a racist", and they don't want me to think that. Or else – one of them told me this – they're not sure in their own minds. They're not sure whether they don't want to fuck with

322

me because I just don't turn them on, or because I'm a black man. They're thinking "What's holding me back? Is it himself, or his blackness? Underneath my white skin, am I still prejudiced in spite of what I say?" And then I taunt them, "A black man is not good enough for you?" And they can only deny it by giving in to me.' He threw his head back and roared with laughter.

'Well, maybe that is just what holds me back,' Indres said.

'What?'

'Just that. I wouldn't want to take a woman on those terms, I don't want to think she might be willing to sleep with me just to prove to herself that she is not a racist, or because she is afraid of offending me.'

Perhaps he and Pila had not come closer because they still saw each other in terms of colour; he had always thought of her as a white woman. Every relationship was poisoned by racism; whether you recognized it or not, it was there. Only sometimes for a very small time, like with this woman whose luminous white arm lay across his dark chest, could they be free of it; because it was for a night, perhaps one more night, and that was all; because they met by chance and would part by necessity; because the purity of his feelings towards her would never be spoiled by all the subterfuges and risks of maintaining such a forbidden relationship. Just for once they were released from the awful weight of all the problems of their land, so that their loving was for now, only now.

He felt healed, as though after a long illness. He turned to her again, and the resurgence of desire was an expression of his passion for living.

# Thabo . . .

'Shall we bring him through, then?'

The young lieutenant had eyes of the very palest blue, and hair so blond that it appeared to be white. He stood at a table playing with the knobs and wires of a machine.

'No,' said the major, 'no Hennie, you've got to use psychology. This isn't one of the real raw type of boy. He's sort of educated – he worked in a bookshop, you know – he even reads books.'

The lieutenant sniggered.

'Oh yes. Look at this.' The major pointed to two large cardboard containers filled with books. 'That's from his house.'

He bent down and picked up a handful.

'C. P. Snow, *Corridors of Power*, *The New Men*, Bertrand Russell, all this political stuff, Russia, Werth, Engels, *Selected Writings*, *The Identity of Man*.'

'You don't tell me a kaffir reads all that stuff,' the lieutenant said. 'They keep it there for show. He couldn't read all that stuff.'

'Well, I'm sure you'll find he has actually read some of them,' the major replied solemnly. 'That's where they get their half-baked stupid ideas from, socialism, revolution. Listen, I know these bastards, I've dealt with hundreds of them. They're not all the same, you've got to know what type you're dealing with. You've got to understand the mind of the Bantu. He reads a few books and he thinks he is civilized, he thinks he's the same as you or me. Now this one: you have to weaken him first, you have to break him down bit by bit. You go at it the wrong way, and it'll only take you longer.'

'But we got to find out where those boys are staying before they leave for the border.'

'There's plenty of time, a few days won't make any difference. If they were leaving soon, he would have told our chap, he would have given the place where they had to be picked up. What did he report? There's been a few days' delay, they're not quite ready.'

'Then it might have been better to wait a little while before taking him in?'

'Well, we didn't know, but it doesn't matter. He's a slippery customer, best to take him when we can. We'll find out what we want, just the same.'

The lieutenant was fiddling with the clips on the ends of the wires.

'That machine,' the major went on. 'Have you ever seen what happens to one of those real raw boys when you try it on them? A boy straight from the country – oh! That's too funny, really. It's not even the pain, they don't feel that so much; it's the fear – they don't know what it is, where it comes from. Magic! *Tokoloshe*! Witchcraft! But this chap here, he knows what electricity is. First, you have to break his morale.'

He got up.

'I'm going to enjoy this one,' he remarked. 'I know the type. They think if they keep their mouths closed it will be all right. First you got to make them feel your strength.'

He strolled through the open door into the next office and stood with arms akimbo, each thumb thrust into his leather belt, and gazed at Thabo. After a moment's silence the round, close-cropped head moved slightly, the suggestion of a nod.

'So this is him, this is the one,' he said. Then abruptly, shouting, '*Wat's jou naam, kaffir?*'

'Thabo Motjuwadi.'

He strode forward and with his open hand gave Thabo a stinging slap across the mouth.

'Is that how you address a white officer?' he shouted. 'What's your name?'

'Thabo Motjuwadi, major.'

'Major!' the major yelled, his face suffused with colour. 'Major! Who do you think you're talking to, your commie Jewish friends? You call me baas like a good kaffir. Baas!'

Thabo remained silent. Breathing heavily, he stood close to Thabo. Then he shot out again, '*Wat's jou naam, kaffir?*'

Thabo did not reply.

'It's all right. We know you Tommy,' the major said jeeringly, 'Tommy. The Reverend Thomas Khumalo. We know everything about Tommy. What we don't know, we'll soon find out.'

The lieutenant giggled.

'All right, we'll give this boy a chance. Listen, *bob-bejaan*, you just talk nicely and you can stay alive, but you try any of your tricks on us, and I promise you boy, you're dead, you're a dead kaffir. We don't waste time.'

He sat down at the desk and pulled a pad towards him.

'Thabo Motjuwadi, alias Thomas Khumalo, alias Tommy,' he said aloud as he wrote on the pad, and added the date, laying down his pencil. He tilted back his chair.

'Now, speak!' he ordered.

Thabo did not reply.

'Speak!' yelled the major, the crimson tide flooding his face once more, 'Speak, *houtkop*!'

Thabo said, 'What must I say?'

326

'What must you say? Everything! Where've you been hiding since you left home? Who's been helping you? Who did you meet last Friday? Who's on the National Committee, every name, every one, and where are they? How did you contact them? Where are the boys who are planning to leave the country? How were they going to get out? Come on now, all the names, we want it all, everything, and we want the truth.'

'Talk!' the lieutenant shouted, hitting Thabo with all his strength across the side of the head. As Thabo staggered under the blow, the lieutenant seized his gun and struck his face with the butt. '*Ek sal jou gal uitrap!*'

The major intervened. 'All right, Hennie,' he said, 'we've given him a chance. Bring him into the other room.'

He was taken to a storeroom with boxes, files and papers stacked on the floor. The lieutenant raised Thabo's hands above his head and handcuffed them to an iron pipe that ran around the top of the room. To do this, he made Thabo stand on a wooden box and when he had fastened his hands to the pipe, he kicked the box away. In this position the tips of Thabo's toes barely brushed the floor.

'You will stay here,' the major said, 'until you're ready to talk, whether you want to or not. You will not leave this room until you talk.'

He felt something pulled over his head, a hood made of sacking that smelled foul. Blows began, from one side, from the other. He was a pendulum swinging with the blows. Each blow was accompanied by a question or a threat. The questions that were reiterated concerned his contacts and the volunteers, but others were thrown in from time to time: 'Who's your contact on the mines? We know you got explosives from the mines. Who supplied you? Where did you get the black powder?'

A part of his mind remained detached and strangely clear. Thabo knew something about the major. He knew he had a hair-trigger temper and from his appearance, he thought he suffered from high blood pressure. He knew from what others had said that in spite of his rapid rise in the Security Force, from lieutenant only a couple of years ago to captain, and now to major, that he was a stupid and ignorant man; his success did not depend on his brainpower but on the simple fact that he was more sadistic, ruthless and violent in his treatment of political prisoners and detainees than any of his associates.

But then, under the bull-like exterior – the overweight body, the small thick head set like an egg directly on broad shoulders – there beat a different ambition: to be thought of as a man with brainpower, who defeated his enemies by a superior grasp of psychology. 'I understand the native mind. I understand the way a communist thinks. That's how I defeat them, I understand them.'

Thabo concentrated on receiving the blows with the least possible strain, trying to maintain some contact with the floor so that he did not become a mere human pendulum with arms pulling out of their sockets. And with the other part of his mind he was listening to the questions that fell, one after the other, into his ringing ears. The questions would reveal what they knew and what they did not yet know; the names they had not managed to get; the people and places that they had not discovered. Surely, they did not have the information they needed about the volunteers. That, and all those areas of ignorance, had to be protected at all costs by his silence.

The blows on his arms and head, kicks in the legs and groin, seemed to go on for a long time. The curses fell with the blows: '*Boesman – Moerskant – fokkenmoer – fokken moerskant! Jy sal jou morer sien, jou fokker.*

*Fokker, fokker!*' He drew in deep breaths of air contaminated by the smell of the sacking. He heard the sharply expelled breath, the grunts, of the major.

After a while it was quiet. They seemed to have left the room. Bruised and unable to see, he stayed suspended.

Perhaps his body stretched a little, or perhaps the pipe sagged under his weight, but after a while the balls of his feet were resting on the ground and some of the agony of the pull of his arms was relieved. Behind the sacking he breathed slowly and deeply, the self-reproach that was inevitable at his capture relieved by one redeeming thought. Right at the last moment, when Sipho had come to the church to receive his orders concerning the volunteers, Thabo had been assailed by all the weight of Marie's doubts and by his own mounting unease; quite without any previous intention, feeling only the responsibility for what they had planned, the absolute need for it to succeed, he had hesitated and had withheld from Sipho the vital information, the time and place. 'There's been some delay,' he had murmured, 'I'll contact you again in a few days . . .'

The thought of this was sustenance. Perhaps, in spite of his arrest, the volunteers would get away. If he could stay silent, he would save them.

'The major says you can bring him down.'

The sack was removed at last and he saw the faces of two white Security men and two black policemen, erect in their stiff-collared uniforms. The black men escorted him to the lavatory. Then the Security men took him along a maze of passages, through corridors that seemed to lead one into the other without end, and finally to a flight of stone steps. At the bottom was a door; he appeared to be in a basement room with windows high up and boarded over. A single bulb hung by a flex from the centre of the room. On the cement floor was a small pile of three grey bricks.

The door was closed; all four men remained in the room. One of the Security men ordered him to stand on top of the bricks. They wobbled under his feet and he overbalanced. The two white men started punching and kicking him, pulling him to his feet and driving him against the wall. Their actions were almost automatic. They did not speak. The only sounds were those of their own heavy breathing, and occasionally a grunt or gasp from Thabo when a blow landed in his stomach or on his chest.

He was once again ordered to stand on the bricks. He realized it was best to balance there.

'Sunday, and I have to waste my day like this!' Schoeman remarked bitterly. 'I have to spend the afternoon with this stinking black rubbish. *He's* gone off' – he bared his teeth as he spoke – '*he's* probably lying in the sun somewhere sleeping. I had a date. Two weeks running I've had to come back on Sunday, and it's not my time on.'

The other man said, 'I was on my way to church. The van comes to pick me up just as I was leaving for church.'

In the corner a tap dripped in an old stone sink. The air was stale and cold. Thabo concentrated on keeping his precarious balance on the three bricks.

Schoeman sent a policeman to bring them some coffee. When it came, he stood in front of Thabo with the steam rising from his cup.

'The human statue!' he said, and the men laughed. 'That's what you are, kaffir, that's where you'll stay. You will stand on those bricks and never leave this room until you speak. *Jy moet praat, kaffir,*' he added menacingly, '*jy sal praat!*'

Thabo set himself a single task – survival. He was in

the hands of the enemy, their objective was to destroy him, he would try to defeat that objective by whatever means were available to him.

Standing on the bricks was just a prelude. Thabo knew this. It was intended to exhaust him so that he would be weak and therefore less able to withstand prolonged interrogation. He realized too, as the night wore on, that the treatment was intended also to humiliate and degrade him.

Three times he asked to be allowed to go to the lavatory. He was ignored, or he was reviled; he was struck in the genitals and fell off the bricks, and punched around the head and shoulders as punishment. Finally, when light was filtering through the planks on the window and a new shift of police had arrived, he said again, 'I must go to the toilet.'

'Piss on the floor,' the tall young policeman said. 'My instructions are that you stay on those bricks until you make a statement. You can get off when you're ready to talk.'

The muscles gave at last, and there was a warm trickle down the sides of his legs, onto his socks, shoes, bricks, floor. *Not since I was a tiny child . . .*

'Sis! Look at that, the filthy dog. *Donder! Jou hondenaaier!* Now he'll shit in his trousers and stink us all out. God! And they want us to give them the vote!'

The two men laughed, and one went and called an African policeman. 'Take his shirt off,' he ordered, 'and make him wipe the floor with it. Decent people have to walk on that floor. They don't want to dirty their shoes with kaffir-piss.'

The shirt, wet and filthy from the floor, was forced back on him.

Later in the day the major came, carrying a *sjambok* which he flicked playfully around Thabo's shoulders. 'You still standing there, *bobbejeaan*? What are you wasting time for? *Jy moet praat, kaffir, jou lewe is niks werd nie. Jy sal vrek. Praat, fokker, praat!'*

There had been periods of blankness during the night, but now his brain seemed particularly alert. The strain of balancing on the bricks had produced excruciating pains in his back and legs, but his mind was alive to everything they said and did.

'Did you bring in his wife?' the major asked.

'No, sir, you didn't say that . . .'

'Oh, that's all right, we know where she is. We can pick her up any time we want.'

*They are watching to see my reactions. This is just part of the whole thing, it's just one of the tricks to frighten me.* But fear shot through him, just the same.

'He doesn't care,' the major said. 'You could bring his wife and put her here in front of him, and then bring in any kaffir passing by in the street and force him to fuck her here, on the floor, and he wouldn't turn a hair. He wouldn't even care – would you, kaffir? Would you, *fokker fokkermoer*? You reds are all the same. Sleep around, this one with that one. One woman isn't good enough for them. Why don't you stick to your own kind then?' he shouted. 'What do you want with our white women?'

Somehow the day dragged on, the shifts came and went. He fell off the bricks and was placed on them again. He collapsed once more, and once more was propped up for a little longer. The third time, as a concession, and to save themselves trouble, the men on duty removed the three bricks and told him to stand on the floor.

There was a night and another day. He had no food, and only a few times was he allowed a sip of water. Exhaustion and pain became a great cloud filling his head, swelling it to enormous size, a head made out of grey mist, a living sponge. Behind his heavy-lidded eyes flashed pictures of the past, of places and people without time, entering and drifting away of their own volition, actors playing out confused and confusing roles.

At night the raiding parties came, night after night, hammering at the doors. At first it had been only in the early hours before dawn, three or four o'clock in the morning, when all the township was dark and everyone asleep. Now each night they came at different times, sometimes at midnight or even earlier, or one o'clock, or two, or three. There was no relief, little chance to sleep. *We sleep on our knees, our wives never take off their dresses, the children are pale and shivering from the midnight fear. Permits, permits, where's your permit?* The permits had been taken from them. The township was disappearing beneath the bulldozers. Their house was reduced to a pile of broken bricks; their furniture and possessions were piled up under a tarpaulin. They slept in different places each night. On a crumbling wall was painted: WE SHALL NOT BE MOVED. But they were moved. The families disappeared, the machines came, the lorries were piled with stoves and clothes and bits of furniture. The hammering on the doors. The hammering on the doors. The hammering inside the crumbling walls of his head.

*They are beating me again – to wake me up, they say. But to be beaten is nothing. Beating is part of our living. Blows and kicks and claps on face and head. When you are hit, restrain yourself from hitting back. Teach your children not to strike back at a white. Preserve yourself – for what? My father was arrested and they beat him while I cried. – Be still, child, he told me – don't anger the whites! I cried for weeks, why did they beat my father? Why is my father in jaul?*

*And then I taught my own children to hold back . . . to survive. Survive? On your knees waiting for the raids every night? Waiting for the bulldozer to bash down your whole life? It was the greatest mistake of all – patience. All of us, too patient; what we are beginning now, we should have planned years ago.*

They were hitting him again.

*Beating is part of living. We were beaten every day on the potato farms. Bethal, Nigel, Devon, there in the Eastern Transvaal, among the rich mealie lands and potato farms . . . One moment's carelessness, walking out without a jacket, leaving a jacket over the back of a chair – for that moment to suffer a whole month's torture on the farms. Never again, never, never. The art is to survive. Never be without your pass, even if you just go out to breathe the air in your front garden. To be arrested for blowing up pylons is one thing, but to be arrested for not being able to produce your pass is just foolishness. Never again. We came as men, dressed like men in clothes, trousers, jackets, shirts, ties, even socks and shoes. We were stuffed together in the back of a van that was made into a cage. We saw the town disappear between the mesh of our cage, the dust swirl up when the tarmac ended. For miles and miles the dust spiralled behind us, obliterating our route, obliterating our lives. They took our clothes away and gave us a sack to wear, with a hole for your head, another sack to sleep on or use as a blanket in the sharp cold of the nights. At night we shivered under our sacks, weals on our backs, chained by our ankles to a post. Never again! Learn to survive in this land, learn to survive in what they have made of our beautiful land.*

A light shone in his eyes. A very tall, thin man, stood in front of him holding a tin up to his face. The light bulb swung across the ceiling, making strange shapes jump back and forth across the room. 'Drink,' the policeman said. Cautiously he took a sip of water, then the tin was quickly withdrawn. 'Enough. You'll only piss it on the floor again.'

He heard their laughter. 'Listen man, he's asleep, or half dead. Wake him up. *Jy sal jou gat sien, sonder 'n spiëel.*'

The water fell like a blow on his face and head. 'Will he speak now?' the voice said.

'By morning, I promise you. *Wil jy praat, kaffir?*'

'Well, just watch him,' said the invisible voice, 'just make sure he doesn't fall asleep. Hit him to wake him up.'

'I don't think he feels anything,' said the thin one with a snigger. 'I do hit him, man, but I get tired . . .'

*The younger man said to his father, – Pappie, it is not worthwhile to bring this boy back to the lands. The father said, – No, my child, this is a strong, healthy, brutal kaffir, and we must make him work. The old man quite freely told the court, – I gave him a couple of blows with the hosepipe and he walked in a slow, insolent way . . . I hit him again and again. He fell in the same way as before and just lay on his side. Then it was clear to me that this was a habit of his. As he lay there, I hit him again. I said,* 'Magtig, man, work!' *and hit him again. It then occurred to me that this kaffir felt nothing with the sack he was wearing and I told a native to remove it so I could hit him on the thighs and see if he could feel anything. I said to Jantjie,* 'Man hit the kaffir until he listens.' *I was very tired . . .*

*A farmer named Snyman. What did he get – one year, two? Or was it just a fine and suspended sentence to set against the death of a black man?*

Never again. He would never be caught without his pass again.

He studied. He wanted to understand. He joined clubs,

335

associations. He talked to others, but they did not know any more than he did. Then at last, Congress. A school in a garage. He had despised all whites until he met Ralph. His hatred switched from individual whites to the whole system. He studied Marxism with the devotion others gave to theology or science. Slavery, feudalism, capitalism, imperialism, socialism, communism. Strive to understand the nature of society. Learn how peasants lived in that distant Europe. The book by Leo Huberman. Then the history of South Africa, kaffir wars, gold, diamonds; the Boer War; hut tax, dog tax poll tax, fence tax, all the ways they had of forcing black men to leave their land and go and work a mile underground grovelling in dark tunnels of rock that they crushed to dust. The violence with which they beat the miners back after the strike. Violence. Hammering on the doors. Pass raids, liquor raids, mass round-ups. They were singing as they marched away: '*Imethetho ka Malani isiphethe nzima, Mayibuy' iAfrika . . .*'

The voices were singing in his head. The silence was singing. The light bulb swung before his eyes. He was lying on his back on the floor.

# *Margie . . .*

'Jack Miller's wife is coming round this evening,' Margie said to Indres. 'I'm going to Pretoria in a day or two, and she wants me to take some things out for her husband at the same time.'

'I'll disappear when she comes,' Indres said.

'Oh no, it isn't necessary. She knows you're here – after all, she arranged it.'

All afternoon the clouds were gathering in the sky, as they had been now for nearly a week. They accumulated until by evening the whole sky was crowded with them, but each evening the storm stayed somewhere else, far away, and at night the sky cleared once more.

This evening the thunder was like a distant and sustained rolling of drums. Lightning flickered along the horizon. By the time Raos arrived, the first large, spaced drops of the summer rains had begun to fall.

'Just in time,' she said. 'It's really going to come down tonight.'

She walked into the room where Indres waited. 'Is she looking after you?' she asked, smiling.

'Very well,' he replied seriously.

'Where are the clothes, Rosa?' Margie asked. 'Did you leave them in the car?'

'No, actually Jack doesn't need anything. I just phoned you to establish a reason for coming here this evening. Asking you to take clothes to Pretoria seemed an innocent enough excuse.'

'Phone-tapping has its advantages,' Margie said, smiling. 'At least, you do use them sometimes.'

'Ah, but not enough! There was a friend of Jack's – I won't tell you his name – he was a real joker, he was always thinking up ways to annoy the Special Branch by the things he said on the phone. One day he phoned about twenty different people, all people whose phones are tapped, and he said, "Have you heard why Spengler's been sent out of town? Colonel Buys is a queer, and he's found himself a new mate – Captain de Villiers, so Spengler's had to go."'

They laughed. 'We all did that sort of thing,' Indres said. 'We used to say the most libellous things.'

'They could have sued you.'

'What, and come to court to say, "Your Worship, while I was tapping the phone in Jack Miller's house, I heard . . ."'

Rosa was fumbling in her handbag; she drew out a large, fat envelope. 'I have something for you, Indres,' she said, placing it on the glass top of the coffee table.

'For me?'

'Yes.'

'What is it?'

'Have a look.'

Indres took the envelope and opened it. It was crammed with five-pound notes. 'What is this?' he asked in bewilderment.

The sky above them seemed to have cracked wide open, and rain beat down on the house in solid sheets. Through the thunder, he heard her say – 'Your brother Joe . . .'

When the peals stopped for a moment, she repeated, 'Your brother sent it for you. He wants you to take it with you when you go over the border.'

Indres looked at her. 'I'm sorry, I don't understand what this is about. I don't understand how you got this money from my brother, and I don't know what you mean by "over the border".'

'The day you escaped,' Rosa said, 'you went to the house of a friend of yours in Vrededorp, right?'

'That's right.'

'Then you had to leave in a hurry because there were SBs in a car in the street outside.'

Indres nodded.

'Well, your friend was very upset about your going like that, and that he couldn't do anything. He sent to your brother in the country to tell him that you were out, and what had happened. Joe collected this money for you, and he sent it back to town. He knew your friend would find some way to get it to you.'

'How did he find out, then?'

'By asking around,' Rosa said. 'Oh, not openly of course; he was very careful. He spoke to someone he knew had worked with you in politics, and asked that someone to speak to others. Eventually word got round to Elaine, and she gave this to me.'

He sat fingering the notes. 'God, all this money!' he said at last. 'How much is it, do you know?'

'Three hundred pounds.'

'Three hundred! How on earth could Joe send me that much? He never had that much money.'

'I suppose he borrowed it. He sent a message with it. He begged your friend to use as much as needed to get you out of the country, and to give you the rest so that you wouldn't be stranded for months in the middle of the desert like some of those refugees.'

'He expects me to go.'

'Of course.'

He said, 'But you must send the money back.'

Rosa was shocked, 'How can you ask such a thing? Your brother wants you to have it.'

'You don't know what it represents to him. So much work – he just can't afford it. He's done enough for me.'

Margie asked, 'He's very fond of you, your brother?'

'He's been father and mother to me. I've disappointed him terribly.'

'If you care about him, you'll take the money. It's what he wants. He wants to help you, Indres. You must accept it from him, I'm sure he wouldn't understand if you sent it back.'

'You'll need it whatever you do,' Rosa said. 'I also have to tell you your friend, the one through whom Joe sent the money, has now found a place for you to stay. He says it's pretty safe. He also says he's trying to fix up a safe way for you to leave the country. We think you should move, in any case. It will be easier to keep in touch with you in the new place.'

The thunder was dying away in the distance, a long mumbling roll that seemed to travel round the rim of the sky. The rain ceased abruptly.

'I'm going now,' Rosa said. 'It's stopped raining. I'll get in touch with Margie about where to take you tomorrow night.

'It's so beautiful out now,' Margie said. She turned off the lights, drew back the curtains and pushed the glass door open to the garden. 'Look!'

Hardened by the dry months of winter, the earth could not absorb all the rain that had fallen, and water lay in shining pools as the dry grass-roots softened and swelled. Rain dripped from every leaf of bush and tree.

'Tomorrow you will be gone.'

They held each other and she cried in distress, 'Oh Indres, what will become of me?'

He stroked her hair, at first unable to speak. He said at last, 'You will stay, you and Jonny. You'll wait for Dick.'

340

'Yes, I'll wait for Dick.'

He wanted to say 'Come with me,' but he knew it was impossible. He wanted to say 'Perhaps we'll meet again sometime . . .' but knew it was absurd.

Later, lying beside him, she said, 'Indres, I want to thank you.'

'Thank me? For what?'

'I had to change. I – you helped me, having you here, taking that step, then this – you helped me change myself.'

'But you wanted to change. I just happened . . .'

'Well then, to thank you for happening.'

He sat up suddenly.

What is it, Indres?'

'Nothing, no, I've just though of something, someone who might help us. I don't mean us personally, I mean what's going on. Tell me, are you busy tomorrow? Would you be able to do something for me?'

# April and Margie . . .

The boy stood on the street corner for a few minutes looking up and down. Then he crossed the street and squinted up at the driver of a lorry parked at the kerb.

Hey, mister!' he called.

The driver took his cigarette out of his mouth and looked down at the thin figure. The boy pulled himself up onto the step under the door of the cab. 'Is your name April, mister?' he asked.

The driver nodded. 'That's it, son, that's my given name. And who're you?'

'I want to speak to you,' the boy said.

'Come round the other side then.'

Sitting next to April, the boy took off his shoe and produced a crumpled piece of paper. 'It's from a friend of yours,' he said. 'He asked me to bring it to you.'

April read slowly and nodded his head. 'Ja, ja,' he said. 'It's all right, it's OK. So you're going to take me to him, then?'

'Yes,' the boy replied. 'I'll take you.'

April grinned suddenly, the fine lines radiating out from his eyes like the sun's rays. 'What we waiting for then?' He turned the ignition key and pressed the starter. The lorry shuddered as the engine turned. 'Which way?' April asked.

'I'm sure glad to see you safe,' he said. 'Oh, I been really worried about you, especially since I seen all that stuff in the paper.'

'April,' Indres said, 'you remember how you said to

342

me that one day you wanted to get your own back against the government? You said you wanted to have a smack at the ones who made the laws? Would you like that chance?'

'I knew it would come, matey, I knew my time would come!' April cried gleefully. 'I reckon I can even guess what you're going to ask me, and the answer, here and now, true's my name's April Petersen, the answer is yes, absolutely and for certain, yes!'

Indres could not help smiling. 'What do you think I'm going to ask you, then?'

'You're going to ask me to drive you some place, maybe pretty far, hey? Isn't that it? Or you just want to come by my place for a while? Whichever, the answer is yes.'

'It's more than that, April, and don't jump to any decision before you've had a chance to think it over, and just what it means.'

'Go ahead, brother.'

'We've got some lads, seven or eight of them, they were supposed to be leaving the country. They're going overseas to . . . study. They have to get across the border, no passports, no papers. No, don't answer me yet, let me explain the whole thing to you. Someone was supposed to take them out in a van, and he's turned informer. The police know there's a plan for them to go, but they don't know where they are, or when they're supposed to be leaving. If you're caught driving these chaps out, you'll go to jail for a long time.'

April laughed. 'Jail, brother? Do you think you can frighten April Petersen with a threat like that? I been inside for every useless thing they ever thought of, every stupid rotten useless law. To go to jail for something like that – that would be worthwhile.'

He shook his head. 'No, listen pal, what've I got to be

frightened of? Who've I got to care about? No one sitting at home worrying about me, waiting for me, what does it matter? It's a pleasure, honest to God, a real pleasure.'

'It's got to be done soon. We can't keep them hanging around, and anyway, arrangements have been made to get them on their way at the other end.'

'Tonight, if you like.'

'Tomorrow,' Indres said.

'I know it's a lot to ask of you, Margie, and I really wouldn't have asked, except that there isn't any real danger to you personally. Less, in fact, than you've had with him in your house these last few days.'

Margie looked around her. It was mid-morning in Stuttaford's tearoom. The clink of teacups and pastry forks accompanied by the hubbub of feminine voices. With their children at school and their babies in the charge of nannies, the women were able to flee the boredom of their suburban homes after setting the servants to work. Dressed in smart and expensive clothes, they had come to eat cakes and talk about diets.

Even Elaine. A waitress manoeuvred a trolley laden with pastries over the carpeted floor, and Elaine said, 'I'll have a piece of that Black Forest cake. I shouldn't really, it does awful things to my figure, and I'm trying to get my weight down. I just can't resist it, all that chocolate and lovely cream. The cream here is very good, you know.'

Margie smiled.

'I do find it extraordinary,' she said when the waitress had gone, 'the two of us sitting here eating cake and drinking coffee just like any other pair of Johannesburg matrons.'

'But we are just like any other pair!' Elaine exclaimed. 'Look, you even wear white kid gloves, and what a nice handbag that is, real leather, isn't it? None of your cheap plastic. And I even have a hat, although I hate wearing it, but it makes me feel respectable and conventional.'

'And all the time you are being unconventional and subversive. Has it been difficult, to lead a double life?'

'Well, it's not just me, is it? It's in the nature of our society. I often think this is what makes the South African situation so poignant. You look around you, and it's all normal, isn't it? Everything's normal, all these women having their cup of tea or coffee in between running up accounts at the stores . . . Of course, everyone in this whole place is white, but the blacks are in the kitchen washing up the cups, and that's normal, too. And while we sit here, people are hiding and running away, and being interrogated and beaten and tortured. Nothing changes. Nothing disrupts the surface. What a grotesque country this is!'

'Yes. We all know it, but we won't admit it. I really want to do what you ask. I'm so happy that you trust me, to feel I'm part of something. I want to do it.'

'What will you do about Jonny? You'll be driving for hours.'

'I'll take him over to my mother and let him stay the night. She loves having him. I can always think up some excuse. If Rosa comes, she'll share the driving. We might go down to Zeerust afterwards and put up there for the night instead of coming all the way back again so late.'

The last crumbs of cake and cream were finished.

Elàine said, 'As soon as our friend said you'd mentioned this farm, we jumped at the idea. And everything seemed to fall into place, this man with the lorry. But we were really afraid they would never find it themselves.'

'Why isn't Indres going out with the other men?'

'No, it's too dangerous, both for them and for him. You see, even if they are stopped before they reach the border, they haven't yet committed any offence, anything for which they could be charged. But if he is with them, that would be helping a prisoner to escape; it would be too dangerous.'

She said, as casually as she could, 'He could travel with us in the car, ahead of the others.'

'Margie, they don't want to do anything at all that might endanger this whole thing. He's safe for a little while, they can't keep up the road-blocks and searches all the time. Perhaps, when the heat's off a bit . . .'

She picked up her handbag. 'So it's all fixed? You'll pick up Rosa at the Springbok Hotel, then you'll drive along the Maraisburg Road and park outside the café just before the turn-off. The lorry should be there at half-past five. He'll slow down, then you pull out, and he'll follow you.'

She walked with Margie to the door and they stood at the top of the stairs. She took her hand.

'I don't have to thank you,' she said. 'You're not doing it for my sake. But all the same, thank you.'

'It's little enough,' Margie said. She walked through the store and stepped happily out into the sunlit street.

# Thabo . . .

He heard the gusts of wind that shook the windows, and after the wind, the first soaking rains of summer. In the night the smell of moisture and dust invaded even the room with the boarded windows. It was the smell of the land, the smell of freedom.

When the door opened, Thabo saw a patch of brilliant white sunlight on the floor outside. The Pretoria sky would be an arc of palest blue; each day now would be hotter than the one before.

The African policemen came to drag him down the corridor to a shower room. His feet were swollen like balloons, his legs as stiff as iron. They supported him while the cold shower revived him, and he rinsed his soiled shirt as best he could, squeezed it out, and put it on again.

He was reasonably clean, he was awake, he was conscious. He was taken back to the basement room.

They made him crouch on the floor, hands clasped in front of knees, and there handcuffed together. They passed a wooden pole over the crook of his bent arms and under his bent knees. In this position he was completely immobilized.

The African policeman removed his shoes and socks. Clips with zig-zag teeth were attached to the big toe of each foot. Wires ran from the clips and to the machine on the table. Trussed and helpless, Thabo waited for whatever they would do to him.

'You'd better talk this time, boy, because the major means business,' said the Security man. 'Let me tell you something. Every single one of you talks in the end, there's not one what hasn't finished by talking. That's true, isn't it, Kobie?' He turned to the second man.

'It's as true as I'm standing here. They all finish by talking.'

'Well then, boy, you heard what he said. Every one talks. Some makes it harder for themselves. The harder you make it, the more we make you talk, in the end. Isn't that a fact, Kobie?'

'It's a fact, it's the truth. The harder you make it for us, the harder we make it for you.'

'And when you've made your statement, then later on you'll have the chance to see a lawyer and you'll be given a fair trial before the courts. A fair and just trial. Every one gets a chance to defend himself. All your friends got their lawyers now, haven't they Kobie? You'll have one too, boy, after you made a statement. The major's a reasonable man. He just doesn't like you playing around with him.'

'All the kaffir's got Jew-lawyers,' Kobie said.

Another man came into the room. He examined the clips, the wires, the machine. He walked over to the door and called, 'He's ready.'

The major swaggered in, the white shirt hanging over his pouching stomach. 'Now you'll speak, kaffir,' he said.

Smiling, the man at the table moved a knob and suddenly there was an explosion inside Thabo's body. He was seized by spasms of tremendous force that seemed to come from within himself and were utterly uncontrollable. The spasms followed one another so fast that they became one fearful stiffening of all his muscles, forced against pole, handcuffs, straps. A sharp penetrating smell as of something burning filled his nose. He heard himself utter a harsh shrill cry.

'Now you'll talk,' said the major. 'Now you'll tell us

everything. Where are the boys who're leaving the country? What route will they take? Give me the names, I want names.'

The shocks stopped suddenly, but he felt his heart racing and pounding in his breast.

The policeman unfastened the clips from his toes, and fastened one to his ear. Forcing his mouth open, he held the other one against Thabo's tongue, then nodded to the man at the table.

'The names, kaffir,' the major said. 'I want all the names.'

And the shocks began.

'The names of the boys, all the names.'

Lightning exploded in great flashes. The waves swept through him interminably.

'You're going to tell me everything,' the major said. 'No lies, you bastard, no lies. You're going to tell the truth. I want to know it all. The truth.'

His muscles were iron transmitting fire, the tearing vibrations of burning agony. When the shocks started and when they stopped he did not know. His body trembled and shook uncontrollably.

'Are you ready to talk now?' the major shouted. 'Are you ready? We'll get the truth out of you, *jou fokker*.'

Fire flashed across his eyes that bulged like huge marbles in their sockets. It was no longer possible to breathe or to hear anything other than the monstrous drill shattering against his skull. The unsupportable waves of agony lasted a minute, an hour, a year. The wire was removed from his mouth. The convulsions of his body went on, as though he could never be still again.

Someone had turned a radio on in the next room. There was a voice speaking, then music. He would die to the sound of music. He could no longer cry out, his throat had turned to stone, his tongue felt as though it had swelled to fill his whole mouth.

The music stopped. The policeman hummed to himself. The major began moving the electrodes, trying out different parts of his body. 'God!' he exclaimed, 'This kaffir doesn't feel a thing! Look at him! He's not a human being, he's just a great lump of filth – look at him, he doesn't care what you do to him! *Swartgat! Bobbejaan! Hondernaaier!*'

He flung aside the electrodes. 'Petrus!' he called. 'Bring me the sack.'

They took the pole out, and forced Thabo to stand. Then the top of his head was enclosed in a thick sack.

'We'll revive him,' the voice of the major said.

He felt himself dragged across the floor, his back was forced against the sink. 'Right over,' the voice commanded, 'look, Petrus, you don't want to make the whole floor wet. There's enough mess here as it is. All right – now!'

Water poured over his face, the sacking clung to nose and mouth. Gasping for breath, he gasped in water, water flowed over his face in a ceaseless fall, filling his lungs. He was thrashing about, trying to save himself from this terrible death by drowning, and the more he struggled the more water he gulped in, he wanted to stop struggling, to stop breathing, to die.

The policeman was hitting him in the stomach. Water shot out of his mouth and nose, air came in. The blows continued. 'Put him under again,' said the voice of the major.

This time he thought he would stop breathing, but it was not possible. The water came rushing down again, the water flowed into his body, into his lungs. The moment came again when it seemed he was seized by a death agony, and beyond his own pain he heard the music playing. *A juke-box playing in a café. Sunday afternoon, a raid, police chasing them across the veld. A man jumps into the dam to get away from the police. The police stand on the bank and watch him drown. Three times he comes up, calling and thrashing around. He was a child, standing on the bank, he saw it all. Three times, and the last time the man's arms were above his head, and they were still like that above his head when the police fished his body out in the morning. Three times, and then he drowned. Death by drowning and the juke-box playing . . .*

Thathumthwalo Bhuti sigoduke
Balindile omama nobabekhaya . . .

*Collect your things and let's go home, brother, our mothers and fathers are waiting for us at home. Tired. Let's go home.*

He was lying on the floor, a black policeman was wiping vomit from his face, cleaning up the floor. The major had left the room, unable to stand the smell and the dirt. 'I want this place cleaned up!' he had shouted. 'These pigs make everything into a pigsty.'

The room was crowded with policemen. They jammed the small space jostling each other for a chance to see the fun.

He was standing, a wood plank was placed upright against his back, his hands handcuffed together behind the plank. A strap was passed over his legs, holding him firmly to the plank. Like a living mummy, he was balanced against the wall.

Someone pulled down his trousers, and the electrodes were fastened to each testicle. The current passed through and through him in shivering waves of agony, one on top of the other, an excruciating torment split into a million

351

separate needles. The sounds he made were only animal-like moans from a throat as hard and dry as if it had been filled with cement. The forms moved around, between the turns of the magneto they pushed each other aside for their chance to have a go. There were pauses so that between the spasms the interrogation could go on.

'You didn't care about harming people, did you? You would have killed thousands with your sabotage if you'd had the chance . . . Soon he'll talk . . . What are the names, kaffir, give us the names . . . You haven't had enough? Then we'll show you. Don't you know you can die here and no one will save you? Your friend Ralph won't save you – all your white friends have run away to leave you to face the music . . . What shall we do with him? . . . Burn him, this time we'll really burn him . . . Let me do it . . . No, come on now, it's my turn, just watch this . . .'

They were experimenting to find the best places, the most sensitive portions of the body; the lips, the ears, the groin, the testicles, the penis.

'They can't feel like human beings, these black bastards. Their skins are thicker, their skulls are thicker. They don't feel it enough.'

'Are you ready to talk now? To tell us everything?'

And suddenly, rigid as his body was and convulsed with the endless spasms that did not cease even when the machine was switched off, helpless in his physical purgatory, he understood quite clearly his own power and their weakness. *How can men who only know how to hate ever discover my secrets, the power that makes me what I am, that makes me feel and think and act out of my deep concern, my respect for human life, my love of all my brothers? Whatever I tell them, they will never be able to penetrate our secrets, whatever I say they can never comprehend what it is to be human. If you want to know, I can tell you, I will tell you – the secret is silence!*

For a few unendurable moments the accumulated agony of rigid and bruised muscles, of flesh raked over and over by the great prongs of pain, was obliterated by a greater agony that started as a sudden and concentrated pain pulsing through him, an acid pouring into every nerve and vein. The buzz in his ears became fainter. 'Who are they? Where are they hiding? What are the names?' They would never know! He would never speak! The knowledge of his triumph combined with a stiletto of pain, unbearably sharp, that pierced his heart in one moment of pure ecstasy before the darkness exploded in his skull.

# Indres . . .

When he heard the old man slowly climbing the stairs, wheezing as he came, Indres knew it was nearly five o'clock. The shop was in a factory area; after the factories closed, there was no trade in the street; it was empty. Gopal would have shuffled to the front door, looked up and down, locked it and bolted it top and bottom for the night.

He brought with him a tray of food, samosas and some of the bright pink sticky sweetmeats that were displayed in the small shop window. 'Eat,' he ordered, 'if you don't, it's wasted, tomorrow I get fresh order.'

The young men would have arrived in town by now. Singly, they would make their way to a point on the western fringe of the city where the office blocks petered out and scrapyards mingled with factories and a few anonymous shops with frosted glass windows. They would be dressed in working men's jeans and overalls, indistinguishable from all the other young Africans who worked in the area. They would not carry anything at all, not another shirt or pair of socks. They were going just as they were. A journey of a thousand miles begins with but a single step . . . their journey was longer than that.

From behind the lace curtain he looked out into backyards full of empty cartons, and overflowing dustbins. The area was run-down. Soon the buildings would be demolished and there would be redevelopment.

Gopal said, 'I live here forty years. It is nice area when we first come here, not like this. White people live here, Indians, Chinese too. Nobody care, it is very nice place.

Now they make it for white buildings only. Group Areas. So us they throw out.'

'Where will you go, Gopal?'

'Where can I go? Do I have choice in the matter? Lenasia.'

'But will you be able to open a shop there?'

The old man shook his head. 'Never,' he said emphatically, 'no, not at all. Too many shopkeepers there already. Who we do trade with then, we buy and sell to each other? What room for small chap like me, with all those big chaps, Fordsburg, Vrededorp, Market Street. There would not be room for me, now, would there?'

That lorry – it looked as though it was falling to pieces, it rattled like an old bag of bones. But April had said the engine was good. He just hoped nothing would go wrong with it. Perhaps it would be steadier when it was loaded. A whole load of big wooden crates, stencilled with the name of a firm of soap manufacturers. April had collected them over a long period and stored them at the quarry. 'Always knew they'd come in useful one of these days,' he had said.

'What are you going to do then?' he asked.

Gopal shrugged and spread his hands. 'I'll live somehow, if I can't, I die. Since my wife die, I do not care so much. I save little money, not much; something. Maybe I can sell a little door to door, that's how I start forty years ago, see? Now I'm back to where I start.'

Ingenuity. He was really clever, that April, he could make things out of nothing. A man with such talents, thrown away in an old quarry because he was coloured. What an inspiration, to load his lorry with all those crates and tie the whole load firmly down; loaded like a child's building blocks . . . and the bottom crates, inside, had their sides removed so they made tunnels, long enough and wide enough for men to lie there . . .

'Is it justice?' Gopal was saying, 'Is it right? Is that white man's justice, to drive people out there to Lenasia, twenty miles? What about schools, what about mosques? What they want of us, we should all die?'

April must have picked them all up by now then. They would drive openly on the lorry through the city, labourers on a lorry with a load of crates, nothing suspicious about that. Down Commissioner Street which would be crammed with traffic at that time of day; all the multi-storey office buildings and the huge mining houses near the law courts would be closing. He hoped the traffic would not delay them too long.

'I knew your father, a good man. He's been spared this, to live to see such things. And your brother Joe. They'll make him move too, they going to make Group Areas for them out on the veld. So what will he do then, build a store in the bush? Who will be customers? What do they care? That's what they want, we should all die.'

Then the road to Krugersdorp, that same road he had walked along, the night he left Essop. April knew every inch of it, and the unmarked tracks in the veld around. He would turn off past the mines, near a grove of trees, take a side off one of the crates; the men would crawl inside. He would batten it down again. Flat in the dark, packed in rows. April hammering the side back on the crate, whistling, humming; starting the lorry up again.

Gopal sat silent, sucking his teeth. After a while he rose. 'I must go down,' he said. 'Got to put stuff away.'

At the door he turned again. 'Anything you want? You got everything? While I'm going down, anything . . . you just say . . . No, it's not for thanks. For your father's sake, for his memory. And for your brother, I told Essop when he came to ask me, all right, I'll be happy . . . Just the same, what can I lose? They take everything. What more?'

Indres heard his slippers shuffling down the stairs.

She would lead the way. The dust would rise along the country roads, spiralling away behind them for miles and miles. The empty roads through the reserves. It would take at least five hours in that lorry.

She would stop before they reached the farm. They would stand out there under that luminous sky, brilliant with stars, far from the lights of any town. The last couple of miles they would do on foot in the dark, through the farm and across the dry river bed. They would be on their own. The night would be intensely quiet, the ground rough, the grass dry and sharp beneath their feet.

They would cross over. People would be waiting for them; they would be the first. It was a long way, through deserts and hostile lands. They would be the first. They would cross over tonight.

# Dick . . .

Once he had liked to think of himself as part of something big, not simply the organization itself that stretched across the country, radiating from the industrial centres outwards to the remote reserves; but part of a movement of ideas, shared by people everywhere. To adhere to such ideas meant that he adhered also to others, that he was an integral part of something good and full of meaning. It meant he had conquered some of his isolation and his middle-class doubts.

Now he belonged to nothing except himself, he was separated from all others, he was alone. He must learn once again to live with solitariness. He would find what he needed in the future only within the confines of his own small family. He and Margie and the little boy . . . perhaps, when it was all over, they would go away somewhere, to a different town. Even a different country. There were other countries where his qualifications would be in demand. He would get a post in some quiet University town with tree-lined streets, he would have a life of routine and order; there would be compensation for the loss of his country. He would move up the scale, he would write a text-book, bring up a family and ultimately there would be a chair – ? Where was this University, in what town, in what country – Canada? No, too cold. Australia then, or even New Zealand? He could not pin it down; as soon as he tried to make the idea concrete, it slipped out of his grasp. The houses, the shape of the trees, the landscape he envisaged belonged only to Africa, Africa south of the Sahara, the flat-topped thorn trees, eucalyptus with bark hanging in strips, the burning flames of kaffir-boom and flamboyants. The earth of that imaginary country was red, like the red earth of the Transvaal; the air was always thin and clear, sparkling like glass, the marvellous air of the high-veld . . .

He had adapted once more to his own immediate solitude; life revolved around the trivia of his personal routines which had developed an importance of their own. The food he ate, the few possessions in his cell, the arrangements of comb, shaving kit, water bowl, the state of his nails, his bowel movements, all these occupied the forefront of his life. The jail routine had become an obsession and he was deeply disturbed by any deviation from it.

From the window of the second-floor cell that he now occupied he could see right over the prison yard, over the high wall surrounding the prison, and beyond that to an area of land dotted with red brick houses where the warders lived. Further still lay an expanse of tawny countryside that soon would become green, and then the railway, and in the far distance, barely visible, the faint outline of the Magaliesburg, blue and beautiful, where he remembered white water fell in deep *kloofs*, and the baboons barked high among the rocks on hot afternoons.

From the wall, where five white pigeons sat, to those far mountains, came the material for fantasies to occupy his mind. He could encompass anything that was sufficiently remote. It was the situation close to him that he refused to examine.

Out they marched every morning – there were six of them now, quite a little army with a warder in front and one at the end and a warder walking between each of them. The yard was entirely enclosed by jail buildings. Two sides of the square were the three-storey blocks of cells; the African prisoners could be glimpsed from time to time cleaning the ablution block, washing the stones in the yard, passing, heads down, feet bare at the end of grey legs; in appearance and demeanour, the very epitome of servitude. The ordinary white prisoners – criminals, not 'politicals' – were housed in a separate block; they never saw them.

Exercise time was the same routine: defecating, the single cigarette, shaving and showering, washing a pair of socks or underpants, pacing the yard – all this within the half hour.

If he glanced at the faces of the other men he saw something of himself, the same grey, tense, self-absorbed look. Hanging on for the end of ninety-days.

Three days before the ninety-days was due to end, as he picked up his clothes, towel, shaving kit, toilet bucket, dixie and water bowl, he noticed in the bowl, now filled with fresh water, a small screw of silver paper. Instinctively he covered the bowl with his towel. Once locked inside his cell he fished the paper out and opened it.

Inside it was another piece of paper, and written on that:

All of us made statements under pressure, we are all going to repudiate them when we come to court. Don't give evidence. Join us. If you agree, tear off a shirt button and drop it in one of the bowls.

His first reaction was one of anger – that they should so breach the precarious wall he had built around himself, that they should so plot to disrupt his life. Then despair. It had all been done; he was committed already to being a witness; it was as though he had made a promise to Margie to rejoin her soon, to end the nightmare for both of them. Now these others asked that he prolong it, that he put himself away for years and years. They had no right to do this to him.

Without thinking, he fingered the buttons on his shirt.

Only three more days. How foolish it would be to make any gesture now.

That afternoon there was a disturbance in the jail. He heard footsteps running along the passage, voices raised in some sort of excitement – but what? He heard doors being unlocked, warders calling to each other. Supper did not come at the usual time. He judged the time by the light and by such routine events as the return of convicts who worked outside. Now it was all confused. He felt a terrible unease. The note, the disturbance of jail routine, had robbed him of the peace and security that he had managed to build for himself.

Food arrived nearly an hour after the usual time. The warder who unlocked the door and placed his dixie on the floor was one of the more easy-going ones. He dared to ask him, 'What's been going on here? Why is supper so late?'

'Oh, nothing,' the warder replied. 'Some kaffir hanged himself.' He banged the door shut.

In the yard the next morning during the exercise period he sensed an extraordinary tension. The men seemed to parade stiffly, like puppets. The pace was faster than usual. And suddenly, just before their exercise time finished, there was a loud noise, a clanging as though someone was banging something metal on the bars. A voice from the main block shouted out 'Thabo is dead! Thabo is dead! Listen – they murdered him, Thabo Motjuwadi, they say he hanged himself but it's a lie, they murdered him . . .'

The voices became part of a tremendous uproar, of warders shouting commands, clanging doors, keys, foot-steps, the sounds of what must have been blows, and the voice still shouting, though muffled.

Then echoes rippled round the yard. The sound seemed to come from all around them, mounting in waves, a clamour that began inside the buildings, in the cells, and burst out in a mutinous roar of human voices mingled with the reverberations of metal bars. The whole prison was alive, crying out. Whatever any man had, he used; angry voice, dish or toilet bucket banged ferociously against barred windows. Amidst the uproar the warders ran up and down screaming, opening cells and batoning the inmates, yelling futile threats against the anger they could not quieten.

They were locked away again, they were not taken out to exercise in the afternoon. He sat on the floor of his cell with his back to the wall, his head resting on his hands. His food was untouched; his heart pounded relentlessly; pictures passed through his mind, a man beaten to unconsciousness being dragged from his cell after he had shouted his news. Beaten bodies. That searing cry 'Thabo is dead! They say . . .'

He got up at the required time and unrolled his sleeping mat, undressed and crawled beneath the heavy blankets.

The prisoners began singing. One voice would start, then others would come in, the harmony of many voices taking up the parts. The songs went on and on, sound coming from all directions. A lead voice would change the words, then came the chorus, over and over, a dozen times until a new voice took up a different theme. They were singing for their brother, for Thabo. He did not understand the words but he heard the name, Thabo, repeated again and again. The warders made no attempt to silence them that night; perhaps the commandant understood enough to know it was better to let anger and sorrow pour out and disperse in the singing. Dick listened to the familiar tunes: hymns, laments, work-songs, then freedom songs. Yes, tonight they even sang those illegal songs that had arisen from the Congress struggles.

For a long time after lights-out he lay awake in the semi-darkness of his cell. The singing died down. At last he rose again. He went to the corner and took his clothes from their carrier bag. He unfolded the clean shirt that Margie had sent in for him; and in the dark he fingered the buttons, one by one. He felt an impulse to tear them off, every single one. Thabo is dead! Thabo is dead!

*At least they cannot do any more to him. At least nothing I do or say now can harm him any more. Would they have taken him if . . ? Why take an irrevocable step now? The buttons. One button. Even one button would mean an absolute decision.*

His head ached. He had some asprins, carefully hidden from their daily searches. He felt for them in the seams of his jacket and swallowed three. Three smooth little tablets, round and small like three shirt buttons. Tomorrow he might see Margie. They might let her come.

He went back to his mat and crawled once more under his blanket.

# *Indres . . .*

Indres heard light footsteps climbing the stairs and then the boy's voice, 'It's me, uncle, it's Cassim.'

He opened the door. 'What's happened?' he asked sharply.

'Nothing, uncle, nothing.'

'Then why are you here?'

The boy sat on the edge of the bed, legs apart, hands lightly clasped.

'I was visiting a friend near here, and when I left him I just thought I would pass by on the other side of the street. Then I saw the light was on inside the shop, so I knocked and he let me in.'

'Yes, he's working down there this evening, taking stock,' Indres said, 'but you know you should not come to me unless it is absolutely necessary.'

The boy looked down.

To soften the reprimand, Indres said, 'But I suppose you were very careful?'

'Oh yes!' The boy brightened. 'I have a system worked out. I keep a check-list in my mind of things to do and things to look for wherever I go.' He paused, then asked the question that worried him most.

'Indres, when will we know?'

When will we know? Indres had found a school atlas in Gopal's shop; he had tracked the journey, mile by mile, always telling himself, if the lorry does not break down, if the tyres are OK, willing them forward . . . these, the pioneers; he could hear them singing. Even if very quietly, surely they would be singing. When they had crossed over, they would sing. The first.

'April should be back some time tomorrow,' he said, 'if all goes well. That's the first thing we must wait for, to see if he comes back OK and to hear his report. If they were not intercepted, if he dropped them safely, then they will be on their way. But it could be a long time before we really know about them.'

Even if they crossed the border, they could be taken back again; it had happened to others. White farmers, hostile officials, South African security men operating on the other side . . . they could be dragged back into the dungeon of ninety days and no one would know for months, perhaps years.

'It might be a long wait,' he said. 'Patience, that's very hard, isn't it? Caution and patience.'

The boy said seriously, 'What is hardest for me is growing up.' Indres did not even smile under the steady gaze of those dark eyes.

'And why do you say that?' he asked. 'I should think you are growing up very well.'

'Yes, but not fast enough. As soon as I am big enough, I shall go to learn how to fight.'

'You've already learned,' Indres said.

They heard the old man's slow footsteps on the stairs.

'You must go now,' Indres said, 'and remember, be patient. Take care.'

'I will,' the boy said, 'I promise.' He stood up and a rare smile illuminated his thin face. Indres drew the boy towards him for a moment and held him against his chest. And felt, underneath the shirt, pressed against his own body, the firm beating of his heart.

## JUNE 1980

Just for a moment, at the first earth-shaking explosion,
Cass put a hand before his eyes as though to shield them
from a light too brilliant, a cloud too rounded which
billowed upwards into the night sky. Then – no more
hesitation – he turned and buried himself in that night. It
was done. Years of preparation, years of training. They
had succeeded; or partially. To survive, to get away
safely, to find the way through the net of security forces –
that was part of the total plan.